Beneath the Ice

Beneath the Ice

CRIME NOVEL

C.M. WEAVER

THE AUTHOR OF SILENT RIVER

Ordering Information:

For orders and inquiries, please contact:
1-888-404-1388
www.goldtouchpress.com
book.orders@goldtouchpress.com

Printed in the United States of America

An author never completes a book by themself. I'd like to thank those who critiqued my posts on The Write Practice. When I completed the manuscript, Molly Gingerich offered to beta read it. Thank you for catching things I missed.

My thanks to my wonderful sisters, Susie Scriber and Kathy Buss, who listen and offer advice from their heart. No holding back.

Chapter 1

Ice cubes floating in a blood-red sea. They were bumping into her head, keeping her from the surface. Reaching up, she tried to hold on to one as a life raft, but her fingers kept slipping off. Kicking her feet hard to stay above the viscous red sea, but she couldn't get her head above it. She was going to die, and no one would find her. If she opened her mouth, the blood would fill her lungs and drown her, but she couldn't hold her breath any longer. She inhaled— air.

Her eyes popped open. She lay in her bed and gasped for air like a fish out of water. She kicked to untangle her feet from twisted sheets. She was alive.

I don't believe in visions. Some things can't be explained. It was a bad dream.

Andrea Watson repeated the mantra more than a few times during the hours, after the dream. She tried to convince herself it was the result of the article she'd read about the Winter Carnival Ice Castle under construction. She'd decided to watch the ice blocks being cut from the lake to build the Castle. It was her subconscious distorting the information. While she drove to work she sang along with the artists on the radio to distract her mind.

1

The squad room buzzed with the sounds of business as usual. Detective Andrea Watson wove her way through desks to her own, in a far corner. None of the other detectives spoke to her or even looked her way. She was used to their misogynist attitude toward women in the department.

"Watson!"

Andrea turned as she set her briefcase on her chair. Across the room, in the corner office, she saw one of the senior detectives motioned to her. Her heart picked up a beat or two. Maybe this time, she'd get a good assignment.

"Yes, Sir." She addressed him as she stopped at Sargent Steve Totts' desk.

"Take these folders and file them." A pile of folders sat precariously on the corner of his desk. He didn't look up to see if she took them or not.

She didn't move. Heat slowly rose from her fingers to her face. "I'll drop these off at the clerk's office. Please sign the proper order form." She remained stiff. He looked up.

"You sign it." He dared her to refuse with the raise of his eyebrow.

Her teeth ground together. She felt the eyes of the other detectives on her. "I'll get a container. There's too many to carry." She turned away and crossed the room, where bins for folders sat on a table. She picked the smallest one up, walked back to Steve's desk. Placing a short stack of the folders in the tray, she walked out of his office.

After she dropped them off at the file clerk's counter, she headed to the restroom. Resting her palms flat on the counter, she glared at the sink. "I'm not his servant. I'm a detective like he is. I may not have years of experience with this department, but I'm a detective too." She mumbled to herself.

She straightened and glared at her red rimmed eyes, determined not get emotional over a jerk.

The door opened and Chrissy, another detective, and her friend on the force entered. She didn't continue to a stall but stood leaning against the counter, her arms folded.

"You aren't going to take the rest of the folders to the clerk, are you." The woman's expression didn't give any personal feelings about the statement.

"I'm still thinking about it."

A slow smile lifted the corners of her lips. "You go, girl. The rest of us want to thwart the mighty STEVE TOTTS." Her tone insinuated the capital letters of his name. "We limit our retribution to small things. I told you about the time we made fudge and put a laxative in his. Everyone else got the good stuff." She chuckled. "We even sprayed pepper spray into his tissue box once. He doesn't get it." Chrissy shrugged. "Don't take all this personally. He's a jerk, and the rest of his little posse follow his lead." Chrissy leaned closer to the mirror. "He's intimidated by you."

"What? I do not."

Chrissy looked at Andrea's reflection. "You had a reputation of being a good detective. Then that thing with your dad. He isn't sure if that's true or not and is worried you'll get more press than he does."

Andrea chucked with no humor. "I get it. You all think I have the same woo-woo my dad does." She returned Chrissy's look in the mirror. "I don't have anything my dad has. He's the one with all the big press. He's an observant detective. He sees things others miss. Details. They labeled him a psychic for years."

"Are you saying he has no ESP? He's not psychic?" Chrissy asked.

Andrea shrugged. "You can believe what you want. Is he psychic when he knew when I snuck out through the window at night? Or when I lied to him? Or when I failed a test? Was it a father who knew his daughter? You've heard the expression having 'eyes in the back of their head?' So, you tell me if he's psychic."

Chrissy shrugged. "What about all those cases he solved?"

Andrea gave her a quizzical expression. "He was a good detective?"

Chrissy gave her a hug. "He was that. What's he up to, now that he's retired?"

"When he's not calling me, he has his routine. He alternates making breakfast at home or headed to his favorite diner. I tease him by calling it ROMEO's"

3

"Huh? What's that? I've never heard of that diner." Chrissy smoothed her slicked-back brown hair, checked for strays in her reflection.

"Retired Old Men Eating Out." Andrea grinned.

Chrissy paused, then burst out in a laugh. "That's good." She held up her hand in a high five. "What are your plans for your day off? I wish we could coordinate our days off. Your birthday's coming up." She tilted her head at her friend. "Twenty-nine. Yipes, you're old."

"Hey, you're a few months behind me." Andrea protested followed by a sigh. "I thought I'd go up to Blue Lake and watch them cut the ice for the Ice Palace. I saw the plans in the newspaper. I'll bet it's a doozie. It looks like it's going to cover all of Harriet Island. I love going to see it at night when they have all the colored lights reflecting on the clear ice. Especially when they change color, lighting up the turrets.

I read one night is a tribute to Prince. Purple lights and his music playing. It's a good thing this January we had our normal subzero weather. No melted blocks during the festival. I'd better head back to the desk. Steve will be down here, to haul me back to work."

"I'm surprised he hasn't texted you to bring him a coffee."

Andrea gave a dry laugh. "Next he'll want me to wash his feet and dry them with my hair." She touched the blond, bobbed cut. "Good thing, it's short."

Chrissy walked down the hall beside her friend. "I don't know how we put up with those macho males. I'd love to file a harassment charge."

"Yes, and you'd have found yourself transferred out of the department, then the station. This is life, good and bad. As much as I despise the culture, it can't be changed. It's too ingrained. See ya. Call me."

Andrea sat at her desk. A text bubble popped up on her computer screen. **Come to my office.** No signature. The message came with its tag Det. S. Totts. She stood and walked across the room. In his office, Steve looked up at her with no expression and pointed to the tipping pile of case files. His eyes never left hers and dared her to say something.

Andrea looked at the pile. *Pick your battles.* She heard her father's voice in her head. She picked up the box and headed to the file room. If she had a top hat, the lid would wail with steam.

As she fixed dinner that night, the phone felt like the elephant in the room. She shook her head. "Why am I thinking Dad is going to call?"

"We eat at the table like a real family. We aren't going to watch TV for dinner." Her father drilled into her, and to this day, she still ate at the table, sans TV distraction.

Once, after an argument over the phone, she'd left the table. In the living room, she sat in the chair to eat her dinner, but she went back to the table after a few minutes. She couldn't break tradition. Here she was, feeling her father was going to call.

She put the empty dish into the dishwasher and checked the clock. She shook off the uneasy feeling. In the living room, she picked up a book and stared at the page without seeing the words. She silently pleaded, "Alright Dad, call me already."

Her phone trilled, as if on cue, "Hello, Dad."

"That was quick. You knew I was going to call."

"How are you?"

"Same-o, same-o. How are tings at da station?"

"Nothing new. Same-o, same-o." She repeated his own answer."

"Any new cases?"

"No." She raised the tone in almost a question. "Are you telling me something?"

Her father didn't answer. Andrea felt frustration grow. Her lips almost pursed, but she forced them apart and asked, "What? You always do that, and I have to pull teeth to get the full story. Just spill it."

She heard his sigh before he spoke. "All I can say is ta step up to da challenge. Don't let anyone put you in da corner, so ta speak."

"Are you saying I'm going ta learn ta dance?" The mix of sarcasm and humor wasn't lost on her dad.

"Glad you still keep your smile. You're going ta need it."

"Dad, stop your verbal dancing. Tell me what's going on." This time it was her sigh that crossed the airwaves.

"I'm glad you're back ta believing. You're going ta need dat faith. Also, when a strong hand is offered, don't push it away."

Andrea dropped her chin to her chest. "Dad, I wish you could give me some hint. I know it doesn't work like dat, but you have to give me something."

"Honey, all I can say. It's going to be the case that launches your career."

"Dat's it?" She waited for her father to continue, but all she heard was silence.

"What are you doing on your day off?" He changed the subject, and Andrea gave a tilt of her head.

"Da Winter Carnival is building an Ice Palace dis year on Harriet Island. Dey're cutting the ice from Blue Lake. If it's not too cold, I tought I'd go and watch for a while." She caught herself lapsing into the dialect she'd worked so hard to change.

"You're hearty Minnesota stock. Bundle up and go. It'll be a sunny day despite da cold. Be sure ta wear dose gloves I gave you, and if you look in dat Christmas box on your shelf, you'll find da fur hat I gave you a couple years ago for your birtday."

"Dad. That hat makes me look like I'm from Russia," she protested.

"But it will keep you warm. Wear it."

She agreed and said her good-byes. Why was it as soon as her dad got her into a conversation, she forgot how to talk right.

The event from earlier from the night before came to mind as she made her way to bed. Why was she even going to the lake? She hated looking at frozen lakes. Maybe she should have told her dad about the dream. She dismissed the thought.

The following morning Andrea geared up for the cold weather and drove to Blue Lake. She joined the few brave who lined the barricades to watch the activity on the lake.

After a few minutes, she wrapped her arms around her body. The thick fur-lined coat with its fur-lined hood kept her warn on this minus five-degree morning. The sun reflected off the ice, and it's dark blue, almost black appearance seemed to invite, yet to Andrea, she felt a chill. Her body became colder, and it had nothing to do with the weather.

A movement in the distance caught her attention. She blinked. It was still there. She rubbed her eyes, then squeezed them tight. *Not now. It isn't real, nothing is there,* her mind screamed.

Through military-grade sunglasses she'd bought from the ad online, she saw ghost-like figures out on the ice. She closed her eyes and opened them again.

This time hands rose from the ice and clawed the air. A pair of skulls emerged from the ice and turned her way. No eyes, the jaws open and appeared to howl.

She groaned and pulled her glasses from her eyes. This time when she looked across the lake, no skeletons and no ghosts. It was her crazy imagination. She'd listened to too many true crime podcasts. She put the glasses back on, took a deep breath, and turned her gaze back to the lake. It was back to normal. She sighed in relief.

Dotted across the lake in groups, ice houses stood as sturdy as the fishermen who sat inside and out, attending their poles. Andrea gave a small shudder at the idea of even being on the ice. She would never go out there, again.

Her eyes turned to watch the action on the lake. Men in heavy suits, covered with chest waders, walked back and forth along the edge of the ice where it had been cut into blocks. They used barge poles to guide the blocks, that floated in the frigid water, toward a barge parked next to the dock.

The ice blocks moved up the gravity roller and into the truck. She knew they'd driven into St. Paul, where they were assembled into the Winter Carnival Ice Palace. She stomped her feet to keep circulation in her feet.

"They sure are beautiful." A man leaned on the barricade next to her spoke out loud.

She didn't answer. She thought he spoke to someone else.

"Do you come here often?" He continued; his head turned to look at her. She looked down at the man and saw the dimple in his cheek as he smiled. He was teasing her.

"No, this is the first time I've been here to see this process. I've seen the result, which is impressive on its own." She stomped her Sorrel boots on the frozen parking lot pavement. "You?"

He straightened. Andrea looked up and raised her eyebrows at his height. The top of her head reached his chin. "No, my first time here. I came from Michigan. This is my first winter in Minnesota. I read about the ice palace, and since I had the day off, I thought I'd check out how they cut the ice. You?"

"Same here. I've seen a few of the ice palaces through the years. They are well worth the visit when they're done.

The castle is made of the most translucent ice blocks. They reflect the colored lights. They have had long ice slides and an enormous throne you can sit on for pictures. I doubt there's much difference in the weather here and Michigan." Her eyes followed the blocks as they floated. Men pushed them to the conveyor.

"So far, there hasn't been much difference, weather-wise. The culture is different thought. I lived near Detroit most of my life. I like it better here."

"Working here?" The words popped out of her mouth before she could stop them.

"Yes." His answer sounded clipped. He raised his hand to shield his eyes as he watched the action. "I wonder what's going on?"

Andrea leaned close to the barricade and watched as men ran back and forth along the edge of the ice. They pointed at the water. Blocks bobbed along as they had but whatever the men saw had them calling to the others onshore. She couldn't make out what they said, but her eyes followed the blocks as the men gathered around them.

The next block of ice came out of the water onto the belt. Andrea squinted her eyes to see what caused all the commotion. When the block reached the top of the conveyor and made the turn, she gasped.

The men standing by the truck moved next to the block, their hands held phones, they didn't hear the calls.

Andrea took the few steps to the end of the barricade and pushed her way through.

"Hey, you can't come through!" The security officer stepped in front of her. She lifted her coat to expose her badge at him, and he nodded. Andrea turned her head, the man she'd been talking to kept pace..

"Police?" she asked.

"FBI," the deep voice responded.

She nodded and made her way to the edge of the barge. The ice block had made its way closer to the truck, and she could clearly see what was causing a fuss. Frozen in the ice, she saw a partial decayed skull and feet encased in a fishing net.

"Look, another one." A voice shouted.

Andrea turned as a second block made its way up the conveyor. She heard a security officer call for help. The people behind the barricade held their phones out to video.

Andrea held up her ID and told the men, "Get these into the truck and out of sight. We don't want this on the news before we can access the situation." She jerked her head to the crowed.

The men did what she said and got the blocks into the truck. The wooden sides on the conveyor kept the ice on track. She'd seen the blocks as they passed the end of the wood and entered the truck. She hoped no one actually got a clear picture of what it was.

She took pictures and texted them to her Chief Conrad Bellows. Her phone rang,

"What is going on?" His rough voice barked at her.

"We have two blocks of ice taken from Blue lake for the ice palace, with body parts in them. I'm sure the local police have been called. There is an FBI guy here too."

"FBI? How did they get there so fast?"

"The same way I did. I was here on my day off watching the ice harvest. I happened to see what's going on." The sound of sirens got louder. "You can hear the police arriving."

"Secure the area. I'll get the guys out here asap." The phone went dead.

Within minutes the parking lot of Blue Lake was filled with policemen. Yellow tape fluttered in the wind. The once quiet morning had been broken by the sound of bull horns ordering the onlookers to get into their cars and move out of the area.

Andrea pulled her knitted scarf over her mouth and nose as she walked across the parking lot to meet her Chief and the officers that arrived with lights flashing and sirens blaring. She counted seven detectives beside herself from the St. Paul Criminal Apprehension Unit.

She sensed someone followed her and turned to see the FBI guy. "I think we have this handled. You can go."

He grinned at her and continued to follow her. She ignored him and joined her fellow officers.

Captain Conrad gave Andrea a nod when he saw her and asked her for a rundown of what happened. She gave him a brief statement.

The crunch of quick steps approached the group. "Watson, fill me in."

"I already gave my update to the Captain; he's handling it now." She didn't look at Steve Totts, who shouldered his position in front of her.

"Who are you?" Steve demanded of the man behind Andrea.

Fletcher remained at Andrea's side. He ignored Steve, and he spoke directly to the Captain, who'd turned at Steve's question. "Agent Fletcher Petersen, FBI. I realize this isn't my jurisdiction, but I'd still like to observe. I've been given permission by my Director."

Conrad's eyes narrowed as he looked at Fletcher then at Andrea. She didn't speak. *I'm not saying anything unless he asks me.*

"So, the FBI wants in?" Conrad asked.

"No, Sir. I observed the activity next to this officer. When we saw the body parts in the ice. I gave a call to my boss. I'm here in case you need our services." He held his hands up palm out in surrender. "I'm new to the area and came to observe the process."

Conrad nodded and Steve snorted. "We don't need any of your sort mucking things up." He included Andrea in the comment.

She held her ground as the group moved to the back of the truck. Captain Conrad squatted next to the blocks of ice.

"There's a skull, it still has some skin and hair attached. One of the feet, cut off above the ankle still has polish on the toes. I'd guess without too much of a stretch it's a woman. Where's the Medical Examiner?" He straightened and looked around as a tall woman with Scandinavian heritage climbed into the truck bed.

"What do you have here?" The woman looked at the blocks in the center of the group. "You couldn't find small enough cubes for a party? You called me here to dissect the blocks into usable chunks?" The lilt in her voice caused a ripple of chuckles through the group.

"Denise, we have two blocks cut from the ice with body parts in them." Conrad squatted next to the cube.

Andrea moved closer to stand next to Denise who looked up at her. "You find these?" She winked at Andrea's nod.

Denise looked back at the ice. "You have a skull, and it looks like three feet encased in a fishnet. There seemed to be a cord attached to the end of the net bag that ends where the block was cut." She sidestepped to the next block. "The cord may have been attached here." She pointed to the frayed bit of nylon sticking out of the ice.

"There's a second bag and this one has two skulls with more hair and skin. I can see hands in that next bag. I hope he was too confident to cut off the tips so we can find out who they are." She stood. "Since the cubes are in a truck, have the guys follow me to the station."

"Andrea was on the scene when the blocks were cut. She called it in and secured the area. I'm sure the media has found out by now."

"Yeah, they have vans set up and are questioning everyone in the vicinity." Steven squatted down and gave the blocks a once over. He straightened and ignored the officers that stood around, "The blocks need to get to the lab so we can find out who they are."

"If you'd get your sorry butts off the truck we could get it to the lab." Denise mimicked his tone. She swished her gloved hands at the group and motioned them to get out of the truck. Andrea allowed the ice workers to help her down.

"Ma'am, can we go back to cutting now?" They asked her.

"Let me check." She moved to the Captain's side. Steve had his attention. She waited for him to take a breath. "Captain, the guys want to get back to work. They need these ice blocks cut for the palace."

Steve interrupted her, "Captain, someone needs to stay here and oversee the cutting. In case more of these parts show up. Also, what about divers? Maybe we should have a crew look for anything on the bottom of the lake."

"You want to go into that frigid water?" Andrea asked Steve before the captain could answer.

He ignored her and continued to look at the chief. "They're trained and have cold water gear. The lake isn't all that deep here. Maybe five to six feet once you get away from the shore."

Andrea stepped back and let Steve run with his idea. "We'd need to look at each block cut to see if any more parts are inside."

"Good idea, take a couple of the guys with you Steve, and keep an eye on the operation." Conrad turned away to face Andrea. "Where's the FBI guy?"

"Right here Sir. Fletcher Peterson," He stepped forward and held out his gloved hand. Conrad shook it briefly. "I contacted the office and they said to offer our help if you need it."

"We'll see if that's necessary. We have a great team of our own." He turned.

"I'd like to observe the process if you don't mind." Fletcher fell into step with Conrad. "I'll stay out of the way. I just moved here a few months ago and I'm learning my way around. I'd like to make any transition or communication between our divisions, as smooth as possible. There doesn't need to be any real hand over of information but, I'm already here to assist if needed."

Conrad stopped, looked at the young man for a long moment then nodded. His eyes moved to Andrea. "You two can work together. Andrea, make sure he doesn't get in our way." It seemed more like an order than a joke.

"Sir, I'll need to be on the case." She bit off the *not babysitting* she almost added.

"You will be. Let's wait for the ME's report. I'm sure we'll have to question the residents and anyone who fishes here regularly. I hope this is a one-time drop," he paused and looked over the lake, "but I have a feeling this is going to be a long case."

"Me too," Andrea muttered.

Chapter 2

Andrea arrived at home, hung her ski pants, down jacket, along with her winter cap and gloves in the front closet. Cold seeped into her bones and the memory of what she'd experienced that day swirled around her brain. While the culture of the department wasn't new, the picture of the body parts in the ice caused questions to run like a litany in her mind.

Once she had a hot bath, dressed in her flannel pj's, and sat in front of the TV to watch the news. When the microwave dinged, she pulled her dinner and sat at the table.

Her phone rang. She smiled. It was no surprise who called her name on the other end.

"Hiya, Dad. Did you see me on TV?"

"Yes. Ya looked nice in da fur hat an' gloves."

Andrea rolled her eyes.

"Who is da FBI guy?" His voice dipped lower.

"He was standing next to me when we saw da-the blocks of ice."

"He may be da one you can use to get on dis investigation. I'd watch for a way to push yourself on to da team.

"It's not that easy, Dad. If I push too hard, Conrad will feel pressured."

"I don't tink dat's gonna happen girl."

"Dad? Your tone sounds like you have a clue?"

"This FBI guy seems to be da key here. Don't push him away if he wants ta help ya, ya know."

"He's FBI. They don't have any jurisdiction over the case unless Conrad asks for them. He's told the Captain he wants to observe the investigation. That's not going to fly with the Captain or Steve. They don't want to share anything."

"Dis is gonna be big. Bigger dan what anyone guesses. You're on ta someting here."

Andrea dropped her head in her arms. Luckily, she wore earbuds. "Dad, all this cryptic talk gets confusing.

"When you're on dis case, you 'll need ta listen to da gift. You deny it, but I see it. We both know it's there, girl, if you develop it. Be sensitive to anyting dat comes to ya and don't ignore it." The tone of her dad's voice made her frown.

"Dad." Her tone warned him, but she softened it with, "I love you."

"Sleep well, sweetheart. I love ya too, dooncha know." He hung up.

Andrea took her empty bowl to the sink. As a child, she'd believed him to have the gift. When she got older and saw how the media both supported him and made fun of him, she began to question his ability. *Was he observant with attention to detail or did he really have a gift? Can I count on him?*

His publicity spilled over into her own life and she'd been bullied by the kids in school. Made fun of. They'd called her the witch or the Voodoo girl. She'd pulled away from all but her best friends. They stuck by her no matter what.

Later she'd joined her dad and become a police officer. What else could she do? She'd hung around the station so much Sally, the clerk, put her to work. It wasn't long until she knew every form and call. When anyone in the office was sick, she filled in.

That night her dreams were filled with arms that reached out of a lake.

The next morning Andrea parked her car in the station's lot and sat for a moment. Vans, reporters, and the curious lined the curb. Reporters huddled in groups; their breath reminded her of dragons breathing fire. They devoured anything they set their eyes on.

After the sleepless night, she didn't look forward to dealing with reporters. She needed to get into the station and get to the daily briefing.

She took a deep breath, kept her expression firmly neutral, and focused on the back of the building. She strode to the station hoping the group would think she was a lowly office worker. At the backside of the building, She saw a reporter, who stood in her way.

She spoke into a microphone. "You're Detective Andrea Watson. You were at the lake when the body parts were found in the ice. Can you tell me what they've found?" The woman in a fashionable snowsuit with a local station logo on the jacket held the microphone toward Andrea. Across from her stood a cameraman focused on the interaction.

Andrea liked the news station. It was her favorite to watch. They tried, most of the time, to report the news without too much personal commentary. Today she wasn't in the mood to talk. "I can't comment on the case. I'm sure the Captain will have a press conference." She waved her card over the sensor and started to reach for the handle when a male hand passed hers and pulled the door open.

"What's your name?" The man beside her asked the reporter while he pulled the door partway open not allowing Andrea room to pass.

Andrea turned to see it was the FBI agent. She sighed.

"Kaeli Meyers, Channel six."

"Well, Kaeli. I can tell you this." Andrea scowled at the agent as he spoke to the woman. "What looked like body parts were found frozen in the ice blocks cut from the lake. The blocks were taken to the Medical Examiner's office. I'm sure she is doing her best to thaw the ice and retrieve the evidence. She'll perform whatever tests she'll need to do to determine who the parts belong to. That is if they are actual body parts and not pieces of a mannequin." He pulled the door open for Andrea to pass him into the building. A slight lift of the corner of his mouth and a dimple appeared as he winked at her. It caught Andrea off guard. *He's cute.*

"Sir, who are you?" Kaeli held out the microphone toward him.

He turned slightly and winked at the girl. "Be a good reporter and find out." He firmly shut the door behind him.

"What was that all about?" Andrea asked.

"You shouldn't leave these poor young reporters with nothing. They're doing their job. So, I gave her something to fill in her time slot. It raises a question that will have her ahead of the rest. Were these real body parts or pieces of a mannequin? If not I didn't tell her anything she didn't already know."

"What was your name again?" Andrea asked.

"FBI Agent Fletcher Petersen at your service." He clicked his heels like a Nazi officer.

"What are you doing here? This isn't the FBI office."

"I've been detailed to your department."

"Good luck." Andrea offered.

Chapter 3

In the squad room, Andrea made her way to her desk. After hanging her coat on the hook at the end of her cube, she looked around. A couple of officers headed down the hall with quick steps. She checked her phone. No message. She took a chance, grabbed a notebook, and headed to the conference room.

Officers stood shoulder to shoulder, blocking the door. Female officers tried to peer over their shoulders. Andrea pushed her way into the room, excusing herself. Two men parted, allowing her to stand in front of them, and she ended being pressed against the conference table. Captain Conrad stood at one end of the room next to Sergeant Steve Totts.

Her eyes narrowed at the second man, and her jaw locked. The guy was a disgusting pig. He and his friends made no secret they thought women shouldn't be on the force except to make coffee, type, and file reports.

The room quieted when Steve whistled for attention. "As you are allaware, we found body parts in the ice blocks cut from Blue Lake." Steve rested his arms on the podium as he spoke. "The Medical Examiner has tested them and corroborated they are, in fact, human remains. We have a total of three skulls, three feet, and four hands, encased in two net bags. The ME's office will match DNA samples to see if they match any known missing persons. Until then, we need to find out what anyone might know about how they got into the lake in the first place." Steve looked around the room. "A team will be with the divers doing an underwater search. It would seem like these can't be the only parts in the water. It's a possibility there are more bodies at the bottom." He looked down at his notes.

"Captain Conrad will be doing a Press Conference this afternoon. Those of you I've assigned to lead a team will attend. The rest of you can start your assigned duties or go back to your normal assignments."

A loud throat-clearing sound came from near the door on the opposite side of the room. Steve turned, along with everyone else.

"It seems you've left out something. I'm Agent Fletcher Peterson. I've been assigned by the FBI to observe this case. It's been cleared with the Chief of Police and your Captain Bellows." He nodded at the Captain, who gave a noticeably short nod in response. "I'm wondering which team you have Detective Watson and myself assigned to?" Fletcher never looked away from the man assuming the leader's position.

Heat rose in Andrea's face as all eyes turned to look at her. She could almost hear them ask, *How does she know this guy? What did she do to get that kind of pull?*

Steve kept his expression neutral, but Andrea knew he'd been backed into a corner. He looked at his notes glanced around the room settling on one,

"Ben, they're on your team. You'll be interviewing the property owners around the lake." He dismissed the group and slammed the cover of his portfolio.

She watched as Steve turned to Captain Conrad. His body language showed he wasn't happy. She hid a smile and headed toward Ben.

Ben held up his hand when he saw her making a beeline for him. "I don't know what we're doing. He may change his mind after the press conference. I'll tell you when I find out." He walked past her to his cube.

The FBI agent arrived at her desk. "I think that went well. At least we're on a team." his dimples showed, and the twinkle in his eyes almost caused her to smile, but she didn't.

She shrugged. "I guess. I almost want to ask why you dragged me into that situation, but I have to admit, it was the only way I'd get on a team. Thanks."

"You're welcome. I've been given this desk to use." He swept his hand to the side of the cube that mirrored hers.

Nodding, she sat at her desk and ignored him. Opening her computer and a pad of paper began to write questions she'd want to ask the neighbors.

"How long have you been on the force?" Fletcher asked.

It took a moment before Andrea answered. "Three years here in St. Paul, seven up north." She didn't look up, hoping it was enough.

"How do you want to approach the neighbors?" The agent asked, changing the subject.

Andrea rolled her eyes and turned her head to face him. Pasting on a smile, she responded, "Any way you'd like, Sir." She went back to writing on the pad.

"Look, I know we haven't got off on a good start. I'd like to help all I can. I'm not the enemy." He leaned on his elbow looking directly into her eyes.

Andrea felt his sincerity. "I'm sorry. You're right. I'm writing questions to ask the neighbors. I'm also trying to figure out who and what we're looking for."

"You a profiler? We've got a whole department for that."

"We have a few here too." He opened his laptop. "Is there a printer I can connect to?"

She held back a sigh and told him the link to her printer. Soon it whirred, and paper spits out. "Here are some questions you may want to use."

"Thank you." She looked at the paper and nodded as she read through the list.

Andrea logged into a site to search the database for missing women in the surrounding counties. She was sure agents were working on the same thing, but she wanted her own list. The question was, did this killer take from his backyard? She doubted it. She'd search in the states surrounding Minnesota.

At the press conference, Captain Conrad Bellows introduced everyone, including Fletcher Peterson, from the FBI, who stood slightly behind Andrea. He didn't mention Andrea or her relationship to the case.

Steve took over from Captain Bellows and went on to explain what they would be doing. When he was done, it was open to questions. Andrea noticed the same reporter, who had approached her and Fletcher, hold up her hand. Steve acknowledged her.

"Kaeli Meyers, KPTV. Is it safe to eat fish caught in the lake?" The woman had pulled her hood off, revealing dark coppery colored hair that almost glowed in the afternoon sun.

Steve looked down at his notes. "If your fish hasn't eaten any humans lately." He gave a laugh that didn't go any further than the woman addressing him. "I haven't heard from the DNR at this time. I suggest you do not eat fish from that lake to be on the safe side."

"Has it been determined if the body parts found are male or female?" Another voice asked.

"The skulls are definitely female. A couple of the hands look to be female as they still had fingernail polish on them. The rest is going to be up to the lab to tell us."

"What is the FBI's interest in this case? Are they taking over? Any indications this might have connections out of state?" Kaeli asked, giving the nod toward Fletcher.

Steve glared at the woman before he answered. "Agent Peterson was on site when the body parts were found and removed from the lake. The FBI knows we have jurisdiction on the case. He's a special agent and will be observing in case we need to call on them for assistance."

"How about Detective Watson, who was at the site when the parts were taken from the lake. Is she handling any part of the case?" Kaeli continued to direct her questions to Steve.

This time Steve glared at Andrea. "Detective Watson will be on a team gathering information." He went on to pick other reporters, and as the conference began to turn into a bunch of regurgitated questions, Andrea slipped behind the officers and headed to the station.

"Detective, are you on this case or not?" A woman's voice stopped her exit. It was that woman reporter, Kaeli Meyers.

Andrea looked at her. "Yes." *There was no way she was going to be caught in a verbal battle with this aggressive reporter.*

Kaeli dropped her mike from her face and motioned to the camera guy to kill the video. She watched until he did so and stepped closer to Andrea. "Officially? Or are you relegated to your desk to type up reports?"

Andrea checked the woman over. She seemed nice but showed an edginess. She was after something; it was in her eyes. "I'm on the case. I'll be interviewing the residents."

"It's been noted that women in Captain Conrad's team aren't given any real detective work. They're relegated to menial tasks, not allowed to go out on cases."

"I'm sorry you've heard that. Some of us have boots on the ground, so to speak, while others help out with reports and research. We are all a part of the team." Andrea responded as if she were quoting from a script.

"So, you're saying the reports about Captain Conrad Bellows and Sargent Steve Totts treating the women in their department like they are clerks are false?"

"I have no comment on that question." Andrea turned to the door leading to the lobby.

"One more thing Ms. Watson," Kaeli called out.

Andrea turned. Kaeli had the mic to her mouth and the red light on the camera indicated it was recording. "Do you have the same psychic abilities as your father? Have they asked you to use them in this case or any other cases?"

Andrea froze. The off the wall question stunned her. Not forming an answer, she pulled open the door and wished it could slam behind her. *What did that question have to do with the case? What was this woman after?* In her cube, she found a sheet of paper on the blotter. Her name scrawled at the top and one line below.

You and Agent Peterson will begin interviewing the property owners around the lake. - Ben

She looked around the room for the FBI agent, no sign of him. She headed to her car and drove to the lake's parking lot.

Chapter 4

Andrea pulled into the public parking lot next to Blue Lake. Yellow tape strained in the wind. Vehicles lined the street next to the parking lot, and men milled around the area talking in small groups. She found an open spot next to a sign stating Private Property that led to a property next to the public parking lot. Before getting out she wondered who lived behind the beautifully wrought iron gate.

Andrea made her way to the officers nearest the dock, watching the ice cutters culling more blocks for the Ice Palace. She could hear fishermen arguing with the police about getting access to the lake.

"How is it going?" She asked the first officer she saw.

He shrugged and jerked his head to the groups standing in the parking lot. "We had some words with them. Most are complaining about not being able to get onto the lake. That group over there wants to talk to someone official," he stressed the last word, "about what they've found. I told them to give it to us, and we'd make sure it was taken to the proper authorities. They said they'd wait for someone with authority. I guess that's you, Detective." The officer looked past her; his gaze didn't waver. She turned her head to see what caught his attention. Agent Peterson headed her way.

"The lost is found, ya betcha." Andrea answered.

"I went looking for you after the press conference. You were already gone." He smiled. His blue eyes and dimples caught her attention again. She looked away.

"We have some people with information they aren't willing to give to our officer here. They didn't think he was important enough. We're going to show them that everyone here is important." She motioned for the officer to follow her. She took care to step around the frozen ground. "What's your name?" she asked the young man judging him to be about her age.

"Tim, Ma'am, Tim Smith."

"Okay, Tim, which were the men who talked to you?" She walked slower, giving him time to look over the groups.

"Those guys over there by the white van. The Asian gooks." He snorted.

Andrea stopped and turned to stand in front of him, preventing him from continuing. In a low, even tone, she spoke his name. "Tim, just as you felt offended when they wouldn't talk to you because of your rank, your tone tells me what you think of them because of their ancestry. Don't make that mistake again. Everyone gets treated fairly. I could have left you standing guard over a parking lot, but I didn't. Tuck your personal feelings aside and hear what they have to say. You don't know if they have a clue that will make you a hero and find who did this or not." She waited for his short nod before turning back to the group, which now had all eyes on her.

"Good afternoon gentlemen., I'm Detective Watson, this is Agent Peterson. Officer Tim informed me you have important information we need to hear. What do you have for us?"

No one spoke. One man looked her over and nodded. "You were the one I saw on TV. You found the body parts at the lake."

"I didn't find them; I was here when they were discovered." Andrea bowed her body slightly in respect.

The man paused. When she looked up at him, he gave her a nod. "This isn't the first-time body parts have been found in this lake."

Andrea stared at the man. He was middle-aged but older than some of the men around him. Some nodded. The rest of the men had no clue what was said. She recognized they were Hmong by their features.

"Where have other body parts been found?" Tim asked as if trying to assert his position.

"In the fish we catch. Some of the larger fish have larger pieces. Eyes, fingers, toes, and chunks of meat. Mostly in the larger Carp. They stay in the deeper parts of the lake along with the bass and muskie caught here."

"How did you find these parts?" Tim asked.

They were interrupted when Tim's radio went off. "I gotta go." He took off back across the parking lot in a jog.

In his own language, one of the men laughed and said, "Stupid cop, he doesn't know anything about fishing. Where else would you find body parts?"

Andrea pasted a smile on her face as she walked the few steps to the man who spoke, standing at the end of the line. In his own language, she said softly, "He's not stupid. He wants to be clear on how you found the parts. For all we know, you're the killer." She returned to stand next to Fletcher.

"You speak our language. How is that for a -a-"The older man didn't finish.

"A non-native to the language?" She answered again in his native tongue. The others smiled. "Fletcher, I'll translate later." She went on to explain in the Dae language. "I lived next to a Hmong family who took me into their home like a daughter, and I learned the language, or I'd not understand anything being said." The men smiled and chuckled.

"You speak like one of us." One of the men spoke in English.

"Thank you, let's keep that little piece of information between us." the men nodded.

"What body parts did you find?" Fletcher asked the men when she stopped to gather her thoughts.

This time a different man answered in heavily accented English. "We found a finger first in the stomach of one of the fish. At the same time, I found a partial eyeball in another fish. We told the Doc about them and showed him. He took the pieces with him and told us to look in the stomachs of all our fish caught. Bring any pieces to him. We did."

"Who is Doc? What did he do with the things you gave him? Can we talk to him?" Andrea asked.

They turned away from her; the discussion was private. Even Andrea couldn't hear what was said. She waited for the men to finish their confab.

The man who had spoken before continued. "Doc is a friend and another fisherman. I'll contact him and tell him to come here tomorrow to talk to you."

"Okay. Here's my card if he wants to call me. I'll be back here tomorrow morning early. One more thing. How long have you been collecting body parts?"

"Four years or so. We'll be here tomorrow." They all gave a quick nod and bow. Andrea nodded and gave a brief but more distinct bow. She turned to walk across the parking lot.

"Now, what was that all about? I take it no one at the station knows you speak that language?" Fletcher guided her to his car. "Let's get warmed up before we start knocking on doors."

In his car, Andrea wrapped her arms around her body and waited while the car warmed. The heater blasted cold air that soon turned to heat. Her butt got warm then hot. "The seat warmer is working; how do I turn it down?"

Fletcher grinned and turned the dial on her side of the console. "Better?"

"Yes. Thanks."

"Now tell me how you knew their language?"

"When I moved to St. Paul, in an area where any Hmong live. Not many of our culture want to live where the smell of garlic and spices permeates the walls. I needed cheap and close to downtown. I often saw the young woman who lived next door at the bus stop. While we talked, I found out she attended a tech school downtown, and we rode the same bus. As we spoke, we got to know one another. After a time, she invited me to meet her family.

Nine people living in a two-bedroom apartment. I hesitate to say two bedrooms. They are so small they were like large walk-in closets. Anyway. They took pity on me. Que, that's her name, invited me to dinner one night. I managed to eat rice and bits of fish. I tasted everything, and some things I didn't question until I'd tasted. Some I didn't want to know. I learned by smell or Que's suggestion when to stay home." She smiled at Fletcher. "They were so kind to me. They talked fast. I had no idea what they were saying."

"I can say a few words in Spanish. I took it in high school for a couple years." He chuckled. "Hola. Como esta? That's about it."

Andrea smiled and continued. "One Saturday, Grandma knocked at my door, frantic. I followed her back to their apartment. Smoke filled their kitchen from a fire on the stove. I ran back to my apartment to get the fire extinguisher and put out the fire. I couldn't understand what she was saying. She pulled me to the bedroom. Que's mother lay on the bed, moaning. I felt Nye's forehead. It was hot. I saw she'd been throwing up in a bucket, and it didn't look good. I called 911, but Grandma cried and screamed at me. Hitting me as I tried to calm her. When the EMS and police came, I took them to Nye, and they put her on the gurney. Grandma was upset. By that time, Que came home and I told her what happened. She calmed Grandma. I stayed with her while Que and a neighbor went to the hospital. Nye had food poisoning from her work. It was then Que, and her mother decided I learn the language. We had a great time with me learning much the way children do."

"You seem to speak it well."

"I got hit over the knuckles with a spoon if I pronounced the word wrong. I got it right. I guess I'm a natural at languages."

"Really? How many do you speak?"

"Four. Dae, Italian, French, and Spanish. I know a few phrases in German, Russian/Ukraine, as well as Croatian. Oh yeah, I also lapse into Nordy speak. "

"You are a smart woman. I'm impressed. I can see why the Captain wants to keep you around." He guided the car to the curb next to the first house from the public dock area.

"You're sadly mistaken. I don't mean to complain, but the Captain is a year from retirement. All he wants to do is collect his pay and leave. He wants everything status quo. Steve Totts is looking to take his place. If that happens, I will look for somewhere else to work. As to my language ability, I have spoken basic Spanish when needed." She pulled on her gloves.

"The pasture isn't always greener on the other side." Fletcher intoned.

She winced, "Let's find out if this homeowner can tell us what goes on around the lake."

Chapter 5

They walked up the steps to the first house. The door hadn't been painted in many years. Cracked and bubbled paint peeled from the door jamb. The siding had warped and pulled the nails away from the house. The once shiny enamel painted porch had been worn smooth from use. The paint on the rocking chairs had long faded in the heat and sun.

Fletcher knocked at the door. "How old do you think this person is?" His head indicated the dead plants hanging over the edge of the pots.

"I'd say his wife's been dead at least five to seven years." She shrugged and pressed the doorbell. She heard a faint old-fashioned buzz resounding through the door.

After a moment, they heard someone call, "Just a moment." The sound of several locks being unbolted heralded the response. The door swung open and a tall, thin man with a blanket over his shoulders peered down at them. Not too far down as Fletcher was almost eye level to the man.

"Good afternoon Sir, We're from the police department. You may have seen the commotion on the lake?"

The man continued to look at them through the glass storm door, then nodded.

Fletcher continued, "Could we come in and ask you a few questions about living on the lake?"

The man's watery eyes traveled from Fletcher to Andrea and back. "What do you want to know?" He didn't move to open the storm door.

"How long have you lived on the lake?" Andrea asked before Fletcher could say anything. The wind rattled the loose shutter on the nearest window.

"Moved here in '89 with my wife. I'd been given a new position as head of a department for 3M. The bonus was good and with our savings, we bought this house."

"So, in forty years or so, you've met a lot of the people who've lived around the lake?" Andrea continued.

"I saw on the news you found body parts in the ice." He nodded to Andrea.

"That's true." She gave a shiver more for effect than what she felt. "We're asking if anyone has seen anyone suspicious on or around the lake."

The man fiddled with the lock on the storm door and pushed it open, "May as well come in. It's too cold to be talking on the porch. A man could catch his death. Now wouldn't that be something after all these years?" He turned expecting them to follow.

Fletcher shut the door behind him and gave Andrea a pained grimace. She was already breathing in short gasps to keep from gagging.

The smell of an unwashed body, clothes, musty uncirculated air permeated the narrow path behind the old man. He moved into what was the living room. The décor had been north woods rustic. Now it was dusty woods.

He fell into a worn recliner that has seen more bad days than good. Stacks of papers sat on two chairs. "Move those on to the floor."

Andrea looked at Fletcher who grabbed from the top of the stack and began to build a paper tower next to the chair. Andrea followed his example.

Her chair had a faded, but intricate afghan thrown over it. Andrea fingered the pattern. "You're wife crochet this?" She asked the older gentleman as she sat down.

"Yes, May was good at that stuff. Every one of her nieces and nephews had one for their graduation, wedding, or as a baby gift." He wiped his cheek, "She got cancer and died."

"I'm glad they have that as a remembrance of her. By the way, we didn't get to the introductions outside. I'm Detective Andrea Watson and this is FBI Agent Fletcher Peterson." Fletcher leaned over to shake the man's hand.

"Harris Ford." The man offered his name. After the long pause, he continued. "I know it sounds like Harrison Ford, but we're no relation and I sure don't have the money he does." He gave a dry laugh that sounded like he hadn't made that noise for a while.

"Have you seen anyone on the lake that might appear suspicious?" Fletcher asked.

"Suspicious? They're all suspicious if you ask me. Who'd want to sit on a bucket over a hole in the ice and wait for fish to bite?" He laughed at his own joke.

"Mr. Ford, what can you tell me about your neighbors? You've lived here a long time, have any of the other residents lived here as long as you have?"

He rubbed his scraggly beard, "Well now there are the Turners, Ruth and Joe, next door. They aren't home now. They're snowbirds. They leave here in November after Thanksgiving. Joe drives their fifth wheel down to California and parks it there until April. They come back for a few days during the week of Christmas then fly back after New Year's Day."

"Has anything unusual happened around their house while they were gone?"

"No. I have a key to the place, and I make sure the papers are picked up if someone mixes up the houses and tosses a paper on their porch. They have their lights on those timers."

"Who lives next to them?" Fletcher was curious about the camper he saw parked along the side of the house."

"Now look here, I'm not the nosey type, I don't go spying on my neighbors." Harris protested.

"I'm sure you don't. They're the Moffit's." He looked at his notebook.

"Yes, they are. They have a daughter in Seattle that had surgery. They went up to care for the kids."

"Is there anything else you can tell us or something you remember that wasn't quite the way it should be?"

Harris shook his head. Fletcher stood and handed Harris his card. "If you think of anything call me."

"I sure will. Everyone here has been a regular on the lake even the Asians. They come like clockwork. I don't have anything against them. They're clean fishermen and have offered me a carp or two when I'm walking by them at the end of the lake. Come here." Harris got out of his chair with great difficulty and walked to a curtained wall.

After a moment he pulled the curtain open a little. "Be careful of that father." He jerked his head toward a house at the curve of the lake. "The man is ex-military. I hear his wife travels a lot. I stay away from him. He's creepy if you get my meaning."

"Why?" Fletcher asked as they looked at the house.

"He's too perfect. He manicures his lawn. He runs his kids like they were his platoon. They march outside in a line. They all sit together in a circle around the fire and I hear them singing. He corrects any of them that don't sing it right. There's something not right about him. Now there's a killer if anyone is."

Andrea wrote it down in her notebook. "Being a strict dad isn't a crime."

Mr. Ford turned to face the two detectives. "I served in the Viet Nam war. I also watch crime shows and listen to crime podcasts. My nephew showed me how to get them on my iPad. Yes, I have an iPad." He hobbled over to his chair and picked up the device. "This guy isn't a normal dad." He tapped the face and turned it to face them. A video played.

Andrea watched as the video focused on a group of children marching across the back lawn in a single file. The man ordered them to do something in the garden. They divided into groups of two and began pulling weeds. Six children. They looked to be four or five to maybe twelve to fifteen. The video stopped and Andrea held the device toward the old man.

"No, wait for the next one." He waved his hand to indicate her to continue watching.

This time the video showed the same children playing a game of croquet. The sound of a loud whistle came through the device. The children stopped playing. They pulled up the metal hoops and sticks and moved in slow deliberate steps to form the same line she'd seen previously. No emotion.

When the implements were returned to the game cart, the oldest pulled the cart along as they all marched back to the house. The video moved away from the children up to the deck where a man, dressed in slacks, shirt, and tie, watched the procession. He looked up toward the person holding the video. He made a short bow, spun on his heel and walked into the house. The feed stopped.

This time Mr. Ford took the device back. "Does that look like the way normal kids act? I have another video of the kids who live on the other side of them. They aren't allowed to play together. Do you see the fence around the yard? The gate is locked on the lakeside."

Andrea looked back at the window. She couldn't see the house in question, but for a moment she had an odd feeling about it. "Thank you for showing that to us. I don't know what we can do about it." She gave a dismissing wave of her hand. Mr. Harris grabbed it mid-air.

Andrea's eyes met his watery gaze. His eyes locked with hers and he didn't let go of her wrist. Fletcher moved quickly to her side, his hand reaching out to disengage the hold. Andrea waved him back, her gaze still connected to the old man.

"I have one more thing to add. You're going to understand when I tell you." The words connected to her mind and the feel of his hand caused a chill to run through her body. She couldn't shake her arm loose from his grasp even if she'd wanted to, which she didn't.

"As you could see, our lots are narrower at the lake as the land curves. I have a compost pile among the grass in my yard. This last fall I went to spread some of that on my raised garden." He let her wrist drop from his grasp, but he didn't move his eyes from hers. "It's what I found in that pile that disturbed me. Buried under the compost near the top I found a dead chicken. It's the manner in which it died that worries me. It was butchered. The head was cut, and I found it apart from the body. The eyes were stabbed out with a sharp object. Maybe an ice pick or something similar."

His expression turned to concern. Andrea felt this was not a joke of some sort. She nodded for him to continue.

"The body had been cut in half and the innards pulled out. The feathers were pulled from the body violently. Not plucked like you would if it were to be cooked. Like someone was angry when they pulled them out. That's not all, the body had been stabbed repeatedly with a knife. It looked like a sharp pocketknife. A short, small blade folding knife."

"Like using it for a target?" Fletcher asked, still standing close to Andrea. His body in protective mode.

Harris looked at Fletcher, his expression cold. "No, savagely stabbed, over and over. I've been in the war, I've killed. Not a clean stab to kill. This was done in a fit of anger. The cuts were close, overlapping. Someone used this bird as a surrogate for the intended subject."

Andrea started to speak, but he held up his hand for her o stop. "I know what you're going to ask. It wasn't the only animal. Further down in the pile I found a cat. This cat may have been a pet as it was fat, well-fed. This cat had been split down the gut. The entails pulled out. They were spread and buried in the pile. The cat was also brutally mutilated."

"Do you think this was done by the same person who put the body parts in the lake?" Andrea responded.

Harris narrowed his eyelids at her. "I don't know what those body parts looked like. Were they hacked in pieces? Where the parts stabbed?"

"No. They were cut by someone who knew what they were doing. The appendages had been cut at joints."

"The parts weren't mutilated or hacked?" Harris asked.

Andrea and Fletcher shook their head. "It's not the same person. The person who did this attacked the cat and hen as if it were the object of their hate. They were taking all their feeling out on the animal." Harris captured Andrea's gaze again. This time she knew what he was inferring.

"You think someone around this lake has issues."

"Yes. Here's the thing. Two families raise chickens. That family," he pointed at his device. "And an old guy at the far end of the lake. What does that tell you?"

Andrea looked away. That chill came back. His words swirled in her mind. Things she'd heard, read came to her mind. *This is a killer in the making. Oh God, who could this be?* Her gaze returned to the old man. "This is disturbing."

Harris nodded. "When you go to the military house, keep your eyes and all your senses open. You may learn something." He motioned for them to move back to the front door. "I wish you luck finding who put the bodies in the lake. My vote is the guy on the video."

"Thank you for the information." Fletcher followed Andrea off the porch.

Back in the car, Fletcher turned up the heat as he drove the few yards to the next house.

"What do you think of the video?" Fletcher asked.

"I think we need to get a copy of it for the file. It may not have anything to do with this case. I get a feeling it may be critical to a future case." Andrea hugged herself. It was what Mr. Ford had told them after the video that caused her reaction.

"Are you thinking what I'm thinking?" Fletcher asked as he put the car in park leaving the engine running.

"Yes." Her voice came out in a whisper.

"Let's put that aside and visit this next house."

Chapter 6

They knocked at the door, but no one answered. Andrea left her card in the storm door in case the homeowners used the door. "Isn't this the couple that went to Seattle?" Fletcher nodded and turned back to the car.

"There isn't much left of the afternoon. Let's hit one more house before we call it quits for the day." Andrea nodded. "I want to leave the family until another day."

As they parked and began to walk toward the front porch, a car pulled into the driveway and stopped beside them. The woman threw open her door, swung her feet out, and stood to face them.

"What happened? Is it my husband? Are my kids okay? Is it my parents?" She clutched the front of her shirt through the unzipped, Imperial purple down coat.

"Ma'am hold on nothing's wrong with any of the people you disclosed that we know of. We want to ask you a few questions." Andrea touched the woman's arm to reassure her.

Her shoulders slumped with relief and the woman stepped back to the car door. "Who are you? Are you sure no one's dead?" Her tone pleaded with Andrea.

"I assure you. We have no knowledge of anyone connected with you that is dead." Fletcher told her. "Are you missing someone?"

"Missing? Someone's missing? Who?" She turned to her car and rummaged around the front seat and stood with her phone in her hand before either Andrea or Fletcher could counter her action. "I need to call my children."

"Where are they?" Andrea asked.

"I hope they're with their grandmother. She agreed to pick them up today from school." She snagged her large handbag and swung it over her shoulder as she turned and slammed the car door.

Fletcher leaned back in a quick reaction or he'd have been smacked with it.

"Mom? Are the kids with you? Good. It'll be a while before I can get them. The Police are here to question me."

Andrea looked at Fletcher who cocked his head.. *She knew we're the police.* She mouthed. He shrugged.

They followed the woman to the door and waited while she stood in front of it continuing to give instructions to the person she referred to as Mom. After terminating the call, she unlocked the storm door and the front door. "Come in. We can talk about where it's warm."

Flinging her purse and coat onto the bench in the foyer, she motioned for them to follow her. "Put your coats on the chair. You won't be here long enough to hang them up." She waved to the chairs facing the fireplace in the family room. She headed to the kitchen. "I know you don't drink on the job. Would you like a cup of coffee? I can pop a pod in." She held up a mug and a pod of coffee waiting for an answer.

"No thanks, we won't be long if you want to sit and answer a few questions." Andrea motioned to the family room so they could continue their conversation.

She paused for a moment, acted resigned to the inevitable and found a seat across from the love seat. Andrea and Fletcher sat side by side on the two-cushion couch.

"Are you here about the body parts found in the lake?" She asked as if piecing a memory

"Yes. My name is Detective Watson and this FBI agent Peterson. You are?"

"Silly me. I'm Carla DeVey. My husband John, is a chemist for one of the medical companies in Minneapolis."

Fletcher wrote the information in his notebook. "What have you heard about the body parts that were found?"

'Not a thing. I saw the report on the news at my mother-in-law's house and then saw the police cars at the dock when I brought the children home. The area had been taped off. Dan and I watched the police talk to some of the men before they all left for the night."

"Did you talk to anyone about what you saw?" Andrea asked.

Carla tilted her head a bit to one side and said, "I called Harris. He's the neighbor between our house and the boat ramp. He said yes the police found two nets with heads, feet and hands." She wrapped her arms around her waist and shuddered. "How awful."

Before Andrea could ask the next question Carla's head jerked up and her eyes bored into first Andrea then Fletcher, "You don't think I had anything to do with it?" Her tone sounded belligerent.

"Why? Do you have anything that could help us find out who out the parts in the lake or committed the crime?" Andrea smiled as she asked.

"Heaven's no. Do you have any suspects?" She leaned forward almost conspiratorial.

Andrea didn't answer. "Have you seen anyone on the lake or walking across your lawn that you didn't know or knew they didn't belong around here?"

Successfully distracted, she tapped her finger on her chin. "Kids sometimes cut across our lawn when the snow is melted. I think one of the boys lives in one of the developments off the lake. He takes a shortcut on his way to his friend's house from school. I don't have any interest in fishing. I see boats on the lake in the summer and the fish houses on the lake in the winter. That's about it." She shrugged.

"Do you recognize the fish houses out on the lake this season? I'm sure many are family-owned and maybe even built. Are they local people, what I mean is do you know if they live around the lake?" Andrea asked.

"No, I don't pay any attention to who's out on the lake. Last year someone didn't get their house off the lake when the weather began to warm sooner than usual. It started to sink into the ice. That was quite a bit of excitement as some of the men took snowmobiles out as close as they could and lassoed the little house and drug it off the lake." She chuckled at the memory,

"How long have you lived here?" Andrea continued.

"We moved into the house after the Parade of Homes six years ago. It was one of the featured homes." She crossed her legs as if that emphasized the importance of the event.

"You must recognize most of the neighbors around the lake."

"Most of them, Harris Ford two doors down. The Moffit's next door. They are in Seattle taking care of their daughter and grandkids. She had surgery, a tumor." The words were almost in a whisper. "The next house is Tim and Mary Jacobs. They have three children all younger than mine. She has quite a handful. The next house is the Nelson's a middle-aged couple. They both work. They don't socialize with anyone on the lake that I'm aware of."

She stiffened and picked at an invisible thread on her designer jeans. "Look at the Richardson family. Now if you're looking for odd, they are the ones to look at. The father, John, is or was in the military. He stays at home. I have no idea why. He doesn't seem to have a physical disability. He could be a stay-at-home-dad." She paused and looked toward the backyard, leaning back a little to look farther along the lake edge.

"Why do you think he's strange?" Andrea prompted. She already knew who she was talking about.

"He gets the kids up early and they are out on the deck. If it's winter, they shovel the deck first. He has them doing calisthenics. They are outside for a good thirty to forty-five minutes depending on the weather. They have six children all about a year or two apart. The oldest must be about fourteen or fifteen. The youngest is about six, maybe seven, four are boys and two are girls. Now that's not all. They sit outside on large stones facing the lake and do artwork. Some paint, others draw, some write in notebooks and the little ones may color in a coloring book. After an hour or so he blows a whistle. They all get up put their things away or put them alongside their bodies, holding the paper, book, or whatever they have, and form a line. The oldest first on down and march single file back into the house."

Andrea looked at Fletcher. "That in itself doesn't seem too odd. If the father is military and that's how he keeps things in order. It's not a crime." Fletcher commented.

"Do you have kids?" Carla shot a question at him, but answered it herself, "No you don't. I can tell. Kids don't like to line up and march in and out of a house. They don't like spending every waking moment with their siblings. They want alone time. Playtime where they can roll in the grass, run, and jump. These kids aren't allowed to do any of that. They come and go out of that house all together in a line. They don't play. None of them." She leaned forward to make her point.

"In the summer they weed and do yard work. All together. They are in the garden or along the path that goes around their house pulling weeds. He whistles and they all get up, line up and go into the house together. I once saw one of the younger boys hide behind a bush and take a leak. No one looked at him or said a thing. I'll bet he wasn't allowed back in the house before the whistle blew. That's not right. The father is a psycho."

"He may be over-controlling, but it's not a crime unless he's physically abusing the kids. If you him doing anything like that, call us immediately."

Carla shook her finger at the two, "You don't get it. He's creating monsters. I watch true crime tv shows. I know things and I will move my family if they ever start wanting to play with my kids. They will kill, and their dad would cover it up. Maybe he's a murderer." She popped to her feet. "Yes, I'll bet he's the killer. He has a kayak or two. He and the older boy sometimes use them in the summer. What if he killed his wife and dumped her in the lake? He has his older son go out after dark and dump the weeds they pull into Mr. Ford's compost pile. I'm sure he doesn't mind, but I doubt they asked for permission."

Andrea froze at the announcement then asked, "Did you see this happen?"

"Yes. I never met the boy. He's got to be in his teens. He's strong with an athletic body like his dad." Carla glanced away.

Andrea watched her thinking the woman looked a bit guilty. Maybe she'd been watching the pair a little too closely?

"We'll look into the situation when we get there." Fletcher stood. "Thank you for all your information."

"Oh, one more person you need to talk to." She walked over to the sliding glass door and motioned for them to follow.

"That big house over across the lake is the Saunders' house. The family was one of the first to buy out here and build. That big log cabin and the smaller cabins are for their families who come and stay during the holidays." She used her painted finger indicate the house across the lake, next to the public dock and parking lot.

"They have big summer parties and invite all the property owners around the lake, over for BBQ. The grandparents don't live there anymore. They had three children. One son died in the war. One son is married, and one is divorced. The grandchildren are married and own each of those houses along the lakefront. I have no idea whose kids belong to whom. You'll want to question. Evan Morrison."

"Why are you concerned about him?" Andrea asked.

"He's too nice to the kids. He takes them out on the family boat and teaches them how to fish. He dyes his hair. Sometimes he's light brown with blond tips. Other times it's so dark brown it's almost black. I've seen him with plain brown colored hair." She shakes her head and waves her hand dismissively. "Never mind. That all sounds so normal when you say it out loud. He gives me the creeps.

Once, I went to find the kids at the BBQ. I knocked at the cabin he stays in when he's in town. The door swung open when I knocked. I called out his name but got no answer. I looked around the room. The cabin is like an oversized hotel room with a small kitchen to one side and the back door opens to a porch you can see from the lake. He had clothes laid out on the bed. Four outfits all different, quite different." She shook her head in disbelief.

"Did he see you in his cabin?" Andrea asked. *Now, why did I ask that?*

"No, I heard the kids' voices outside. I shut the door and left. I've never heard what he does for work. I've seen his car next to the cabin then gone. He could live somewhere else and use the cabin when he's passing through."

"We'll check on him," Fletcher stood, waited for Andrea to stand too. "We've taken enough of your time."

She followed them to the door as they donned their coats and scarves. "Come back any time." She looked at the card, Andrea hesitantly handed her. "Can I call you if I think of anything else?"

"Sure."

Back in the car, Fletcher pulled away from the curb and drove back to the parking lot. He parked next to Andrea's car. "I don't know what to think about what we learned today."

"It's a lot, yet it was nothing you can write in a report that would be useful information. How do you write that one person thinks there's a killer in the making? That both contacts think their neighbor is possibly the killer?" Andrea shook her head.

"I guess, it will have to be just the facts ma'am, just the facts." Fletcher winked at her.

"Agent, I'm glad you came with me. It was definitely an interesting morning." She pulled the handle and opened the door. "I'll see you back at the station."

"I have to go to the FBI office. I'll talk to you later."

Chapter 7

Andrea drove back to the station. In her cube, she pulled her notebook out and stared at what she'd written. Loading the form on the computer she typed in what they learned. She tuned out the buzz of conversation around her. Most of it involved personal situations in which she had no interest until she heard something about the lake.

"That water was cold." she heard one of the officer's remark. "I stuck my hand in." He shivered. "No way I'm getting in that lake."

"Yeah, the temperature they took was the same as the ocean when the Titanic went down. Think of trying to swim, finding a boat that would let you come aboard. When you do, they row away. When I put my hand in the water and left it there for as long as I could stand it, it didn't take long to go numb."

Andrea recognized the voice belonging to Bruce. He sat in the cube across from hers. Now he leaned on the dividing wall looking at her.

"I'll bet. I saw the movie and my dad took me to the exhibit one year. I've been fascinated by the story. I've watched all the documentaries they have. Still, it's the stories told by the survivors that get me. Survivor's guilt."

Bruce leaned over to her with a smile. "I didn't know you liked movies."

"Sure, what else do you do for eight months of winter?" She grinned back at him.

"What movies do you like?" He responded.

"All kinds. Movies that focus on the fighting and not how much they can show off the carnage. I want the story. I've seen Pearl Harbor enough times I don't watch it anymore. The same with Bridge over the River Kwai."

"So, you like war movies." He cocked his head looking at her with a frown. "I didn't take you for someone that would like that kind of movie."

Andrea gave a short huff of air. "You do know who my dad is." She raised her brows in question.

"Yes."

"I've watched all the old war movies from Guns of Navarone, Dirty Dozen, The Escape, Stalag 17 to K-19, and Hunt for Red October. We watched them all."

"What did you think of K-19?"

"I can't watch it. I cried from the middle of the movie to the end. My dad made me watch until the end. We weren't in the theater, but he said I needed to toughen up. I was too sissy." Andrea turned back to her desk. "I'm not a sissy. I have a lot of compassion. I cried for the dedication those men had for their country. If the sub would have been one of ours, it would have been the same. Our men would die for our country and their Captain. I still hurt for the families of those men." She lifted her head a bit to allow the excess moisture in her eye to dissipate.

"You're a good woman Andrea. No matter what people think or say around here." He whispered at her. "Don't let them change you."

"Meeting in the conference room in fifteen!" Steve Totts' voice blasted across the room.

Andrea pressed the save icon, grabbed her notebook, her coffee mug, and headed to the conference room. Of course, all the chairs were taken. He must have waited until all the guys arrived then shouted announced the meeting. *Men.*

Steve cleared his throat indicating he needed their attention. "Here's what we have so far. The lab hasn't had enough time to process the parts. The divers found another net, but this one had bones with little bits of muscle and tissue attached. That's been taken to the lab too. The media is on a need-to-know basis. I don't want anything being said to the media about this case. Got that?" Steve looked straight at Andrea.

What was he inferring? She hadn't talked to the media about the case. Kaeli! What had she written? Andrea didn't take the paper, so she never read the news. She watched a little news either at night or in the morning while she dressed for work. The local stations ran on a couple of screens in the squad room. She had a news stream on her computer that notified her if breaking news came across the wire.

Steve continued, "The rest of you have your assignments. I need those reports every day. What's been said and who said it. We need to find out who did this."

Andrea walked back to her desk. What was Steve's problem with her? He didn't treat other women as bad. They did their jobs. Typing reports, making coffee, running reports, and researching cases. She wanted fieldwork. That's what Captain Conrad promised her. Her ranking and recommendation from the academy had put her at the top of the recruiting list. She'd wanted to stay in Minnesota, so she took the best offer and stayed here. She wanted to be close to her father, but not in the same town. Conrad knew she'd turned down more lucrative offers out of state.

"Next time you see a reporter, keep your mouth shut." Steve's voice hissed from behind her as she finished her reports.

Turning to face her accuser she looked up at him, "What are you talking about?"

"You know what I'm talking about. You and that nosey reporter. It's all over the papers and the news."

"Steve I haven't watched listened or read the news for three days. I have no idea what you're nattering about."

Steve looked at her calm expression and turned to walk away. He was back in a minute tossing the paper at her. The newspaper, unfolded as it fell on the desk beside her and left.

She picked it up and read:

Daughter of Bemidji Detective on the Ice Cube Case.

The article told how her dad was known to solve his missing person's cases and bring in murders. Was his daughter following in his footsteps? She was seen questioning fishermen near the dock where the body parts were discovered and then asking questions of property owners around the lake.

The article wasn't long, but it insinuated she had inside information she wasn't telling her team members.

Andrea headed across the room and tossed the paper into the garbage can next to Steve's office door. "You believe this stuff? Steve, there is some truth about my dad. He was good at his job. He retired and he's puttering around looking at cold cases. Furthermore, I didn't talk to her or ask for her to confront me."

"You didn't talk to the reporter?" Steve pressed.

"She stopped me and asked if Donald Watson was my dad. I said yes. That was about it. We came inside and left her standing outside."

"We?"

"Fletcher and I."

"He was with you?"

Andrea crossed her arms. "You—assigned—him—to—me." She spoke as if to a small child reminding him of his own actions. "He arrived after I did."

He paused. "Okay, don't tell that reporter anything." He started to turn away. "You got a call from some guy to meet him tomorrow at the Blue Lake parking lot at nine AM. He has something to show you." Steve made a face at her. "Who is it?"

She wanted to tell him if he kept making that face it was going to freeze like that forever. She resisted the urge and schooled her expression to a blank stare.

"One of the fishermen," she stressed the distinction, "told me he might have something to show me." She shrugged.

Steve continued to stare at her as if he wanted to say something more but turned away. "Give me a report on it as soon as you get back."

Andrea remained in the office for a minute longer. He'd dismissed the call as unimportant or was it that he was giving her the message that he was in charge?

Andrea returned to her desk. What did the Hmong fisherman have to tell her? Did he still have the body parts he'd collected? If he did, how had he preserved them? She let all the possibilities run through her mind. What about the chain of evidence? Would it hold up in court if they ever found the guy?

When her shift was over, she headed down the corridor to the lobby. Before pushing the door open she peered through the side window. No reporter insight. Giving Bobbie a quick wave as she passed the front desk she hurried to her car and headed home.

Chapter 8

Fletcher stood next to his car when she pulled into the public parking lot next to Blue Lake. The meteorologist reported the wind chill was minus five degrees. She pulled on her fur-lined gloves and reached for the fleece Balaclava fitting it over her head. Taking a quick glance at herself in the mirror, she grimaced at her reflection.

Her boots crunched in the ice and hardened snow. Gazing for a moment at the lake, she wondered if more body parts would be found. Almost as if she answered herself she heard *yes, lots*. Now that was creepy.

"I brought you a coffee." He handed her a steaming thermal travel mug. "Thanks for calling me to tell me about the meeting."

"Thanks, and you're welcome. I was pretty sure Steve wouldn't call you."

The men at the camper greeted her and told her the Doc was inside. She nodded and grabbed the handle with one hand. It wasn't going to work trying to balance the mug and pull herself up the step ladder.

"Here, give me the mug." Fletcher took it and guided her up the steps into the camper. His manners didn't bother her like it did when other men grabbed her and tried to control her.

Inside, two men sat in a small booth. She slid across from them. Fletcher's legs were too long, so he sat sideways next to her.

"Hello. I'm Detective Andrea Watson and this is Agent Fletcher Peterson. I was told you have more body parts. How did you come to get them?" She spoke in his language.

He sat back for a moment, surprised, and looked at the man next to him who laughed out loud. "I didn't tell him you knew how to speak our language."

"You speak it quite well." The man surprised Andrea. He spoke English without an accent.

"You do too. Are you American?"

"I'm Joe Vang. Doc to some. I came here for an education. I was able to stay on the ally program."

"How did you come by the nickname?" Fletcher asked.

Joe shrugged one shoulder. "I helped fix a broken leg and the nickname stuck."

"Back to the body parts. Joe," Andrea pushed her hood off, her balaclava down, then unzipped her coat. The camper had heat. She sipped her coffee. "Sorry I don't have any coffee for you."

"Not a problem, we brought our own." He lifted a similar thermal cup. "I was here fishing and one of the men brought a finger to me. I questioned him and he showed me he'd found pieces of flesh and tissue as well as other body parts in the stomach of some of the fish he caught. After questioning the fishermen, I found they all had bits and pieces they'd found. Most of them were tossed in the garbage. I told them to bring me every piece, they found. Not to touch them. Bring it to me as they found them."

"What did you do with them?"

"Right after I saw the parts I called the police. They referred me to another department, and I talked to a detective. He came to the lake but never got out of his car. He wanted to see what I had found. At the time I had a few bits of skin, fingernails, the acrylic kind attached to a fingertip.

He didn't look at them much, just glanced at the case and said he wasn't interested. I told him I had more items, like bits of tissue and muscle. He shook his head and said they were the guts of an animal. Now if I found a body to go with it, I could contact him. He drove off and never came back or called me."

"Do you remember who that officer was?" Andrea asked.

"Oh yes. He's in charge of this investigation. It's that red-headed guy that was on TV."

Andrea looked at Fletcher and they both said "Steve" at the same time. I'm sorry he gave you the brush off. When was it you showed him this?"

"Two years ago."

"TWO years ago? You've kept this evidence for two years and never said anything about it?"

"Who would I tell?" He answers softly brushing his fingers through thick salt and pepper hair. "If he didn't think what I had was important who would?"

"Me!" She responded. "When can I see what you have?"

"You can come by on the day after tomorrow. I have some appointments tomorrow. Here's my address." He presented her his card and she took it with both hands bowing the best she could from her seated position. "Thank you." She in turn dug into her pocket and handed him one of her own, presenting it in the same manner. He nodded and smiled.

"WE can come by on Friday at nine am. Would that work?" Fletcher asked. Joe nodded.

Back at the car Fletcher shielded his eyes with his palm and looked across the lake. "Maybe we should go and talk to some of the owners of the ice houses." He got into the car and started it.

"Wait!" You mean right now?" she'd shut the door, but her hand remained on the handle.

"Yes, what better time than now? I see a few trucks and snowmobiles. We can question the owners." He put the car into gear.

Andrea pulled the handle, flung open the door and started to get out.

"What are you doing? Get back in here." He ordered.

"No thanks. I'll go back to the station in my car." She stood away from the car. Her arms folded and her back to the wind.

Fletcher looked at her and put the gear into park. "Get in and shut the door."

"Fletcher, I'm not going out on that lake."

"Get in the car." Fletcher's voice rose as he ordered in a standoff.

Fletcher stared at her for a long moment. "I won't go onto the lake."

Andrea eyed him between narrowed lids. When she saw he meant it she sat back down in the car and shut the door.

The silence felt like a giant curtain had fallen in the car between them. "Are you going to tell me what that was all about?" He asked in a low calm voice.

"No." She didn't look at him.

"Andrea. We need to question those people. There isn't any different way to do it but to drive on to the ice. Nothing is going to happen to you. I promise."

She didn't answer. Heat rose in her body. Blood raced through her veins. She began to shake. Holding herself she took deep breaths and laid her head against the rest. After what seemed like ages, she calmed down.

"You can go out on the lake. I will keep my feet firmly planted on solid ground."

"The ice is solid."

"Try telling my mind that. No matter what you say it will not make the fear go away."

"Tell me why you're afraid. What happened?"

She always wished she could have talked to someone about her fears. Would he tease her and laugh at her as much as her father did? Would he tell her to grow up that fears like that were for children and not almost thirty-year old's?

"We all have fears. Some we can hide others we can't. I want to know what caused this fear of going out onto the ice. We'll figure out another way to deal with the questioning."

Fletcher reached out and put his warm hand over the cold one that clutched at her coat. She didn't resist. Something about him gave her a feeling. What was the feeling? She pushed the thought aside to deal with the question.

After a long silence while she argued with herself she turned to Fletcher. He wasn't laughing. "I was about ten and my friend and I went ice skating after school. The ice on the lake looked like this lake. It wasn't all white and snow-covered. Most of it was black, yet clear enough to almost see the bottom once you got away from the bank."

She turned to look at Blue Lake. Where the men had cut the ice blocks, yellow tape flapped in the wind. The lake had already begun to freeze forming a thin layer that grew as the water froze onto the layer with each lap.

"We skated in circles, trying to do all the things we'd seen the figure skaters do on TV. We laughed as we fell trying to do a sits spin or what we called the flying camel. In a moment of stupidity, we started spinning and holding hands in a circle. I lost my grip and Helen flew out of my grasp and headed away from me. I tried to reach her, but she laughed and let her momentum take her." Andrea took a shaky breath and continued.

"I had a sudden feeling of fear and danger. I called for her to stop. I screamed at her at the top of my lungs. Over and over as I skated toward her. I heard it. The cracking of the ice. She heard it also and tried to change course, but she was going too fast. She did a fast break , her ankle twisted and she fell screaming in pain. I stopped while she lay on the ice holding her leg.

The cracking sound didn't stop. I saw it. The ice opening and it headed right for Helen. I tried to get to her, to pull her back, but a chunk of ice broke up with her on it and bobbed in the water.

She tried to call, to move. I told her to stay still." Andrea wadded her scarf around her wrists so tight she wasn't aware it was cutting off her circulation.

Fletcher took her hands and worked the scarf off as she talked, her eyes staring at the lake, his hands holding hers as he rubbed the backs with his thumb.

"I whistled with all my breath to some skaters at one end of the lake. They turned and began to skate toward me. I laid on the ice and tried to throw my scarf to her to hang on to, but the ice wobbled and almost dumped her in. I heard more cracking and this time I was dropped into the lake. The cold water made me gasp and almost froze my throat. I kicked and bobbed up, but my head hit the ice. I pounded at the ice and felt someone grab my jacket. I could breathe but they lost their grip and I fell back into the water." Andrea rubbed her arms as she took a moment to catch her breath.

"I was finally dragged from the water and onto the ice. Someone pulled me across the ice to a safer spot and put me in a toboggan tied to a snowmobile. I looked back and saw Helen lying on the ice. They were giving her CPR. They pulled me to shore and I was taken to the hospital." She turned to look at Fletcher, tears streamed down her cheeks. "I've never gone on to a frozen lake since."

Fletcher let a few seconds pass then asked. "What happened to your friend? Helen."

Andrea squeezed her eyes shut. "She died."

"I don't think you should drive. Leave your car here for now. We'll come back and get it later."

Fletcher drove her home. She didn't resist when he held her arm as they walked into her house. She answered his questions about coffee and cups. While it was brewing he pulled an afghan from the back of the couch and wrapped it around her.

Why had she had such a violent reaction to the lake? She'd been around them before and not become almost catatonic. What was it about this lake? She shuddered.

"Are you okay?" Fletcher pressed the hot mug of steaming coffee into her hands and sat next to her.

"Yes. Thank you." She sipped the hot liquid. Her face heated. It wasn't from the mug. "I'm sorry about all this. You don't need to babysit me."

Fletcher chuckled. "No, and I didn't need to drive you home and follow you into your house. I could have left you, but I didn't." He didn't add anything more.

Andrea sneaked a peek at him. He was smiling at her, dimples, and all.

"If you're okay, I can leave."

Andrea nodded. "I'm fine, really. I'm a little embarrassed at how I reacted."

"Don't worry about it. It's between friends." He stood. "I can see myself out. I'll come by and pick you up to get your car. I'll bring coffee."

"I can make our coffee."

"My treat." He waved and she heard the door shut.

Chapter 9

The following morning Fletcher picked Andrea up at her house, taking her to her car. She headed to the office and worked on her research.

The first thing she did was to make a list of missing women in the area. She created a map of the Twin Cities and put a dot on each place where they'd last been seen and how long they'd been missing. She noted the list of missing women was long.

Andrea sent a text to Fletcher telling him she would be unavailable in the morning.

Is everything okay? Do you need anything I can help with? Fletcher responded.

She texted back, *NO,* and left it at that. It was the way Dr. Vang had said he couldn't meet today that bothered her. What could he be hiding? It didn't matter to her that he said he had appointments that day. When the men grinned at each other and whispered, she had suspicion something else was up.

She typed in the house address listed on the card into her GPS and drove to the house.

The address was in the northern suburbs of St. Paul where older homes, were well kept. The narrow streets of the day didn't leave much for parking, but she found a spot in the next block where she could still see the front of his house.

A split level where the main level opens to the garage. Two cars occupied the driveway. The camper truck she'd been in the day before, and a smaller import car next to it.

From her vantage point, she watched a van approach the driveway, stopping as close to the approach as possible. The passenger door opened, and an older Hmong woman got out. She helped a man, stooped over holding a cane, to the driveway. She helped a younger woman with a baby out as well as a couple of younger children under school age out of the van. The group walked toward the garage then disappeared from her sight. The van pulled away and left.

Another van arrived at the same spot a few minutes later. More people exited this van. They were all ages and the younger people assisted the older ones. All disappearing from her sight around the back of the garage.

Cars and vans came and went dropping off and picking up people at intervals over the couple hours she watched the doctor's house.

What is going on here Doc? Are you practicing medicine? Do you have a license?

A knock on the passenger window startled her. Heart racing, she saw Fletcher's face, and he wasn't smiling. After she unlocked the passenger door, he slid next to her and gave her a questioning look."

"What?" she asked.

"You couldn't trust me to tell me what you were doing?"

She looked down at the steering wheel. "I'm sorry. It wasn't that I didn't trust you. I had no reason to be here. It was a niggling question as to why we couldn't meet today. How can I explain to you it was a feeling?"

"You just did." Fletcher rested his arm on her the back of the seat as he turned to face her. "I know you think no one understands you. I've read about your father. Do I think he's psychic? I do however think he has a gift or enhanced instinct about things. Did he always know what you were up to when you were growing up?" He smiled at her.

Andrea looked away. How much should she tell him? Maybe a little. "Yes, but it isn't like that, or maybe it is we didn't talked about IT."

"Your father and you never discussed this ability you both have?"

"No. We never talked about IT. I asked him questions about how he knew things and he'd say, 'I just knew'."

She watched as a different group in a car, arrive and depart. "Why were you spying on me?"

"I wasn't. I had the same feeling, that something was off. I decided to come over to his house and check it out. I saw your car parked down the street. I drove around the block and parked behind you. You never even looked." His voice accused her of not being diligent.

"I wasn't hiding. It didn't matter if anyone saw me."

"Right." He snorted. "That's why you're hiding down the block and not parked across the street. What do you think is going on?"

"My guess is our Doc is operating a clinic without a license."

Fletcher nodded. "He could have a chiropractor's license or even a homeopathic license. I've known doctors who have come to our country but aren't allowed to get a license unless they take all the classes over again. Not only is it expensive but it's time-consuming. They already qualified."

Fletcher looked at his watch. "Are you going to work today?"

"Yes."

He got out of the car and gave her a salute.

She started her car and watched him in her side mirror. Even bundled in a winter coat with a hat and scarf, he looked fine as he walked away from her. One last look as he opened the door. She allowed her lips to relax into a smile.

Later, Andrea tried calling Fletcher when he didn't come into the station. A breaking news story caught her attention on the TV across the room. The story showed how surveillance cameras helped catch a murderer. The idea came to her to check with any of the neighbors to see if they had cameras outside their homes.

"Hey, Bruce." She turned to the officer in the cube across the aisle.

"Yep." He called back.

"How long do you think people keep data from their surveillance cameras?"

He turned to look at her with a thoughtful expression. "I get what you're asking. It's a good thought. The thing is, I doubt anyone keeps them more than a month at the most. Unless you have someone who saves them just in case." He shrugged, grinned and jerked his head at Bob's cube. "Andrea, you might want to call those neighbors and ask if any might have a saved video of the lake. You could get a good tip that would break the case." He gave her a wink and turned back to his computer.

Andrea watched from the corner of her eyes with her head bowed. After a couple minutes passed. Bob hurried past her and Bruce and headed toward Steve's office. Bruce gave her a low fist pump and winked at her.

She worked on her research and tried again to call Fletcher with no answer. At the end of her shift, she gave up, swung her bag over her shoulder, and headed to the side exit. Still cautious she checked the outside to find no one waiting for her.

At home, she dialed her father's number. He didn't answer. She left a message. Her phone rang a half-hour later.

"Hello Kid. What's new?"

"Not much. I have a long list of missing women from the Minnesota area. I have them broke down by age and location. By breaking them that way the lists are easier to process."

"You'll have a lot of runaways. Some women walk away from their families, become prostitutes and disappear into the underground. They become Jane Doe's."

"I get it. I should match some Jane Doe's with my missing person's list."

Don't waste your time. They have already done that. Leave it to the Cold Case guys."

"Right. I'd better get to bed. It's going to be a big day tomorrow."

"Good luck Honey. Keep an open mind tomorrow."

"Dad, are you telling me something's going to happen tomorrow?"

"You don't need my help; you already know what to do. Gud Nite" The line went dead.

Chapter 10

Fletcher met Andrea at Dr. Vang's house. The street in front of the house was empty of cars today. She parked at the curb and Fletcher pulled in behind hers.

Fletcher pushed the doorbell and the door opened. A young woman stood staring at them.

"Hello, Is Dr. Vang in?" Fletcher asked.

The sound of hurried steps sounded in the hall and Dr. Vang arrived. He placed his hands on the woman's shoulders to move her aside. "Come in."

He pushed the storm door open and guided the woman back from the entryway. Andrea entered first and smiled at the woman and Dr. Vang. Fletcher closed the door behind him shutting off the cold air.

Andrea noticed shoes at the front door lining the wall.

"Do you want us to take off our boots?"

"If you would please." The doctor responded. The woman held out a basket with knitted and crocheted slippers inside zippered bags for them to choose from.

Andrea took a pair in the color she liked and returned the bow.

"What do I do?" Fletcher whispered.

"You can take a package of slippers or wear your socks." Dr. Vang answered before Andrea could speak. "We wash them after each person uses them. Binh puts them into clean bags each time."

"I'll wear my socks, thank you." He made a stiff bend with his body. Andrea smiled, but felt good he followed the protocol.

"Come." Doctor Vang gave a slight bow and put his hand behind the woman's back gently guiding her past the entry to the dining room. He stopped, faced the woman, and signed to her. She turned and went into the kitchen. Andrea heard the sound of cups and saucers rattling.

"Follow me. I will show you what you, but first, we talk." He motioned them to sit in the family room area.

Andrea smiled. This was Asian decor. Pillows lined the walls with small tables, about a foot high, set next to them. Andrea found a large, overstuffed pillow in a deep red velvet and sat down. Luckily, the center had a large button from the front to back. It gave her a way to balance.

Fletcher squatted and fell onto a cushion next to her. He started to tip, and she chuckled grabbing his arm before he fell over.

"Sitting on these isn't as easy as it looks." Dr. Vang noted as he gracefully sat on a cushion with no wobble at all.

Andrea started to giggle. "What's so funny?" Fletcher demanded looking like he thought she was laughing at his expense.

"I got this thought. I've no idea where it came from except I remember hearing about these as a kid." In a slightly sing-song voice, she recited, "Weebles Wobble but they don't fall down." She tipped back and forth on the cushion.

Fletcher didn't laugh. Dr. Vang's lips gave a hint of a smile.

"You have samples or evidence taken from the lake." Fletcher had his notebook in hand. Andrea fumbled for hers. The older man nodded.

"You said you told someone at the police station about what you found. Who did you tell?"

Andrea looked at her partner, Joe had already told them he'd spoken with Steve Totts.

"When the men first came to me with the body parts, I was skeptical. Did we have a killer among us? After questioning the men, they told me they had found the parts in the stomach of the fish they caught. I went to their trucks and cars where they cleaned the fish and it was true. Some of the fish they'd caught had bits and pieces of human body parts." Dr. Vang folded his hands on his crossed legs.

"What did you do about it?" Andrea asked.

"I didn't know what to do. I was afraid." He tilted his head. "You know how we're treated. If I brought the parts in. We might be questioned then with no proof how they were found; we'd be dragged off to jail and into court and someone would be put in jail for murder."

Fletcher nodded his head. "I'm sorry that you thought that. I'm sorry there is such a lack of integrity at times anyone would feel they couldn't trust the police with the truth."

Dr. Vang tipped his head down to accept her apology.

"You said you did approach the police." Andrea prompted.

They were interrupted with the sound of a clatter of cups. The woman descended the stairs carrying a tray with two teapots, cups, and a tray of assorted sweets. She set the tray on the low table between the three.

Andrea signed 'thank you.'

"You can sign too?" Fletcher asked.

Andrea laughed. 'Not much. I can say thank you, good morning, good night, I love you', and basics like 'father', 'mother,' I learned in school."

The woman watched her. "Does she read lips?" Andrea asked.

"Not so much. She knows English since signing is the American Sign Language. We translate what people say from our language to English then to ASL for her. You can say she's multi-lingual." He signed as he spoke.

The girl smiled at him. He signed something. She bowed and left.

"Please pour." He indicated Andrea to do the honors. She did and they sipped tea and had a sweet. The sesame balls were her favorite.

The Asian man leaned back and hooked his arms around his knee pulling it to his chest. "I asked the men to leave the fish's stomach intact and bring them to me. I put them under a microscope and found ones that indeed have strange things in them.

I went to the police and asked to talk someone in the Medical Examiners' office. I admit I was a bit vague with the woman at the front desk. She finally called to a cop walking by to come over. I explained again that some of the fishermen had found what looked like human parts in their fish. He laughed. "Now that's a first." He said to anyone listening. "Body parts in a fish? Are you joking with me?" I assured him I wasn't.

I explained I had some samples of fish stomachs I thought the Medical Examiner should look at. They may or may not be human parts."

He let his leg drop and crossing the left one, resting his forearms on his thighs. "He made a joke to the woman clerk, 'I doubt if they're human parts, but if you want to wait, I'll have Nancy here call down and see if one of the lab people can come up.'

I sat in the lobby for two hours. No one came to me no one spoke to me. I asked the woman at the desk to check what the problem was. She finally made a call and turned away from me to speak on the phone. She told me the ME was busy today but someone might be able to come shortly.

After an hour I left."

"Do you know who the officer you talked to?" Andrea asked. The words came out of her mouth before she could stop them. "Not that it matters, I was curious."

"I told you before. That red-headed guy that was on TV. I wasn't going to bother when the men at the lake called me and said body parts had been found in the lake. I wasn't surprised. I drove over and watched what was going on from my truck. I saw you two. I saw you talk to the fishermen and the cop. The men told me what happened. They trust you."

Andrea flushed and fiddled with her pencil. "Thank you."

"That's why I came down and talked to you. If it had been that loud-mouthed redhead, I wouldn't have bothered."

Fletcher and Andrea looked at each other, "Steve."

"I didn't ask his name and he didn't offer it," Joe said.

"What did you do next after no one would talk to you?" Fletcher asked

"I researched how to preserve human flesh as evidence. I found a small dryer cabinet someone was selling. I cleaned it out to be as sterile as I could. I placed the pieces in small, brown bags, labeling them the day they were found. Do you want to see them?"

The two nodded and stood to follow Joe.

They took the few steps down to what would be under the entry and kitchen. Andrea noticed the hall had a closed-door to back part of the basement. The doctor unlocked a steel door on the opposite side of the hall and motioned for them to follow him.

Andrea stepped into the room, moving aside for Fletcher to stand beside her. A humidifier ran softly in a corner of the ten by twelve room. The finished walls had been covered in heavy-duty plastic and the seams sealed with a tape of some sort. She walked around the stainless-steel tables. Microscopes and vials sat in metal holders. She saw a sterilizer machine, a refrigerator, and two cabinets lined the wall. Dr. Vang opened what looked like a large food dryer.

On the racks lay paper sleeves with dates on them. Dr. Vang handed latex gloves to the two, then handed them a sleeve.

"Female fingertip – 3/22/2018." She picked up a different card, "femur bones – 3/25/2018". He flipped through a few on a lower shelf. "Here's one that I think will prove a good piece of evidence." The brown kraft bag had been labeled "eyeball-1/2 blue in color -8/05/2019"

"This is pretty recent. The men have been bringing you lots of fish entrails." Fletcher counted the shelves and flipped a few of the bags as if he were counting.

"I have one hundred fifty samples. I have them logged and cataloged as to where the men were fishing and the date. I also noted the temperature of the water at that time."

"You're very thorough," Andrea noted looking at the logbook. "You said *where* the men were fishing. How did you log that? Did any of these come from other areas?

"No, just Blue Lake. The men began giving me GPS coordinates each day they fished out in the lake."

Fletcher gave him a thumbs up. "Again, you are very thorough."

"I was a doctor, log ago. We had to be." He didn't smile. It was a statement, not a joke.

Andrea looked at Fletcher. "We have to get these to the lab." She rolled her eyes. "I suppose we have to pass this through Steve first."

"How about we take one or two samples I'll take them to the Medical Examiner's office." He slipped the bags into a brown lunch bag marked evidence he'd pulled out of his pocket, and taped it closed. He wrote January 17, 2020, on the outside.

Andrea looked at the room. "You know what you're doing. You've preserved the evidence better than some of our labs have. Thank you for doing it despite the initial resistance."

"I knew someday they would be important. I've been scared thinking I might have prevented the murder of someone had I been able to get the police to listen to me." He shook his head.

"I wish you would have been taken seriously. It will be taken seriously now. You have my word." Andrea gave him a low bow of respect then turned to leave. She didn't comment on what she'd seen the day before. That was a conversation for another time.

As the two walked back to their cars Andrea turned to Fletcher. "Are you thinking what I'm thinking about the chain of evidence?"

He nodded. "I thought that even though he's documented each piece, in court the defense is going to challenge the chain of evidence."

"No matter what, it makes the St. Paul PD look bad." She sat in her car and Fletcher closed her door patting the top before walking back to his own. She watched him in her side mirror. Bundled in winter garb he walked with confidence. A similar feeling coursed through her body. She chided herself for gawking, as she pulled away from the curb.

Chapter 11

"**W**atson, you're wanted in the conference room." Someone shouted across the squad room.

"Ooo—what'd you do now?" Bob commented from his desk on his side of the cube.

"Nothing, but that doesn't make a difference." She muttered a response grabbing a pad and pen and headed to the conference room.

She pushed the door open to find Chief Conrad sitting at one end of the table and Harold, the head of the ME department, sitting next to him. His eyes stared at the pages in front of him. Next to him sat Steve Totts. Andrea didn't see Fletcher.

"Come in Andrea." Conrad motioned for her to take a chair on the opposite side of the table. "Have a seat."

She sat and looked at the two men who didn't speak.

"There has been a miscommunication here." Conrad leaned on his elbows and tented his fingers over the paper on the table.

Andrea said nothing. Conrad continued. "Did you bring evidence in this case to the ME's office without giving notice to the lead on the case?" His serious gaze pinned Andrea in her chair.

She didn't want to admit to anything. "What exactly are you talking about?"

Conrad continued to hold Andrea's gaze.

Steve couldn't let her silence pass. "You gave the lab samples of body parts and didn't inform me, the lead on this case, where you got them or anything about them."

Andrea continued to look at Chief Conrad for a long moment then looked at Harold. "Did I give you any samples that had anything to do with this case? Did I give you any indication of where these came from? Is it possible they could have come from somewhere else and part of another case?" She didn't look away from Harold.

Steve interrupted, "You said the samples were from the lake."

Harold slouched into his chair and didn't look at her.

"Let's clear this up. Where did you get these samples? Where did it come from?"

Andrea paused and looked at Steve. "Let's let Steve answer the question. He seems to know more about this than I do."

"Me?! What do I know about this?" his lips pursed as he dared her to drag him into something he didn't anticipate.

"Let me tell you a story." She turned slightly to face the Captain and crossed her arms on the table. "Two years ago, a man came to this station and asked to talk to someone in the Medical Examiner's office."

Harold's head jerked up and his confused expression almost caused Andrea to smile.

"It's okay Harold, you aren't responsible," Andrea assured him and watched his body relax.

"The man had body parts that were given to him by fishermen at Blue Lake. He wanted them tested to find out if they might be something the police should investigate. He was sure they were body parts and hoped the police would be interested in what he had." She turned to Steve. "Sound familiar?"

He didn't respond.

"He was left sitting in the lobby for three hours. No one talked to him, no one checked his story and no one from the ME's office ever came to look at what he had. He'd left his name and number as a contact when he first got there, but no one ever called him. Two years have gone by and I was given samples he'd collected and preserved. Does it have anything to do with this case?" She shrugged. "That will be determined by the ME's lab. So, I didn't feel the need to make it an issue until I knew for sure."

"What did you find out?" Conrad asked Harold.

"The samples she sent us were indeed human. They're being tested for DNA. The other samples—'

"What other samples?" Conrad roared looking at both Andrea and Harold. Steve looked like he wanted to crawl under the table.

"Sir, I got a call from Harold's office. Simone told me the samples were human. I told her I had more, two containers full. She said she would test them as soon as they were brought in."

"I made arrangements for them to look at what Dr. Vang had and bring the containers in. They did that and I'm guessing they must have found something interesting?" Andrea looked at Harold.

Now that he wasn't in trouble Harold straightened and looked down at the pages in front of him.

"Yes, in fact, I found many interesting things here." He smiled at Andrea. "The good doctor knew what he was doing. He said he'd read about the preservation of human specimens online. His research was spot on. He did what we would do. The parts are not contaminated."

"Harold we don't want a lesson in preserving samples. What did you find?" Conrad asked.

Harold nodded and continued. "We have about one hundred fifty different samples. I pulled everyone I could to work on them and we have about sixteen different DNA's. This is one of the largest body dump sites I've ever seen. What if there are more? We have a prolific serial killer here." His expression turned to worry, and his voice lowered to a whisper as he spoke the last words.

Andrea watched the Captain. He wasn't stupid. He could put two and two together. If Steve had done his job and taken the samples two years ago, could they have stopped the deaths of women during this time frame?

Conrad's eyes narrowed as he stared at Steve. Steve didn't lift his head.

"Steve, you personally order those DNA profiles uploaded and check if they connect to any missing persons we have on file." Conrad pointed his pen at the team leader.

Steve nodded. He stood and left the room with long strides.

"Thank you for bringing these in." Conrad shook his head. "I fear when this gets out, the media will have a hay day."

"Sir, I have a list of missing women in Minnesota and what information we have on them. As soon as we have any DNA on them we can match those."

"Andrea, thank you for following up on this. What connected you to this Asian man?"

She fingered her notebook and pen for a moment. "I don't want to get Steve in trouble, but he is the one who dropped the ball on this. I was at the lake going to question some of the fishermen. A group of Hmong men said they had information on body parts. They connected us to Joseph Vang."

"Good follow-up." Conrad stood. "Keep working on matching any of the DNA to the missing women on your list. Let Totts know you have a list and I said to work with you. Better yet, I'll tell him." Without another word, he left the room.

On her way back to her desk she stopped to fill her water bottle. Steve came to stand over her.

"Don't get too smart. You're nothing. You'll never be anything around here. No matter what your father did he's nothing but a drunken loser. You'll end up like him."

Andrea turned and capped her water bottle before she gave in to the urge to toss the whole thing at his red face.

"If you weren't so pitifully jealous and loathsome, I might be scared of you." She smiled condescendingly, "As it is, I work smart. I listen to people and I don't overlook details. I don't steal from others to make me look good. Hmmm, doesn't sound anything like you does it?" She stepped around him and walked back to her desk and sat down. She grabbed her knees to keep them from knocking together. *Had she said all those things out loud?*

That night she got a phone call from her father. She filled him in on what had transpired.

"I told you dat dere would be some new clues. You did right. Don't worry about Totts. How is your partner?"

"Dad, he's not my partner." Andrea couldn't keep the flood of heat from her face. It was a good thing her dad couldn't see her.

"He might be."

"Dad! He's FBI, not regular police." Her voice gave a resigned sigh.

"Hmm, dere are many types of partners." He muttered.

Andrea changed the subject. "Dad, two of the people we interviewed indicated one man, the father." She stopped. Would telling him this be breaking the code of silence?

"No, tell me." Her father asked after a moment of silence.

She didn't respond. Andrea was used to her father answering her as if he could read her mind. "Both people talked about the male neighbor and his actions with his children." Andrea went on to give the same description of the father's actions. "Then the man we were talking to said he found mutilated animals in his compost pile." She described the mutilation Mr. Ford described. "Dad, this sounds bad."

After a pause. "You're right. It sounds like a killer in da making. Tough call. Dere isn't any evidence ta connect ta someone. What did you tink of about dat type of mutilation?"

"I kind of thought, from the way Mr. Ford described it, the person was angry. He was taking his frustration out on the animals. It was Mr. Ford's observation too. He was worried."

"I tink you're right. It's a tought, but my guess is it's a young person, not an adult. If da udder neighbor says she saw da son trowing weeds in da compost pile dat could be da perpetrator of da mutilation."

"That's not good either. What if he finally had enough and took that anger out on his family or his neighbors?" Andrea pleaded. "What can we do?"

"Noting right now. Who has da chickens?" Donald asked his daughter.

"Da-that military man and a family at the opposite end of the lake. None of the ones we've interviewed said anything about chickens gone missing, but I'll keep my ears open. Maybe ask that question to the next people we interview."

"I heard dere's going ta be anudder Press Conference tomorrow. Are you gonna speak?" Donald enquired.

Andrea gave a dry laugh, "Me? Not likely. Chief Bellows and Steve Totts will be doing that."

"You'll be dere though?"

She sighed, "Yes, I'll be there."

"Good, I'll be watching for ya." After some small talk, they said good-bye.

Andrea still felt uneasy about the animal mutilation. What if this wasn't a young person? What if this had been placed in the pile by someone who knew the Richardson males, routinely put their yard clippings into Mr. Ford's compost? After all his yard wasn't all that well kept. Who would know, even himself, what was new compost and old? Anyone around the lake could access his yard from the lake or land.

Chapter 12

Fletcher and Andrea stood inside the lobby area the next morning. The bitterly cold wind stopped the press conference from being held outside. A few reporters sat waiting for the conference to begin. The cameramen filled up the remaining area.

Chief Conrad Bellows entered the room and addressed the reporters. "Thank you for coming. I'm sure you have questions about this investigation. We've discovered fragments of body parts and the lab is testing them. We have had one match to a woman missing in Kansas and a woman missing in Missouri. Their families have been notified. We are continuing to match evidence to any missing people in the system."

"Where did you find all the body parts you're testing?" A reporter asked. She stood a little in front of Andrea.

The woman's hair looked familiar. Andrea bent to one side to look at the woman's face. She was right it was Kaeli Meyers.

Conrad leaned into the mic. "They came from the lake."

"How are you obtaining these samples? It's been too cold for the divers to go into the lake?" Kaeli continued.

Conrad gave her a tight smile, "We can't comment on an ongoing investigation. Any other questions?"

"When do you think the divers will be able to go into the lake?" A reporter asked.

"As soon as the ice comes off the lake. We have another month or so."

The reporter continued. "Is it true you are going to be using underwater drones or cameras to look for anything that might be in the lake?"

"Yes, that has been discussed. Nothing's been confirmed." Conrad answered.

"Do you have any new leads in the case? Are you looking at a local killer?" Kaeli asked.

"We aren't' making any assumptions. We have no reason to believe the killer lives here. This may be a dump site."

"You expect us to believe the killer doesn't live here and somehow found this little lake in the middle of the city?" Her tone registered complete disbelief.

"Somethings we can't discuss Ms. Meyers. I suggest you wait until we have concrete evidence."

"Concrete? More like waterlogged evidence. I hope you have more proof and are close to catching the killer before another body or parts show up." She snorted.

Conrad glared at the reporter then at Andrea who stood in his line of sight behind the reporter. He turned and walked away. The media liaison moved to the mic, "That will be all today." He walked toward the hall Conrad had passed through.

Fletcher angled forward and whispered somewhere near her ear. "Your little friend seems to know something or has made an educated guess."

"I haven't talked to her." Andrea moved away from the group.

"Detective!" Someone called. Andrea didn't turn but kept walking. It was a female voice and familiar.

"Andrea Watson." The tone was all business.

Andrea turned to face the young woman. She was hungry for a lead and story. "Yes?"

"I'm running a story on the Hmong fishermen. They are more willing to talk than your Chief." She still held her mic and the cameraman trailed her.

"What do you want from me?" Andrea kept her tone from encouraging more conversation. She continued toward the hallway opening.

"The fishermen at the lake said they collected body parts they found inside fish and gave it to a Dr. Vang. When I tried to reach the doctor, he wouldn't answer me. His neighbors said an ME's van came and took some boxes from the doctor's house. Now I wonder what was in them?" She waited for Andrea to fill in the blank.

"I've heard curiosity killed the cat." With a smile, she left the reporter standing in the lobby.

"You're evil." Fletcher chuckled. "I wouldn't want you as an enemy." He followed her as they entered the squad room.

Steve stood at her desk. "Sargeant?" Andrea addressed him.

"What did the dragon want?" he sneered.

"What dragon?" She asked and pulled her chair out, hoping he'd leave.

"That reporter. Where did she get the information? How much does she know?" He directed his questions to Fletcher.

Andrea seethed with his dismissal and sat at her deck ignoring him. The two men remained behind her.

Fletcher answered. "My guess is she did what a good investigative reporter would do. Since fishermen are at the lake more than anyone else she talked to them. Everyone wants their five minutes on TV, she gave them that and they gave her what they found. It led to Doctor Vang and when he wouldn't talk, she went to the neighbors. They got their ten seconds of TV and spilled their guts that the ME's van came and carted off boxes from the good doctor's house. Maybe you should hire her on your team." He emphasized, "your".

Steve showed his bottom teeth like a bulldog, then stomped toward his office.

"Ouch, and you think I'm the bad girl?" She pointed her finger at Fletcher.

Fletcher sat across from her tapping on his computer. It felt good to have a friend she could tease. He'd make a good partner if she wanted one.

When Andrea worked deep in her research she became oblivious of those around her.

The authoritative voice of Steve interrupted her concentration. "Watson, you and the agent finish interviewing the property owners.

The officers got halfway around the northern part of the lake, there are a few houses left. I figured you two would enjoy getting out of here for a while." He slapped the top of the cube wall and walked off.

"So much for that. Let's go. No time like the present to get it done." Fletcher stood. "I'll drive."

Andrea nodded and gathered her things.

"What's this guy's name?" Fletcher pulled the car to the curb of the address on their list.

"Joseph and Mary Pickett. How sweet."

"What?" Fletcher asks.

"Joseph and Mary."

He gives her a quizzical look.

"The parents of Jesus." Her tone made a question.

"Okay, I wasn't thinking along those lines. Give me a break."

"I would think the two names together would be an automatic trigger, bacon and eggs, peanut butter and jam." She took out her notebook and checked to make sure her pen worked.

He held up his hands. "I give in. I must have missed the big Jesus test." He turned away, they walked to the porch and knocked at the door. After no answer he rang the doorbell. Still no answer Before they leave a voice from the doorbell monitor.

"What can I do for you?"

"We're with the police department we need to ask you some questions." Fletcher held his badge up to the camera in the upper corner of the porch.

"Just a minute."

Andrea noticed the curtain next to the door move and a small face appeared. The child suddenly disappeared, and a low deep tone came through the wall.

A man opened the door but didn't unlock the storm door. "Yes?"

Andrea and Fletcher held up their ID badges. The man still didn't open the door.

"We are asking questions about any unusual sightings in the area."

"I have nothing to say. I didn't see anything. We don't know anything."

"You are Joseph Pickett?" Andrea asked, never taking her eyes from his.

"Yes." The answer is short.

"How long have you lived in this house?" She continued.

"Look I said I'm not answering any questions."

"May I ask why? What are you hiding? Are you being held against your will?"

He gave an exasperated sound. "No, I don't talk to the police. You don't need anything from me as I don't have any information that would help in any way."

"Do you own chickens?" Fletcher asks.

The man's gaze reveals surprise as he looked from Fletcher to Andrea. "Yes, why?"

"Have you had any that are missing?" Fletcher continued.

Joseph gave her a quizzical gaze. "Why yes, I have two gone missing. I thought they got out of the cage. Since you asked I'm thinking they didn't leave on their own."

Andrea and Fletcher continue to stand at the door.

"What does this have to do with the police asking me questions. Am I a suspect?" Joseph's eyes narrowed at the two.

"No, at least not at the moment, although everyone is a possible suspect until we find the killer," Fletcher added.

"If you have anything pertinent then I'll answer your questions. Good day." Joseph nodded and shut the door.

"Well, we have been dismissed." Andrea turned back to the car.

"Yep, and he's been moved to the top of the list."

"Right. This next house is the Richardson house. The one with the military man. "Not that I feel in any way inferior to you, but I want to be the observant in this inquiry."

Fletcher looked at her. "Are you sure?"

"I want to get the feel of what's around the house. You can focus on questioning the man. I'll jump in if I have something."

"Good idea. Okay, here we go." Fletcher rang the doorbell.

Heavy steps on hardwood flooring were heard and the door opened. A tall muscular man stood looking intently at the two outside. After a few seconds, he flipped the latch on the storm door and pushed it open. "Come in."

They stepped into a foyer. Andrea immediately cringed at the stark white walls and parquet floor. Beyond the wood began immaculate white carpet. The man motioned them into an office to the right of the door. The carpet was dark navy and lying on top an Aubusson Rug. Money.

The two are motioned to sit in the chairs on one side of the ornate walnut desk while the man sat behind the desk.

"What can I do for you? I assume this has to do with the report on the news about the human body parts found in the lake?"

Fletcher and Andrea nod. "We'd like to ask you some questions about what you or your family may have seen."

"My children haven't seen anything. They stay in the house most of the time. I don't want them exposed to germs. "

The homeowner pulled a bottle of hand sanitizer from his desk and rubbed it into his hands as he sat across from them.

"To be clear you are?" Andrea has her pen poised over her notebook.

"You don't know? You come here and have no idea who I am?"

"We have a list of all the property owners. However, we like to be sure to whom we are speaking. You could be a friend or relative who doesn't actually live here." Fletcher responded his tone sounded professional and neutral.

"Oh. Alright. My name is Frank Richardson. I own this house."

"You mentioned children, how many do you have?"

"Five."

"Ages?"

After a hesitation, he answered. "Fifteen, thirteen, eleven, eight, and five."

"Thank you." That matched her sheet she'd pulled from tax records. The children didn't attend public or private school.

"Would you like to meet them?"

Andrea schooled her surprise. "Yes, we would." Andrea wanted to observe them for herself.

"If your ears are sensitive, please cover them. I'm going to blow a whistle." Before Andrea could move her hands to her head a piercing high-pitched sound came from a thin whistle.

The sound of soft footsteps, on wooden treads, could be heard announcing the arrival of children, "we're here father." A girl's voice sounded from the hallway.

"Enter."

The children marched in a line by height and age. They stood at attention with no expression, staring straight ahead.

"Very good. These are my children. I've told the officers that you do not know of anyone or any strange things that happen on the lake."

Andrea ground her teeth. He's coaching them. Fletcher asked the second to the youngest, a girl. "Who do you play with when you're outside?"

"My brothers and sisters." She answered without looking at him.

He looked at the middle child, a boy. "What is the name of the family that lives two properties down. They have a large playground in their backyard."

"I've never played with them." The answer was like the next sibling, monotone.

"I'm surprised. When I spoke with that mother, she said she'd invited the kids to come to their house to play and for a birthday party. She'd heard one of your children shared the day with one of hers." Fletcher turned to the father.

This time Andrea asked "She said she'd met your wife. Is she here? Could we talk to her?"

Frank frowned and waved his hand dismissing the children. They left the room, in the same manner, they came in. A single line. She could see them turn to the stairs and heard the soft steps on the tread. Their muted voices could be heard before the sound of doors shutting.

"I'm sorry she's out of town. She works for a medical company and travels for them."

Fletcher nodded. "I noticed you have a beautiful telescope. When I was outside at your neighbors, I saw you have a small deck built off an upper level and a large telescope is mounted there. I'm sure you can see stars and galaxies. You must be interested in astrology?"

Frank preened a little. "Yes, I've seen all the galaxies. I've charted stars and planets.'

"I'm interested in stargazing. Could I see your setup?" Fletcher acted eager to get a look. "I've never seen a telescope like that except at planetariums. To be able to put my hand and eyes on one would be a privilege."

"Of course. Come with me." He gave a tight smile and stood. *I have nothing to hide,* Andrea thought she heard him say. He didn't say anything out loud. She shook her head, dismissing the thought.

They walked up the steps. Family pictures hung on the wall arranged by age. She saw one of Frank and his wife. The woman's eyes were unfocused. She stared at the camera and her lips lifted enough to give the impression of a happy person. Was she on medication?

As Andrea walked by the picture, she got an eerie feeling about it. Were those eyes crying for help? Where was the wife now? Was she out of town or buried in the basement? If she worked, her job would be calling for her whereabouts.

All the doors to the hallway were closed. Frank opened the double doors which would be over the den and one end of the living room.

Andrea took in the spacious room. A king-size bed with a white cover took up one wall. Andrea glanced into the open door of the bathroom. The white rug and the towels were perfectly folded and evenly spaced on the bar. The larger towel with a hand towel and washcloth lay over the rod. No personal items sat on the counter.

At the door to the deck, she zipped her coat and stepped out. They were three stories off the ground. She stood still and gripped the railing. The deck didn't budge. No loose boards. It was sturdy.

Fletcher stood next to the large telescope. It wasn't tilted up. Frank pulled off the canvas cover. "I leave it pointing to the ground when I'm not using it. I don't want the lens to get broken if something should fly through the air."

Fletcher bent to put his eye to the eyepiece. Gently turning the handle and looking at whatever the scope was previously set to.

"Here let me show you some of the stars you can see in the daylight."

"Thank you. I think I've seen enough." Fletcher smiled at Frank whose expression went from friendly to hostile in seconds.

"What are you doing? Are you playing with me?" He pulled the cover on the scope in such a hurry it didn't slide easily down. Angry he turned. "Get out of my house."

Fletcher didn't say anything. Andrea followed him and saw two of the hallway doors open a crack, eyes peeking through the openings. The doors closed when she made eye contact with both viewers.

Outside, Andrea said nothing until Fletcher pulled away from the curb. "What was that all about?"

"Mr. Richardson is a Peeping Tom. He could be a pedophile also. The way he treats his kids is almost a profile for one of them. But some are control freaks." He guided the car onto the freeway toward the station.

"Tell me what I missed."

"I saw the large telescope. It wasn't pointing at the sky or down at the ground. When we were on the deck that day the lens glinted in the sun.

After Carla described the father and that she rarely if at all saw the mother, I investigated the family. He's a graphic designer and works from home. He has an apartment in downtown Minneapolis. His wife works for a local medical company, which he told us, and travels a lot."

"I have the kid's age, I wanted to see them. They could either be abused or over-controlled, which is a form of abuse but one not easily defined by the law. You can't jerk kids from their homes if there's no evidence of physical abuse."

"What about the telescope? You said he was a peeping tom."

"He's narcissistic and needed to show me his BIG telescope. It was leveled and locked. When I turned it, it looked into the windows of the bedroom of his neighbor. Close up and personal if you get my drift."

"Disgusting."

"That's not all but you may not want to hear the rest."

"Shoot."

"Funny you should use those words. That's what I saw on the deck. Dried-"

"Never mind I get the idea." Andrea wanted to gag. "I'm surprised as he's such a clean freak."

They walked into the station. When they entered the squad room a buzz of conversation rose that had nothing to do with cases. Officers rested their arms on the cube walls or stood in the aisles. A general movement of eyes following the two as they headed to Andrea's cube.

"Do you get a feeling something's up and we're it?" Fletcher muttered as he passed her and stopped in front of her desk. "No summons."

Her phone began to ring. She picked up the receiver, "Detec-"

"Get to the conference room" Steve's voice barked through the receiver, "Bring the agent." The call was disconnected.

Chapter 13

Andrea led the way into the conference room. Chief Conrad, Steve Totts, and Harold watched the two enter. Harold nodded at them. Andrea sat across from them and Fletcher took the seat next to her.

Pictures of past chiefs and mayors lined the wall. Andrea ignored the decorations and concentrated on the three across from them.

"Here's what we have." Steve stood at one end of the table. "The lab came back with the results from the evidence they collected from the doctor. A number of them matched the same person, a few were loners, no match to any specimen." He handed a folder to Andrea, Fletcher, and to Chief Bellows. Harold held one of his own. "It's all yours Harold." Steve sat down at the head of the table.

"As Steve said, some of the pieces matched to the same DNA. We have about ten individuals with common parts. The parts that have been tested are numbered and their matches are listed in a single column. Ones that had one DNA match are listed separately."

Harold turned the page and continued. "We ran the DNA through the missing person database We've contacted NamUs in hopes they have matches.

Here's where things got interesting. We found two women in the database who matched the DNA samples. Column five and Column eight." He looked at the page and waited for the rest to catch up. "Their families had contributed to help find their missing family member."

"The next page gives the donor's information and family contact that we have. Since they are both out of state, we informed the FBI. That's you, Agent Peterson." Harold nodded at Fletcher.

"Not me," He waved his hand to dismiss the idea. "You need to contact the office downtown St. Paul."

"I know, I was joking. We did that this morning. You're to report to them as soon as possible."

"See ya." Steve Totts rested his elbow over the back of his chair, waiting for Fletcher to go.

Fletcher didn't move. He looked at the Chief.

Chief Conrad straightened in his chair. He rubbed his chin which pulled the deep lines on his face down. The older man looked tired. Andrea could tell he didn't want this meeting, but it was his responsibility. She felt a bit sorry for him.

"Thank you, Harold, for the report and humor. I got a call from the Director of the FBI and he does want Fletcher to be on the team going into the field. One of the women is from Missouri." He looked down at the paper, "The other one is from Kansas. You'll get your orders from your superiors." Conrad stood up. "Thank you both for following through on getting these samples. I don't understand how we never heard about this doctor and what he had. Someone slipped up." He gave them a nod and walked out.

Andrea didn't say anything but looked at Steve, who stared at the folder in front of him and said nothing.

Andrea stood and walked out behind her boss. She fumed at Steve's audacity.

"Leave it be." Fletcher's voice whispered above her ear. "He's not worth it. I'm going to talk to my boss and ask if you can on the team as an observer. Maybe a coworking thing between our departments as a gesture of goodwill. A partnership. Your side pays your way and gets half the credit if we find anything."

"Good luck with that thought."

Fletcher stopped and pulled her in front of him. "Are you sure about that?" He tilted his head a little.

"What do you mean? Of course, I'm sure. First, there isn't any money in the budget to send me off to Kansas on a goose chase.

Second, do you think Steve is going to let me go and not him?" She snorted in disbelief.

"Are you willing to bet on it?" This time his eyebrows raised in a challenge.

"Sure, you can buy me dinner at that Brazilian steak place everyone talks about."

He crossed his arms, "Okay if they don't let you go I'll take you. If not, you lose, my choice."

"I'll agree but no underhanded discussion about this. It's strictly between us and you can't prime the pump on your side."

Fletcher threw up his hands in surrender. "I don't have a problem with it. I'm not going to be out the money." He leaned a little closer to her, "Don you want to know what you have to do if you lose?"

Andrea felt fission of fear cut through her body. She tried to shake it off, but a flash of ice and lake rushed through her mind. "NO!" She glared at him.

He bent to look closer at her face. "You cheated."

"I did not. How can I cheat?"

"Did you read my mind?"

"I can't read minds." She protested and fiddled with her pen.

"But you knew. Somehow you knew what the consequence would be if you lost. How?" The last word was a force of air at her.

"I don't know what you're talking about." She glared at him.

"Yes, you do. For a moment you didn't care about losing all that much, then in a second, I saw the stare and fear in your eyes. Tell me, what you saw Andrea?"

She turned to walk away. Fletcher put his hand on her shoulder, "Stop, I don't think you want Bob overhearing this." He pulled her into an office. He shut the door keeping their conversation private. "Tell me what you saw in your head when I asked you if you wanted to know your consequence."

Turning her back to him she stared at the window on the opposite wall. The blinds were shut against the afternoon sun. Silence filled the room. He sat on the corner of the desk. Waiting.

Now she was angry and scared. "If I lose you want me to go out on the lake. I hardly think that's fair. Dinner would cost you a few hours of work but if I lost it would cost me everything." Her voice trailed off into a breathy whisper as she couldn't form the words.

He didn't answer. Anger still filled her, and she stuffed her fists into her jacket.

Fletcher's voice sounded low and calm. He didn't laugh at her. She saw compassion.

"Yes, that was my immediate choice. I think when you make a bet it has to cost you something or you shouldn't make it."

"I should have picked a restaurant with a higher price tag."

"How much do you think I make? The FBI doesn't pay any more for low-level worker bees than your police department. I'll bet I make as much or a little less than you do. I live in a studio apartment off Maryland Ave, in an attic. I don't have AC, I'm in a sweatbox year around. A friend says he's going to fix me up an AC unit this summer. Right now, it's eighty degrees in the place. All the heat from downstairs floats up the floor register. Even though I have it closed and covered, it's still getting hot. It's all I can afford right now."

Andrea stared down at the floor thinking about her comfy townhouse. She didn't feel guilty enough to offer to rent out the spare bedroom to him. "You're right, I saw the ice and the lake when you asked me. I don't know why it came to my mind. Maybe it's a logical deduction considering how adamant you were about me going out on the lake."

"Yes, I can understand how you might come to that conclusion, but you didn't go through a process to arrive at that conclusion. It appeared to you out of nowhere and it was a picture of the ice and the lake, not a thought of me telling you to go."

"You're right. Now what? It comes down to I'm not going out on that lake."

"What to bet on it?" Fletcher stood and motioned her to the door, and he followed her out.

"No, I'm not going to bet on it."

Chapter 14

A newspaper fell on her laptop. Andrea jumped her heart thumping. "What's this about?" She demanded of the team leader whose expression was anything but happy.

"What do you and that reporter have going? You two have a hard-on for each other?" Steve Totts sneered.

"Knock it off Totts. That kind of talk will get you into trouble." Fletcher ordered turning to face the man.

"You soft-touch guys have it easy. You have no idea what it is to work for a living." His fists opened and closed at his side as if he fought to keep from swinging at Fletcher or Andrea.

"Steve, knock it off. What's this about?" She hoped the distraction would defuse the situation.

Andrea opened the paper and read the headlines. Her lips pressed together in a straight line. *What was that woman up to?*

The header announced the latest success of Donald Watson of Bemidji. He found a woman lost in the woods. She'd been missing for about three days and within a few hours of him arriving at the site, he'd taken his dog, Sanford, and found the autistic woman.

A picture of him from a few years back shaking the new Chief of Police's hand accompanied the article. It stated Donald announced it was the dog that deserved the praise. He'd given her scent to Sanford and he found her. This reporter wonders why former detective Donald Watson can find people when others have completely lost the trail.

The article went on to state a man had gone missing in the pacific northwest and no one could find him. A lone search and rescuer brought the missing man out of the mountains. The man said he was lucky to be going along a ravine and saw a cave. Calling out he heard a faint cry and found the young man almost dead.

The lost young man had camping gear and was warm, but his leg was broken, and he couldn't get down to the river to get water.

The reporter, Kaeli Meyers, stated she was able to talk to the rescuer and he told her he'd gotten a call from a man in the Midwest. This man told him exactly where to find the lost man. Phone records show the call came from Bemidji, MN and the number belonged to Retired Sheriff Donald Watson.

Andrea heaved a sigh, "Steve, talk to my dad, maybe he's been giving her the interviews." She tapped the article. "If you want to know what's going on with him, call my dad. I'll even give you his phone number." She reached for her phone.

Steve waved his hand dismissing her offer. "Who's been telling him what's going on down here?"

"I haven't talked to my father in a week. You can check my phone records if you want. I've spoken to this woman twice in the last few weeks. Once was outside the station and the other was at the press conference. Did you see us all chummy? Because I certainly wasn't feeling it."

"She seems to have a lot of inside information." His light brown eyebrows creased over the bridge of his nose.

"You might want to ask her if she's psychic. Maybe she and my dad are hooking up to listen in on your conversations." Andrea handed the paper back to him.

"It's not funny it's serious. Things could leak out to the killer. He would know how close we are to finding him."

"Do you have any information about who the killer is?" Andrea asked keeping her tone friendly and inquisitive.

"Don't get smart with me. I don't know who it is, but if we did we'd want to keep it from the media." He looked down at her as if she wore a bug and was recording.

"I can assure you it's not me. I don't even care for the woman. Imagine insinuating my father and I are psychic. Does that sound like me?" She asked Steve expecting an answer. "I've never met one, have you? Have you ever been to one of those fortune tellers?" Her eyes searched Steve's for an answer. He blinked and looked away.

"As a kid at someone's birthday party. Those are people dressed up. They might have been given cards about the kids, so they'd be prepared." He slapped the rolled newspaper on his hip and walked away without another word.

"Yeah, Steve that sounds like what it was." Andrea shook her head. The guy was a nutcase.

That night her phone rang. She wasn't surprised it was her dad. "Hello, Dad."

"Hi, girl. How are you?" She didn't detect a slur in his voice, he was out of money for the week or it was a good day,

"I'm fine. We got some good news."

"I read the article. You helped find some woman. Dad, what are you doing?" She shook her head.

"You're going ta be traveling soon. You and da boy from da FBI."

"Fletcher? Yes, he's traveling to either Kansas or Missouri to follow up on the girls whose DNA matched."

Silence followed her statement. "You're traveling too."

"Dad stop this. Do you have a mole in the FBI? How do you know these things?"

"You know. It was never a secret between us even dough we didn't talk about it."

"Dad I don't have any woo woo stuff. It's all made up."

"I'm not going to argue wit you. At some point, you will have ta accept what you have. Call in intuition or logic or even instinct. It will come to your aid when you need it. If you don't push it back. Use it or lose it. Anyway, I called ta tell you ta keep in touch. When you get ta wherever you are going, ask ta look at the reports on da missing women. Pay close attention to da description of da men at the places da woman were taken from."

"Why?"

"Not sure."

"Okay, Dad. I'll maybe do some research here since I won't be going anywhere."

"Pack your winter boots."

"There's no snow that far south."

"I know it, not for snow it's for water."

"Good night, Dad."

Chapter 15

Two days later Conrad called Andrea to his office.

"Have a seat." He motioned to the chair across from his desk.

She searched his face for some clue of his intent but got nothing.

"It would seem you've made an impression with the FBI." He tapped a paper on his desk. "They want you to go to Kansas on a trade. We've had Agent Peterson here and now they want you to accompany him." He paused and waited for her reaction.

Andrea had no words.

He wagged his finger at her. "There's no extra pay. We're covering your expenses. You get a minimum per diem plus your hotel. You'll fly to Kansas and back. I don't know how long you'll be there. Maybe a few weeks. All I can say this is an excellent opportunity for you. Learn all you can and come back ready to work." He slid the letter with the FBI seal on it. "You and Fletcher need to finish questioning the fishermen on the lake before you leave."

"You mean at the lake Sir."

"No, I mean on the lake. We had an emergency, and the other officers couldn't get out to contact the fishermen on the lake. You two will finish the duty." he asked.

Did she dare say yes and ask to do something else? That would give Steve another knife to stick into her. "No Sir, I wanted to clarify that."

"Good. I'll see you before you leave for Kansas."

An hour later Andrea pressed her feet straight into the floorboard as Fletcher drove down the freeway towards the lake. The closer they got the faster her heartbeat and her breath came.

She felt every bump from the ice as they drove down the drive to the boat ramp. The 4x4 stopped at the edge of the ice, Fletcher put the vehicle into park. The engine idled as he turned to face her.

"I'm sorry. I didn't mean for this to happen this way. I'd planned to try this over a day or so. Now we don't have the time. We leave for Kansas in two days. The people on the lake are our job. Sometimes we have to do what we don't want to, what we fear." He put the truck into gear. "Hang in there."

Andrea squeezed her eyes shut and felt her heart pounding in her chest. She could feel the tires roll and bump then the sound of crunch beneath them. Her fingers gripped the armrests until her knuckles hurt. She peeked through her eyelashes. The lake lay before her, they weren't sliding. She forced her fingers to gradually release.

In the cab they heard a whine of a snowmobile and the machine flashed across their path. Fletcher slammed on his brakes. The backend fishtailed. Andrea squeezed her eyes shut and screamed. Her feet braced her body back into the seat. Then the back end fishtailed and straightened out to a stop.

Tears leaked out of the corners of her eyes. She tilted her head back and stared at the ceiling, feeling the banging of her heart in her chest, her fingers shook even though they gripped the armrests.

"I'm sorry. I didn't see the snowmobile. He must have come at an angle and then cut right in front of me. Are you okay?" He leaned across the console and peeled her fingers from the armrest and held them in his. She felt the strokes on her hand as he warmed her fingers and he massaged them from their death grip.

She heard his door open and close, then hers opened. His hands peeled her body from the seat, turning her to face him, and arms wrapped around her. "I'm so sorry."

She hadn't expected this, his strength and support cut through her wall and she clung to him burying her face into the fur of his collar. He held her tightly and rubbed her hands up and down her back as if warming her.

Gradually her heartbeat returned to normal and her mind stopped its frantic replaying of the incident. The present came crashing down. She realized she was in the arms of a handsome man who held her as if he didn't want to let go any time soon. *Because I was afraid, not for any other reason* that inner voice chided. What was she thinking still holding on to him? She had to move. With deliberately slow movements, she pulled her arms from around him and adjusted herself back on the seat.

He let her go but didn't move. "You okay now?" his voice a hoarse whisper.

"Yes. I'm sorry for falling apart like that."

He brushed a stray lock from her eyes and smiled showing those heart-stopping dimples.

"Don't apologize."

"I'm okay now. We should get to work." The corners of her lips lifted to a slight smile. It was all she could manage as her blood pumped hard, but not from fear.

"Good." He waited until she swung her feet back into the truck and shut the door.

They drove to where trucks had parked in a row behind the houses. He started to pull into a space between two of the buildings.

"Please. Can we park away from them? Maybe on the opposite side of the houses?" A picture of a crack appearing in the ice because the vehicles had parked too close together in one spot came to her mind. A cold shiver ran through her body.

"Sure." He moved the truck a distance from the vehicles and houses.

She fished around the console and found a few napkins folded. Blowing her nose and wiping her eyes she hoped anyone they talked to would think her red eyes came from the wind. She tucked the unused one into her pocket along with her notepad and pencil. Ink didn't do so well in these frigid temperatures.

He was at her door helping her onto the ice. His arm supported her until she got her balance.

"It's not that slick. Don't look down."

Andrea didn't need to be told. Most of the time lakes are piled with packed snow and look white. The wind had swept the snow off the lake into piles at the edges and along crevices. The ice itself looked black. She knew that under the clear ice was cold water and a lot more bodies than were accounted for.

Fletcher walked beside her but kept his hand firm on her elbow. It looked natural. Andrea wanted to pull her arm away and walk confidently beside him as an equal. Her nerves and fear kept her right at his side. *You like it, admit it,* her conscience taunted her. She didn't push the thought too far away, it felt comforting.

Ice houses sat spaced a few yards apart, across a large area. "Watch where you're walking." Fletcher admonished.

Andrea stopped. Fletcher turned to see why. "Fletcher. I was raised in northern Minnesota. I know what ice fishing is even though I haven't been out on the ice for years." This time she held on to his arm which he bent to bring her closer.

"Okay."

Andrea took interest in the fishing process. Her father had explained it all to her. Holes were drilled into the ice either by hand or with a power auger. Lines baited and dropped into the holes with a bell or flag that popped up to announce a bite.

"There is a code of respect among the fishermen," Andrea told Fletcher in a low tone as they walked. "You don't fish in another person's hole unless they aren't around. If they leave it's fair game. If lines are left unattended you might holler at the person to get their attention, but you don't steal their catch."

Fletcher nodded as they walked. He didn't respond but looked at the group with interest.

"Unfortunately, this code is on the honor system, and not all the fishermen are honorable. Booze sometimes plays a part and fights break out. Usually, it's men who don't want to drill their own fishing holes or have any way to do so. If someone isn't actively tending their hole, an unscrupulous fisherman might move in and commandeer it. You might lose your line, bait, and fish if you or your friends aren't watching. That's the worst case, my dad told me, it's not the rule."

"It's quite a cutthroat sport." He looked down at her with a smile.

She looked up at him. "You knew all that didn't you?"

He squeezed her arm. "I enjoyed the refresher lesson. You told it so well."

"Next time tell me to shut up." Andrea realized she didn't feel embarrassed or upset he'd let her ramble. It was a good feeling.

Andrea eyed the group of men ahead of them.

"Morning." Fletcher greeted the group. He showed them his ID and she held up hers. "We have some questions."

"About the dead women." One man responded.

"Yes, about the dead women, but not specifically. We're asking around if any of you have seen anyone acting more covert than usual?"

The men looked at each other then laughed. One of the men stepped forward. "We've talked about nothing else around here since bodies were found. We have no idea or any clue who the killer might be. In fact, we all could easily be the killer." He looked at his buddies and nodded.

A man with his eyes visible above a ski mask laughed in response. "We're all a little odd if you get right down to it. We're mostly retired or work odd shifts. We come out here to stay for a day or even longer. The generators power our lights, heaters, hot plates, and small refrigerators. This is like a small town in a way. We all know each other, our families, wives, and lovers."

Another man in a thick snowsuit that made him look like the stay-puff mand spoke. "If truth be told, we have figured out how he did it." They all nodded. "You see it would be pretty easy to bring a truck or snowmobile out here and set up a tent or pull a house out here. Drill holes in the ice from inside the house and drop the weighted nets into the water. Quite ingenious, we thought. That's why he's gotten away with it all these years."

Andrea's head jerked up. "All these years?" She pinned the man with a gaze that had him backing up with his hands in the air. "I didn't mean to sound like I was confessing or anything. We figured the two women they found; one had been missing three years the other four years. So, it didn't take a rocket scientist to figure he's been doing this for a long time."

A fisherman pushed his way forward, his loud laugh cut across the space. "It isn't like we have anything else to do while we're checking our lines. I think we've solved the mystery for you all."

Andrea grinned at him, "Pray tell, kind Sir," She gave a slight curtsey.

"Now doncha be laughin' at us. We kinda went over every possibility. He could easily do it like Gary said, during the winter. If he kills in the summer, he could row out here at night. No one would see him if it was the dark of the moon. He could easily drop the nets over the side, row back to the dock, and be gone before anyone would think anything about it."

Andrea nodded. "That's a possibility. How many of you fish out here at night in the spring through the fall?"

Most of them shook their heads.

"Not at all?" She asked.

"Sometimes. It's too noisy here with all the families out at night until late. Then the adults put the kids to bed and go out and make whoopee in the hot tub." Gary guffawed at his own joke.

"Then there's the weird guy with the telescope." The man in the full ski-mask lowered his voice. "Now if you want to look at a possible killer it's that man."

"Who?" Fletcher didn't look at Andrea but pretended he had no idea who they were talking about.

"Don't look now, but I saw the flash of the lens. He's outside watching us." Dan jerked his head in the direction of one of the houses behind him. "He's creepy. How he treats his kids is odd too."

"Have you seen him on the lake?" Fletcher asked.

Roger spoke up. He turned his back to the house in question and stomped his boots as if to warm up his feet. "I haven't, except to swim with his kids in the summer. The lake is shallow at that end for a few feet then gets deep at a steep angle. If you aren't careful and don't swim you could get into trouble fast. He's been teaching his children to swim."

"I thought you didn't fish in the summer," Andrea spoke to him.

"No, but we come out with the family. I have a pontoon." Roger answered.

"Yeah, it sure takes a long time for the girls to learn. The boys seemed to pick it up pretty fast when you're left to sink or swim." Gary's tone sounded hard.

"Care to elaborate?" Andrea asked.

"Gary." The rise in Roger's voice admonished him to either be quiet or careful about what he said.

The two officers waited. Gary's mouth tightened. "It frosts my cookie." His arms crossed his chest. "I live a few houses down from him. If I'm on my deck, I can see everything the neighbors do in their backyards. It's when I take the family are out on the pontoon swimming and relaxing that I've seen him and his kids." He stopped and looked around for confirmation. One of the men shrugged and nodded. He continued to speak.

"I'm not going into details, but he teaches the girls to float. Now we've all taught our kids the same way, they lay on their backs and you support them for a while and when they get the hang of it you take your hand away. Only this creep doesn't take his hand away. How he "teaches" is borderline sexual abuse." Gary gave air quotes to the word teach.

Fletcher nodded while Andrea wrote in her notebook what he said.

"Now this isn't going to go public is it?" Gary lowered his voice sounding worried.

"No, you aren't alone in observing inappropriate behavior," Fletcher assured him.

"Good. We talk, but I wouldn't want to speculate without proof. I doubt the kids know any different." Gary looked at the guys.

"Since you live here on the lake, is there anyone else that might act suspicious?"

"No, people do things differently. The old guy at the end is a Vet. He collects stuff and makes yard ornaments. Stuff I wouldn't put in my yard, but he does quite well selling them at flea markets." Gary shook his head.

The sound of a bell ringing had the men all running to check their lines. Andrea and Fletcher walked to the next group of men and women standing outside their houses. None of them knew of anyone they could pinpoint that acted differently or suspiciously on the lake. Newcomers made friends or were shunned for bad behavior.

After they'd talked to most of the groups and the lone fishermen, the two returned to the truck.

"How do you feel?" Fletcher asked.

Andrea rested against the back of the seat resting on the headrest. She turned to look at him. "Better. I don't feel the fear I had before. I still don't like the sound of the ice cracking."

"You held up well. If anyone were watching they'd have no idea you were terrified."

"Not even the death grip I had on your arm as we walked around?"

Fletcher chuckled. "There was that. I may have a bruise for a while."

"Sorry about that." She didn't sound too sorry.

Fletcher started the truck and steered toward the shore. Even though she felt more comfortable in the vehicle as it moved across the ice, as they neared the shore she saw the sun had melted some of the ice near the edge. Her fingers gripped the armrest and she stared at the sky rather than what was ahead of them.

She squeaked when she felt the tires bump over something and slide a bit. She squeezed her eyes shut.

"Andrea we are in the parking lot. You can open your eyes now." Fletcher's voice was soft and encouraging.

She opened her eyes to the familiar road leading around the lake to the main street. "Thank you," She whispered.

At the station, Andrea wrote her report leaving out Gary's interpretation of the swim lessons. Those she'd keep to herself.

Chapter 16

Andrea drove to her friend Chrissy and Dave's house. She smiled to herself as she pulled into their driveway and smelled the scent of a grill going. *I wonder what the neighbors think?*

Pulling the carrier she'd brought with her from the front seat, she headed to the side door. After a firm knock, she opened the door. "Honey, I'm home."

"Come on in," Chrissy answered.

"I brought chocolate cherry cake." Andrea set the carrier on the counter.

"Oo-oo You know how to make a woman and man happy." Chrissy turned from the stove, laying the ladle down on a holder. She reached out and hugged her friend. "How are you? We haven't talked much since this case started."

"It's been crazy." Andrea ran her finger across the substance on the ladle and licked it. "Oh yum, marinara sauce, or is it spaghetti sauce?"

"It's not for tonight unless you want it over your chicken. It's for my family. They're having a big birthday for my aunt and my mom says my sauce is better than hers." She rolled her eyes but Andrea could tell she was proud of the compliment.

"It is good. I can't say it's better since I've not tasted your mom's."

"It is better, but that's between you and me."

"And me," Dave announced entering the kitchen holding a plate of meat.

"Dinner is ready. I got here in time." Andrea teased.

Andrea turned to the table to pick up a stack of four plates. She froze. "Are you expecting anyone else?"

"No. Why?" Chrissy asked.

Andrea stared as the stack of plates.

Dave picked up the plates. "I guess I picked up four instead of three." He gave Andrea an inquisitive expression. "Did you think we'd invited your FBI friend?"

Andrea felt her face get hot and she turned away. "No."

"You did." Chrissy chuckled. "Now the truth comes out. You like him."

They sat at the table. "I think he's a good agent."

"That's not what I heard." Chrissy raised her eyebrow at her friend. "I heard you went onto the lake with him. Now that is something. You never go out on the ice."

Andrea stared at her plate. The perfectly grilled chicken and golden potatoes once tempted her more than talking. The piece she chewed seemed dry in her mouth.

"What?" Dave asked in a tone that expected an explanation.

"I heard through the office grapevine that Andrea and the agent questioned the ice fishermen." Chrissy waved a fork of vegetables at him.

"What's the big deal?" Dave looked from one woman to the other.

"Andrea doesn't like to be on lake ice," Chrissy answered in a lower tone.

He cocked his head as if re-emphasizing his last question.

"I mean she REALLY doesn't like going out on a frozen lake. When she was younger she fell through."

"Ah, now I get it." Then after a moment, he looked at Andrea. "So, the FBI agent got you to go out on the lake?" He sounded impressed.

Andrea wagged her finger at him. "He pushed me because I had to do it. It was the job or I'd..." She paused. She couldn't continue.

Chrissy patted her arm. "We get it."

"Where are you in the case?" Dave changed the subject.

Andrea heaved a sigh. "We got a bunch of pieces of body parts. Doc had been getting these bits and pieces from the Hmong fishermen. Stuff found in fish stomachs."

"Ugh!" Chrissy faked a gag.

"Think of all the people eating fish from that lake that ate human flesh." Andrea laid her fork down.

"Please," Chrissy begged, "No more, I'm eating."

"How is your boss taking all this?" Dave put his fork down and rested his elbows on the table.

"Which one? Chief Bellows or Steve Totts?"

"Both." Dave and Chrissy answered at the same time.

Andrea hung her head. "The Chief is doing his best. He's caught in the middle."

"You're being too kind," Chrissy interjected.

"He's retiring in about eighteen months, and he wants to go out on a good ticket. He'd like to get this case buckled up." She paused and when neither spoke, she continued. "He hired me because of my dad. He made only one comment when he hired me. 'Let's hope you have the same success as your father.' Andrea held up her fork to make the point.

"He can't expect you to be your father. He's had years of experience." Chrissy responded.

"I think he was hoping."

Dave shrugged and dismissed the comment. "How is the Agent?"

"He's fine. He's good at his job I guess. He lets me work the case on my own." She shrugged and took a drink of the soda. "I think I'm on to something."

"With him?" Chrissy smiled at her friend.

"No, with the case." Andrea took her knife and made a jabbing motion at her friend.

"What do you have?" Dave sounded interested.

Andrea pushed her almost empty plate aside. "I think this guy is a serial killer who brings the bodies away from the kill zone. He thinks after all this time he's gotten away with murder."

"It sure looks like he has up until now. If those two bags hadn't gotten loose and somehow ended up in those ice blocks..." he stopped and shook his head.

"Why?" Andrea asked him.

Dave looked at her with an incredulous expression. "We know what he did."

"So? We found a dumpsite. We don't have a clue who he is or where he is or how many he's killed. He's laughing at us."

Dave and Chrissy were quiet for a few moments. Chrissy got up and took her and Dave's plate to the counter. Andrea followed her. "I didn't mean to be sarcastic."

"You weren't," Dave called from the table. "It's true. IF that's a big if, he lives around here, he's watching the news every day."

They cleaned up the dishes. Andrea cut the cake handing each a plate then moved to the family room by the fireplace. Andrea sat across from her two friends and stared into the fire.

"I have something I want to tell you." She didn't look at the two. "I didn't drop this info on you before because I knew we needed to catch up."

"You sound serious. Does this have something to do with the FBI guy?" Chrissy teased.

With a sly look, Andrea turned to her friend, "Now that you brought him up I guess we can talk about Fletcher first."

Chrissy leaned forward. "NO WAY! The two of you haven't moved that fast!" Her eyes were wide with surprise.

Andrea burst out laughing and wiggled her fingers at her friend, "Gotcha!"

Chrissy fell back against the cushions. "Foul!"

"You fell for that, woman." David joined the laughter.

"No, tell me, what's the news?" Chrissy asked.

"I'm going to Kansas with Fletcher. Not together, but as part of the team. I got a letter from his boss. I have no idea how this worked out and I think Conrad was glad for me to be out of the office and Steve's control."

"You think? I've seen Steve walk by you many times and give you dirty looks. Then times he goes out of his way to avoid you."

Chrissy took another bite of the cake. 'I love this cake. It's almost better than sex."

The two laughed. "No, that's a different cake." Andrea waved her fork at her friend.

"I'm happy you get this opportunity. I'm not sure what you'll do but learn all you can." Chrissy admonished.

They were silent finishing the cake.

"I want to look at the case files of the two women we found." Andrea continued.

"Good luck." David shook his head. "You know these guys. They don't like outsiders. You may be in a situation that's worse than here."

"Same song, different songbook." Andrea laughed dryly."

A short time later, Andrea said goodbye to her friends and headed home. As she passed Blue Lake she wondered if the killer lived on the lake. Maybe he was familiar with the area and dumped the bodies then went on his way.

If the latter was the case, they might never find this killer.

Chapter 17

wo days later Fletcher and Andrea walked into the Police station in the city of Winfield, Kansas. They landed that morning in Wichita, were picked up by an officer, and driven to their hotel an hour away. Now they followed another officer to a conference room filled with people.

Some sat at the large table and stared into laptop screens, tapping keys now and then.

"Wait here." Fletcher left her near the door while he made his way across the room.

The room hummed with activity. Everyone seemed to move in a synchronized dance. A couple of large whiteboards on the wall were filled with words, lines, and arrows. Andrea managed to make her way across the room to stand in front of one of the boards.

The names of the women, dates, and the location they were found had been printed. She'd looked up both cities on the map checking for common traffic lines.

Beneath each name was the place they were last seen. Peggy Hicks, Hitchin' Post, Winfield, KS 2017, and Jenny McNabb, Katie's Diner, Carthage, MO.

The memory of her father's admonition came to her. "Look at the reports from people who had been with Peggy Hicks, the missing woman, that night.

She didn't know who to ask her questions. Fletcher had disappeared. The rest were busy. She headed back to the lobby and stopped at the main receptionist desk.

"Pardon me. Who in this office worked the Peggy Hick's case?" Hoping her smile might get her the name.

"We all did." The woman's answer sounded short and abrupt. She didn't look at Andrea.

"I'm sure you did. I'm wondering where I can find the officers that personally questioned the customers at the restaurant that night."

"Restaurant? The Hitchin' Post isn't a restaurant, it's a dive bar and pub." The derision was evident.

"Okay. Who were the officers on duty that night?" Andrea pressed.

"Who are you?" The woman eyed her with more suspicion.

"I'm Detective Andrea Watson with the St. Paul CAU. I'm here with the FBI task force. I have some questions for those officers. I think they can be more helpful to the case than they are aware of." Andrea kept her voice professional but courteous.

The woman continued to stare at her for a long moment then picked up her phone and pressed a couple of numbers. "You busy? One of those FBI Officers is here and wants to talk to you. How should I know, get over here!" She dropped the receiver back onto the cradle.

"Mark will be here." She turned away to her computer.

Andrea looked out the window. The cold drab colors of winter were evident even this far south. Trees were bare and the shrubs had lost any semblance of what they would become once spring hit.

"Ma'am?" A deep voice asked. Andrea turned.

An older man in his mid-fifties, with silver hair and a round face, gave her a quizzical expression.

Andrea held out her hand. "Hello, I'm Detective Andrea Watson, St. Paul CAU." He shook her hand.

"Mark Steele."

"I'm sorry to bother you. I have some questions about the night you questioned the patrons at the rest--Hitchin' Post." She corrected herself.

"Sure. It was a long time ago. I hope I can remember anything."

"Is there a place we can sit and talk?" She looked around the lobby.

He sighed, and motioned for her to follow him, "Come back to my desk. It's not quiet, but we can talk." She followed him down a long hall opposite the rooms the FBI used.

They entered a room with pairs of desks filling the area and officers looking at her as she followed Mark to his desk along a wall with no windows.

"Have a seat." He indicated to the one next to his desk. "What can I tell you?"

"I'm sure you have reports of all the people you talked to and what they said. Do you remember anything they said about who was in the bar that night?"

Mark rubbed his face. "No way. That was three years ago."

"Where are the reports you wrote? All of the reports taken from the patrons."

"You can read them online; everything has been digitized."

"That's convenient, but I have no computer or access to one. Are there paper copies?" She continued to be pleasant and courteous.

"In boxes down in the cage." He shook his head at her as if she were crazy.

"How can I get them?"

"I can request them. If anyone is around that can get them." He didn't look too helpful.

Andrea moved close to his desk and whispered. "I don't want to go over anyone's head to have some FBI yahoo demand someone bring them to me. It would be better if you looked like you were part of the investigation and helped me out by getting those boxes brought to me." She kept a smile on her lips.

He took a long look at her weighing what she said. He turned and pressed a few buttons on the phone and spoke into the receiver. "Mary, tell Kane to come to my desk. Yes, now." He grimaced as he replaced the handset.

It didn't take long until the sound of swift-moving footsteps could be heard on the linoleum. Mark had a sheet of paper and pen filling in the lines on the request form.

"Sir? You asked for me?" A young man in his late teens or into his twenties, dressed in an ill-fitting police uniform slid to a stop next to Andrea.

"Kane, this is Detective Andrea. She's with the FBI."

Andrea started to correct him, but he waved his hand at her and continued. "She needs to look through the boxes in storage that pertain to the case they're working on."

"The Peggy Hicks case?" his voice sounded as if he knew the investigation.

"Yes, that one. She wants to look through the case files. Can you go and bring them up?" Mark looked around the room. "Bring all of them to that desk." His voice remained firm and he spoke slowly as he pointed to a desk in a dark alcove.

"Yes Sir. Ma'am, I'll bring them up right away." Kane took the paper and gave them a short salute, then jogged down the hallway.

After a brief pause, Mark sighed. "He's the Captain's grandson. A little slow on the uptake but diligent and wants to be a police officer." He shook his head. "Please don't judge him or us too harshly. He knows he's not a real officer because he hasn't been to the academy. He wears the "pretend" uniform when he works here in the office. He changes before he goes home. He's proud of it and takes meticulous care that it isn't wrinkled. It was his dad's. God rest his soul."

"His father died in the line of duty?" Andrea queried.

"Yes. He was called to a house for a domestic. When he arrived, the man opened the door and shot him."

Andrea felt a wave of shock pass through her. "I'm sorry."

"So were we. Chief is raising Kane, no pun intended. We all give him projects to help him out."

"I understand. Thank you. Is a coffee machine around here?" She looked around the room.

"Down that hall." He jerked his head toward a short hall off the end of the room. "Bathroom's down there too if you need. You'll see coffee mugs but, I wouldn't take one if you get my drift. Foam cups are in the cupboard."

"Thank you, Sir." She stood.

"Call me Mark or Sergeant." He nodded.

Andrea headed down the hallway.

It was a good hour before Kane brought up a hand cart with boxes stacked so high he had to peer around them to move. He set them on the floor next to her desk.

"I'll be right back." He hurried away driving the two-wheeler like it was a drunk-on Saturday night.

She started going through the files in the boxes. She found the box marked #1 had some files with the investigator's notes. She began reading them. The stacks of boxes multiplied.

When she was almost surrounded by boxes she stopped Kane.

"Are all these boxes from Peggy Hicks?" She walked around to look at the boxes.

"No. When I told Gus what I was after, he told me to bring these up too. They have files from missing women in the county."

She opened the next box. Some had accordion folders with a few files inside and others had two or three large folders. "All these women are missing?"

"I guess so. He said to bring them up."

"Kane. Check back with me later this afternoon. I may send some of them back. "

He shrugged "Okay" He went back down the hall with the cart weaving back and forth.

She spent hours reading different officer reports. The patrons each described those in the bar. She made a list of the names and made tick marks after them each time they were mentioned and described by the officers. Also made notes of different observations.

Four officers questioned the thirty people. Reading all the names. The patrons described a single man with no name. Their memory of him had been listed as:

> He looked familiar. I've might have seen him in the
> bar a few times but was never introduced.

One patron described a man in a flannel shirt and jeans wearing a baseball cap.

No, he didn't remember if there was anything on the hat.

He bought a round or two for everyone at the table. I've seen him in here before, but I don't remember his name.

Turning the page, she read:

I think his name is Joe or George. He's been in the bar before. I'm sure of it.

Their descriptions varied. One said they saw a man with a jean shirt and quilted, hunting type vest. Another said he wore a polo style shirt in a dark color. Were they all describing the same man or bringing up a memory of the man wearing different clothes at different times?

All the patrons remember seeing this guy before, but he wasn't overly social. He blended in, there, but not SEEN. Who was this man?

She continued reading, looking for any descriptions of the man called 'Joe or George.' Nowhere did she find a report of the man being questioned. *Where did he go?* She read on. She found one report, handwritten, stating the officer followed up on the missing man. No report gave his follow-up.

"Hey! What are you doing here?" Fletcher stood between two stacks of boxes, looking down at her.

She grinned up at him. She was tired and her eyes hurt. Kane had brought her a lamp as the ceiling lights didn't reach her corner. "Hi. Are you going to lunch?"

"Lunch?! I stopped by the hotel and knocked on your door. It's seven-thirty. We went out for dinner already. I couldn't find you. You didn't answer your door or your phone. I came back here to meet HD. I asked if anyone had seen you. For a moment I thought you might have been kidnapped."

His expression warmed her heart. He'd been worried about her. He continued. "A young man said you were way back in a corner. He brought me to you."

"That was Kane, the Chief's grandson. He brought me all these boxes." She waved her hand at the stacks.

"I see. What are they?" Fletcher looked inside one.

"They are case files on Peggy Hicks. I'm reading them."

"What for? They're all digitized. You can read them on a computer." He flipped through the folders.

"I'm sure they are, but I don't have a computer here. I don't have access to the files. This was the only way I could read them." She didn't allow her voice to sound like she was complaining or that she'd been forgotten for the whole day. Her stomach rumbled. "Can I hitch a ride back to the hotel?"

"Of course. You haven't eaten all day, have you?" He took her hand and pulled her gently away from the corner and all the boxes. "I'm so sorry. I feel like a big jerk. I got you here and then I left you to fend for yourself. I apologize for being so selfish." He unlocked the car and waited until she was seated and shut the door.

His apology sounded sincere. She knew he was caught up in the case and all that was going on. He had to brief everyone on what they had found in Minnesota and be in on how to proceed. She didn't hold it against him. She was hungry and tired.

"What do you feel like eating. I'm sure there's a chain restaurant open." He turned the car down the main road and pulled into the parking lot of a familiar building.

"This sounds good." She gave him her favorite menu item and waited while he went in to order. She put her head back on the headrest and closed her eyes

The interior light going on woke her. Fletcher climbed back in the car with a bag he sat in her lap. "Here's a large soda." He set it in the cupholder.

She smiled her thanks.

At the hotel, she pushed her room card in the slot to open the door. Fletcher followed her into her room. "Andrea, I'm sorry."

She turned to him. "I know you are. I'm too tired and hungry to even be mad about it. I'm not mad, it was as much my fault. I was so deep into the case files I never even went outside. Kane came in and brought me fresh coffee. I think he thought of me as his special project. He brought me water." She tilted her head. "Now that I think about it, he did mention something about going to lunch. I told him to go."

"Okay I'm not going to beat myself up, but I promise to take better care of you."

"Fletcher, it's not your job to TAKE-CARE of me." She bristled at the innuendo. "I'm a big girl, I can take care of myself. Now go." She swished him out with her hands.

He smiled and shut the door. She locked it and pushed the security bar over the door.

Tomorrow she'd show him what she found.

The next day she waved at Fletcher as she headed to her office. He insisted she come with him to the conference room. Entering the room Andrea stayed for the morning meeting. When they dispersed, she started to leave.

"Where are you going?" Fletcher asked.

"I need to get back to the files."

"Come on, I want you to meet the head of the team." He led her to a group of men. "Sir, this is Andrea Watson who was at the scene when the evidence was discovered in the ice. Andrea this is Harry Devereau."

"HD." The man interrupted Fletcher and held his hand out to shake hers.

She shook his hand and stared into his eyes. He was tall, thin, and peered at her with dark eyes under bushy brows. Creases at the corners of his eyes and mouth had come from many tense situations.

"Pleased to meet you, Sir. Thank you for allowing me to join your team. I hope I can help."

He nodded. "You're here as an observer. Agent Peterson is your contact. He'll make sure you are informed of what you are cleared for." He gave her a nod and turned away.

Fletcher turned her away, "Well, you have been officially introduced to HD. You won't be talking to him. I don't even talk to him." He gave a dry chuckle. "I'll find an extra laptop for you." His eyes scanned the room.

"Fletcher don't make a fuss. I'm sure those agents are doing what I am. Let me stick to the hard copies for now. I like holding paper." She gave him a wink as she rubbed her fingers together.

"You're sure?"

"Yes." She smiled and headed down the hall to the squad room.

Back in her corner, she arranged the things she'd brought from the hotel. This time she had a large container of coffee, rolls, and a breakfast sandwich to snack on. Kane came by every so often to make sure she had everything she needed.

He came by at lunch to tell her it was time to meet Fletcher. She entered the conference room where sub sandwiches, chips, and beverages were provided. She brought Kane a couple of cookies and a sandwich. "You're on this case too buddy. What would I do without you checking on me?"

He puffed his chest as she watched him strut down the hall munching on the cookies.

Late that afternoon she left her corner to look for Fletcher. He'd introduced her to a few of his coworkers, but other than a nod, they ignored her.

She found him at his computer. "How's it going?"

"They're going through the files too. They haven't found anything but what the original officers found. What did you come up with?" Fletcher stretched his arms above his head. It pulled his shirt tight over his muscular chest. Andrea noticed and looked away taking a deep breath.

"Is your Superior available? I don't want to have to go through this twice. If he thinks it's nothing I'll drop it."

Fletcher nodded and led her to an office where he knocked on the door jam. "Andrea found something she thinks we should know." HD motioned them to enter.

"If you don't mind, do you have space for me to spread out my notes so you can see them?" Andrea held up a sheaf of legal sheets.

He nodded. At a long credenza, he pulled on a handle, a board extended making the space larger. She laid her yellow legal pages out side by side.

"Here are the questions the police asked. Most of them were the same so I condensed them to the basic ones. Each page is the answers to the questions by each person. Now I'm sure your people have read all these."

Harry nodded and looked at what she wrote. "We have all this stuff. It's on the computer.

"What about the man in the flannel/jean/polo shirt? Who questioned him?" She stood a step away from the table and didn't point to the papers.

"What man? We have all the police reports." His gaze scanned the pages.

There isn't a report from the man in flannel. I showed Mark, one of the officers who questioned the patrons. I asked if he remembered questioning this man. He didn't and then asked around. None of them remembered a particular man in flannel. Flannel shirts or plaid ones are common in that group."

HD looked again at the pages. "No statement came from the man in flannel?"

"No report taken from a man called Joe or George. I'm not sure, but I guess he was never called or found. He wasn't someone in town that anyone recalled. As each person came into the room they sat with an officer, then left. They figured he'd already been questioned and left. I don't believe he ever came in. He had to have left town, or he isn't from Winfield. From the patron descriptions my guess he'd been to the bar more than one time to set up his alibi.

I'm not pointing fingers at anyone. It was an honest mistake. Now it's three years later and will you be able to question these people about the man in flannel? You might. It might be worth a try.

HD straightened but his eyes were still on the pages. "You put all this together? How come it's on legal sheets?"

"That's what they gave me to use."

He shook his head. "I haven't seen this concise report for a long time. You did a good job in two days."

"Whoever filed them did me a favor by putting all the interrogations into three boxes. Once I figured out how they filed them, I started with those." Andrea waved her hand at the table. "It's a bit of a mess. I sat up last night and rewrote it all."

He shook his head. "Old school. I think we can fix that. You won't have to retype it. I'll have someone else do it in our typical format. Is there anything else you thought about while you were reading?

"The other woman was from a city not far away."

"Yes, Carthage, Missouri is about three hours away." HD rested his elbows on the desk.

"Not far. What do the two cities have in common? Both aren't far from the main highway. Both highways converge in Oklahoma City. We have Kansas City to the north and Oklahoma City to the south with two women, we know about missing ."

"One went missing three years ago, the other disappeared two years ago." Fletcher put in.

"I'm assuming you agree this was done by a man, I wonder if I looked at the interrogation reports from that missing woman I'd find a similar man in that bar?" She watched the head of the regional FBI rub his face and neck.

"Why does all this sound so routine, but it wasn't done?"

"I'm guessing different jurisdictions. The departments don't share information." Fletcher stood relaxed with one hand in the pocket of his slacks.

"I hate to ask, but would you be willing to have a go at those reports too? I'll get you a computer so you can access them online. Let's hope they have them online otherwise you may have to do it old school." His expression showed his confidence in her and an apology before they knew what she would be getting into.

"Yes, I'd be glad to help." A warm feeling spread across her chest. The Regional head of the FBI had asked for her help.

Chapter 18

HD told her it would be a while before he could set her up with a computer. She left the building and walked through the city of Winfield, window shopping. At a deli, she bought food then continued to her hotel. Munching on her sandwich she began to get a familiar itchy feeling. She ignored it and kept walking. It got worse. It was almost like a buzz in her head.

"Stop it, Dad," She whispered. Her father would ask her about things on a case he was working on. Eager to help him and sit with him she'd do what he said. She'd read the reports. Words or phrases would stand out to her. When she'd point them out to her father he'd pat her on the back of her head or shoulder and nod. "Good job. You saw what I saw."

Later she figured out, he didn't always "see" the same things she did. Sometimes she'd get an itchy feeling about what she was looking at. What she saw put a different light on the case and he was able to get a different clue. It was how she found the missing notes on the Flannel guy in the bar. She shut her mind against work thoughts and looked at the almost bare storefronts as she walked.

Many of the stores along this stretch were closed. Boarded up or the windows covered with faded butcher paper or old newspapers. In the window of one store, she paused to look at the display. A movement in the window's reflection caused her to look at it more closely.

A man carrying a large duffle bag walked down the sidewalk across the street behind her. That itchy feeling got worse.

"Oh, come on!" She spoke out loud as she turned and continued down the sidewalk looking where he went. No one stood across the street. She pursed her lips. *Not now.*

She walked to the corner. Still no sign of the man with the duffle bag. *Where could he have gone so fast?*

A sign on the corner pointed to the high school football field down the side street. Crossing the street, she kept an eye on the few houses along the way, looking for the man.

At the field, she followed the moving hat as it bobbed through the brush. She needed the exercise. It might get rid of that itchy feeling.

She reached the track and followed it toward the far end of the field. She told herself the itchy feeling was a nervous reaction to her job.

Once she got to the end of the track she didn't follow the curve but stepped off the pavement and continued toward the blackberry and brush filled edge of the mowed field.

She heard a hum behind her and whirled to face the intrusion. An African American man driving a golf cart pulled to a stop beside her.

"Hello. Are you taking your constitutional around the field?" He grinned a wide smile filled with straight white teeth.

"I guess so. I'm tired but for some reason, my feet want to walk around a bit."

"Now that's a new one. You're a visitor here?" He crossed his arms on the steering wheel.

"Yes, one of the detectives on the Peggy Hicks case." She looked along the brush line ahead. "Did you by any chance see a man walking along here carrying a duffle bag?"

He looked around the field then shook his head. "No. No one's been here for a couple of days. Usually there are runners, joggers, or walkers, but it's Saturday and everyone's at the football game up at the College field. Were you looking for someone?"

"I—" She stopped. Could she say she'd seen anyone, for sure? Could he be in her imagination? "I guess not. I thought I saw him turn down here, but he could have been going somewhere else." She rubbed her arms. "What's over there?" She pointed to the overgrown vegetation that marked the edge of the track field.

"You mean the Commissioners Folly." He gave a dry chuckle.

Andrea gave him a questioning look without answering.

"That's Walnut Creek. The brush and trees line the back along the creek. It snakes through the entire town. The kids were skipping out of class and heading down here to do whatever teenagers do when adults aren't looking." he waved his hand, then continued. "Several years ago, the Commissioner, had a meeting when his son was caught drinking, smoking, and let's say dallying with an under-age female. He said the area attracted the wrong kind of crowd. He told the Public Works to leave it alone. Don't cut the brush or weeds. That should stop the kids from being able to reach the creek around the school."

"Did that stop them?"

"I'll show you. Hop in. By the way, my name is Craig Brown. I'm the groundskeeper here. What's your name?"

"I'm Andrea Watson." She answered as she slid next to the man. He pressed on the gas while she hung on to the bar to keep from falling out as it bumped over the uneven ground. He came to a stop at the end of the field.

"This wooden bridge spans the creek to allow kids from that part of town to walk to school without walking all the way around to the main road to cross it."

He stepped out and walked to the brush. "Did you see the church cross?"

Andrea turned to look and saw no church cross, she turned back. Craig was gone. She looked around where he'd been standing. Her heart began to race. Had he also been a figment of her mind? No, she'd sat in the golf cart and talked to the man.

"Over here." Craig stepped out of the bushes. "This is how the kids hide." He waved for her to follow him.

She walked to the place she'd last seen him. No matter which way she walked, the path appeared invisible until she pushed between two bushes.

Craig led the way as the path curved then gradually sloped down to the creek bed.

There was no shoreline at first. The brush grew almost to the water's edge. After a few more yards path opened to a cleared area.

"See what I mean?" Craig swept his hand around the area then over his head. "This place is pretty private."

Andrea nodded, then noted planks had been nailed on top of stumps or chunks of wood. Some logs had fallen from trees and been brought here to sit on. An old aluminum lawn chair had been reinforced with what looked like a plastic screen.

In the center, a circle of rock had been built up with mud that dried to look like concrete. Ashes and partly burned wood remained sodden in the center.

Craig pulled a cooler out of the brush and opened it.

"Nothing, but empty cans and bottles." He closed it and pushed it back where it had been.

Andrea walked around the area. Her nerves hadn't quit buzzing. She rubbed her arms again.

"Is there something wrong? Are you cold? We can go back." Craig asked.

"No, I want to walk around here for a few more minutes. I wonder if the kids are the only ones who come here. Do you think the homeless might come here to hide?"

Chapter 19

Something here that wasn't right. She pushed the thought out of her mind. She didn't want this right now. Why am I here? *This is why you were sent here.* "No!"

"No what?" Craig turned to ask her.

"Nothing, a thought. What's up there?" She pointed up the bank.

"Nothing, but more brush." He moved toward the exit path.

Andrea walked along the edge of the elevated bank. It felt like someone guided her eyes and steps. Pushing some of the branches to one side she saw they had been bent and broken at one time.

"Does this look like another pathway here? Like it was used at one time but now the weeds and grass have begun to grow?"

"You may be right." He pushed branches aside as Andrea followed him. "It's different, not like it's been used for parties and such." He started forward but Andrea grabbed his arm.

"Stop. Don't move." Andrea ordered.

He obeyed but looked around for danger.

"Something is buried here." She looked at the ground.

"How do you know?" He stepped back and looked around the small area.

"Notice how the grass is greener here? There isn't much light, but it looks like someone might have dumped fertilizer here, or something is dead under here. Can you smell something odd?"

"DEAD? As in buried?" He looked around like a ghost was going to jump out. "Are you serious? How do you come here and think dead things are buried here?

"Don't ask me. I could be all wrong." She turned away.

"Wait." He gave her a hard look, "You're serious. You think something is buried here." He sniffed the air. "It does stink. I thought it was the creek."

"I don't think so." She continued to walk back to the edge of the bank leading down to the clearing. She stopped at the edge. Why did she think something was buried? She was far from her home. She'd never been here before in her life. It's that itchy feeling. Like something is rubbing you the wrong way. It led her to this spot. Can she walk away? She gave a mental shrug. Maybe there's nothing here after all.

"You have a tool belt on. What's in it?" She walked back towards him.

He reached around and pulled out a forked tool for digging weeds. "Just this, a knife and my phone."

She held out her hand for the tool. Bending down she poked in the dirt. It wasn't loose, but it wasn't packed the way dirt would be if it were undisturbed. She continued to dig letting the tool move as if on its own. Then she felt the tool hit something. When that happened, it felt as if a shock went through her body. Sitting back, she waited for the feeling to leave.

"What is it? Did you find something?" Craig bent to look at the area around the tool sticking out of the earth.

"Come here, do you want to look?"

"No." He stepped away from her.

She brushed the dirt away from the area. Craig handed her his work gloves and a piece of flat bark. She used it as a shovel.

"Look, there's something here. It looks like cloth." He bent over her shoulder. "It is cloth."

Andrea pulled it, lifting it so the dirt fell away. She dropped it again when she saw what looked like bones roll out of the fold. "We need to call someone."

"I'll call 9-1-1."

"No! Let me call my FBI friend." She took out her phone and pressed Fletcher's speed dial.

"Hey, where are you?" He sounded cheerful through the phone.

"You need to bring your boss and come to the High School practice field."

After a slight pause. "Andrea, are you okay?"

"Yes, but what I'm seeing isn't okay."

"What did you find? Where are you?" His voice was lower like he was trying to downplay her call.

"You need to come. I think I found a place where a body is buried."

"WHERE ARE YOU?" Even with his voice low the intensity cleared her mind.

"Go to the High School Track and we'll meet you there."

"WE?"

"The groundskeeper and I. Please come. Don't make a big deal about it so the public is alerted. Especially the media. Bring a medical examiner and your boss, possibly a CSI unit."

"Okay." He disconnected the call.

"Let's go back to the cart and wait." Andrea began walking toward the path that led to the field.

Craig pulled his phone out.

"We can't tell anyone until the FBI gets here." She tapped the phone in his hand. "No calls."

"Okay." He pocketed the phone. They made their way back to the field and sat in the cart.

"How odd that you saw that clearing. I wonder if the kids know about it." In a softer voice, he added. "I hope it's not something they are a part of."

"Me too."

They had an uneasy silence. She wasn't in the mood to answer questions. What was she going to tell Fletcher and HD? She happened to be in a woods and found a body dump? Would he or any of the team buy that? She hoped Kalie never found out. She'd be spilling it all over the paper. What was it about her father that set Kalie off? It was almost like a personal vendetta.

Forty-five minutes later a van and a few police cars turned the corner at the small parking area and onto the grass. Craig winced.

"It will get worse before the end of this." She advised the older man.

Fletcher was out of the car and striding toward her. "Where is it?"

"Wait here," She responded and sat in the cart until the rest of the group arrived.

HD glared at her with part irritation and curiosity. "What is this all about? I hope you didn't waste our time."

Andrea explained. "Craig was showing me the creek. I wanted a better view, so I climbed the bank and smelled something. We found a cleared area where the smell was strong. I dug a bit and found a bit of cloth and what I think might be bones. I didn't want to make a big deal in case it was a prank."

The group followed Craig through the brush to the clearing. He showed them the piece of cloth and the bones protruding from the dirt. The Medical Examiner nodded and asked his assistant for some tools. It wasn't long until he confirmed a body was found.

"She said it was possible there could be more." Craig offered to the ME and HD who stood at the edge of the clearing.

HD turned and gave her an unreadable glance.

"I'm guessing he doesn't think this is a dumpsite. Just wait for it." Andrea spoke under her breath.

"You smelled something?" Fletcher asked, sniffing the air.

"It does stink around there. Even Craig thought it smelled bad."

He gave her a look that boarded pride.

"Maybe this will be a prank and the bones are a Halloween decoration." She crossed her fingers and walked back to the creek bank while the rest of the group climbed up to observe the process.

Before too long Fletcher came to the edge of the drop-off and looked down on her. "It's not just one body."

Andrea nodded and made her way back up to the field. She wondered if Craig would mind if she nabbed his cart to ride back to the hotel. She felt wiped out. She could walk the mile to the hotel from here. She started walking toward the short street where she'd entered the field.

She glanced at her watch, four-thirty. She hadn't eaten when she left, planning on grabbing a bite before going to the hotel.

A few blocks away she found a gas station with a food mart inside. Several cars filled the spaces in front and at the pumps. She went inside and found a counter of hot food displayed at one end of the room. Booths lined the windows and a couple of long tables next to them.

The glass display showed hot dogs, jo-jo potatoes, fried chicken, burgers, chili, and pizza.

"What can I do for ya, Honey?" The woman behind the counter asked.

"A couple pieces of chicken and Jojo's to go. I'll have a Coney dog with the works to eat here."

She took her tray to a booth and felt her phone buzz.

"Hello, Fletcher."

"Where are you?" His voice sounded gruff, frustrated, or both.

"I'm at a little gas station food mart on the main street heading toward the hotel."

"Why did you leave?"

"I didn't think I needed to stay. The local police and FBI were swarming. There wasn't enough room to stand around and watch. I'm tired and headed to the hotel for an early night."

"Don't go anywhere. Wait for me!" It was an order.

She ate her food. It was good. Just the right amount of chili and beef dog topped with thick grated cheese and finely chopped onion. They'd even put a couple of jalapenos on top.

"Is it good?" Fletcher eyed the last bite on the paper boat.

"Yep. Sorry, I'm not sharing." She pushed the bag towards him. "There's a couple pieces of chicken if you want."

"I don't want to eat your food."

"It's yours. You can take me to dinner tomorrow." She grinned at him.

"So that's how you roll." He pulled the foil-wrapped pouch from the bag and sniffed the aroma when the steam escaped.

"Smells good." He bit into the crisp chicken and groaned. "M-M-M."

"How's it going? Do you know how many bodies were buried?"

"No. They had to bring in dozers to dig a path. They arrived as I left. Like you, there were too many people. On the way here I got a call from HD. He wanted me to tell him how you found the dumpsite. You haven't been here long enough to talk to anyone or looked into researching the area." He took another bite and chewed. "He seemed surprised, but I think he's heard something because he gave me an expectant look. All I did was shrug." He swallowed.

"I went for a walk. I asked Craig what was past the bushes at the edge of the field. He showed me the secret entrance. We were looking around to what kids do down there. After I walked along that higher ground I thought I saw another clearing through the trees. It wasn't a clearing, so I was going to leave when I thought. What if this guy had a local dumpsite. One he could get to easily, yet it was so hidden no one would even look. That was the perfect place. Far enough the kids wouldn't stumble on it. So overgrown adults never went. He could access it in two ways."

"How?" Fletcher wiped a bit of chili from his chin.

"Walk over the wooden bridge or park in that lot on the short dead end. He could carry the bodies in a duffle bag. If anyone did see him. He could say he was going jogging or coming in from a run."

"You have it all figured out." He finished picking the bones clean and wiped his fingers. "You're something else. I'm still trying to figure you out."

"Thanks, I guess."

"HD wants to talk to you. What are you going to tell him?"

"I thought that story sounded pretty good." She sipped her soda.

"I guess. Let's get you back to the hotel. I have a laptop for you, and you'll need to get set up with security access." Fletcher guided her out to the car.

Chapter 20

The following morning, Fletcher led Andrea to the new room the FBI team had been allocated. She looked around for a chair and a spot at a desk or table to sit. No one looked her way, no one moved over to allow Fletcher the chair he pushed, to a table. Her eyes searched the room no available space. She didn't feel the usual rejection. Instead, she turned to Fletcher and smiled.

"Fletcher, I'm going back to my desk." She jerked her head for him to follow. He left the chair right behind two agents with their heads buried in their computers. Neither could move unless one of them or both moved the chair out of the way.

"I'm sorry." Fletcher shoved his hands into the pockets of his slacks as they walked down the hallway. His expression showed his frustration.

"It's no big deal. People are people and they need to protect their space. I have a perfectly good desk with a light, and you can't discount a helper who loves to bring me coffee and makes sure I get to lunch." She nodded toward the young man standing guard outside the squad room.

You're back." Kane grinned. A bit of relief in his expression. "You didn't move to the new room."

"I am, Kane. They wouldn't let me sit at their table." She grimaced. "What do you think about that?"

"That wasn't nice." Kane shrugged. His eyes searched her face.

"That's exactly right, Kane, Miss Watson didn't care. She knew she had a good desk with a lamp she didn't have to share with anyone." He nodded at the young man; whose smile couldn't have gotten any bigger.

"Kane, make sure she drinks water and she has her coffee. Here's five dollars. She may need a roll or treat about ten o'clock. You can get her one and one for yourself."

Andrea held up her water bottle. "I can fill it."

"I'll do it." Kane offered, whisked it out of her hand, and loped off to the water cooler.

"I'll see you at lunch or so." He winked at Andrea.

Andrea set up her new computer under the watchful eye of her young guardian. "Kane, I think you have some mail deliveries this morning?" He nodded. "You can come back when you're through." He nodded again and gave a skip as he left.

After logging into the system with the passwords she'd been given, she began looking into the reports from the young woman in Carthage. Jenny McNabb was forty-eight. Much older than the twenty-five-year-old Peggy Hicks. Neither had similar features or anything that might trigger a killer. One Blond, one dyed black. One five foot three the other five foot five. One single and going to college, the other divorced with three kids.

Both had been taken outside their work. Both worked late nights at a bar with a restaurant. Andrea began reading through the reports. It wasn't a good way to search to find duplicate descriptions. She had to read what each patron saw in the restaurant and told the officers.

In these situations, what was written was sometimes interpreted by the officer not written verbatim. That could cause problems. Especially when the devil was in the details.

The people at the restaurant where Jenny worked, all said the same thing those did at the Hitchin' Post. They knew everyone at the restaurant. There wasn't anyone new. They named all the patrons including Joe.

JOE? She read on looking for any reference to Joe. The police did their work and tried to locate the missing Joe. Could they be describing the same man as the one at the Hitchin' Post?

The patrons told what they knew about the missing Joe. He didn't come by often. His wife had cancer and he had to bring her to the hospital nearby. No one knew where he stayed. Andrea recognized their descriptions. They described a man about five-eleven or so. One said black hair, one said dark brown. Another said he had bleached blond hair. He wore a flannel or polo shirt, cowboy boots, or sneakers.

Everything about the two men matched. A picture flashed into her mind. Carla, the neighbor. She'd recounted to Andrea and Fletcher about the guy in the cabin across the lake. He'd had three outfits on the bed. They were the exact match to the ones these people described both in Winfield and in Carthage. How had she remembered that?

Could there be any correlation or connection? She'd have to ask Fletcher if anyone back home questioned him. What was his name? David? Bob? Evan. It was Evan, Evan Morrison.

That afternoon she and Fletcher drove to the dumpsite.TV vans with their satellite dishes pointed to the skyline filled the parking lot at the High School. Craig stood directing traffic while local officers kept the gawkers behind yellow tape and barricades.

Andrea caught bits of news anchors saying the Medical Examiner and forensic department excavated three bodies from the site. Meanwhile, the lab did quick work to extract DNA and get it matched. That still would take a while.

Andrea followed Fletcher to the conference room the next day. HD stood at one end next to a whiteboard with a list of the newest information. He gave a loud whistle that quieted the buzz of conversation.

"Thank you all for your help in this case," HD said. "As good as the information that's been massed, a dumpsite has been discovered. Thanks to Detective Watson's eagle eyes, she spotted a depression and disturbed ground. She dug around with the help of the Maintenance man and found cloth with bones in it.

The team has excavated the area and so far they found the remains of three women found. One body quite decomposed, but still enough to identify. A young girl, highly decomposed also the bones and the mostly decomp'd body of a third woman. A rough guess is they were killed at least five to eight years ago." He pointed to a list of women, their details on the whiteboard, and continued.

"It's possible for more bodies. We've ordered a ground-penetrating machine. It will show if there have been buried under the ones we found. The dogs are scenting more bodies, but we can't confirm that."

"Do we have any identifiers or matches yet?" A voice across the room asked.

"We have had a possible hit from a woman in Des Moines. The clothing and hair match the description of what she was wearing the night she was abducted. We're pursuing that. One of the women in the Winfield PD has come forward. She thinks the woman and girl maybe her aunt and cousin. Six years ago, they went missing. They had been ready to leave for Dallas where her aunt got a job. They stopped by the Hitchin post to eat before leaving town." He tapped his pointer on the board.

"After three months went by and no one had heard from them. No answer to their phone calls. Her aunt and uncle filed a missing person report and tried to contact the company they thought she had gone to work for. The manager at the company said the woman never arrived at her new job. The man thought she must have changed her mind, so never reported it."

Fletcher raised his hand when HD acknowledged him. "We're doing a DNA match with her family."

"Is there forensic evidence this is the work of our serial killer?" Another agent asked.

"No, it could be a copycat."

The meeting broke up. The group moved off murmuring amongst themselves, Andrea grit her teeth, not one of them took notice she found the bodies. She tried to convince herself it didn't matter; she didn't want the notoriety.

"I think the woman in Carthage was taken by the same man as the one in Winfield. I bet if we looked at the reports on this new woman and daughter who were at the Hitchin' Post we'd find that "Joe" was there that night." Andrea spoke in an even tone.

"Go take a look." Fletcher gave her arm an encouraging squeeze and followed HD for the update. "I'll take you to dinner."

Andrea smiled and she felt a warm feeling again. He liked her. He wanted to be with her. It was a good sign.

Andrea looked through the reports searching for Flannel Man any reference to a Joe or George. She ended up with multiple hits, but none matched her perp. She kept looking. Someone had to match her man. He may have used a different name and look.

Every man at the bar had been questioned. She made a note to call that police department to see look at the list. He had to have been there.

A sat in a chair in her hotel room. "This guy is the most prolific serial killer I've ever heard of. More than Bundy, Dahmer, Gein, or even Gacy. He might be on the level with Ridgeway though. We have no idea how many are in the lake."

"How can you eat when you're talking about serial killers who cut up their victims' bodies?" Andrea pushed her Rueben aside as he talked. She'd been about to take a bite of her pickle when he went on about Dahmer.

"What does HD have to say?" She changed the subject and bit a chip.

"He says they have a profile created. He's giving it to the department tomorrow morning. Then doing a video conference for the Minnesota division."

Staring at the sandwich she asked, "Do you remember Carla, the mother we interviewed?"

Fletcher wiped his mouth and took a drink from his cup then answered, "Oh yes. Quite the busybody she was. Why do you ask?" His expression showed his interest.

Andrea pulled some sheets of paper from a file and handed them to him. "Remember what she said about the Saunders family in the big log house across the lake?"

"Yes, she was being very nosey if you ask me." He wiped his hands and took the paper from her. "You're thorough." He raised his eyebrows at her.

She waved her finger at him to read while she ate.

Watching him brought that feeling to well inside her. This man treated her as an equal. He cared about her more than just a fellow detective. How did she feel about that? *You trust him* she heard her subconscious tell her. *You're falling in love with him.* Her eyes went to his face. He continued to read. She hadn't said that out loud. Her heart pounded in relief.

"You have something here." He looked up at her. His expression gave her more than a feeling of camaraderie. "You see things others miss." Fletcher paused for a moment and asked. "Will you do something for me?"

Andrea answered with caution. "Yes."

"I want you to close your eyes and think back to the figure you saw in the reflection."

Andrea opened her eyes and stared into his. His voice and expression encouraged her to continue. She closed her eyes and cleared her mind of all fears and recalled the moment she stood in front of the window.

"Did you see his reflection?" Fletcher's low voice asked.

Andrea smiled a little. Was he trying to hypnotize her? Pushing the thought away she concentrated on the figure.

"He's near six foot."

"How do you know?"

"He passed a doorway. His head almost reached the door jamb."

"Good. What color is his hair?"

"He's wearing a baseball cap, dark color with a matching brim. He has a slight beard, maybe a few days growth, but neat."

"Do you recall an insignia on the front?

"I can't tell, I'm sorry."

"Andrea there's nothing to be sorry for. What about his clothes? Shirt?"

Andrea squeezed her eyes. She could see the figure walking with long strides. "He is wearing a dark shirt, possibly black or dark blue.

The sleeves are long and he's wearing a vest, also black or dark blue, quilted. He's wearing jeans, well worn."

"How did you figure that out?"

"The fronts of the jeans are lighter than the back. A circle or something on the back pocket. It could be a chew box or a logo." She drops her head and shakes it. "It's fading. I'm not sure why but I can't see him any longer." Looking up at Fletcher her brows furrowed into a worried expression. "Why did that happen? Why did it seem so clear at first then fade away?"

Fletcher pulled her into his arms, and she let him hug her. It felt good. "Maybe you could ask your dad. He might be able to put it into perspective."

That would be admitting something she wasn't ready to do. She pulled away and he let his arms drop.

"It's a start. You're pretty smart. Are you the new Sherlock Holmes?"

"That's the nicest name anyone has called me."

"What names have you been called?" He asked while he still read from her notes.

"When your different in any way from others you're shunned."

"For being observant?" This time his gaze met hers.

"More like speaking those observations out loud. People like their secrets." She looked away and picked at a thread on the bedspread.

Fletcher put his hand over hers. "Andrea, do you mind sharing?"

Andrea shrugged. "I'd already been labeled a freak. I was in class and I saw my teacher's car in an accident in the reflection of the window. I knew she wouldn't believe me. I asked her if she'd help me with a problem I was having with math. She didn't believe me. I'm good at math and she knew it. I was agitated. I finally told her I thought she might be in an accident and go home a different way. She laughed and said I was sweet." Andrea paused to take a drink from her water bottle. When she finished she didn't immediately resume the story.

"What happened? Did she have an accident?"

"No. I checked with my dad. There was an accident, but she wasn't in it. She must have gone home in a different way."

"She never said anything to you?"

"No. She looked at me funny from that time on. The other teachers did too. She must have told them."

"What about the kids?"

"I don't want to talk about that. You can imagine the harassment when one of the kids found out my dad was labeled a psychic. They twisted it to psycho. I got the brunt of it."

"Your dad has unusual powers of deduction, like you, from what I read." He held up his hand to stop any comment from her. "I was told about your father from the men on the team. I looked up the newspaper reports. He seems to weather the confrontations."

"He loves the notoriety. He's able to handle that he's called a psychic. He laughs and says he finds people, not things."

"What do you find?"

"Nothing. I look at things differently." She shrugged, gathered her trash, and his, walking to dispose of it. Using a bit more force than needed, pushed it all into the small basket.

"Andrea your gift is nothing to be ashamed of."

"That's fine for you to say. You weren't the one being made fun of." She looked away and stressed, "I don't have a gift."

Fletcher stood, took three steps to her side, and reached for her hand. Turning her around to face him he tilted her chin up so he could look into her eyes. "You're important. What you do may save lives or at least bring closure to families. Don't let anyone tell you any different."

Andrea remained still. Waiting. Would he kiss her or move away? She didn't have to wait. The look in his eyes caused thrills to race up her spine. "Andrea, I'm going to kiss you, if you don't want that you'd better move away."

She didn't move except to bring her hands alongside his waist. His lips met hers. She felt the kiss from her head to her toes which brought her closer to his body. He deepened the kiss drawing her against his body.

She almost sighed, he was feeling that attraction too.

Chapter 21

Andrea pulled into the parking lot of her St. Paul, Minnesota police station a week later. She sneezed wiping her nose. Her head felt fuzzy and her sinus's tingled. Resting her head on the steering wheel she willed herself to not be sick. She didn't need a cold at this time in the case.

Fletcher knocked at her window. "You okay?"

She forced a smile and nodded. Opening her door, she grabbed her gear and got out. "I'm a little tired."

Fletcher and Andrea approached the police station. Satellite vans lined the parking lot and reporters bundled in down coats and lined boots huddled in groups clutching microphones.

Andrea kept her head down and pulled her hat over her eyebrows hoping to disguise her face from the media. Fletcher wore his fedora pulled down. He bent his head against the wind and held Andrea's elbow as they strode past the crowd. She thought they'd made it by when she heard, "Ms. Watson." The strident nasal voice cut through the noise.

Fletcher's fingers gripped her elbows tighter picking up the pace. Kaeli's voice gave an incite for the others to call her name as they rushed forward. The sound triggered a sound bite memory from a movie with seagulls calling "Mine, Mine, Mine." In chorus.

"Did you use your ESP to find those bodies?" Kaeli called?

Andrea's steps faltered.

"Don't fall for it. Keep walking Andrea." Fletcher ordered as he pulled the door open and almost pushed her through. She heard the sound of rapid footsteps following them.

The security door shut behind them with a loud bang shutting out the shouts. Andrea turned her head, Kaeli stood looking at her through the glass. When their eyes met she saw the corner of Kaeli's lips raise in a smirk. Andrea looked up at Fletcher as they walked down the aisle to her cube. "I don't trust her. She's one that would take a truth and twist into a question."

"Leave it. We need to concentrate on what Carla said and look into Evan Morrison."

"What about creepy Joe?" Andrea set her new FBI laptop on her desk. She smiled releasing the weight. She was still a consultant to the FBI. HD said she could use the laptop to do research.

Fletcher hung his coat on the hook attached to her cube. She hung hers next to his. She liked the way it looked. They were in this together.

"You made the watercooler talk." Bob's head popped up over the cube wall, his fingers gripped the edge.

For a moment she thought about Tim Allen's neighbor in the TV series, Home Improvement.

"Watercooler talk?" Fletcher looked at Andrea.

"You know the scuttlebutt." Andrea winked at him.

"I know what both words mean, I wondered what was said." He looked at Bob for an answer.

"Captain said you found a body dump. Was it one of our guy's sites?" His curiosity evident as he propped his arm on the dividing wall.

"It could be another killer's dump. There are other killers out there." Fletcher pulled papers from his bag, not looking at the man.

"Yeah, but who else could it be? In the same area as the two women from here?" He gave them a quizzical look.

"Bob, the Bureau is looking into it to coordinate any connections. That's not our jurisdiction." She turned hoping it would be a clue for Bob to disappear into his cube.

He did. She went back to opening the laptop and powered it up.

"That was a bit cold," Fletcher whispered.

Andrea shrugged. "I need to start looking at those two perps."

Before she could sit down, Steve's sharp voice called out across the room. "Watson. Conference Room."

Andrea sighed and walked with measured pace to the room. Again no empty seats around the table, and she didn't care. She felt tired and didn't want to listen to one of Steve's droning speeches.

After a bit of general information about other cases, Steve turned to Andrea. "Now that Detective Watson has returned, she can fill us in on what happened in Kansas."

Andrea winced at the cutting tone of his voice. "A dump site was found and--." She began.

"Who found it?" Steve crossed his arms as he asked.

"I did." She continued, "The FBI thinks it could be our guy from Blue Lake. We can't figure out why he has two dumpsites. There isn't a firm forensic connection. They are looking for any common evidence in the remains."

"Didn't you ask them?" Sneered Steve in a low voice wiggling his fingers like she could speak to the dead. The officers laughed, nudging each other.

Andrea stiffened and felt Fletcher gear up to respond. She pretended to move and stepped on his toe. She heard his intake of breath. She shook her head a little. "Don't," she coughed in her hand.

"The FBI will send anything they find that might match what we found here. These could be two different killers." Andrea continued. "The F-B-I is handling the case down there. Any evidence or clues this department gets will be filtered through them as needed." Her gaze locked with Steve's for a moment then he looked away. "I'm sure they have sent you a copy of the profile. If you have questions about it, you can ask them or Agent Fletcher."

"It's good to have someone who can find these killers. Who knows what would happen if they kept killing." Steve retorted putting the emphases on *someone* indicating her but not complimentary.

Andrea turned and walked out of the room. Steve called her name, but she didn't stop. Her head hurt, her body ached, walking to her desk she picked up her laptop.

"Fletcher, I'm not feeling good. I'm going home." He'd followed her back to her cube.

"Andrea don't let him get to you. He's not worth it." Fletcher admonished.

"I'm not. I don't feel well. I'm going home."

Fletcher stopped her. "You look tired. I'll tell the Conrad you went home sick."

"Thanks. A good rest and some chicken noodle soup will put me back on track tomorrow." Smiling at him. Normally she'd be offended he thought she LOOKED tired, but she felt worn out. Without speaking to anyone else, she left.

Starting the car, she waited for it to warm. Her phone rang. The familiar ring tone caused her to smile. "Hello, Dad."

"What's going on down dere?" His voice boomed from the car speaker.

"Nothing. I don't feel well so I'm going home." She put the car into gear.

"I tought so. I got a feeling you were stressed. Are you sick?" The concern flowed through the car's speakers.

"Yes. Dad, I don't want to talk about it."

"De man is a Troll, no brain, and a few muscles dat don't reach above his neck." He referred to Steve without using his name.

Andrea's lips spread into a smile in spite of the rumble in her stomach. "Yes. Can I call you later? I'm not in the mood to talk."

"Sure Honey. Rest. Warm-up da soup in your frig." He rang off.

Andrea wasn't surprised at the comment.

After a long nap, she ate chicken noodle soup and searched the internet for anything on the Saunders family.

She didn't find anything new. The family had been around since the early 1900s. The ancestor bought the land and farmed the area. They owned the lake and fished it. Later they sold some of the property off as the children married and moved away.

One of the grandsons gained the land in the will, His family owned what wasn't sold. Nothing in their history indicated anyone being a criminal. They seemed like the all-American Midwest family.

She closed the computer headed for bed. She called in sick the next day and sent Fletcher a text that she had a cold. She'd agonized about doing it. He wasn't her boss or partner, but he was sort of. She convinced herself of the relationship and sent the text.

Her phone rang. Fletcher's ID showed on the screen. She smiled. "Are you alright? I can do anything for you?" His concern came through the phone.

Holding a wad of tissues to her dripping nose she answered, "No, I'll be fine. I don't get these colds often but when I do they are usually a doosey." She began coughing.

"Go back to bed. I'll bring you dinner tonight and leave it by the door." He promised.

"No, Fletcher. I'll be fine." She tried to dissuade him.

He laughed, "It's spicy Chinese. I'm also bringing you some cough syrup with a small bottle of cinnamon liqueur. It helps."

"Sounds like you're trying to burn the cold germs out of me." She tried to laugh but it ended in a cough and a sneeze.

"I'll ring the doorbell in a few hours. You can come and get it."

"Thank you." She hung up. The thought he cared enough to do that soothed her more than the tea she sipped.

The sound of her doorbell ringing woke her. Who was at the door? Fletcher. A text pinged. *Your dinner is delivered*

Getting out of bed she made her way to the door. A quick peek revealed no one waiting. She opened the door and found a picnic-style basket on her mat.

Fletcher stood on the drive next to his car. He waved when she picked it up signaled he'd call her later.

Once inside she put the basket on the counter and opened it. Hot and spicy soup and an egg roll. Another container held noodles. The soup warmed her, and the yellow mustard cleared her nose. It was good and though she didn't have much taste, the effects gave her some relief when she crawled back to bed.

She sent Fletcher a text. "*Thanks for dinner. Sinuses are clearing for the moment. Still don't think I'll be back to work tomorrow. I'll work from home when I can.*"

I'll bring you coffee tomorrow morning. Sleep well.

His response gave her lips something to do rather than stifle her coughing.

Chapter 22

hree days later, Andrea had recovered for the most part. She and Fletcher left the station making their way north on I-35N. She stared out the window at the familiar scenery. Dirty snow stuck to the bridge railings and shoulders of the freeway. They'd left the station with Steve Totts barking orders. Since they'd returned from Kansas he'd been on the warpath with Andrea in his sights for some reason.

Here they were on the way back to the lake to interview David Saunders, the owner of the big log home on the east side of the lake. Fletcher had set up the trip by calling David, who finally agreed to the meeting.

Andrea hadn't spoken much on the short trip to the lake. After Steve's diatribe at the station, she didn't feel like talking, let alone rehashing the meeting. The whole incident had left her skittish.

"You're awfully quiet. You can't let that jerk bother you. He's jealous." Fletcher turned on his blinker and changed lanes to take the Larpenter exit. A car horn blasted beside her and she jumped, her heart beating fast as she looked to see why. Fletcher pulled the car back into his lane.

A small car sped up and cut them off. Fletcher slammed on his breaks honking his horn. The car sped off not stopping but wove in and out of the traffic erratically.

Fletcher's arm had flung out across her chest to protect her. "Are you okay?" He glanced at her.

"That guy almost sideswiped us!" Andrea bent her body still gripping the armrest. "I'm fine. Thanks." She looked at him with a slight smile.

"He wasn't there when I signaled the move, I looked. He must have switched lanes or sped up from that on-ramp. Good thing we're getting off here."

He signaled and took the exit. At the top of the ramp, he turned left across the freeway overpass. The service road to the lake area wasn't far off the freeway.

Andrea watched the road as they passed the tree-lined highway and turned onto the access road that led to Blue Lake Ave. A couple of cars and a camper were parked at the back of the lot. The chain barrier with its STOP sign swung in the breeze across the boat ramp. The whole place looked abandoned.

Fletcher pulled to a stop facing the lake. The cold night froze any melted sections from the bright sun shining the day before.

Andrea tensed, gripping the armrest. Reassuring messages screamed inside her brain. *You'll be okay. No, you're not, the truck will break the ice as you drive out there and you'll sink. No, I won't, Fletcher would never do anything to harm the two of us.*

Fletcher's voice interrupted her internal conversation. "Relax. We're not going onto the ice." He pried her fingers from the armrest and held them massaging them as she willed herself to relax.

Knocking on her window startled her and she whipped her head to whoever stood beside the truck. She had to look down as the four-wheel drive sat up high. The person's face looking up at her barely cleared the window.

"Dr. Vang." Andrea rolled the window down canceling any warmth that built up on the ride over. "How are you?"

"Fine, it's good to see you both. I was going to call you today. I have more samples and something else. If you don't mind coming to my camper."

"Sure, we'll be right there." Andrea rolled the window and turned to Fletcher. "That's okay with you?"

"Of course. I'll park closer to his camper. We have an hour before we meet Mr. Saunders."

Inside Dr. Vang's camper, he motioned for them to look at a cooler sitting on the floor. Two fishermen Andrea recognized from their previous meetings greeted her with a smile and in their language.

"These two men brought something to me that's very interesting."

Fletcher and Andrea lift the lid to the cooler. Inside they saw a net bag with another skull with bits of hair and skin. Eyes are gone. There are bones of hands and feet. Some bits of muscle and flesh are stuck to the bones.

Andrea kept her expression neutral. "How did you get this?" She asked the men in Dae.

"We're going to drag the bottom of the lake, we might hook something." They answered in the same language.

Fletcher squeezed her arm.

Andrea responded, "Oh, sorry. I asked them how they came to find these items. They said they dragged the bottom."

"Dragged the bottom through the ice?" His thick brows raised..

Andrea repeated the question in Dai.

"We understand and speak English." They gave her a look as if she had underestimated them. She could read the unsaid finish of the sentence. *We aren't stupid.*

"Right. Sorry."

"Explain how you did it," Fletcher ordered.

When they were finished, both Fletcher and Andrea were amazed at their ingenuity.

"It worked," One of the men offered. "We hooked this one and managed to pull it *and* the block it was attached to."

"Where's the block?" Andrea looked around the small space.

"Outside. We didn't have room for it here. "

Worried they might have compromised the DNA, Andrea asked, "Did you touch it?"

One of the men smiled at her. "I work at the forensic lab. I've seen you come at the station. I was going to bring what we found, but Dr. Vang saw your truck come in and said to call you to verify the find. It would take me off the suspect list."

"Again, I'm sorry about that. The doctor is right. This way we'll be responsible for calling the medical examiner to bag and tag." She pulled out her phone and paused.

"We need to meet Mr. Saunders. What if we wait until after our meeting?" She looked at Fletcher for his opinion.

He cocked his head, and then looked at his watch. "You're right. We hate to impose but we have a meeting in a few minutes."

Doctor Vang waved his hands at them. "Go. We'll sit here and talk until you get back."

"I'm not sure how long we'll be." Fletcher bent his head as he walked to the door.

"We aren't going anywhere until these are in proper custody."

Andrea turned. "To save time, if you have any paper, write what you did, how you did it, and where you were. Put the GPS in to be extra thorough." The men gave her a thumbs up.

Back in the truck, Andrea asked, "Do we need to have the police tell the public not to eat fish from the lake?"

"We can ask."

Fletcher pulled into the driveway leading to the open gate. They were expected. He parked behind an expensive SUV in the circular drive and looked over at Andrea who gave him a slight smile.

"Let's go." Opening the door, Fletcher got out and came to her door to help her from the high truck.

"I love this house." She whispered as they ascended the log steps to the porch.

The door opened and a man as tall as Fletcher stood looked at the two. He didn't smile but he wasn't glaring at them either. "Hello, come in." He stepped back as they walked in. "Right this way." He led them into the living room and Andrea took a deep breath.

This was the house of her dreams. A log home that exuded family, love, and warmth. Pictures of family members grouped on tables. The long couch showed its use. Throw rugs, pillows, and blankets added to the Northwoods decor.

"Please sit. What's this all about?" He swept his hand to the chairs and sat in one across from them.

"My name is Detective Andrea Watson, and this is FBI agent Fletcher Peterson. "We'd like to get some background on anyone who lives here and the dynamics of your extended family," Andrea asked. "For the record can you tell me your name?"

"David Saunders. What is this all about? Am I a suspect?" He turned toward them with a worried expression.

"You heard we found body parts in the lake?" Fletcher asked.

David nodded.

"That makes everyone with access to the lake a suspect. We're questioning each family and anyone they allow on to their property to get to the lake. I'm sorry we have to be so invasive, but we have a serial killer out there."

"They could drive up to the public dock, put a boat in and no one here would have any clue who they were." David crossed his leg and rested his hand on his knee.

He was relaxed. Andrea watched him. He didn't appear to be deceptive, but he was interested.

"True, that's why we want to rule out anyone living on the lake and their friends so we can concentrate on one area of access." Fletcher folded the yellow ledger paper over leaving a clean sheet for his notes. Andrea held her notebook and pencil.

"Would you tell us how your family came to acquire this large piece of land?" Andrea asked.

"My grandparents owned the land around the lake, back when the city limit was miles away. As time went on and the city expanded, they were forced to sell off land for roads, highways, and such. My grandfather wasn't a dummy by any means, he made good money. He bought and traded for land elsewhere. Then he built a trust for the family. My aunts and uncles either didn't marry or have children so my folks inherited the trust. I'm now in charge of it."

"I'm guessing it's sizable?" Fletcher asked.

"Yes. My parents had six children. I'm the oldest and the youngest is Nancy. They all live in the area, but their kids are spread across the states. I can get you that information." His eyes narrowed.

"What we're looking for is someone that has access to the lake, has a job, or may have a reason to travel to Kansas, Missouri, and on south to Texas," Fletcher offered.

"I could name about twenty-five men that fit that description in some capacity or another. Some family, some are friends. Are you going to question every one of them?"

"The longer it takes to find this killer, the more people we'll have to question. Any of the men you'd consider close enough friends to allow on your property at all hours of the day or night?" Fletcher asked in a dry tone.

"I'd hate to make a list of all my friends who come here on vacation. I don't want to sound cold, but anyone can come and go on the lake. A lot of people use it." He crossed his arms.

Andrea watched him. *He knows someone. He's thinking about him.* The thought came to her.

"I guess what I'd like to get from you is a list of the family members who have access to this property on a regular basis. I you have a pretty sophisticated security system here so I'm sure you keep track of who comes and goes. If you don't mind, I'd like a list of who has been on the property as far back as you have records."

"Should I ask for a warrant?" David asked.

"You can," Andrea offered. "But why? We aren't asking if we can search your property or to even look at anything you aren't willing to show us. If you had something to hide, I could understand you'd want one, but we want records of anyone who came and went that you don't know or didn't give consent to. Do you have it?" she paused and looked at the collection of family pictures, "say for a year or two?"

David bit his lip and stared at the paper. "I can give you that. How do you want it?"

Andrea handed him her card, "You can email me."

"Is that all? I mean is that all you want from us or me?"

"Mr. Saunders, I have no reason to believe you're a murderer. I can't rule out that you aren't or anyone else with access to this lake. I can tell when I asked you a question something triggered in your memory. You recognized something."

She watched his expression freeze with no response, not even denial. "I would appreciate it if you would share what you think or if you have questions. If it comes out you're hiding information or a criminal, it won't go good on your end." Andrea pressed.

David almost jumped to his feet. "I think we're done here. I'll email you that report, but that's it. Anything else you want, call my lawyer. I'll include his information with the report."

The two officers stood and followed him to the door. "Mr. Saunders, I'm sorry this turned out like this. I was hoping we could work together to find a killer." Fletcher held out his hand. David hesitated but shook his hand with a quick motion then pulled the door open to avoid Andrea's outstretched hand.

"You have a beautiful home and property," Andrea told him as she stepped out on the porch. The line of trees at the edge of the road buffered some of the road noise. They did own a lot of property around the lake area. "I take it your siblings own those houses along the lake." She pointed down the small, paved road from the entrance away from the house."

"Yes, they were given property as long as they didn't sell it. They could live on it or use it for vacations. We have a service that takes care of the landscaping and snow plowing."

"They do a good job. Please include that information in your email." Fletcher took the steps with Andrea right behind him. "Thank you for your time."

"Wait." David stood at the top of the steps. He gave a pained expression. "I'm sorry this couldn't have been under different circumstances."

"Please work with us on this. We aren't the enemy. We want to help and stop a killer."

David's head drooped then he nodded. "Have a nice day."

"That was sad," Andrea spoke as she stared out the truck window. Fletcher turned out of the property and into the frontage road. The big gate closed behind them.

"He's a nice guy and I think he loves his family. He seemed to struggle with something. It may be someone in his family or he's friends with, that could be a suspect. Let's have a look."

Fletcher parked next to the camper in the public parking lot.

Dr. Vang opened the door and let them in. He was alone. He indicated Fletcher should sit. Andrea stood as her head didn't reach the ceiling.

"Do you want to take these body parts in? Nye was going to take them with him to work, but I think you need to bring them in."

Fletcher nodded and picked up the container and took them to his truck. Andrea bid the doctor good-bye thanking him.

Andrea contacted the medical examiner, letting Harold know they were bringing in more samples pulled from the lake.

"More bits and pieces?" Harold sighed.

"Not this time. It's another net and with a skull, hands with no fingers, and feet. There are toes. Do toes have prints that we can use?"

"In theory yes. File aren't kept on toes or body parts. However, if you had someone to match it to, footprints have been used in court."

"Well, this could be one of those times." Andrea rang off.

At the station, Fletcher carried the cooler to the lab. Harold met them as Fletcher sat it on the counter.

"These are fresh samples?" He asked as he walked to meet them.

"Take a look." Fletcher pointed to the cooler.

Harold stared at the box for a moment. Then looked at the two officers. "This is untouched?" He pulled on fresh gloves.

"As clean as it came from the bottom of the lake." Andrea offered. "The men who found it, put it in the box and taped it. No one has touched it." She moved to one side of the container and looked in. "In fact, Harold, one of the fishermen works for you."

Harold's head jerked up to look at her. "Works for me. Who?"

"A man called Nye." She watched for his reaction.

"Nye. Yes, I know him. He's a tech here. He found these?" He indicated the samples.

"Yes, he and his friend dropped a hook down and snagged a net."

Harold made an appreciative expression and nodded. "He does think outside the box. That's why I like him."

After cutting the red tape he used his gloved finger to lift the lid. When he saw what lay inside he shook his head. "What is this man doing? We need to catch him quick. I don't think I can take much more of this."

He indicated his assistant to pick up the handle. They carried it to the stainless-steel table.

"That's not all," Fletcher announced to Harold.

"Not more parts," the man queried.

"No." Fletcher motioned for the two men at the door to carry the bags in. "Two cement construction blocks. It's the best we could do to keep them clean."

Harold shook his head and motioned for the men to put them to one side.

"No more please." Harold waved a finger at them.

"I wish I could promise you that. I think we'll find more down there." Andrea spoke in a low voice.

The following day, Andrea jumped at the sound of a loud clap behind her. She whirled to find a red-faced Steve Totts glaring down at her.

"What do you think you're doing? Did you get made the lead on this case and I didn't know about it?" The sound came forced through clenched teeth.

Andrea took a breath and forced the muscles in her face to remain in a neutral expression. "Not that I know of. I'm still hunting down leads."

"Why wasn't I informed about these additional pieces of evidence? I was informed Harold has more evidence you brought in." Now his body leaned forward so his face was close enough to almost feel his breath.

"I didn't find them. I spoke with the men who found the body parts and called Harold with what they found. I assumed the good doctor called you. We were questioning David Saunders."

"From now on you sit your butt in that seat. You aren't going out interviewing anymore." His voice rose. Realizing the squad room was silent and listening to him he clamped his lips shut and strode away.

Andrea remained frozen in her chair. The force of his anger jabbed at her like a battering ram. Her hands shook. She and Fletcher did their job. She shook her head a little and her eyes narrowed as she stared at the computer screen in front of her. It was her JOB. She would do whatever it took to find this killer and hopefully before he killed again.

Chapter 23

Kaeli Myers stood next to Andrea's car the next morning when she arrived at the station. "Detective Watson. Can I have a word?" The woman held a microphone in her hand.

Andrea got out of the car and faced the woman. "Go ahead."

"What is the task force doing about the missing women?" Kaeli asked.

"We're looking to find anyone who had contact with the missing women." Andrea gave a simple answer.

"Can you give us more detail about what you are doing for the task force?"

"Miss Myers, what are you asking? We have a press liaison you can ask these questions." Andrea shut the car door and adjusted her computer bag on her shoulder.

"They are giving the same pat answers you just did. I know you have found a dumpsite in Kansas. How convenient." Her sarcastic tone wasn't lost on Andrea who didn't answer.

Kaeli waited then pressed on when Andrea didn't respond. "Have you gotten any "feelings" about who this person is? I mean have you and your dad talked about who is doing all this?"

Andrea pressed her mouth into a grimace and turned to walk to the station. Kaeli kept right with her, this time the mic bobbing next to Andrea's chin.

"Come on Miss Watson, we come from the same small town. I know how difficult it is to break into the big city politics. Can't you give fellow Northerner something to report?" This time she'd stepped faster and now faced Andrea forcing her to stop.

"Miss Meyers. I can't tell you anything about what we are working on. You will be told whatever the liaison gives you. There are things we are working on that are sensitive." Andrea stepped around the reporter.

"What is the answer to my other question? Are you and your father working together to find this killer?"

Andrea turned her head, "No."

She'd reached the door when she heard Kaeli say "We will be questioning Miss Watson's father, Retired Sheriff, Donald Watson, later on, get what information he may have sensed about this serial killer. Stay tuned for that interview."

Andrea jerked the door open and stormed through the lobby to her cube.

At her desk took deep breaths to calm herself. What did that woman want? What was her issue with Andrea and her father? After sitting down, she searched her memory for any clue as to what Kaeli's issue with her might be. Did her father has some contact with this woman? She pressed his number on her phone and waited, but he didn't answer. Was he avoiding her? She'd call her dad about it later.

Andrea looked at her email to see David Saunders had sent the list. It wasn't as long as she thought it would be. The family didn't use the property all that much.

After creating a list of card numbers. She used the spreadsheet to coordinate times and dates each card had been used. One person used the gate code every day. Sometimes three or four times a day during a specific period. Then nothing for several weeks and the pattern repeated.

Who did this card belong to or had someone been using a stolen card? It was something she and Fletcher would have check into. The thought stuck in her mind. She thought of them together. As partners? Something more? She had that feel-good emotion again. She smiled.

"Hey, you still here?" Fletcher entered their cube and sat at his desk.

She looked up at his handsome face and smiled. "Yes, I am. Look at this." She pointed to her laptop. "One code is used to access the gate at regular intervals. During any given month that person may come and go two to five times a day or not at all. They don't use the code for three to four weeks."

"I agree. My guess someone lives there part-time and is on the road the rest. Maybe a salesman."

"We need to call David and find out who uses that code." Andrea closed her laptop. "What are you doing tonight?"

He shook his head. "Another microwave dinner and either a movie or a book."

"If you don't mind sharing, I have a pork loin in the crockpot with some potatoes."

He grinned. "I don't mind sharing if you don't. Any home-cooked meal is better than frozen."

"Okay, let's go." He held her coat while she slipped her arms in the sleeves. After she zipped the front he wrapped her knitted scarf around her neck and took her laptop case from her hand. "Do you want me to follow you or do you want me to drive?"

"I don't want to drive back here tonight to get my car."

"I didn't mean that. I'll come and pick you up for work tomorrow."

"Fletcher I know you like conserving energy, but that would cause the gossip mill here at work to explode. You are the hot topic around the ladies." She grinned as she heard the door unlock on her car.

"You don't say?" He acted like it was news to him. "Here I thought all those women were just being nice to me because I was FBI."

"Oh, that too. You can follow me. I hope you can keep up."

"Ha!" He laughed as he waited for her to settle in her seat, then shut the door.

Fletcher followed her to the townhouse and parked in her driveway as she pulled into her garage. She waited for him to join her before pushing the garage door closer button.

They entered the warm hallway and she hung his coat next to hers in the closet. There was that feeling again, not itchy, but more pleasant. This time she didn't try to hide the smile and shut the door.

"Have a seat anywhere you want. The bathroom is around the corner. The remote is on the coffee table." she waved her hand at the living room.

"Coffee?" She called.

"Sure."

She pressed the button to heat the water on the machine.

"Smells good." Fletcher sat on the high stool across the counter from her as she prepared the meal.

It wasn't long until she had the food plated and they were seated at the table. "What did you think of David Saunders?" Andrea asked.

Fletcher finished chewing and looked at her. "Would it be alright if we didn't talk shop? We've been working together for about eight weeks. Can we just get to know each other? Every time we had to grab a bite or ride somewhere, our focus was on the job. I clocked out at five, mentally that is. How about you?"

Andrea felt the heat rise to her face. "Sure." She stuffed a bite into her mouth. *Why was she feeling embarrassed about him wanting personal time with her? She wanted that, didn't she? Yes.* came the answer.

Silence prevailed while she ate and thought of some witty comment to break the moment.

"Is your mother alive? I never hear you mention her." Fletcher broke the silence.

So much for witty starters. "No. She left us when I was about three years old." She took another bite.

"Andrea, you're going to run out of food or get sick if you keep shoving it into your mouth to avoid talking. Was this a mistake? Do you want me to go?" He set the cup down.

"No!" She answered a little more forceful than needed. She sounded desperate. She was. She wanted to be with him. "I feel so nervous about talking to you."

"Why? We've been doing it for weeks now."

"Yes, but as colleagues, not as..well…" she paused.

"Friends?" He interjected. He'd rested his elbows on the table and folded his hands above his plate.

"Well, yes." Now she was embarrassed. She'd wanted more and was caught in a web she's created.

"Andrea. News flash, I like you, a lot. I can say I've never felt quite like this with women."

"Are there many?"

"You fishing? You want to know if I've had lovers before?" Fletcher grinned at her.

She nodded.

"No. I didn't date all that much. I was focused on college and the academy. I'm thirty-three. I've dated. Let's leave it at that. You?"

Swallowing her tepid coffee, she answered. "I'm twenty-nine. I too have been focused on getting into the academy and did my stint as a police officer in Bemidji, then transferred down to St. Paul. Time flies when you're having fun, or so I'm told."

"Any siblings?" He asked.

"No. You?"

"Yes, three younger. My mother remarried after my father died in a domestic shooting. I was already in the academy; she found a policeman to fill in my dad's place." He pushed the chair. Backward, balancing it on two legs. "I don't have any bad feelings about him. He's a great guy and we get along more like brothers in arms than stepfather and son. He helped me get accepted into FBI training. He's the Chief of Police in one of the suburbs of Detroit."

"That's a good person to have at your back."

"Yeah."

"You don't sound so thrilled about it."

He let out a long breath and rubbed his hand around his neck as if it had become stiff all of the sudden. "He is strict, has high expectations, and demands instant obedience."

"A control freak."

"Yes. My mother loves him in her own way. He's the stereotypical cop. He drinks, is tough on the job and off. He knows if he ever laid a finger on my mom or the kids I'd beat him within an inch of his life." His eyes narrowed. "Sorry, TMI."

"I understand that." Andrea nodded.

"I don't always like how he treats her, but they have a good marriage."

"It's not your place to judge. If that's not the relationship you want then don't do that. Find someone that fits your life." She stopped. *What was she saying? Did she sound like an advert for his wife?*

"You're right. When I go home I get a little tense knowing what I have to face."

"Don't expect, accept."

He looked at her and smiled. "Should I quote? 'Physician, heal yourself?'"

"Maybe. It's easier to teach than to do it." she grinned.

"I take it your dad is a little like that?"

"Quite the opposite. He's too laid back for me. I wanted structure and he wanted to teach me to use my inner feelings to deal with things."

"Did you? Use those inner feelings?" He pushed the empty plate to the side and looked into his cup.

"Let me make you another cup."

He waved his hand, "No thanks, too much coffee today."

She took the plates to the sink and started to rinse them. "I can help." Fletcher started to stand.

"No. It's not much. I'll do it later. Let's go to the living room."

He turned and waited for her to follow.

She paused. *Awkward* If she took the chair she'd be saying stay away. She detoured to the couch and sat in the middle of the last cushion. He sat at the next cushion a couple of hand lengths away and rested his knee on the cushion facing her.

"Tell me about your dad. The real story." He laid his arm across the back of the couch.

Andrea reached for the fireplace remote and turned it on before facing him. His eyes shown compassion and warmth. She felt safe. When was the last time she'd felt like that? "I don't remember my mother. My dad raised me like he had a son. I learned all about tracking, shooting, survival, and eventually police work. In all of that, I later realized he was testing me to see if I had the same ability he did." She rubbed her left thumb over the base of her right thumb.

"Are you admitting to it?"

"What?"

"Have some psychic ability?"

Andrea searched his face for some idea of what he would do with the truth. *Truth,* what was it?

"I don't judge. If you want to keep it secret, that's fine."

"Fletcher, it isn't that." She rubbed her skin harder. And glared at the red spot.

"You don't even know what it is." He spoke into the silence.

She let out a rush of air from her lungs. "I saw what the town's people and the media did to my dad. While he let the naysayers and the mocking roll off his back. It bothered me. I came under the spotlight a few times. I rejected the accusation until a teacher I'd had in first grade was interviewed." She bit her bottom lip. "I told you about her. She outed me to the media, and I became a freak like my father."

"Words can't kill you," Fletcher spoke.

"Right, that old saying *Sticks and stones can break your bones, but names will never hurt you.* That's a farce."

Fletcher scooted closer to her and took her hand in his. "I don't want you to rub the skin off your hand." He smiled. "No, it's true. Name-calling by kids never killed anyone. I'm sorry you had to go through that. You can't ignore what you're able to do.

Look at people who are gifted like Sherlock Holmes. He's a mythical character, but his accomplishments are based on truth. Some observations can be taught. In the FBI we're taught to look at the way people act, their body language, and what they say. We have FBI agents with a sense about people, or they can read a crime scene the way others at the same scene can't. They aren't freaks; they're valued members of the team.

Never downplay what you think is important. You found that body dump. I'm not going to ask you for details you don't want to talk about, but you did it. Those bodies might never have been found. Now we either have another killer to look for and prevent from repeating his kills or we could be looking for the same man."

"I think they're the same man," she whispered.

"Why?"

She took a deep breath. "This is between you and me." She waited until he nodded. "I stood on the sidewalk looking at a display when the movement of a man across the street caught my eye. I didn't turn around but watched a man with a duffle bag turn the corner and disappear from sight. I stood there. I wasn't sure if he was real or something else. Something about him compelled me to follow him."

"Why?" Fletcher still held her hand in his. She didn't pull away. His grasp gave her a feeling of comfort.

"I got that nervous tingly feeling. An urgency that I should go down that street. I debated on whether to go or not. I felt I needed to look for him. When I turned the corner, no one was on the sidewalk. I walked to the field looking at the houses along the street. No one walked between any of them. He wasn't that far ahead of me. Even if he'd ducked between the houses I should have seen him. Before he could get to the back."

"Why did you go through the track field?"

"I'm not sure. When I didn't see the man, I kept walking. I thought I saw someone in the woods along the brush line, then they disappeared. That's when Craig came along and gave me a tour. I questioned the overgrowth at the edge of the field. Craig showed me the kid's hideout."

"When you were at the party area, what made you go up the bank to that specific area?"

"You want to hear it all?" She questioned him wondering what his motive was.

"Yes, I'm curious. You're fascinating."

"Moi?" She acted surprised pointing to her chest.

"Yes. I've never met a woman like you or one who makes me feel the way you do."

"Is that good or bad? I can be downright irritating." She teased.

Fletcher gave a laugh. "No, you make me want to get to know you more. I want to hear what you think about things."

His smile made that itchy feeling rise from her toes to her face. *Not now* she didn't want anything to interfere with this moment.

"Tell me what made you go to that spot?" He'd adjusted his position and sat in the middle of the couch, his knee resting next to her bent leg.

She took a deep breath. "I stood looking around the area and thinking this was well hidden from the rest of the town. No one but the kids came here, and it was a perfect place to bury anything you didn't want to be found. Like a body.

The bank had worn away to the to a drop about waist high. For some reason, I walked up the bank and looked at the forest.

The trees were bare except for a few evergreens." Andrea rubbed her face.

"I'm not sure why but I pushed the bare branches aside and saw a clearing. It looked natural. The leaves lay thick on one side and almost non-existent in the middle. The leaves weren't as wet or compact as I'd thought they should be, and it was easy to move them. That's when I saw the disturbed ground.

It wasn't a fresh dig, but an indentation. I think animals had been digging. I smelled death. I know that smell.

When I knelt next to the indent I saw the fabric sticking out of the dirt. Craig joined me and we discovered the bone. He couldn't smell anything but a strong stench of old moldy leaves and such."

"We know the smell of death." Fletcher nodded.

"I'd say your find was about twenty percent woo woo as you call it and eighty percent good detective work." He let go of her hand settling her palm on his thigh while he rubbed the back of his neck.

"Andrea, I think you're too sensitive about the "label." You need to accept the detective work first and your 'instinct' later. If anyone asks if you have psychic abilities, ask them "What are psychic abilities?" Ask them to define in their words what that means. It means different things to different people. You are overly observant of details. If that's being psychic, then say yes."

She thought over what he said. "You're right. It's perception. If I present the idea that I'm no different than say the upper level of average, then that's all it is. Try and prove it's any different." her voice sounded more convincing as she said the last part.

"That's my girl!" He grinned at her.

Andrea looked into his eyes and felt a connection that had nothing to do with observation and everything to do with her blood pounding.

"I think I'd better leave," he whispered. "What I'm feeling has nothing to do with friendship."

"Me either,"

"I enjoyed having dinner with you and talking to you. The more I'm around you the more I like you." He stood and pulled her to her feet, tucking her arm through his as they walked to the door.

He pulled on his coat and faced her. "Thank you for dinner." Then he cupped her shoulders and bent to give her a firm kiss. Not too long and not a peck. It wasn't long enough for Andrea. She stood in the same spot as he opened the door and closed it behind him. She didn't move until she heard his car engine start. She stood there letting the kiss settle her before locking the door.

Chapter 24

After a hectic day of pouring over missing person reports. Andrea left the station and headed home. She heard a ping and glanced at the meter, she needed gas. She pulled into the station a few blocks ahead and pulled up to a pump. With her credit card in hand, she fumbled with the cold handle and shoved it into the gas spout.

Even with the chill in the air, the sun heated her face as she faced its warmth. The smell of donuts and coffee filtered across from the doorway as patrons entered and left with their purchases.

"Miss Watson, fancy meeting you here." The familiar voice of Kaeli Meyers cut into her reverie.

Andrea nodded a response, hoping it would drive the woman away. No such luck, she sighed as the woman walked toward her. A glance at the digital counter showed she had half a tank to fill. The cold weather slowed the filling process a bit.

"How is the case coming? I got a press release there might be a suspect being brought in for questioning. Care to comment?" Kaeli stood between her and her car door, cutting off any escape.

"No." Andrea shot back.

"How did they come up with a suspect?" Kaeli crossed her arms over the puffy knee-length down coat.

"You seem to have the info on it, why ask me?" Andrea eyed her. "But then you're fishing. Can you produce the PR? I didn't think so."

Kaeli ignored the comment. "Who could possibly be a suspect in this case? How would you find him?" She leaned closer to Andrea as if to share an intimate conversation. "Did you have something to do with locating a possible suspect? Have you questioned him?"

Andrea heard the click of the gas hose and sighed in relief. She grabbed the handle, pulling it from the car and shoving it into its holder. After twisting the cap on she ripped the receipt from its slit. Kaeli blocked her from reaching the handle.

"Excuse me?" Andrea questioned her.

"I asked a question. It's rude not to answer." Kaeli moved closer.

"Whoa, personal space please." Andrea held up her hands in surrender. Her voice attracted attention from customers, filling their tanks.

Kaeli saw they had also drawn attention and stepped back but not beyond the driver's door.

"Kaeli what do you want from me?" Andrea matched her step moving toward the door. Kaeli took another step backward.

Kaeli's eyes bored into Andrea's and she barely opened her lips to speak. "I want you to admit you use your psychic ability on this case."

"No one would believe it, even if I were to admit it." Andrea lowered her voice in response.

"So you're saying you have no extrasensory perception? No inkling about things you can't explain? No gut feeling?" Kaeli moved her hands to her pockets. Andrea could tell they were balled into fists. *I hope she keeps them there.*

"All good cops have gut feelings. I'm sure you've had a thought and later it came true. Maybe you had a bad feeling about something? Does that make you psychic? A good cop learns to read people, situations, and a crime scene. That feeling is honed to notice things. We aren't psychic. You're trying to get a hot story."

Kaeli took a step back at Andrea's passionate speech. It was far enough that Andrea reached for her door handle and opened it effectively putting a barrier between the two. "You'll understand if I don't continue this conversation. Have a nice day." Andrea buckled up and started the car. A sudden feeling of hatred slammed into her. It oozed over her like slime. Andrea grabbed her chest taking a deep breath as if it were her last one.

The woman stood beside the car glaring at her. Kaeli's expression changed and she grabbed the door handle opening the door.

"You saw something. Your expression changed. I saw it. What did you see?" She demanded.

"Nothing." Andrea hoped the sick hatred wasn't coming from Kaeli. She pulled on the door to shut it, but Kaeli held it open.

"Kaeli, let go!" Andrea growled at her. "Go find a story someone wants to hear and leave me alone." This time the door slammed shut and she locked it.

As Andrea waited for traffic to clear the feeling of ill will subsided. Looking to her left at traffic, she saw a man standing next to an SUV parked in the lot. The sun shone behind him and she started to shield her eyes to get a better look, but he got into the car.

Why did he look familiar? Or did she just sense it? Was his car familiar? Her thoughts were interrupted by a long insistent horn, She waved an apology and pulled into the lane.

Heading for the station, she tried to think where she might have seen him.

Andrea looked around the station parking lot to make sure she wasn't going to ambushed again. No sign of the reporter or anyone else. At her desk, she ducked her head behind her computer,

"What did you do to that reporter?" Fletcher asked as he sat beside her. The smile on his face reflected hers as he laid the newspaper in front of her.

"Kaeli Meyers? I have no idea. What's she saying about me this time?" Andrea looked away from the Saunders' report she'd been reading.

Fletcher unfolded the paper. "She's on the kick you're physic. She thinks you are hiding information from the department because you want to make a big reveal."

"She said that?" Andrea held out her hand for the paper but Fletcher continued to read the article.

"Not directly, but she has it in for you." Fletcher read a short blurb from the article. "Better read it before the Team leader sees it.

"I can't figure her out or why she's doing this. She stopped me in the parking lot, going on about whether I had any feelings about the missing women in the lake or anywhere else. I told her I didn't know what she was talking about." She stood and checked who was in the cubes next to her then sat down. She lowered her voice to a whisper, "I'm not sure if she'd stalking me or if it was a coincidence, but she cornered me at the gas station."

"Have you ever sat down and talked it out with her?" Fletcher leaned forward and spoke in a low voice to keep anyone next to them from hearing.

"No. When she shoved that microphone in my face I get a little testy. She went on asking about finding that missing little girl back home. Then today she went on accusing me of being a psychic." Andrea shook her head in frustration.

"Did you know her back then? How did she hear about that case?"

"No, I had no clue who she was. It was one of my father's cases. I was fifteen or so." Andrea shrugged staring at her screen. "I told her I didn't have anything to do with that."

Fletcher folded his arms. "She seems to think you did have something to do with it. Why?"

"I had been at the site where they were looking for the little girl. I don't know what caused me to walk away from the group and cross the highway. There was a dirt road, mostly overgrown with weeds. I followed the road for a ways and heard a dog whimper. When I called out, I heard someone crying." Andrea rubbed her hands up and down her arms as she spoke. "That was it."

"So, you found the girl?" Fletcher wheeled his chair closer to her so that his knees bumped hers.

"I found my dad and told him I heard someone crying down a hole. He came with me calling the girl's name. She called back to him. Everyone converged on the site and they dug the girl out of the well."

"Was your part finding her in the papers?"

"No. Dad told the reporters, I thought I heard a dog crying and he should check it out. He made it look like it was his find and I was glad. I hate all the cameras and questions."

"Kaeli acts like this is personal. Was she there?"

Andrea shrugged. "I've no idea."

"Andrea I think you need to talk to her. Find out what she really wants." He tapped her knee with his fingers.

"I don't want to talk to her." Andrea pursed her lips. She looked at Fletcher with pleading eyes. She wanted to cover his hand with hers but they were at work.

"Do you want me to come with you?" He kept his voice low.

"Would you?" She gave him a hopeful look.

"Of course. Do you have her number?"

"I have her card somewhere." Andrea opened the drawer in her desk and pulled out a small stack of business cards. She handed him the card Kaeli had given her.

He handed it back. "Call her."

Andrea stared at the card. That fear from her childhood rose in her chest. This wasn't the time to give into it. She had to take a stand. She punched the buttons and heard the ring.

"Kaeli here."

"Miss Meyers, this is Detective Watson. I'm wondering if you're free today to meet me here at the station?" She kept her tone even and professional.

"Do you have a lead you want to share?" Kaeli's tone sounded almost aggressive.

Andrea didn't answer her question. "I'd like to discuss a situation with you. Do you have time today or would another time be more convenient?" Andrea heard a short breath of frustration than a sigh.

"Sure, I can be there in an hour or so."

"Thank you, Miss Meyers. Check-in at the front desk."

Andrea disconnected the call. "Why am I doing this again?" she looked up at Fletcher. His smile of encouragement warmed her heart.

"You need to face uncomfortable things. Things you aren't in control of. Call the front desk and reserve an interrogation room. That will give you a bit of confidence."

Andrea gave him a wry smile and picked up the receiver again.

She got the call Kaeli arrived and was waiting for the two of them.

"Fletcher she's here." Andrea set the receiver down and took a shaking breath.

"You'll do fine." He encouraged.

Andrea looked up at him pleading for him to tell her she didn't have to go."

"It's up to you." Fletcher rested his body on his hands, next to her on her desk.

She stood straightened her spine and headed to the lobby.

Andrea froze as she took in the tableau. The woman had two cameramen and was speaking into her mic facing away from the front desk.

The desk clerk that morning gave Andrea a look that she wasn't a happy person.

Andrea turned and walked back through the doors to the squad room, Fletcher right behind her.

"What is she doing?" She ground out between clenched teeth.

Fletcher looked through a window to the lobby, then at Andrea. "Here's your chance to show what you're made of. You can hide in here or you can walk out there and face her."

Anger and fear stiffened her resolve. She pushed the door open with a thrust and strode to the front desk.

"Miss Meyers,. Thank you for coming. If you'll come this way, we can talk."

The woman turned to face Andrea and motioned for her entourage to follow. Andrea held up her hand. "No one else is invited. If you want to talk to me, we do this my way." She folded her arms and waited.

Kaeli locked her gaze on Amanda. "I want this interview recorded."

Amanda let her lips rise a little at the corners, "Oh it'll be recorded, but not on your cameras." She tilted her head a little, "Are you coming?"

Kaeli didn't respond then nodded and moved to the door.

Andrea motioned for the officer to open it. Kaeli entered with Andrea following her. "This way." Fletcher waited for them at the door to the interrogation room.

"Is he going to be there for this meeting?" Kaeli asked.

"Yes."

"Why?"

"So there isn't any question about this meeting being official."

"Official? What's this about? Why are you questioning me?" Kaeli stopped in the middle of the hall not entering the room Andrea had unlocked.

"Why not, you ask me questions all the time." Andrea threw the question back at the reporter.

Kaeli didn't move. Andrea continued, "Do you want your questions answered?" Kaeli nodded. "So, do I," Andrea responded.

Kaeli moved inside the room and stood at the end of the metal table. "Are you going to handcuff me to the desk?"

Andrea gave a harsh laugh, "Am I in any danger?"

Kaeli shook her head.

"Have a seat. Before you do, please remove your mic and any recording device you have." Andrea put the tray she'd grabbed from the shelf as they passed, on the table. "Do you need another female officer to help you?"

She gave Andrea a long look then reached under her top unhooking the receiver attached to her waist and pulled the wire attached. She set them in the tray. Fletcher took it outside the room.

"Hey, where's he going with that?"

"He's going to put it outside the room. You'll get it back."

Kaeli sat down in the chair and Andrea sat across from the reporter.

"Kaeli, what do you want?" Andrea sat stiff; her hands clenched under the table.

The woman didn't answer for a brief moment. "How did you find those bodies in Kansas?"

"The field manager was showing me an area along the creek where kids hung out." She took a breath. "We smelled something odd and went to look where it was coming from."

"Why did he take you there?" She narrowed her eyes.

"I went for a walk around the track." She didn't say anything about the reflection in the window. "He saw me and came to talk to me. We were talking about the High School and I asked why the area around the grounds had been left overgrown. He explained why then we laughed that it didn't work because the kids found a way down there." She kept her voice even and friendly.

"So, you had no prior knowledge of the area?"

"No." Andrea let her continue to question.

Kaeli paused then asked. "How did you find the little girl in the well?"

Andrea knew who she was asking about. She retold the story to Kaeli as she had to Fletcher.

Kaeli's expression showed her disbelief. Andrea finished then asked, "What is it? What do you think I'm not telling you?"

"You have the same gift as your dad." Her tone accused Andrea of some misdeed.

"Why do you think that? Why do you think my father has some psychic gift?" Andrea queried.

"Don't you?" she shot back.

Andrea paused for a moment then measured her words. "Kaeli, my father has a gift of perception. He always knew if I wasn't telling him the whole truth. It didn't do any good for me to lie, so I didn't. He observes people and things that you and I might miss."

"Me yes, you and him no." Kaeli interrupted.

"Thank you. I'd like to say I have that same gift. I'm still developing it." She made it sound like they were talking about something else.

Kaeli shook her head slightly. "Stop playing word games. Your father found missing children when no one else could. He caught thieves when they thought they were well hidden. How did he know where they were?" Kaeli moved so she was a few inches from Andrea. "There is no way he knew where all those criminals were."

"The question here is Kaeli, do you believe he has some psychic ability? Why can't you believe he's a normal guy with a good eye and a knowledge of the area?"

Kaeli sat back in the chair. She crossed her arms and stared at Andrea. "I'm not sure what to believe. I don't know if people are psychic. I've read a lot about it and I'm not totally convinced either way.

"I've exposed some frauds and I've questioned people I think are real psychics, or at least I can't find any way they are cheating. Your father is one of them."

"You've questioned my father?"

"In a way."

"That's all fine and good, but what does it have to do with me and your harassment of me? Why are you badgering me with questions and accusations about having some sixth sense?"

Kaeli unfolded her arms and gripped the edge of the table. Her eyes narrowed. In a low voice, she answered, "Because you and your dad didn't find my brother." She spit the words out between clenched teeth.

The words sunk in and Andrea realized this was personal. "Who was your brother?"

"Tim Reid. He went missing twenty-two years ago."

Chapter 25

Andrea stared into Kaeli's eyes. Her brain processed the information. Running through the files of her past memories. *Tim Reid* -Twenty-two years ago she was ten years old.

"Do you remember him?" Kaeli's soft voice penetrated her memories.

"Not at this moment. I was young. I don't remember all the cases my dad was on."

"You were there. You and your father searched the woods for my brother." Kaeli's eye's narrowed as they burned into her own demanding her to remember.

"Do you have a picture of him?" Andrea asked keeping her voice professional.

Kaeli pulled open her purse and withdrew her wallet. She extracted a small picture and pushed it across the table to Andrea. "This is the one my mother used on the missing posters."

Andrea put her hand on the picture and immediately something flashed across her vision. *Not now* her mind screamed. She bowed her head over the picture as if to study it, but all she saw was a movie in fast forward in her mind. A car, a boy on a bike, the boy in the car, then in a trunk. She shook her head.

Kaeli sighed, "I guess you don't have psychic ability."

"I told you I didn't," Andrea whispered. The vision moved so fast she almost missed the sign to the boy scout campgrounds. Then darkness. Bound in a small closet. Hunger, thirst, then nothing.

Andrea stood up. "I'm sorry. I need some air. Can I get you something to drink?" She'd already turned to the door.

"A bottle of water," Kaeli answered.

Andrea pulled the door open and headed to the break room where they kept water for these occasions. She pulled a paper towel from the roll and dabbed her forehead. What was wrong with her? She'd never had a reaction to an object like this before. Most times she'd notice things in the crime scene photos. Sometimes she'd connect them with things in the crime that wasn't in the picture. *How?* She had no idea. This time the picture flooded her mind.

"Are you okay?" Fletcher stood in the doorway. His concerned expression pinned her until she answered.

"No." She looked at his handsome face and felt his compassion flow over her.

"What happened?" he stepped toward her, but she held up her hand for him to stop. "Take her the water. I need a minute."

"I think we need to talk." He didn't move.

"About what? "She snapped at him.

Fletcher didn't react. He continued to look at her. "What was that about? She noticed you had a reaction to the picture. If you hide out in here it will cause more questions. You need to face her and let her know why you reacted as you did. Even I saw you felt something as you looked at the picture."

Andrea squeezed her eyes shut for a moment. Pictures of the boy flew through her mind. She gripped the back of a chair. She felt Fletcher's hand on her arm. The vision disappeared. The feeling of vertigo left her.

"Let's go. I'll talk to her." She pulled away from his touch.

"Good. Then we need to talk."

She nodded and took the bottle of water with her.

Andrea opened the door and entered the room. Kaeli looked up keeping her eyes on Andrea. Andrea ignored her questioning expression. "Sorry. It must have been something I ate. Here's your water. Where were we?" She sat across from the woman.

"I asked if you remembered my brother."

"I didn't remember him from the picture. I do remember going on cases with my father. As part of the search teams that looked for missing persons. He didn't allow me to go when it involved a criminal case." Andrea let a slight smile lift the edges of her lips. "I'm sorry I don't remember your brother. If you'd like I could talk to my father and ask if he remembers anything."

Kaeli stood up. "No thank you. I've spoken to your father several times. He remembers my brother. He remembers looking for him. He doesn't know what happened to him. There were no clues or evidence of what happened." She moved away from the desk. "I'm sorry to have bothered you." Then she whirled to face Andrea slapping her hands on the table and leaning forward. The words came through clenched teeth, her eyes light with an inner fire. "You know something. I saw it on your face, you remembered something or felt something. Tell me!"

Andrea scrambled out of the chair and moved to the end of the table. "I-I."

Kaeli moved with deliberate steps toward her. Then stopped when Fletcher blocked her path and held out his hand keeping her in her place.

He spoke to the reporter. "Hold on Kaeli, this isn't the way to handle this. If Andrea saw or felt anything that would help you find your brother, she'd have told you."

Kaeli snorted in disbelief. "Fat chance. She's always trying to come off as some goody-two-shoes cop. Well, I don't believe it. I think there's more to you than you let on."

"You can't have it both ways. Either you believe she has some sort of ability or you don't. Which is it?" Fletcher continued.

"I believe she got something. I saw it in the way she reacted when she touched Tim's picture. Did you or did you not get something when you touched the picture?" Her words came out spaced as if speaking to an imbecile.

"I'm not sure what happened. Yes, I had a sense of something, but I have to piece it out to see if it was real or a mixture of memories convoluted in my brain." Andrea's voice was low as if she were out of breath.

"When will you be doing that?" Kaeli's voice remained choppy.

Andrea shrugged. "We have a lot going on right now with this case."

Kaeli slapped her hand on the table for attention. "I've waited for twenty-two years. I think that is long enough. Tell me what you saw or felt or anything."

Andrea stuffed her fists into her pockets. She turned away from the two. If she admitted she saw something she would have to admit she had some sort of ability. She'd been protesting it for so long, it was time to admit she had a vision.

Andrea turned to face Kaeli. "I don't know what it was. They were flashes of a boy on a bike. A passing car. That's it." She looked at the girl across the table. "Now did that help you any, answer any questions, solve what happened? It could be something I have in my memory as a child that popped up."

Kaeli picked up her purse. "I'll have the case files sent over to you. For now," she pushed the flimsy picture of Tim across the table. "Take this and see if you get any more clues."

Andrea gave her a short nod, but she didn't pick the picture up.

Fletcher squeezed Andrea's arm with reassurance and escorted Kaeli out the door.

Andrea stared at the picture of the boy then using a glove from her pocket, she picked up the picture and put it in an evidence bag she kept in a pocket.

Chapter 26

"**H**ey Watson, how are you coming with the questioning and research?" Steve's voice jolted Andrea from her reverie.

She turned to face him. "Working on something."

He ignored her response and rested his arm on the cubical wall. His expression turned hostile. "We're working on tracking the remains of the other body parts to missing women." His tone sounded his frustration.

"Any ideas of where they came from?" She prompted.

Again, his response sounded forced. "The FBI has us running down any missing women down the I-35 corridor. Do you know how many women are missing along that freeway?"

"I can imagine. Are they matching any existing DNA to the DNA they collected?"

"Yes, that's the data we're working from. We're looking for families who've submitted samples for matching. So far we've found one possible match." Steve thrust his fists into the pockets of his uniform slacks. "You'd have thought every family would want confirmation one of these were their missing members."

Andrea rolled her eyes. "Steve, think about it. All that DNA to go through and match. You'd have a lot more work than you have now." She laid her arm on her desk and lowered her voice. "Maybe some of these families don't want to know."

"No way." Steve burst out waving his hand to accent his point. "I would think anyone with a missing person would want their DNA on file in case a match was needed someday."

Andrea looked directly into the man's eyes. "Would you want to know your beloved family member was tortured, then cut up, put into a bag and dropped into a lake where fish ate their flesh? I think some people would rather live with the hope their loved one ran away and will return someday." Her voice became a whisper, "Hope is all we have. It's good enough for most people."

Steve didn't respond. He stood still, a perplexed expression on his face as he mulled over her words. "I guess it's a possibility." Shrugging his shoulder, he turned and walked toward his office.

Fletcher stood and moved next to her. He gave her shoulder a squeeze. "You're right. Hope is all we have."

Andrea turned back to her screen. She needed to find this killer. He needed to be brought in and made to face the people he harmed.

"Andrea, I have the list you gave me for the people we questioned. I've put their movements down for the last year or so. None of them traveled that extensively. Except for Peeping Tom's wife. The rest of the people on the list are retired or homebodies." Fletcher sat back down at his desk a few feet from hers. He leaned back in the chair and laced his hands behind his neck. "I'm stumped. What've you got?"

"Did you get a list of the Saunders family members from David?"

"No. I made one based on tax records, DMV, and School records. Three girls and four boys make up the Saunders family. David being the oldest and he said Nancy is the youngest." he handed her his copy.

"How many kids does Nancy have?" She asked using a highlighter to fill in a square.

He reached for his iPad. "It says she and her husband have three kids the oldest is a teenager, a boy."

"I've been looking at the list of times and codes showing entry and exits to the property. One code seems to enter and leave the property often. I wonder if it's one of the kids. I wonder if their parents know about it. It's both after and during school hours." She gave the list a hard look.

"Could be someone is having some afternoon hanky-panky on the side." Fletcher wiggled his eyebrows at her.

Andrea chuckled and shook her head at him.

"It shows, one of the cards or code key was used to access the property one day in the afternoon at three-thirty and then didn't leave until the next day at about one o'clock. Then returned at five and stayed all night, not leaving for two days." She ran her finger down the page to see if the number appeared again. "Here it is two weeks later. They're in and out of the property for two weeks then don't come back for three weeks. Then again in and out for another three weeks and gone for two weeks. This isn't a teenager; this is an adult. Something isn't sitting right."

Fletcher leaned over her shoulder to look at the list. "Do we have any dates that cover any of the missing women?" he asked.

"No, it doesn't go back that far, it covers the last two years, No wait, it does cover three years. What days did Peggy go missing?"

Fletcher went back to his computer and tapped on his screen. "Three years ago, in August."

Andrea flipped the page over to the bottom one and looked at the entries, "The card wasn't used at the property on that day but was there four days later. Whoever this card belongs to, checked in at ten o'clock that night and stayed for a day, left, and returned a couple hours later and stayed for two more days. We need to have a talk with the owner of this card."

"We'll need to find out from David whose card it is. That's not going to be easy and we don't want to tip our hand." Fletcher closed his iPad.

Andrea looked at the dates, especially the last ones they had.

"What if we set up a stakeout and watched to see who goes in and out over a few days? It could be a reasonable reason. I'd hate to start asking pointed questions and end up with egg on our face."

"I'll bet whoever is using the card is at the property now or will be soon. It seems they are on the road a few weeks as time and home." She looked at Fletcher." I'll need to analyze the dates for a more concrete home and away graph."

"Right. You crunch numbers and I'll clear it with the boss." Fletcher pressed numbers on his phone.

"You sure are getting a lot of screen time." Bob's eyes appeared above the wall between them. He waited for her response.

Andrea kept her eyes on her computer screen, hoping he'd go back to his own screen.

"I'm not talking that screen time; I'm talking TV screen time. Did you see Kaeli's report on you this morning? I don't know if the department can take much more of her rants against it and using you as the jumping board." He disappeared without waiting for a response.

Andrea sat up and turned her chair, so she faced the cube wall, with his balding head clearing the top. At times she thought he'd make an excellent prop for her target practice.

Heaving a loud intake of breath and letting it out as loud she responded. "Bob, since you seem to take great pleasure in this, what is it that Kaeli said that has your panties in a wad?"

He waved the paper he held. "You're on her bad side. I don't think the meeting you had yesterday did any good."

Andrea smiled though her teeth were clamped tightly shut. "She may have recorded that sound bite before our meeting."

"Nope. She stood right outside the building early this morning. It went live as she was speaking." His malicious grin irritated her.

Pain shot through her head and scenes flashed behind her eyes. She rubbed her forehead then asked, "Bob? What do leather pants, a blond wig, fake white teeth, and spray-on tan have to do with dancing?" She cocked her head and watched his expression change to surprise then horror. "What?"

Andrea turned back to her computer. *Where had the picture of Bob ballroom dancing come from?* Why had she said that to him? Now things would be worse between the two of them.

A ping on her computer popped up. It was a message from Bob. **How did you know? Why are you spying on me?**

She answered. **Then it's true?**

No response. She deleted the message from her computer.

Chapter 27

Andrea pushed the car door open and a strong wind almost closed it on her, The anticipation of having Fletcher over for another dinner warmed her even as she pulled her hood around her face to keep the wind from drying her eyes.

The doors to the store opened to welcome her as hot air blew down from a heater above. Slinging her bag strap over her head she grabbed a cart and headed to the produce section for salad fixings.

She opted for the bagged salad instead of making it herself. Pulling items from the vegetable selection, an ominous feeling overcame her. She shook her head. A feeling that wasn't a chill, but what she felt when watching a horror film as the action intensified. Her fingers pulled the item from its place, she turned and dropped it in the cart.

Taking a deep breath, she looked up at the other shoppers moving past her. The majority of the group were women.

"Excuse me." A man's arm reached past her to grab an item from the shelf. She felt no reaction to him as she pushed her cart out of his way. It was someone else. Someone with bad ju-ju.

She moved along the display cases. A reaction like this had affected her once before. She'd stood in the doorway of the jail where her father locked a man who'd killed his parents. He'd been a mentally challenged young man who did odd jobs for the community.

People felt sorry for him and ignored his outbursts and reactions to situations. Her father or one of the officers would go get him and bring him in. She never had any interaction with him until the morning the neighbors called to say Efton was out wandering along the road crying. They found him sitting on the curb covered in blood.

She'd come to the station to bring her father his lunch when the van backed up to the jail door and her father escorted Efton in. She couldn't explain what happened, but there was something in him that wasn't right. Anger, and something she didn't recognize then but knew now, was evil. It was the killer inside him leaking out and touching her. His eyes met hers and it was as if he had strangled her. She'd run out gasping for breath.

Someone near her. The feeling became more intense and she pushed her cart along the bins picking up tomatoes, cucumbers without checking them as she usually did.

Dropping peppers into a bag she began to systematically observe the shoppers. A woman with children-pass. An older woman wrapped in a long heavy coat with a colored scarf tied around her head-Russian, no.

Her eyes slipped to a man with a heavy build, a well-known brand work jacket, and overalls. *He works outside. Construction of some sort.* He held a basket in his hand not serious about anything he picked up and put back. He felt the vegetables, caressing them then gently returning them to the bin. He turned and she looked at the apples in front of her. No feeling from him.

He moved on down the aisle toward the deli. Andrea took a deep breath and moved along the opposite side of the area toward the meat. The feeling resided a little.

She loved the way this store prepared ready to cook meats. The butcher behind the counter joked with her as he wrapped her choice offering suggestions for preparations. The bad feeling slammed her again and she almost dropped the bundle when he handed it to her.

"I'll have what she's having. It sounds good. I'm sure my girlfriend will love to make it." The man in the overalls stood a foot from her.

She turned the cart and pushed it away almost colliding with a cart. "Oh, sorry," came the automatic response from her shaking lips. She backed up colliding with a body. This time there was no denying the fissure of fear and "something" she couldn't identify.

"I'm sorry, I guess I need a rearview mirror or a back-up signal." She spoke over her shoulder.

"You're fine." The man answered. She tried to maneuver her way around the woman who blocked her exit, but several people who wanted to order or choose their meat blocked her escape. She felt panic rise.

"Here," a man reached for her cart and pulled it next to his. He pushed both out of the area. "Whew, it was like we opened the floodgate." He smiled down at her.

"Yes, thank you." She gave him a weak response and tried to get out of his way.

"I'm Jim. Do you come here often?" He asked before she could make her escape.

"Sorry, I have to get this home to start dinner for my boyfriend." Her gaze met his and locked.

His eyes went from easy interest to hard slits. "Boyfriend, or did you make that up?"

Her heart stopped. He still held on to her cart. He wouldn't do anything in the middle of a crowded grocery store. Would he? "Yes." She gestured to her cart, "I'm not eating all this by myself," pasting a smile on her face.

"You have beautiful eyes. I'm wondering if you'd meet me for coffee. They have a cafe at the front of the store." He moved to stand as close as the cart would allow.

Andrea backed away. "I'm sorry, I already have a boyfriend and I'm not interested." She turned her cart and pushed past him turning down a crowded aisle. Her heart beat hard against her chest. Stopping half-way down the aisle, she stared at the shelves, her eyes unfocused. Her vision blurred and she clutched the handle of the cart with one hand and steadied herself on the shelf.

The boxes waivered and in their place, she saw the man in the overalls, standing in the dark outside a window peeping at a woman undressing inside. She squeezed her eyelids shut to block out the vision. It swirled to thick hands full of blood as he cut the skin and flesh from something.

This time she forced her eyes open. *Was this the killer they were looking for?* Was it the same man or two different men? Sweat ran down her face and she wiped it away with her hand then stared at it. What was wrong with her?

"Ma'am are you okay?" A motherly woman stopped next to her. "Are to a diabetic?"

Andrea shook her head. The woman pulled a mini bottle of water from her bag. "You look like you could use this." She pushed it at Andrea and passed her with no further comment. Andrea gulped the water down, not stopping until it was drained. She threw it in her cart then scrambled to dig it out and put it in her bag. *They'll think I stole it.*

At the end of the aisle, she turned to the registers, but her gaze passed the cafe and saw the man who'd spoken to her, sitting in the corner drinking his beverage. *What if he is our killer? How can I let him slip by?* She diverted to the self-check-out and when the machine spit out her receipt, she pushed the cart to the Cafe.

"Hi," she gave him a weak smile. "I had a change of heart. If you'll give me your phone number, I'll call you if things don't work out with the boyfriend."

His smile lit his face and he dug in his front pocket extracting a card. "Here's my business card, call me."

She took the card dropping it into her purse as soon as possible putting as much distance between her and this man's effect on her.

In her car, the panic attack subsided. She'd not felt that in years. Why had this man caused it? Why was he different than the criminals she'd come in contact within the past? A flash of men she'd apprehended and taken to jail flit through her mind. She'd been able to control any reaction to them. Why this man? Was it because he was the killer? Her hand hovered over her purse.

Andrea started the car and headed home. Safety. Catching herself checking her mirrors for any suspicious cars following her.

A few hours later her doorbell rang. She stopped. Had she locked it behind her? She realized; it was always locked since she came in through the garage.

She checked her app and found Fletcher's face pressed almost against the doorbell camera. The distortion caused her to burst out in a laugh as she unlocked the door and opened it.

"You don't look your best when you do that." She laughed.

Fletcher kissed her cheek, "I thought I looked good no matter what. I'm sure I heard you say that a time or two."

Andrea flicked him with the towel as he proceeded her to the kitchen.

"How was your day?" She asked. He'd been in meetings and they'd only greeted in passing.

"We put together a nice profile of sorts. We need to get a little bit more information. The fact you pulled that dumpsite for us helped a lot. HD is quite impressed. He asked a lot of questions about you." Fletcher leaned on the counter dividing the kitchen from the dining room.

"What did you tell him?" Her curiosity pricked she folded her arms across her waist and gave him a look.

"I told him." He paused and looked at her. "I told him about you."

She snorted, "What about me? Come on give it up. Did you have me checked out?"

He wigged his brows at her, "I always check you out."

She tossed the potholder at him when he wasn't expecting it. He fumbled to catch it. "Hey!"

"What do you know about me?" Her voice carried a bit more demand with it.

He held up his hands in mock surrender. "Nothing."

This time she turned away and began to check the stuffed pork rolls in the oven. "They're done."

"I'll set the table." He pulled the drawer out next to her and fished out the utensils, then grabbed plates from the cupboard above, scooting out of the room.

"You're not getting out of it that easy." She warned him. Pulling the tender rolls from the pan she set them on the platter and added the two foil-wrapped baked potatoes.

"How was your day?" He asked relieving her of the dish while she picked up the bowl of vegetables.

"Fine. I worked on looking for missing girls along the main routes out of MN. I'm reading police and news reports for MO matches up. I've found three reports between here and Madison that fit. Last seen in a diner/bar or truck stop. If it's the same unsub, we have a traveler. I'm guessing a trucker or LTL with a regular route." she remembered the card in her purse. She would need to find the man's job was." She sat next to Fletcher.

"There are similarities with missing women. It's finding the common male among them. Anything along those lines?" He chewed and rolled his eyes at her motioning with his fork, he was pleased.

"There's something else." Andrea set her fork down and laced her fingers together under the table. She felt Fletcher's eyes on hers and his hand reached under the table to cover hers.

"What?" he asked.

"I was in the grocery store and this guy came up and tried to pick me up." lifting her gaze to meet his, she begged for understanding.

Fletcher rubbed his thumb over the backs of hers. "Tell me what happened." His voice stayed even and low.

"It wasn't what he said or did, creepy as that was, it was what I felt." She wasn't sure how to continue. She'd never shared this with anyone, not even her father.

"Tell me." He prompted.

She recounted the feeling she had and the vision she'd seen. She pulled her hands from his and sat back in the chair rubbing her upper arms as if she were cold.

"Andrea, how did you feel about the vision?" He didn't touch her though she could tell he wanted to.

"I hadn't had a vision like that. What caused it?"

"You're opening up to the possibility and letting it through. It's also possible you've insulated yourself from any connection with people. Now that you've opened the door, those senses are allowing more to filter through. It will be up to you to decide how you want to control it and use it or keep fighting to keep it under wraps. It's your choice."

"I'm afraid," she whispered.

"Of what? Tell me exactly what you're afraid of?" This time he sat back. He pushed the almost empty plate away.

She paused a moment pushing her food around the plate. "First. I'm afraid of people's reactions. This isn't normal you know, hearing and seeing things no one else sees. My father—"

"Hold on, this isn't about your father. He has his own reactions, let's talk about you." He waved his hand for her to continue.

"Okay. I don't want to be the brunt of jokes, or weird people asking me all kinds of questions about their dead relatives."

"Fair enough. Then you control how much to tell and how much to use to your advantage. Have you ever felt anything about people other than that teacher?"

"Yes." The answer came out in a hiss. "At least not the killing kind. I heard that little girl crying and I once saw a boy be taken by someone, but my dad found him without my help. Today was different."

"You reacted to Jim. He made you feel creepy and then you saw visions of him. What are you going to do about it?"

"I don't know." She felt ready to cry.

"Andrea. You put him under a scope and look at him. Profile him, look into his background. Is he our killer?"

"He's not a suspect, I can't go digging around someone's life." She rejected his suggestion.

"Why not?"

"Because he isn't a suspect."

"Yes, he is. You need to treat him like any other person who came to YOU with that story. A guy tried to pick a woman up and she felt creepy about him. With a serial killer on the loose women have to be careful. You have more information about this guy than the average woman would. Do you want to protect people from a possible crime? It has to be done carefully. The FBI can do that. Give me what you have on him."

"I don't have anything on him but his name and phone number." She defended.

"That's enough for me. I'll have it all by tomorrow. Finish your dinner." He swirled his fork at the few bites left on her plate.

"I'm not hungry now." She pushed it away.

Fletcher carried both plates to the kitchen. He cleaned up the dinner and wouldn't let her help. "Go wrap yourself in a blanket and watch TV. No Crime TV. Watch Hallmark or something."

She laughed and did as he ordered. The TV flashed a movie, but her eyelids drifted closed after a few minutes. What played on their backside would have sent most people screaming. Andrea held the vision and looked at the man she knew as Jim. His back was turned, he was cutting something, then tearing at it. The scene went black. She opened her eyes, Fletcher squatted in front of her.

"What happened?"

"He, Jim, was cutting something up in a shed. It's not hunting season so might this be a past action or present?" She shivered. Then relaxed as Fletcher hugged her to his warm body and held her.

The next morning, she woke in her bed still in the clothes she had on the night before. Heat flooded her face. She'd fallen asleep in Fletcher's arms.

Cautiously she looked around her room and listened. Nothing moved in the other rooms. Sliding out of bed she tip-toed to the door and looked around. She was alone. For a brief moment, she felt disappointed before heading to the bathroom to take a shower before going to work.

At work, she kept her head down while she tapped away on her keyboard. She remembered the information from the business card, Jim gave her. The man's job was a delivery driver. PnD. She'd had to look it up. It referred to Pick-up and Delivery drivers for local businesses.

She'd looked at his public social media account and found he posted pictures of dogs who greeted him on his route. I saw videos of the dogs and selfies with the dogs. His smile was genuine. He worked for a national delivery service.

Was this the man she'd met at the grocery store? The one who's inner darkness frightened her? No one looking at his page would think he had a dark side. Was she mistaken?

His last post was the night before when he was finished with his route with a selfie of him and a dog. He'd been in town last night.

Not out killing anyone. He couldn't be the killer they were looking for. *What does a serial killer look like?* Her mind reminded her. None of the men that were famous killers, LOOKED like criminals, that's why they weren't quickly found.

What would Fletcher find on the guy? He didn't drive out of town. He had regular routes in the city.

This wasn't their killer. Andrea hesitated, was he a killer in the making? It looked like he fit the profile of a killer. The horrible thing was, he had to do something to be apprehended. Then it became too late. What do you do when all the signs are there?

Andrea closed the file and took her mug to get more coffee. Passing Chrissy's desk, she whispered over the cube. "Can I buy you a coffee?"

Chrissy looked up and searched her friend's face. "You sure can." At the sight of Andrea's mug, she shook her head, "I think this calls for a walk to the coffee shop."

Andrea gave a weak nod, "I'll get my coat."

Chrissy listened to Andrea tell her about Jim and her suspicion he was a killer in the making. "I understand your frustration. We can only do so much. You can't yank people off the street for suspicion." She angled closer to her friend and whispered, "Or visions."

"That's why I hate them. I don't want to know what I can't fix or change." Andrea's voice rose to a cry. She looked around the busy shop. No one paid attention to the two women.

"Put it in a mental file and shut the door." Chrissy admonished. Picking up her cup she waited for Andrea to stand. "Back to work girlfriend."

Chapter 28

That night as Andrea checked the roast and potatoes cooking in the crockpot, Fletcher took his coffee to the living room and turned the TV on to watch the news. Andrea looked up when she heard Kaeli's voice speak her name.

The police are still not talking about the killer we may have in our midst. I did get a confirmation from the Press Liaison. They do not think the killer has targeted anyone in this area. They aren't putting out any warnings. What does that mean exactly?

I tried to contact one of the detectives on the case, Andrea Watson. You may recall she's from Bemidji MN and her father is a retired Sheriff there. He was involved in solving many cases and dubbed the Psychic Sheriff.

It was a little odd that Ms. Watson was on hand when the body parts were found in the lake. She also happened to discover another body dump while investigating the serial killer connection in Kansas. I'd say she has plenty of mojo when it comes to finding dead bodies, but can she find the killer? That's what we want to know. She won't talk about what she's working on or if the FBI is using her abilities on this case.

Let me tell you about a time when she was a young girl, and a child went missing. No one could find the missing child. A couple of days went by with search parties combing large areas. Ms. Watson was on hand with her father and told him she thought she heard a dog crying in a field across the street. He headed into the area and found a well the searchers missed. The cover was off and the little girl was inside. She was found safe.

Is it possible Ms. Watson is using her abilities to find this killer?

"Turn it off," Andrea ordered.

Fletcher looked up at her. "Okay, but the segment is over. I wanted to see what the hockey score was."

Andrea turned back to the kitchen. She felt cold. Fletcher came into the kitchen and put his arms around her, pulling her into the shelter of his body.

"Why is she doing this? Why is she bringing all this out into the public? What does she hope to gain?" Andrea pressed her cheek against his chest. She could hear his steady heartbeat. A little fast, she smiled, but steady.

"I think she wants you to find this guy, and for her to be the one who scoops the story. If you talk to her and she can quote you she will have the public wanting to know more. She has a connection to you and she's using it to keep in contact, so you'll have to let her in on what's going on."

"I haven't even talked to her except those few times and you were with me."

"Yes, that's why she's giving you airtime. She's going around Lindsey. As Liaison, he told her no comment on an ongoing case. She's frustrated, so she's using you."

"Well, good luck with that direction." She wrapped her arms around his waist, and he bent to kiss her. The kiss deepened and went on for a few more minutes until she gently pulled away. "Dinner's ready." Came out in a breathless sound.

"I was enjoying the appetizer." He bussed her nose. "I'll set the table."

While she took the food from the crockpot and cut the meat, she thought about what Fletcher had said. How else would a reporter get information when the Public Affair's liaison doesn't talk? Talk to the source.

"Fletcher, does she think putting my name out there and telling the public I'm some sort of freak, I'm going to tell her anything about the case?" She brought the meat plate to the table and returned for the bowl of potatoes and carrots.

Fletcher didn't respond.

After pouring them both a drink, he sat across from her and served himself. "I don't think you should worry about her. What she's doing is trying to get you to respond on camera. If she can create a mystery about you, the public is going to demand to know more about you. That will create demand and move her up the ladder."

"That's what I don't want!" her voice rose in frustration. "I want to be left alone." She attacked the pork with her knife.

Fletcher reached for her hand and squeezed it. "I think it's too late for that. Since the station ran the video, they think it'll work too."

"What am I going to do?" her eyes pleaded with him.

"Wait to see what she does next. We'll deal with that."

The next morning when she opened her garage door, a swarm of reporters with cameras crowded in. Fear and anger caused her heart to beat faster, and she got into her car and slammed the door shut. Putting her car into gear she backed slowly toward the street. The reporters and cameramen barely moved out of the way. Two of them blocked the driveway. She held her badge facing the window, "I have a direct line to the station. Keep this up, and you'll all be in jail for trespassing and harassment." The men beside her signaled the others to move away. The reporters stepped back a pace or two but continued to yell their questions at her.

She waited for the garage door to close, making sure no one hid in her garage while it shut. She backed out of the driveway and left the group in the street. She wanted to call Fletcher but decided not to talk while she drove. Her apprehension might affect her concentration.

As she pulled into the station parking lot, Kaeli stood waiting by the back door. Andrea ground her teeth. *I'm not in the mood this morning.* A new thought came to her after a deep cleansing breath. Be sweet and act like the victim. Shed a tear at the harassment.

Exiting her car she headed to the station entrance. Fixing a sad expression on her face. Kaeli came to meet her.

"Ms. Watson, do you have anything to say about the case you're working on?"

Andrea paused and looked straight at the camera. "Yes, I do."

Kaeli pushed the microphone close to Andrea's face, her expression alight with satisfaction.

"I would like to tell your fans that what you are putting me through is a horrible way to have to live. I am harassed by you and those like you. I can't eat or sleep constantly worrying that someone is trying to break into my house or peeking in my windows."

Kaeli tried to pull the mic away but Andrea held it to her mouth. "You don't know how hard it is to come to work when I'm accosted here at my job. There are more newsworthy events the public would like to hear than when I leave, get home or what I cook for dinner."

She turned her tear-filled eyes to the camera, "I hope your station runs this video to show the police are doing everything they can to catch this person. We need clean evidence to put this person away. Tampering and putting out there what we have may cause the person to go into hiding." She continued to pull the mic to her mouth while Kaeli tried to pull it away.

Andrea continued to talk; her expression pleaded with the viewers. "We, at the station, try so hard to keep the public safe. We do everything in our power to catch criminals. Having to defend ourselves to reporters isn't fair to you or us. It interferes with our job." She let go of the mic and Kaeli barely stopped the reflex action of the mic from hitting her face.

Andrea turned to walk the few steps to the door. She slid her card over the reader and opened the door.

At her desk she let out a long sigh, waiting for her heart to slow down and her breathing to calm down.

"I heard that sigh." Fletcher raised his eyebrows at her.

"I was accosted at home and here at work." She informed him. "I played her. Kaeli was waiting for me outside the backdoor."

"She has a lot of guts to do that." Fletcher rolled his chair closer to her. "What did you do?"

"Played the victim. I got teary-eyed, looked at the camera, and said the woman was harassing me and now all the reporters were harassing me. I gave them a sob story." She shrugged and turned to her desk and turned on her computer. "We'll see if it makes the news tonight. I have leftovers. Would you like to join me for dinner and the news?" She wiggled her eyebrow suggestively.

"Me? Are you propositioning me?" He feigned surprise then laughed. "Yes, I accept your offer. I'll bring dessert."

"You're on, I love chocolate."

After lunch, she checked her phone. She had a text from Kaeli. *You win. This time. Check the 6 pm news.*

"I made the 6 pm news." Andrea grinned at Fletcher, holding up her phone. He gave her a thumbs up.

"That's two-news promo's." Andrea pulled the warmed leftovers from the oven.

Fletcher started pointing to the TV. "You're on!" Andrea saw Kaeli standing in front of the station.

"We've been following the case of the ice cube killer. Working on the case along with the FBI is Ms. Andrea Watson. I've known this detective when she worked with her father, a detective on the Iron Range. Her father, as I've mentioned before, uses a unique ability we sometimes refer to as ESP to locate criminals or find those gone missing.

It's come to my attention that his daughter may have the same ability. It isn't clear if the Department is using her abilities. She was able to find those missing women in Kansas. I had this conversation with Ms. Watson. Earlier."

The entire clip ran next. Andrea was happy with it. Even her action of letting the mic go and Kaeli's reaction hadn't been edited.

"Sometimes as reporters, we have to press the police for answers to keep the public informed. There is a fine line between their job and what we do. As we all know, the police need to be held accountable for keeping us safe. Are they telling us everything we need to keep our families safe?"

When Andrea arrived at the station and headed for her desk an odd feeling settled over her. Hanging up her coat the vibe in the office felt subdued. She heard the normal buzz of phone conversations, the tapping and banging of keyboarding, a tap on her shoulder surprised her. She came face to face with Chrissy.

"Hi." She greeted her friend.

"Walk to the bathroom with me?" Chrissy didn't smile.

"Sure. What's up?"

Chrissy didn't respond as she walked toward the bathroom. Inside she checked the stalls and when she was satisfied the room was empty she turned to Andrea.

"Chrissy, you are scaring me." Andrea moves closer to her friend fearing bad news.

"Andrea. There is a buzz in the office. Steve is out to get you not only off the case but out of this precinct. He's putting the pressure on Conrad to transfer you." Chrissy laid her hand on Andrea's arm. "I want you to be aware of what is going on behind the curtain. The rest of the department is divided. Some of the men are siding with Steve since it means their job might be in jeopardy if they don't. The rest of us are keeping a low-profile hoping Conrad will step up and put him in his place."

"Why? I'm not threatening him. He does his job and I do mine." Andrea supported her body on her hands facing a sink and staring at the polished metal that served as a mirror. "Why do some men have this macho attitude? Do you think this has something to do with my dad?" This last sentence came out between clenched teeth.

"Yes and no. He could ignore your connection to your dad, but in this case, it's that reporter that keeps putting you on TV and that he can't ignore. When you're in the news, he becomes more upset."

"Yes, I noticed he's been cranky lately. I thought it might have to do with the case."

"It's because the public wants whoever put those body parts in the lake caught."

"Chrissy, we all do." Andrea looked at her friend who nodded. "Thanks for telling me."

"It doesn't help that Fletcher is backing you up. He rubs Steve the wrong way every time he walks in the door."

"I can't help that. I didn't ask him here." Andrea stepped into the hall.

"True, but you seem to have a relationship with him that is outside work." Chrissy grinned at her.

"I'm not allowed a personal life?" Andrea whispered back.

Chrissy shrugged and turned toward her desk.

Chapter 29

The rest of the week passed with little advancement in the case. The task force worked on their projects, looking for clues they could match with anything on file.

Andrea's desk phone rang Friday morning. Steve's ID showed on the screen. "Come to the conference room and bring your little buddy." The tone sounded terse and condescending.

"We're being summoned to the conference room." Andrea stood and waited for Fletcher to close his computer and follow her.

"What's up?" He asked, leaning down to whisper.

"I'm not sure, I didn't get a sense from Totts."

"Oh, so he called us in." Fletcher reached the conference door first and opened it allowing Andrea to pass him.

Conrad, HD, Steve, a few other FBI officers, and internal affairs sat or stood in the conference room.

"Please sit." Conrad pointed to two empty chairs.

Fletcher looked at Andrea, who looked back at him in question. They sat.

"We've been made aware of a situation this morning that hasn't been given to the media yet. We'd like to have your input on it."

"Sure, whatever I can do to help." Andrea nodded.

"Same here," Fletcher added.

"Funny you accept the offer first without knowing what it is," Steve responded in a low voice.

Conrad gave him a dirty look.

What is going on here? Andrea thought.

"We've been informed that Kaeli Meyers has been missing since yesterday morning. She didn't report to work. She'd had an appointment at nine o'clock with the initials AW circled and a question mark. Did you have a meeting with her?" Conrad asked.

"No, we met with her earlier in the week," Andrea offered.

"What did the two of you meet with her about?" Conrad asked.

"You're aware of her attitude toward me in the media. I wondered if we could come to some understanding." Andrea kept her gaze on her boss.

"Did you?" He paused. "Come to an understanding?"

"Of sorts. We planned another meeting sometime in the near future if anything in the case broke."

"You haven't seen or spoken to her since?" HD's thick eyebrows almost connected as he frowned.

"I haven't seen her since that morning except once on TV and I told Fletcher to turn her off." She ignored the snort from Steve.

Conrad ignored her comment. "Her boss called in to report her missing and that he suspects you might have had something to do with it. Who was she meeting with the initials AW?"

"It wasn't me. Maybe she was going to confront me and record another interview on TV. I heard she put up a video with the station about me. I'm not sure if it was recorded before or after our meeting. Something to check out." Andrea turned her gaze to Steve.

"We have a team of people on it right now. We don't want you on the street or anywhere this could be compromised." Conrad told her.

"We're setting up a meeting today. It's important," Fletcher interrupted.

"Fletcher, take someone else or give it to another agent to do," HD ordered.

"No. This is our lead." Fletcher protested.

"Fletcher, go ahead. I've got things I can do." She turned back to Conrad. "How long do I have to stay low?"

"I think you can leave at a normal time." Conrad stood. "We need to get on this." The other officers nodded and left.

"Sir, I have a feeling if this gets out into the media, her missing, I will be bombarded with reporters. Should I take a couple of days off or possibly hideout at a hotel?"

Conrad looked at HD, who turned his gaze to Andrea. "I think you need to keep your regular schedule. Any deviation would seem like you were hiding something. It's going to be a tough go. Stand straight, don't look any of them in the eye, and if you have to say something, "No comment' is the best route."

Conrad nodded and left following HD with Steve right on their heels.

Fletcher stood and put his hand on Andrea's shoulders. "I'm sticking close. I want to find out what's going on out there. Where could she have gone to? Did she have a family?"

"I have no idea. You need to go and stake out the Saunders property. At least have someone watching it. Who comes and goes for the next few days." Andrea suggested.

He nodded and left after giving her a quick kiss on her forehead. Andrea sat in the empty conference room. *What happened to Kaeli? Who had anything against the reporter?* Nothing would get solved sitting here. She headed back to her desk. She got the distinct feeling she was being watched. *Do they honestly think I have anything to do with the Kaeli missing?* She wanted to stand up and yell, *I called my father, and he sent a ghost to put her down a hole.*

Andrea opened a window on her computer to watch the newscast Kaeli worked for. She watched the video on the reporter's disappearance.

As the afternoon passed, the TV station had no news she'd gone missing. It had been over 24 hours since someone had last seen the missing reporter. Kaeli could be anywhere.

She turned her attention to the computer printout of the entry and exit codes she'd been given. The last date on the sheet was last week. Whoever used that card drove through the gate and left. There were no entries after that.

Four days passed with no news of Kaeli. The TV station gave a newscast she was missing. A few reporters waited outside her house.

She drove past them with not stopping, ignoring the questions shouted at her window.

Andrea ignored team meetings on the missing reporter and continued to look at the numbers she'd crunched. She still needed Fletcher to tell her who owned card number four.

She aligned its use with the dates women went missing along I-35. The more she scrolled through the lists of missing women and filtered the dates on both spreadsheets, the more they began to match.

Her eyes hurt from the glare of the screen. Cells on the spreadsheet appeard larger than others. She rubbed her eyes and reached for the bottle of lubricating drops in the drawer. After a moment of blinking and dabbing a tissue to collect the excess, names and dates aligned on the screen. It wasn't evidence, but it was too similar to be coincidental.

The station felt quieter than usual when a figure stopped next to her. Fletcher touched her shoulder. Andrea looked up and placed her hand over his and squeezed.

"No news about Kaeli. The force is out looking for her, but there aren't any leads. Lucky you have an alibi." He winked and smiled as if he'd told a joke.

Andrea returned a weak smile at his lame joke. "Did I need one?" Her tone sounded a bit terse in her ears. They'd gone to dinner the night Kaeli went missing. Fletcher had driven her home then stayed a few hours talking before leaving. She looked at him, "You told them."

"I had to. The task force wanted me to quiz you about where you were and your activities."

She slumped into her chair. Now she knew what it felt like to be a suspect. "I have nothing against the woman. You were there when I talked to her. We didn't leave on bad terms, albeit a touchy one. What about you? Did they ask about your time from leaving me to getting home?"

Fletcher rested against the back of the chair, "Are you dragging me into the suspect pool? Now that you ask, they didn't ask me what

time I got home or anything about me. I guess I don't fit the profile."
He pulled something from his pocket and handed it to her.

"I think you might want to read this. It was provided by her boss
at the station. I think it kind of explains a little."

She pulled the contents from the worn manila envelope on her
desk. There were news clippings and typewritten pages. She picked
the largest of the news clippings out first. "Missing girl from Aitkin"
The paper was dated nine years ago.

"Did you read this?" She asked him.

"I saw it while it was on Steve's desk."

Andrea gave him a surprised look, but he shrugged.

"What does this have to do with me? Aitkin is two hours away
from Bemidji." She pulled another article out about her father.

Fletcher reached across and shuffled through the papers, pulled
a stapled group from the rest, and handed it to her. "Maybe read
this first."

The top sheet was a photocopy of a letter addressed to her father.
It began:

Dear Sir,

I know this is a lot to ask, but I've followed your
career in the newspapers. You have an inordinate
ability to find people. I've enclosed some of the news
clippings where you found missing people."

Andrea sorted through the papers, and several
articles reported her father's successes. She looked
back at the letter.

My friend's daughter Annie has been missing for
three days now. I know I've asked our local Police
to contact you, but they're too busy. I don't know
if they did and didn't want to tell me, but would
you please come and see if you can find her. I don't

know what you call it ESP or what, but please look into this missing child.

Kaeli Meyers

Her phone number, address, and a picture of the little girl were stapled to the bottom of the sheet. She turned the page; the date was three days later.

Mr. Watson,

I've tried to call you, but you're not taking my calls and not returning my messages. Why won't you come and look for this little girl? Her family is devastated. We need to find her."

The letter went on about how much the little girl was loved.

The last page detailed Kaeli's brother, Tim's disappearance, and blamed her father for not finding her brother in time. Then she added, his non-response to her letters show what an uncaring person he was.

Andrea laid the paper down. Now she understood why Kaeli was so mad.

"I feel bad for her. I don't know why my dad didn't answer her. My father told me what he gets doesn't come on some demand. If he feels it he helps, if he doesn't he can't feel bad about it. That's why I don't think it's a real ability. Look at all the mediums on TV that talk about people's dead relatives." The sound of her own voice didn't sound as convincing as she would have liked. "Do you think they channel dead people?"

"No. I have my own theory about those charlatons. That's a conversation for another time."

She picked up the other articles and read their headlines. They were all about the missing little girl from twenty years ago.

The news articles listed other psychics that offered to find the little girl, but none were successful. Reporters wrote about groups of people who searched for days, weeks, and months. She picked an article where five years later. No more leads surfaced.

Unfolding an aerial map of the the county, she traced the the marked sites that were searched.

"What's that?" Fletcher asked when she laid it down and turned to her computer.

"It's a map of the areas they searched for the little girl."

"What are you looking at?" He rolled his chair next to hers and watched her key in a map search.

"Just a satellite view of the same area." She zoomed down on the view to match the one in the picture. It was a more detailed view than the printed one. She zoomed as close as she could with area A1. Then moved on to A2 and so on.

"Are you looking for something?" He stared at the screen.

"I feel bad. Kaeli hated me for something out of my control. Who knows what happened to that little girl?"

"When you picked up the paper, did you have the same reaction as you did when you touched Tim's picture?"

"No." She didn't want to deal with what that single question implied. Fletcher picked up one of the police reports from the file. "It says she and a friend were playing in the fenced-in yard. They were behind a three-foot chain-link fence. Her sister Kaeli was in the house when it happened. She had checked on the girls and went to get them a treat. She heard the friend scream for her mother, and Kaeli came out. There was no one in the yard. The neighbor girl was crying to her mother that a bogey man came in and grabbed Helena and told the neighbor girl if she cried or screamed, he'd come back and kill her and her mother. Kaeli sat still until he was gone then began to cry. Her mother came out to see what was wrong." She finished reading and laid the paper down on the desk.

"Fletcher, I get it. Kaeli felt responsible."

Fletcher flipped through the faded papers. After a minute or so he held up a full page. "Read this." He pointed to the page.

Andrea read the title in large bold print. "6-Year-old girl found after two months. A trucker found her behind an abandoned gas station in an oil drum. The trucker drove to get his tractor and go out to throw some trash in the barrel. He happened to look inside and saw the remains of the little girl."

Andrea sat back in the chair. "They found the girl. I'm sorry she died.

"Kaeli blames your father for not coming and looking for her right away." Fletcher looked at Andrea with that quizzical look.

"You think she's holding a grudge against my dad all these years?

Fletcher shrugged. "It looks like it. The girl then her missing brother. She's had to deal with a lot. I guess we need to cut her some slack."

Andrea picked up her phone and pressed her Dad's number. It rang and rang. "Come on, Dad, pick up." She spoke to the phone. It went to voicemail. She hesitated but went ahead and left a message for him to call her as soon as he could. She added, "Dad, I need your help on this. Someone is missing."

Fletcher put his hand on her arm. "Do you think he'll call?"

She sighed. "He's been bugging me about this case. Maybe he'll call to have an excuse to help me."

"I get that Kaeli misses her brother. She feels guilty about her part in what happened to the girl, but why come after me?"

"That's up to a psychiatrist."

"Do you think she staged this to get at my father or me?"

"I don't think she'd go that far. I think someone has taken her. What do you think? Are you getting any feelings about it?"

The question was casual. Anyone listening wouldn't have thought anything odd about it. To Andrea, the problem was one of confirmation. She had to choose. To accept whatever IT was or keep denying it. There wasn't much of a choice. She looked up at Fletcher, who watched her every move. She shook her head. He squeezed her hand and smiled.

"You can do it."

Chapter 30

While Andrea continued to focus on matching dates women had been reported missing to the exit codes from the Saunders's property, Fletcher and the FBI team worked on the questioning any lead called in.

Steve stood to one side of the conference table, glaring at HD and Andrea. Conrad wasn't in attendance, and Steve barely held the fact HD had called the police to the FBI task center.

"There are too many things that don't fit." HD spoke to the group assembled." What can you tell me? What does anyone have that might fit." He sat on the corner of a desk.

Andrea looked at Fletcher. He nodded and motioned for her to speak up. "Sir," Her voice came out and a whisper, and she cleared it to speak again. "Sir, I may have a suggestion."

"Go ahead. What do you have?"

"Fletcher, Agent Peterson, and I spoke to the owner of the large property on the east side of the lake. He sent us a list of times, dates, and codes his family uses to go in and out of the property. "May we use the projector?"

HD nodded. Andrea moved around the desk, past Steve, who barely moved. "Why wasn't I notified of this first?" She felt the spit as he whispered the words.

She plugged her laptop into the machine while Fletcher made the proper connections. Andrea explained, "I entered all the times and codes and separated them by numbering the cards. We don't have the names of the people to whom these codes belong to yet. I focused on one card. This card," pointing to the card, she'd numbered S-4.

"It has accessed the property more times than the others. You can see that the owner enters and leaves at pretty regular times." She changed the picture. "This is a graph. The entries follow a pattern over the months, and then here is the graph for the three years we have data for." Andrea changed the graph.

"The card wasn't used during the five days of the missing women we know about from Minnesota to Texas during these three years. I'm not saying this person is a viable suspect. I can say whoever uses this card has returned to the property within a day or so of each date the women went missing. He doesn't leave the area for at least three to four days or more of returning. That may be a coincidence. I hope this is enough to get a warrant to get the owner of that card."

HD looked at the screen and then to Conrad, who nodded. "Let's make it happen. Who does the property belong to?"

Andrea moved to the next screen. It was an aerial view of the property with the houses. "The property belongs to the Saunders Trust. The big house is used by David Saunders, his siblings, and their families. The four houses along the lakeshore," using a pen she pointed to the houses, "Are also the property of the trust but are used by each of David's siblings. They don't own the houses, but they are used exclusively by that sibling's family." She moved to the other side of the screen, "These three houses or cabins are guest houses."

Fletcher stepped forward. "When talking to neighbors, we were told a man comes and goes from one of the guest houses. He doesn't interact with the neighbors, but they describe him as friendly when he's attends community parties the family sponsors each year. One in June after school is out and another in August before school begins."

"What do we know about this man?"

Andrea responded. "His name is Evan Morrison. He's the brother to Mrs. Roxanne Saunders, known as Sandy. "

HD spoke directly to Andrea. "Do you have a background on these people?"

"Yes, we do." She looked at Fletcher, who took over.

"Roxanne met her husband, Darren, at College in Austin, TX, they fell in love. Roxanne had a younger brother she was close to. When Roxanne and Darren Saunders were engaged, he and Roxanne moved to Minnesota. Evan was accepted into the family as a brother and moved with them." He put pictures of the family on the screen, including a wedding photo taken on the property. "Darren and Roxie were married at the house, and the reception was held there too. A small affair for family and close friends. Evan was a groomsman at the wedding and also gave a speech." He pointed to a bearded man with a full head of dark brown hair standing at the end of the back row.

"Are you saying you have proof one of these family members could have be the serial killer?" Steve asked. He leaned against the wall; his arms crossed over his chest. He raised one eyebrow as at the question and barely kept the sneer from his tone.

"I'm not saying anything of the sort. We need to do more research. We do have a possibility of someone that may have connections that correspond to the dates the girls went missing. We aren't finished with that research."

"I'd like to see what you've got so far," Steve looked Andrea in the eye. She didn't respond.

HD cleared his throat. "Continue working on that aspect. We have one more issue to speak of—the missing person of Kaeli Meyers. Who is working on this case?"

A few hands went up about shoulder high. Those officers looked around at who else was working on the case. Andrea busied herself, disconnecting her computer from the projector. The feeling of eyes watching her made her feel uncomfortable. She wanted to yell; *I was told to stay away from the case!* Instead, she picked up her computer and left the room.

Fletcher and Andrea were called to go to Conrad's office. "Bring your computer," Conrad told Andrea.

He wasn't alone. HD sat on the corner of a low file cabinet. He nodded to Fletcher, who greeted him.

"Andrea, fill me in on what you have so far on the man you feel is a good suspect."

"I have two. One is a man I met at the grocery store." Andrea hesitated as she pressed the on the button of her computer. "I have no real evidence he's connected, but he approached me a number of times for a date." She cringed when she saw Conrad frown. "As I said, I don't have any concrete evidence, a hunch."

"You need to cover everyone who has given a lead on this case," HD added. "What else do you have?"

"Evan Morrison is Roxanne Saunders' brother. Darron and Roxanne have their own "cabin" along the lake." Fletcher pointed to the house near the lake. "We don't have an apartment or house that Evan pays for. I'm guessing he uses one of the guesthouses on the lake as his home.

The neighbors thought he worked for a medical appliance manufacturer as a salesman. I found out this man travels from St. Paul to Milwaukee, Wisconsin. Then from here to Dallas, Texas, and all points in between. He does visit as far west as Omaha, and he covers western Iowa along the I-35 corridor, down to Dallas."

The next map showed red dots of missing women during the last three years inside those areas.

"This isn't a complete list of women. It's still a work in progress." Andrea interjected.

"One man can't be killing all those women. We took the women whose body parts were found, created a composite type, and matched it to any missing women. We came up with ten. There were more, but the parameters we used were tight. I limited it to any found in the I-35 corridor."

"You two have done a lot of work on this." HD sat on the edge of the table; his arms folded. "Do any of these have DNA we can match to the parts we have?"

"We haven't got that far." Andrea answered.

"We're going to need a warrant to find out who is using that code to go in and out of that property, but we need confirmation of this guy's movements. Where is he now, and where has he been in the last six months."

"Sir, we did surveillance at the house. We found Evan accesses the house regularly. He hasn't been out of the property for two days. We're not sure if it's his card that is used in these cases or if it's someone else."

"We need eyes on that cabin too," Conrad added then turned to discuss the situation with the head of the FBI.

"Good Job," Fletcher whispered to Andrea as they headed back to her desk. "Steve left the room sometime during the presentation."

Chapter 31

Conrad called Andrea to the conference room the following day. "I know you're busy on the serial killer case, but we need you to answer some questions." He gave Steve Totts a nod.

Steve sat across from Andrea. His expression exuded an arrogance. *What was he up to now?*

He picked up the sheaf of papers and, after banging them on the desk to straighten them, asked, "How well do you know Kaeli Meyers? Do you socialize with her?"

Andrea looked at Steve then at her boss. "Is this an interrogation? What's this all about? No, I don't socialize with her."

"The missing reporter sent you a text," Steve answered.

"I didn't get a text from Kaeli. I don't even have her phone number."

Steve pulled a sheet of paper from the folder in front of him and pushed it across to Andrea.

She didn't touch it as the paper slid to a stop in front of her. It was a list of texts from a phone carrier, and her number was listed at the top. Below a text was highlighted.

Andrea, we need to meet. We have to talk. There's something you are hiding, and if you don't talk, I will.

"I never saw this." She looked up at the two men. She pulled her phone from her pocket and set it on the table and pushed it across to them. "Check it out. There will be no text from this woman to me.."

Conrad leaned on the table. "Andrea, please. We have to do this. We know you didn't receive the text. It wasn't sent. It was still on her phone when we found it in her apartment."

"What was she talking about? What does she think you're hiding?" Steve asked. His tone sounded classic "good cop."

"Steve, if you know something, tell me. I'm not playing the fishing game. Remember, I attended the academy too. I know how this works."

Steve sat back into the chair and gave her a suspicious look. "She's missing. You're the one person had in her planner to contact that day. The text she didn't send. She may have been interrupted before she could send it."

Conrad pushed her phone back across the table. "What does it mean?" he tapped the paper.

"I told you, we talked when she came into the station. Fletcher was in the room the whole time and can verify there was nothing untoward said by either of us. We left amicably."

"I know all about it. The interview was recorded." Conrad tipped his head to acknowledge the fact.

Andrea felt the rise of anger but held it down, keeping her voice even. "Then you know what we talked about."

"Everyone saw her come in, and the three of you go into the interrogation room. I don't know who flipped the recorder on. I was told about it later." Conrad's gaze turned to Steve, who stared at the space between herself and the door.

"This is a checkup on me?" She directed her question to Conrad.

"Not personally. I'm glad this time it was done. We have proof there was no ill will between the two of you.

Steve leaned forward, resting his arms on the table. "Why did she act like that? Why did she think you weren't doing your job or maybe doing it too good?"

Andrea thought about the envelope Fletcher showed her. How did he get it and not the police, or had they?

"You've been to her apartment? You must have looked at everything she had there. Including an envelope of news clippings."

"You saw them? How did you see them?" Steve asked. He looked at his boss. "Sir?"

"I talked to agent HD. He said to give them to Fletcher to have Andrea to look at it."

"Sir, that was evidence." Steve glared at Conrad.

Conrad chewed his lip then addressed Andrea. "What did you make of the articles in the envelope?"

"Not much. Fletcher and I read through them. She had some misconception that I'm like my father." Andrea leaned forward. "I'm not." She let the words drop into the silence with a profound exclamation. "He has his issues and feelings. I never question them. If they work, then what's the problem? If they don't, there's always good detective work. I pick the latter. It's more trustworthy."

"Then you don't have the same ability as your dad?" Steve's question was more of an accusation.

Andrea didn't answer. The two men across from her stared at her waiting for her to continue.

"Sir, we all have different skill sets. We've discussed this before. My father has his, and for whatever reason, they work very well. I use the tools I learned at the academy. If I have some way of thinking outside the box that works for me, it's a skill. I don't claim any woo-woo power." She sat back in the chair, closing that issue.

"Then let's take a look at what we have and work with. You have no idea why Kaeli wanted to talk to you? Nothing about the conversation the two of you had in the interrogation room. You have no inkling?" Conrad leaned forward, resting his crossed arms on the table.

Andrea let a short time pass before answering. "She had an issue with my dad." A long breath passed between them. "She insisted that I was somehow using this ability she claims I have to find the killer. It was going to be her big scoop, is my guess. Since I wasn't playing her game she is insisting I'm hiding it."

Conrad and Steve looked at each other. "Okay." Conrad nodded at her. "Andrea, we had to follow up on this lead. We don't think you had anything to do with Miss Meyers's disappearance. We have to clear everyone, including you."

Andrea nodded. "Is that all?"

Conrad nodded. Andrea followed Steve and Conrad as they returned to the squad room and joined the rest of the team, "What do we have on Kaeli Meyers?" Conrad asked the group.

One of the women, seated at her desk, looked up from her laptop. "We know she left the station at about five-thirty that night. We have her car stopping at a chain restaurant to pick up food, then at dry cleaners to pick up her laundry. After that, we don't have any camera's where she shows up. We don't know where she went. We assume she went home. One of the officers is checking neighbors for home mounted cameras."

"So, at, say six-fifteen in the morning, give or take, she is missing." Conrad looked at the team, "Come on, people. This is the twenty-first century. People don't disappear off the face of the earth."

Andera leaned over to Fletcher, "Maybe they should look into Ethan's movements today."

"Miss Watson has a suggestion." Fletcher raised his hand. Conrad and the others looked at Andrea, who felt her face heat from the attention.

"Go ahead, Miss Watson." Conrad gave her a look she couldn't read.

"Here is the address where this vehicle was at some point yesterday. We may need to track its owner's activity."

"Why this guy?" One of the men gave her a quizzical look.

Why indeed? What made me say that? Why would Evan have anything to do with Kaeli's disappearance? "It's something we're working on. He is a possible person of interest." She shrugged and wished she'd kept her mouth shut.

"We need evidence." Steve retorted.

Andrea started to turn away. *I don't need this. I have better things to do.*

"Steve, we need to check out every lead," Conrad ordered. "Andrea, give the team what you have so far."

Andrea stood with all eyes in the room on her and provided the data she had on Evan Morrison. "We can't pick on people because they fit the profile. They can become suspects because they have motive and opportunity. We aren't sure what this serial killer's motive is. I don't think anyone knows for sure. Keep your eye out for his SUV.

Steve dismissed the group after agreeing with Andrea.

Andrea joined two officers looking at videos from CCV cameras. It was tedious work. She moved to stand to one side so she could view each of the screens.

She recognized the streets and landmarks. They began to fly faster as they looked for cars matching Evan's.

One of the videos on a screen slowed and a black SUV turn a corner and pull into a pharmacy parking lot. She pointed to the screen, "That's him."

"We're on it." The woman said.

"Can you tap into the Pharmacy video? The screen went blank and Andrea ground her teeth in frustration. The view came back as a man that looked like Evan entered the drugstore. It was a half an hour later he exited the store. He wore a thick winter coat and a knitted scarf tied around his neck. His hat, a fur lined trapper's hat, covered most of his face. He stood at the curb, then turned to walk down the sidewalk to the vehicle.

"It's him." She whispered.

"How can you tell?" Fletcher joined her after her exclamation. "With all that winter wear on we can't get a positive recognition,"

The view changed and flashed fast again.

"Wait! Go back. "She moved to the screen. "Go back to that guy in the trapper hat."

"Why? We don't have any confirmation." The woman shook her head. HD waved his arm for her to continue. The screen sped up.

"Please, I need to watch that video again. I need to see where he went."

"I'm sorry, we don't have time to watch home movies. We have a killer to catch. Unless you have some positive reason, we'll continue."

Andrea wrapped her arms around her waist. What was she to do? "Can I access this video in a separate feed?"

"You're wasting time." The other man turned away. "I'll email you the link."

She went back to her desk. She sat down and wiggled the mouse. How to access the video?

Two hands settled on the back of her chair as she tapped on the keys. A video feed box appeared on the screen.

"Which one do you want?" The man behind her intoned.

She'd seen him working. Jimmy rarely spoke and he was always tapping on a computer. She smiled at him and started to get up.

"Jimmy, stay I could use your help." Andrea pulled the chair closer to her desk. "I want the feed from the pharmacy."

Reaching across her, he pulled the laptop toward himself. In a few seconds, the screen showed a four-camera view. The feed sped by, but none were one she wanted. Then the view of the pharmacy appeared. She pointed, "That one."

He tapped the bar, slowing the feed until she could watch it again. Something was odd about the man leaving the pharmacy. His walk was slower and not as steady as the man who'd entered the building.

"Go back to where he comes into the building. Can we follow him until he leaves?"

"Sure." Jimmy pulls up the four videos and they watched each one as it tracked Evan through the store. He stops an employee who points toward the back of the store. Evan enters the restroom. Jimmy starts to change the view.

"Stop. Wait a minute." Andrea lays her hand on Jimmy's arm. "Who is that?" She points to an older man hurrying toward the back of the store.

"Look how he's walking. Odd." Jimmy observed.

Andrea felt a small smile grow on her lips and she stopped it. "He's on a mission to the bathroom."

"Now you see through walls?" Jimmy looked up at her, his eyebrows raised.

"I've been with a friend who sometimes has bowel issues and we've had to make sudden stops for her to hit the bathroom. Here he enters the bathroom." She directs the focus to the screen.

"Ok, now what?"

"Let's watch where they go when the two men leave."

The two men were in the bathroom for about fifteen to twenty minutes when the man wearing the fur hat and overcoat leaves and heads to the front of the pharmacy.

"There he is, let's move on."

"Jimmy, if that's Evan, he'll go right to his car." Andrea watched the man leave the building and stop on the curb. He looked around the parking lot then headed to an SUV and when the lights on a different SUV flickered, he changed course and entered the vehicle. The camera caught the front of the car and they watched the man adjust the seat before starting the car and leave the lot.

"That wasn't Evan."

Jimmy swore and turned back to the camera facing the restrooms. The man leaving wore an ill-fitting jacket that wouldn't close and a stocking cap. He didn't buy anything but went straight towards the front of the store.

Jimmy flips to the front view camera as the man leaves the store. The outside camera shows the man, with a stocking cap, walk to a car parked in the handicap space after the front lights blink.

When he sat in the driver's seat, he adjusted it after clipping the seatbelt and backed out of the space. Andrea and Jimmy followed the car's progress as it left the lot.

"We need to follow that car to the old man's house."

Jimmy nodded. "I'll go back to my desk and check ccv cameras."

"What do you have?" Fletcher asked when he returned to his desk. "Steve has been eyeing you the whole time Jimmy's been here."

Andrea stood and looked across the room as Jimmy spoke into his phone. He looked up at her and frowned. She turned back to Steve's office and saw him on the phone also. He gave her a sneering smile. She sat down hard on the chair.

"What's wrong?"

Andrea felt anger flow through her then turn to frustration. "We're a team here, we share everything we find. Then Steve gets this idea that he has to be the hero in the story."

Fletcher didn't answer. "I get it. He's not a team player. It's something you'll have to deal with. Knowing you may have found an important clue is going to have to be enough." His voice calmed her. She let her head drop back on her shoulders and stared at the ceiling. The frustration eased and she went back to work.

Jimmy called her to come to his desk. "Look at this. I followed the SUV and the car to the same area. We need to look if any of the houses in that development have that car in their driveway."

"I'll check it out."

She headed back to Fletcher and told him what they found. "Let's see if we can find the car if we drive around the neighborhood." She grabbed her purse and keys.

"Hold on. Are you going to tell Steve?"

Andrea's lips pursed in frustration. "Do I have to?"

He cocked his head and raised his eyebrows at her in question.

"Alright." She picked up the phone and punched Steve's phone button.

"Watson."

"I've got a lead I want to follow. A car that one of the suspects drives. Not sure if he tried to throw off suspicion or not. Could be a wild goose chase." She kept her voice casual.

Steve paused for a minute then said, "Fine. Let me know what you find out. Does this have anything to do with the man in the drug store? Jimmy said it was a dead end. The guy left the store and drove home."

"Yeah, well I want to make sure he went straight home."

"You think he didn't?"

"Don't you think we need to follow a lead until we rule all the suspects out?"

"Yes. Go ahead. I need that report when you get back." He hung up.

"Let's go." She returned the phone to its holder and headed toward the door.

Fletcher and Andrea searched each street in the area Jimmy indicated. They looked at each driveway for the car in the video.

After a few blocks, a police car lit up behind them, and Fletcher stopped.

The officer came to the window. Fletcher showed his badge, and Andrea showed hers

"What are you doing driving around here? I got a call a suspicious-looking vehicle driving slowly up and down the streets." The officer looked at Fletcher's ID and back to him.

"We are looking for a sedan with a possible handicap license or tag that matches what we found on a surveillance video."

The officer looked them over. "Okay, tell me what you're looking for and I'll help. That should satisfy any neighborhood watchers."

"That would be great." Andrea sent a picture of the car to the officer's phone. He drove off.

It wasn't more than an hour later; Andrea got a call.

"I think I found it." The officer gave them the address.

"Do you want me to question the owner?" The officer acted eager.

"I think we'd better do it. We have some information we need to corroborate. The FBI thanks you for your help." Fletcher saluted the young officer.

"Any time you need help, call me."

"We may need to." Andrea smiled, waving to the young officer as he drove off. "How do you think we should handle this?"

Fletcher grinned at her. "We're a team?"

She smiled back and nodded. "All for one, one for all." She got out of the car and waited for him to join her.

The car they'd seen Evan driving now sat in the driveway.

Andrea rang the doorbell, and she could hear a faint "Just a minute," coming from inside. The sound of a couple of deadbolts unlocking preceded the door opening, and the same man who'd entered the bathroom stood on the other side of the storm door.

"We're from the police department. Could we ask you a few questions?" Andrea smiled.

"What can I help you with?" His watery eyes moved from one to the other.

"We are looking for a—a missing woman. We are questioning anyone who might have seen her." Fletcher offered.

"Who's missing?"

"Could we come in? It's pretty cold out here." Andrea held her badge out and Fletcher showed his.

The man opened the door. "Come on in." He moved away, allowing them to enter and follow him to a seat in the living room.

"Who are you asking about?" He repeated.

"I'm Detective Andrea Watson, and this is Agent Fletcher Peterson. Can I have your name?"

"Brian Wilson and not the singer." He grumbled.

"Mr. Wilson, did a man approach you in the pharmacy restroom and ask you to change clothes and car with him?" Andrea figured she wouldn't beat around the bush with this guy,

Brian stared at her for a long moment. At first, she thought he wasn't going to answer. "How do you know this?"

"Big Brother," Fletcher answered. "His eyes are everywhere."

"In a public bathroom? My goodness, this world is going to hell fast." The words spat from the old man with such heat, Andrea thought he would have a seizure.

"No, Sir, not in the restroom. We saw a man go in then you went in. When the two of you left, there was some question as to whether you went to your own cars." Andrea explained.

He didn't answer, watching the two. Andrea added. "You do admit to that fact?"

"I don't admit to anything. If you have something on me, then arrest me." He held out both of his hands to be cuffed.

The sound of the storm door being opened then the front door flew open. A woman almost to a stop at the entrance to the living room. "Dad, what's going on here? I got a call from Joe some Dicks, pardon me, police were here. What do you do want with my father?" she asked the two.

"Calm down, Mary. It's nothing to worry about. They have some questions they thought I could help them with. Right?" He looked at the two with a smile pasted on his lips.

Fletcher stood and turned to the woman giving her his best-dimpled smile. "Mary, I'm Fletcher Peterson. We are asking your father a few questions about someone he may have seen while he was at the pharmacy."

"Pharmacy! What were you doing at the pharmacy? When was this?" She directed the questions to her father.

"A couple of days ago, after I left your house," Brian spoke up.

"You were supposed to go straight home. What were you doing at the pharmacy?"

Brian didn't answer. A long uncomfortable silence filled the room.

"Mary, I think it was an emergency stop. You know how we all have those moments when we have to make that decision to take care of business right away, or we'll be taking care of business long after we get home." Fletcher spoke in a whispered tone to Mary.

Brian stared at the floor.

"Oh." She turned to Andrea, "What did he see? How do you even know he was there?"

"We were asking him about a man he saw at the store." Andrea turned to Brian. "What did Evan say to you?"

"You seem to know more about him than I do. I didn't find out his name until he picked up the SUV."

"What?! Dad, what were you doing?" Mary moved to stand next to her father. Her arms folded under her ample breasts, she glared at him.

"Ma'am, this is a sensitive case. Could I ask you to give us some privacy?"

"Does he need a lawyer?" The woman looked at Andrea.

"Oh, no, not that. I need Mr. Nelson to confirm a man's identity, but as I said, this is a special case." Andrea left the sentence hanging while she looked at Mary.

Mary looked at her father, then at the two officers. Neither looked as if they were going to speak, she turned to stride down the hallway. They heard a door slam. Andrea turned back to Brian.

"Please tell us what happened." Fletcher held his notebook and pen ready.

"All right. I was in a hurry to get to the bathroom. I went into a stall. After a moment, I heard a toilet flush and movement at the sink. The person didn't leave. When I stepped out of the stall, a man stood there as if waiting for me.

I nodded at him and washed my hands. While I was drying them, he asked me if I wanted to make a couple of hundred dollars.

I thought he was joking or propositioning me. I told him I wasn't interested, ja know.

He laughed and said he wasn't either. He needed to ditch his ex-wife, who was stalking him. He told me if I'd trade coats and hats and drive his SUV to my house, he'd drive my car home. I looked at him and thought an extra two hundred would be easy money, so I agreed.

It all went as smoothly as he said. I walked out, keeping my head down, and found his car. I drove home. I was a little scared he wouldn't show up with my car or the money, but I had his nice SUV, so I was sure he'd be there ya know.

He drove up and came into the house, where we changed coats and hats. He gave me three hundred and fifty dollars for trusting him and left."

"Did he tell you his name?" Andrea wondered aloud.

"No, but I looked at his registration. It said, Evan Morrison. He lives off Rice Street or up north. I think the address was Lino Lakes."

Andrea nodded. "That's him, alright."

"What'd he do?"

Fletcher answered his question. "I can't say because we have some questions for him. What he did has us suspicious. Did you notice anything in the vehicle that looked out of place?"

"Like what?"

"Any woman's things, like he might have had a wife or girlfriend in his car?"

"Well, now that you mention it. There was a tag stuck between the seat and the center console. It had a woman's picture on it and a TV ID. I thought lucky him to be dating a big TV personality."

"Did you recognize the name or picture?"

"Oh yes, it was that cute little reporter, Kaeli Meyers."

Chapter 32

April brought days of sunshine that melted the ice on the lakes. It didn't warm the water by any means, but plans were made to use the underwater robots to look for any other body evidence that might be in the lake.

Andrea stood on the deck of the pontoon, watching the screen of the computer. One of the officers tried to elbow her out of the way several times, but she held her ground until the man running the machine gave him a job away from the computer.

"You can see how clear the water is? That's why they use the ice from this lake for the Palace. The people around here are adamant about not throwing trash or garbage into the lake. The homeowners association hired off-duty wardens to police the fishermen. There are motorized restrictions on the lake." The man in front of the screen gave her a wink. "By the way, I'm Greg."

"Andrea." She answered, her eyes still on the screen. They'd pulled away from the dock a few yards and put the robot camera in the water. Right away, a clear picture of the bottom of the lake came into view. Curious fish bumped the new object, and she'd laughed when one found the camera's eye and tried to eat it.

Her eyes followed the optical path the rover took as it made it's way back and forth in a grid they'd marked on the map. The grid covered a stretch from the dock to the deepest part of the lake. If they found nothing in that sector, they'd move to the next sector. Andrea felt confident they would find what they were looking for in this sector. She had no idea why she felt this way. She told Fletcher that morning in the office, "It's a gut feeling. You know, all cops and most moms have it."

Fletcher raised his eyebrows at her. "Yeah, we have them, and if we're lucky, they pan out fifty percent of the time. On the other hand, I've heard that in your case, it's at least seventy-five percent or more correct."

Andrea shrugged. "Dumb luck."

"If you say so. Still, I'll stick with your feelings." He'd been called to a meeting so didn't go out to the lake with her.

Now, after two hours had passed and there were no signs of anything on the bottom of the lake, she wasn't so sure she was right.

She rubbed her neck and stretched. Turning toward the shore, she scanned the Saunders's property. Kayaks and canoes were stored next to the house. Other houses along the lakefront had similar storage stands.

The dock had been pulled from the water and lay like a beached whale alongside the ramp.

Movement caught her eye. She saw a man standing on the porch of the cabin nearest the lake. He leaned against the wall watching the action on the lake.

She knew who he was even though she'd never seen him personally. He watched the action on the lake.

The man stood over six feet tall. She compared him to the windows behind him. He was solidly built. She took note of his jeans, a turtleneck with a sheepskin-lined vest. He wore a baseball hat pulled down over his forehead, sunglasses were visible under the brim. His arms were folded. Defensive as he watched the proceedings.

She didn't know how long he'd been there, but she knew when he looked at her. An eerie flowed through her body. She turned back to the screen, but the feeling didn't leave. That man hid his true self from others. She felt as if she were in the presence of evil.

She shut off any inner connection to the man on the shore and focused on the screen. The rover pushed its way along, stirring up silt in its wake. She saw something. "Stop! Go back," she ordered.

"What? What did you see?" Greg asked as he used the joystick to turn the rover around. Silt obscured the camera lens. He brought the robot up away from the bottom and waited while the water cleared a little.

"I thought I saw a cement block in the mud. It was partly covered with mud. It was half of a cement block." She leaned closer to the screen.

The silt cleared. Greg guided the robot down to the mud. The visibility was still low, but her eyes scanned the screen as it moved slowly through the water.

"There!" She pointed to the screen. Greg stopped the rover and brought it up to allow some of the silt to pass by, then brought it back over what she'd discovered.

Others gathered around; their gaze locked on the screen. A net tied to a cement block and enclosed was the outline that left little to the imagination—a skull. Long hair moved inside the sack as the rover disturbed the water.

Greg grabbed a different type of controller. A mechanical arm extended from the rover while a scissor-like device sawed at the cord. No one moved or said a word. When the last strand broke, a few of the men clapped. "Don't get too excited. We still have to see if Rosie can extract the net from the block and pick it up without spilling its contents."

No one moved, making sure the pontoon didn't rock. Time crawled by as Rosie-the-Rover floated to the surface with the bag in tow. When the evidence had been safely bagged and tagged, a roar and shout went up from the team members.

Andrea looked back at the shore. The porch was empty. The SUV that had been parked next to the cabin was gone.

The search wasn't over. A small rowboat sporting a small, electric motor attached to its side idled next to the pontoon. Andrea sat down as Steve exited the pontoon with the evidence bag in tow. Andrea stifled a grin as she watched Steve, perched on the bow, as it put-ted its way to the dock. She could have swum the distance faster than the small motor moved the boat.

She turned back to the screen. "Has the silt settled any?"

"I think I'm going to move out a little into deeper water. Not much, but the water is clearer and deeper. I'm going to turn on the light and give a general sweep across the bottom but not close enough to stir up the silt."

Andrea nodded and pulled her coat tighter to ward off the cold.

"You're cold. How about a cup of hot coffee? I think the excitement has cooled the adrenalin that warmed us up for a while there." Greg pulled a large, insulated container from under the table and a small cup with a lid.

"Thanks, I could use it. You're right, I was warm while I watched the screen. Now I'm cold." She took the cup and sipped the hot liquid.

He opened the lid to another box and pulled out a small tube. Unhooking the clasp, it unrolled to a lap blanket. "Here, wrap this around your legs."

"Hey Greg, you got one for each of us? We're cold too." Whined, his coworker then followed with a laugh.

Greg waved his hand for them to get back to work. They put Rosie back into the water and fed the line out so it wouldn't tangle.

Greg and Andrea watched the screen as Rosie's lights came on, and she moved through the water, her GPS recording where she was on the map. When she reached where Andrea had thought she'd seen the block, Greg moved the robot further out and down into the fading light.

The bottom dropped off a few feet past where they'd found the head in the net. Rosie sank into the darkness.

The light from the robot illuminated a muddy bottom. Several fish swam passed the light as it cut through the darkness.

Andrea pointed to something on the screen. "Can it go back?"

Gary turned on a second then third light to illuminate the bottom. Andrea gasped. Her fingers curled around the edge of the blanket, and she couldn't tear her gaze from the screen.

Greg softly swore the same word over and over, catching the attention the other officers, who came to stand next to them. Their swear words filled Andrea's ears, and she shut them out.

Concentrating on what she saw, she swallowed hard a few times. A dumpsite, unlike anything she could imagine lay revealed in the robot's light.

Not a couple of blocks outlined in the mud, but many of them. Some had landed on top of others. Some of the nets had been pulled by hungry fish, so the mud hadn't settled over them.

This dump field contained more than a couple of bodies. The silence stretched as Rosie-the-robot made her way across the dumpsite, illuminating the multiple net bags of partially decayed or consumed body parts.

There's no way to determine how many bodies are here. Andrea's stomach clenched, and she pressed her arm against it. This had to be the worst serial killer known to man.

Cars and vans filled the parking lot at Blue Lake. Men and women in white hazmat style gear ran back and forth from the dock to a box van. Andrea watched them carry plastic totes as she found a parking spot.

She found the FBI men huddled on one side of the big van and local police in mass on the other. She smiled for a moment. Where did she belong? She was a police detective. The FBI could fend for themselves.

"What's been brought up so far?" She asked Ben, who stood to one side of the group.

"So far, they've brought up enough to fill half the van with totes. Now they aren't full totes. Some had one or two bags in them. I saw an arm, a leg, or a head in one." He nodded at the pontoon out in the middle of the lake. "The divers have been going down in teams. They take time out in the trailer." He jerked his head to the long, Crime scene trailer parked at the back of the lot.

Andrea thanked him. She moved to the back of the truck and looked inside. Plastic strips hung over the opening. The drop-down lift was suspended halfway between the ground and the bed. Masked and suited personnel passed clear plastic totes from the back of an ATV in an assembly line into the van.

She stepped closer to the plastic totes on the ATV. She was curious. Inside the first one lay what was left of an arm encased in a crafting net. The arm hadn't been completely decimated by fish.

The netting had held the flesh together. It looked like something had tried to tear a hole in the net but failed.

Had he run out of fishnet and had to buy crafting net? She looked at one end. There were no fingers: a palm and the rest of the arm up to the elbow. The arm had been cut at the joint. The tote was whisked away.

She moved to the next tote. This one had the same netting, but a head lay inside. The hair looked to be dark blond or light brown. The skull turned away from her.

When one of the other totes was moved, this tote rocked and started to fall. Andrea grabbed the plastic and righted it onto the bed. Before she could let go, her vision blurred. She closed her eyes and steadied herself. A flash of feeling she was drugged came over her. The blurry image of a man, with a large build, stuffed the body parts into the bags. Then she was choking, fighting for breath. Tearing at whatever was cutting off her breath. Black rimmed glasses, her fingers grabbing a plaid flannel shirt.

"Andrea!" Her name being called broke vision, and she was staring at one of the officers. "Hey, are you okay?"

She shook her head. Heat rose to her face. "Yes, I must have stood up too fast. I got a little dizzy."

"Come and have a coffee." He took her arm, supporting her back to a tent where coffee and food were distributed.

"Thanks, Joe, I can make it. I'll get something to eat that will fix it." He nodded and turned away.

Warm air hit her, and the chill slowly seeped from her body. A woman with a broad smile she recognized from the cafeteria at the station handed her a cup. "Here, honey, you look like you could use a drink and a cookie. Are you okay? You look pale."

"I need something to eat." She smiled back and took the food to an empty table in the corner of the tent.

"Here's a sandwich. I think you need something more than a cookie." The cafeteria lady set it down in front of her. "If you're still hungry, tell me."

"Thank you." Andrea knew she would ask for the woman's name. One needed all the friends she could get at the station.

The hot coffee warmed her insides, and the sandwich tasted good despite the effort it took to chew it. On the napkin, she used her pen to draw what she remembered.

She wasn't an artist, but she drew the old style, black plastic frames. The eyes. What did she remember about the eyes? They looked round rather than elongated. Was it because of the lens's thickness or was it his eyes were like someone with Downs Syndrome. She was afraid to close her eyes even to think.

Next, she tried to recall his features. Nothing. She thought about the shirt. Plaid. No color, but the collar was torn. Like it had been pulled or ripped, a shirt underneath—dark-colored, crew neck.

"Andrea. What are you doing here?" Steve's voice broke the vision, and she looked up at him. "I came to see what was going on. It seems a lot of parts are being brought up. I noticed one or two wrapped in craft-type netting rather than the fishnet that the first parts were found in."

He gave her an inquisitive look. "I hadn't noticed." He looked around the room for a moment, then back at her. "Andrea. What that reporter said. Do you have-ah-uh-the ability to see things?"

"See things? You mean ghosts?" She kept her voice neutral.

"Yes." His response sounded like he was grasping at anything.

"No. I don't see ghosts."

"Are you-are you-what she said? Psychic?" He whispered as he leaned on the table beside her.

She lowered her voice. "No, I don't think so. Why?"

"Just curious." He straightened and adjusted his belt while looking around the room. "If you get a "feeling" about anything let me know. We'll run it down. We're a team, right?"

"Clues about the killer or clues about Kaeli?" Taking another bite of the sandwich she hoped to keep Steve from asking more questions.

Steve ran his hand through his hair. "Both. We have no clues, no one saw her at home. She lives alone, and no one saw anything."

"Steve, didn't she have security cameras?" The words popped out before she could stop them.

"Yes, but she didn't come home. She didn't tell anyone she was going somewhere or meeting anyone."

"You are checking for her car. I told the FBI we found her car being driven by some guy."

"What car? What guy?" Steve leaned down. "When did this happen?

"The other day, when Jimmy and I were looking at the video. We saw her car and a guy we couldn't identify driving it."

"How come you didn't tell me?" He growled at her.

"The FBI team said they'd get on it and coordinate with the team. I thought you were already working on it."

Steve swore, turned, and strode out the tent.

Chapter 33

Andrea left the tent and made a tour of the parking lot. Heading for her car, she turned toward the grove of trees dividing the parking lot from the Saunders' property. A movement caught her eye. An ATV stopped on the other side of the closed gates. After a moment, it headed away from the entrance.

Who was driving the ATV? The only car on the property was Evan's. If his car was there. Where was Kaeli?

It had to be Evan Morrison. He wouldn't park Kaeli's car next to his house. He'd have to hide it somewhere.

She called Fletcher. "Are you at the station?"

"Yes. Where are you?"

"At the lake. Are you anywhere near Jimmy?" She whispered.

"He's in the room. Why are you whispering?"

Andrea chuckled. "I have no idea. I'm in my car. Tell Jimmy to hack into the monitors at the airport. It's the best way to hide a car You can take the Light rail back into town and pick up your car and go home like it was a normal day."

He paused, and she could tell he was walking. "Jimmy, I have Andrea on the line." She heard muffled sound then Jimmy spoke.

"Hello Andrea, what do you have for me?"

She repeated what she told Fletcher. "Sure thing. I can do that. We know what the car looks like."

"Are you coming back to the station?"

Andrea paused. "No, I'm going to hang around here for a while. Call me if Jimmy sees anything."

"Andrea, don't do anything on your own. Call me. First."

"I won't." She gave the pat answer.

"I mean it. If you get any thoughts, inclinations, call me."

"Fletcher, I'm trained. I don't need a shadow."

"I'm your partner, don't forget that."

His voice made her smile. "Thanks, partner."

Across the parking lot, she saw the officers flying a drone. Once in the air, it flew over the lake back and forth. She headed over to where they were working.

"What's going on here?" The man staring at a laptop urned to look at her from her head to her boots. Then at the metal badge at her waist and back to her chest area. "Watson. Thee Detective Watson, from the news?" He raised his dark arched brows.

"That depends on what news you're referring to." She backed up a step, so he'd have to turn his body in the chair to look at her. He didn't and looked back at the screen. "I know who you are."

"Are you finding anything interesting?" Andrea questioned.

"No."

"May I ask you for a favor?"

He gave her a look through narrowed eyes, "Like what?"

"Can you swing the drone over the beach area next door and see if a car is parked next to one of the buildings?" She didn't smile but kept her gaze locked to his. It wasn't a request. He could have refused, but he gave a brief nod and picked up the two-way.

"Joe, swing Buddy over the cabin next to the lake."

"What?" the question squawked through the speaker.

"Just do it." The officer next to her responded.

Andrea moved behind the man and watched the screen. The image went from water to land. The guest house next to the dock showed up in full color.

Next to it sat the dark blue SUV. No one came out of the cabin when the drone swooped over it.

"Enough?" Came the operator's voice.

"Could he run the drone over the whole area from high up?" She gave him a weak smile.

"Sure." He gave the order.

Andrea watched the picture. There were no cars on the property except the SUV. The small forest area between the developed area and the dead-end road covered about an acre or two. She leaned over the man staring at the screen. Was that a building in the woods?

"Can you have him back the drone up to the dead end on the property?" She indicated the area at the edge of the road. There looked to be a small ATV hidden in the brush, she leaned closer, her cheek near the seated man.

"Do you mind?" He growled at her.

"Oh, I'm sorry. I wanted to see what that is." She pointed at something outlined in the viewer. "Doesn't that look like a shed?"

This time the man beside her leaned closer to the screen. "Tom, can you drop the drone down closer to the trees?"

"No! Don't! If he's there, he'll hear it. I don't want him to figure out we've found that building."

"Tom, you heard her."

He hovered above the area. The man focused the lens to zoom in and it was the roof of the well house.

"Thanks," She saluted him. "Thank the operator too."

Back in her car, she thought about what she'd seen. Could he be holding Kaeli in that shed or would she be in his cabin instead?

At home she assembled the ingredients for her favorite chili, the phone rang.

"Hello? —Hello?—Hello?" No answer, but she heard breathing. She listened to every breath, and a picture came into focus. She stared at the image. Thick, dark, glasses, small eyes, and then it faded in and out. She tried harder to focus on the image, but it disappeared. She heard a dial tone and hung up the phone.

Walking back to the kitchen, she felt a little dizzy. Gripping the counter, she grits her teeth, pushing back the feeling. The phone rang again. Hesitating, her hand hovered over the receiver, but she picked it up.

"Hello?" No response. She hears the slow deep breaths on the other end. "Hello? Who is this? Why are you calling me?" Still no response. The breathing deepened and quickened. Andrea disconnected the call and waited.

This time when the image came, it was a full figure. Evan. She recognized him as the man who stood on the porch of the lake cabin.

Andrea gripped the chair arms as she sank into the seat. Closing her eyes, she waited and fought the queasy feeling. Her head throbbed as another image took its place.

An implement she recognized as a hand-operated auger. A hole in the ice and gloved hands pushed net bags of body parts into the hole. Through the killer's eyes, she saw the head and face of a young woman. She didn't recognize the white face.

Another bag went into the hole, but she also saw this head with short, brown hair. A flower earring remained in the ear.

A phone ringing interrupted the image. This time Andrea picked up the phone. "Hello."

"Honey, what's going on? I'm getting an odd feelin' about you." Her father's concerned voice came as a relief.

"Dad." Her voice quivered. Her breaths were ragged.

"Talk to me, Andi." Her father's pet name for her.

"I saw him."

"You saw who?"

"The killer, Evan."

"How did you see him?"

"I saw him. I SAW him, in my mind."

"Oh. What exactly did you see? Tell me."

Andrea told him her vision in detail. "What do I do with this? Just because I saw him in a vision doesn't mean I can prove he's da killer." She rubbed her palms on her legs.

"All I can say is da more you open your mind and accept what you see, da more information you may get. It isn't always clear. You don't always get da one conclusive clue. It will give you a person ta follow up on. Did he have da opportunity? Where does he find da woman? How does he get dem? Focus your research on da physical evidence."

"Is that what you did? Did you get little bits here and there and match them to the evidence?" She stood and went back to the kitchen to check on dinner. Glancing at the clock, it was passed when Fletcher should have returned her call.

"Dad, one more thing. I got two weird calls. The person on the other end doesn't speak. I'm sure it's Evan. I got a flash of his round face, black glasses, and a plaid, flannel shirt. I could hear his breathing. It's not heavy sexual breathing but natural heavy breathing from someone with asthma or a nasal issue."

"Is your security on?"

"Yes. That's not his modus operandi. He gets friendly with his target then gets them alone. The women from Kansas and Missouri, if he's their killer, he took them on their way home. I'm guessing he offered them a ride. The police found one where her car wouldn't start. Someone had removed something."

"Probably da distributor cap.' Her father mumbled. "Be careful, Andi. When a serial killer is hunting, ders no one safe."

"I'm a public servant. I'm out in public all the time, you know dat." Andrea moved around the kitchen, wiping the counter after she'd already wiped it. She stopped and put the rag away and sat down in the living room.

"Andi!" her father shouted through the line. "Go to your bedroom now!"

Andrea reacted as she had as a child. She ran to her bedroom. Grabbing her service weapon from the nightstand, she flew to the closet and shut the door.

"What did you see, Dad?" She whispered into the receiver.

"Someone outside your patio door. Is it locked?" His voice registered his worry.

"Yes. It has the door bar on it, and I activated the security video. I'm in my closet with my weapon."

"Don't go nowhere tonight."

"Dad, I can't do that. I'm meeting Que at the Hmong Community meeting. They are discussing issues with Police harassing dem and their children being pulled into Hmong gangs."

"Don't go. Let someone else go and speak on behalf of da police."

"Who? Da Hmong people already don't trust da law. They do trust me, and I need ta be dere." Andrea stands and eases the closet door open. She didn't hear anything and holding her weapon ready, she moved through the house. She switched to the video mode, no one stood at her door.

"Can you call your FBI friend to go wit you?" He asked.

"I invited him to dinner, but he hasn't called me."

"Call him. If he can't go wit you, get anudder officer to come and get you." Her dad's voice didn't brook any argument.

"Dad?" her voice rose with the question.

"Andrea," Using her full name, meant he was serious. "I felt someting evil about your house. It's aimed at you."

"Okay, Dad. I'll call Fletcher."

"Be safe girl." Her dad hung up.

She called Fletcher's phone, and this time he answered.

"I'm almost there."

"Okay. Check around when you get here. I tink someones hanging around my house."

"You've been talking to your dad?"

"Yes, he called me. How did you know?"

"When you talk to him, you revert to sounding like you're up nort."

"Oh, yeah. I do that."

"I'm here. I'll look around before I come in."

There was no one around the house. He drove her to the meeting.

"I'm calling the station to have a couple of officers over to patrol the meeting. We'll keep an eye out for Evan." Fletcher gave her a quick but hard look as he drove. "You sure it was Evan Morrison you saw?"

"It wasn't me that sensed him. It was my dad. Who else would it be?" She didn't add that she trusted her dad even when she didn't admit that he had a sixth sense.

Andrea spoke to the Hmong people who packed the room, in their language. Their response to her speech gave her and the other officers a good feeling about moving forward.

Fletcher drove her home. "Are you okay?" He checked her house and cleared it.

"I'll be fine, but if you are concerned, maybe you can stay here?" Andrea laid her hand on his chest.

"I can do that." Fletcher bent and planted a kiss on her forehead.

The next morning, Andrea found Ben putting a coffee pod in the machine. "Ben, do you remember interviewing Ron Cox?"

"Who's Ron Cox?" He pressed the button to activate the water.

"The guy near the cul-de-sac."

"The old guy with all the carvings outside?"

Andrea shrugged. "I didn't question that neighbor."

"Yeah, the old guy didn't have anything worth following up."

"Did you notice if there was a road or driveway off the cul-de-sac?"

"What are you getting at?"

"I read Mr. Cox's interview, and I wondered if there was more than one way on to the Saunders' property? You wrote in your report that kids used the woods at the edge of the property next to his, to smoke dope. He'd run them off for fear they'd start a fire."

Ben stared at the machine as it dripped coffee into his cup. "If that's what I wrote that's what he said." Ben shrugged. The old guy didn't look like he had it all together.

"You wrote he told you an original house was torn down and all that was left was a well house."

"So? What does that have to do with the dead bodies and the missing news reporter?"

"I don't know" Her upper teeth worried her bottom lip.

"Are you getting a woo-woo feeling or is it your famous 'gut feeling'? he crooked his fingers as if the term was in quotes.

"Thanks." Andrea barely got the words out before she turned and left the break room.

"Who's property, was it? Could she go and check it out?

Chapter 34

When Andrea arrived at the station, she called Steve. "Fletcher and I followed up on that video we looked at the other day."

"What? What have you two been up to?" his tone was short and clipped.

"We should call a meeting of our Kaeli team and the task force."

"Are you calling the shots here?' He snapped at her.

"No. You can do what you want. You've been informed." She hung up, making sure she didn't slam the phone down.

Steve called a meeting, and the two groups gathered in the squad room as they couldn't all fit in the conference room.

"Miss Andrea." Steve called across the room, "Do you have something you want to share with the class?" The room seemed to go silent as all conversation either ceased or got softer.

Andrea froze, embarrassed at his calling attention to her. She looked at Fletcher, and he nodded at her with a smile.

Steve stared at her. She looked him straight in the eye. Her hands shook, and she hoped this wasn't the mistake of her career.

Stepping forward, she reported what they'd found on the video and the interview with Brian Wilson, not the singer.

"How did you find all this out? What was your research process? I think we'd all like to know how it was done." Steve stood next to Conrad and challenged her.

"While we were looking at video's, Jimmy found one with the suspect's car turning into the parking lot. The suspect went into the pharmacy. I continued to look to see when he left and if we could track his car."

"So, you thought to follow some guy into a store?" Steve continued.

"Yes. That's exactly what I did."

"Why?'

"Curiosity."

"You said he went to the bathroom. Why did you continue to wait for him to leave?" The way Steve worded the question sounded like she was a pervert.

Andrea let the corners of her lips lift to a slight smile. "We were watching the man wearing a coat and hat. It was his walk as he left the store that struck me odd."

"So, you followed a man you thought looked odd to his car?" Steve leaned forward; his arms crossed.

Andrea took a deep breath and widened her eyes a little. "Yes, Sir, we did. As I said before. Brian told us how it went down." She recounted Brian's story and how it matched what they'd seen on the video.

After a moment of silence, Steve straightened. "Dave, you and Ronnie go pick up this Evan. Bring him in for questioning."

Andrea stepped forward, "NO!"

Everyone froze then turned to face her. Steve glared at her. "Excuse me?"

"I'm sorry. I didn't' mean to shout. We can't pick him up. We may never find Kaeli. We don't have enough evidence on him." She looked at Conrad for help.

He looked at Steve. "You might change the pick-up order to a tail order. We need to find out where he goes and what he does."

Steve's jaw clenched and unclenched, then he said, "Dave, Ronnie, you go tail the guy and keep me informed at all times." He turned to Andrea, "You, report anything you find on this guy to me before you do anything.

It felt as if everyone heaved a sigh. The rest of the officers moved back to their cubes and cases. Andrea followed Jimmy to his computer.

"Jimmy, work your magic." Fletcher leaned over the tech's shoulder while Andrea stood on the other side of him.

"The camera didn't show anyone else in the car with him. She has to be at a fixed location. If he's the one who has her." Andrea bit her lip. Where was he keeping her? Could she be at his cabin on the lake?

They followed the car on the video cameras until there wasn't any more to access. The three of them sat back. "He was heading south, not north toward the Blue Lake property. Did he have another home?" Fletcher offered.

"Where does his sister live?" Andrea asked out loud. "I need to get to my computer."

"Wait. What's her name?" Jimmy pulled up a screen with an official logo. He typed in his access.

"Her name is Roxanne Saunders."

Fletcher tapped on his computer, and after a minute or so, he turned the screen to show Andrea and Jimmy.

Jimmy typed in the address. The blip on the screen expanded, and the street and address showed.

"Is there any way to log into any of the personal cameras on the street? She asked.

"Not without permission," Fletcher responded.

"Is there a patrol in the area that could do a visual?"

"You think he'd leave the car at the curb?" Fletcher answered a bit sarcastic.

Andrea pressed her lips together, then stood up.

"I'm sorry, Andrea, that wasn't called for. I just reacted. I didn't mean it to come out like that," his expression pleaded for forgiveness.

She took a deep breath, nodded, and walked to Steve who stood talking to the other agents. "Yes, Miss Andrea?"

"I think we need to have a patrol car cruise, David's sister's house. He may be there."

He smiled at her, "You're catching on. HD told me already. We have a patrol there and watching the lake property. We think he's the possible person of interest."

While she stood there, a call came from the patrol. One of the detectives called out of a cube, "No one is at the Saunders's residence."

"Which one?" Steve called out.

"Darren Saunders."

"How about the lake property?" she asked.

"Call the patrol at the lake. Any sign of our guy yet?" Steve asked out loud.

"Nothing yet." she heard someone call out.

"What is going on here? Why is everyone shouting?" Conrad called out, his heavy tread heralded his arrival.

"We're checking with the surveillance teams," Steve answered.

"How come I'm not in the loop?" His voice rose slightly.

"You are holed up in your office, Andrea mumbled as she leaned over Jimmy looking at his screen.

"Something's not right. He's had plenty of time to get to either property. Where else would he go?"

"What are you looking at? How are we seeing this property so close?" Conrad looked at the computer screen.

"Drone."

"Drone? What drone?" Andrea pulled a chair from the next cube to sit next to Fletcher.

It was almost four o'clock. "Where's the guy running it?"

"In the public parking lot. He's in an unmarked car. He's parked near the bathrooms." Jimmy showed her the portion of the parking lot in the view.

The drone passed along the trees at the end of the parking lot. No cars were visible in the Saunders compound. The drone looped over the four guest cabins. No sign of life. Andrea shivered, but not from the cold.

"What now?" She asked Fletcher and Jimmy.

"We keep looking." They all stared as the drone flew over the Saunders' property then around the far end of the lake properties. No sign of Evan's SUV.

Andrea walked away from the group to her cube. Where was Evan? Where could he have gone?

She opened her file and turned the pages, looking for some clue that would put more of the puzzle together. From the early days of the search, she'd been given a map of the property around the lake. She and Fletcher, as well as the other officers, had questioned everyone who owned lakefront homes.

She opened the file again and looked at each report. She matched it with the property owners. She looked at the information given to them by Ron Cox, the old man at the end of the lake.

He's been one of the first to buy a lot from the original Saunders. What had he said? She turned the page, reading what had been typed. There it was a paragraph. "The original house was torn down. All that's left in the woods is the well-house. They left it to protect anyone from falling into the well. It's been boarded up, but smart kids can get in there."

Andrea leaned over Jimmy's shoulder to view the screen. The drone circled the lake and now headed back to the parking lot. It made a wide swoop over the property and though the evergreens covered some of the land, the bare aspens and birch trees revealed a leaf-covered roof of a small building. The well house.

Andrea returned to her desk in long strides. She sent Fletcher a message stating she'd call him later. Grabbing her coat and bag, headed to her car.

Turning on to the frontage road, she drove away from the Sanders property. Following the road around the lake until she passed the old man's house. He wasn't on his porch today. No one was outside their home today. The snow melted rapidly in the warmer spring weather.

After passing the second entrance, the road ended at the cul-de-sac. Blackberry bushes over six feet high lined the curb around the circle. She parked, got out, and followed the curb until she saw a small path, almost imperceptible to anyone using the turn-around. Unless a person knew the opening was there, it was sufficiently hidden from the casual drive-by.

Pulling her coat close and tucking her red gloved hand in her pocket, she followed the well-used path into the wooded area. She smelled the sweet scent before she saw the two boys huddled in a makeshift fort under low hanging tree branches.

"Hello." She greeted them and almost laughed when they jerked back so fast they fell over each other. They couldn't have been more than fourteen or fifteen years old. "I take it you two don't mind breaking the law. You just don't want to get caught."

The two boys sat like lovers staring at her. Their eyes were huge. A slow grin appeared on their faces. "Hi. Do you want some? We'll share."

"No, I think you've had enough."

"How'd you find us? No one knows about this place." One of them tried to stand but fell over his friend's feet, then lay there laughing.

The other boy stood and knocked his head on the roof of the fort, causing a cascade of slush to cover them. This set the fallen boy to laughing even harder.

"Jim, knock it off." his friend ordered.

"It was too funny." Jim tried to brush the icy snow from his jacket.

"What are you going to do?" The one standing asked Andrea.

"I need some information. Do you come here often?" Andrea asked.

"Not too much. Just when we want to get away from our parents."

"Where do you live?"

"Why do you want to know?" Jim stood next to his friend.

"Do you explore the woods around here?"

"Yes. We've been all through these woods. Someone built this fort years ago. We kind of took it over and fixed it up."

"No one but the two of you use it?" She continued.

"There are a few other kids that used to come here. Some have moved. Others are older, and I guess they don't want to hang out here anymore."

"So, what else is in these woods?" Andrea turned from them and peered through the dense underbrush.

The two boys looked at each other, then at Andrea. "Trees." They giggled.

She folded her arms and gave the boys a look. The boy named Jim continued. "There's nothing else here except an old well house. You can't get into it because it's locked."

"Have you ever seen anyone go into the woods or use it?" She raised her eyebrows.

"No, but there is a guy that walks in the area a few times. I've always hidden, so he's walked past me."

"Did you ever spy or follow him?"

"No. He walks around but never came over here. He seemed to be on a mission or something." The boys looked at each other. Andrea wondered what the inside joke was.

"This guy parks over here and walks into the forest and never saw your fort?"

"No. He never comes this way."

"How do you get around? How would I find that well-house?"

"We could take you." The boy whose name she didn't know offered.

"I don't think so. Not this time. Both of you need to skedaddle out of here and head for home."

"Who are you? Why are you asking all these questions?"

"My name is Andrea. What's yours?" She smiled at them.

"I'm Jim, and this is Bobby." Jim moved to shake her hand.

Andrea pulled her hand out of his and held it out again, palm up, "I want your stash. All of it."

"What? I thought you were going to be a cool adult and let us be." Jim's cocky attitude became evident.

Andrea unzipped her jacked part way and pulled out the chain with her ID.

The boys swore and back peddled a few steps.

"I don't think smoking weed is cool. If you had a medical condition, we could talk about it, but that's not the case. Hand it over and head for home."

The two groused for a couple of minutes, then handed her the small baggies. She sniffed at them and then said. "Is this all you have?"

"Yeah, we smoked the joint," Jim said, shoving his fists into his coat pockets.

"Well, boys, that first one might have been the real deal, but this," She held up the baggies, "This is a tiny bit of weed and oregano."

"What?" The two boys burst out at the same time. They continued to swear.

"Hold on, that kind of language doesn't sit with me. Clean it up, or I'll tell your parents. There is no reason to use that kind of language. Get over it now before it becomes so ingrained you can't stop, then no one wants to be around you, especially employers. Tell me how to get to the well-house."

The two boys gave her basic directions. She watched as they made their way back down the path and disappeared into the bush. She hoped they continued out to the road.

It took her about fifteen minutes of trying to find her way. She ended up going down to the lake and walking along the shoreline. As the treelined moved away from the shore, she found the brush cut revealing a path. The remaining piles of snow had been disturbed. She looked closer and found boot prints in the mud, leading up the hill between the trees.

Careful not to step on any branches, she followed the boot prints walking as close to the edge and around the path until she saw where they turned up the hill.

She stopped about few steps from the building. It wasn't as small as she'd thought. A little bigger than the fishing cabins she'd seen on the lake. The wall facing her had new boards between the weathered ones. There were no windows on the side she stood, and no door.

The itchy feeling began to crawl inside her. She sensed someone watching her. She should go back to her car and call Fletcher. Her hand felt for the handle of her gun. *Go back now!* That inner voice told her. She started to turn and make her way back to the lake.

"Put your hands in the air." A deep voice ordered her from behind. She stopped and turned her head.

The figure between her and the well-house was Evan Morrison, and he held a gun pointed at her.

Chapter 35

Andrea didn't move. Evan had a firm and comfortable grip on the Ruger. He watched her, and she watched him.

"Put your hands in the air. I know it sounds corny, but I don't trust you not to whip out that gun and shoot me. Put your hands on the railing." He waved his gun to indicate the porch railing.

She walked up the incline to the porch and stepped onto the porch and gripped the smooth log that made up the top rail. Evan pulled the gun from her holster. He put the muzzle of his gun at her back. He laughed, a loud harsh laugh.

"You thought we were going in here? Nah, but I want you to see my first butcher shop." He gave another harsh laughed.

Andrea swallowed hard. Thoughts of escape swirled in her head. She needed to figure a way to get out of this.

"Stop. Move back and face the end of the deck." His voice sounded pleasant. Not too deep, not too high. Just even, like Evan. If her heart weren't beating so hard, she'd have liked to talk to him. That's why women went with him.

He pulled a key from a retractable holder and unlocked the door. "This way." His hand gripped her arm and roughly guided her through the door. He turned on the single, overhead light. "Welcome in."

She stumbled from the push and grabbed the back of the chair to keep from falling. Fear rose in her throat and she swallowed repeatedly to keep from throwing up.

She took in the chains hanging from the ceiling. Ropes and pulley decorated the walls. A covered well occupied the middle of the room. What could be interpreted as a field dress shed.

"What were you thinking, Andrea?"

"Nothing."

"You were too. I could see it in your eyes and the way you reacted. This was my first place." He leaned against the wall. "We aren't staying here. With all the cops around, I'd be a sitting duck. You were curious about this place, now you've seen it. Let's go."

"What if I didn't want to move. Are you going to kill me here?" Her voice broke a little as she tried to sound confidant.

Evan's eyes narrowed at her. "Are you going to resist? It wouldn't take much to put you down the well." He jerked his head to the object in the middle of the room.

She needed to figure a way out. He stood between her and the door. The window had wooden bars covering the opening. She could use her martial arts expertise to outmaneuver him. She sized him quickly and she had a fifty-fifty chance and if she could get him off balance.

Evan moved so fast she didn't have time to react. He wrapped a rope around her neck before she could stand and tightened it, cutting off her air. How had she not seen him get it?

"Don't move. I don't want to kill you, but I will if you do something stupid." His breath whispered into her ear.

She tried to tug at the rope, but he tightened it. "It takes about ten minutes to actually kill someone by strangling them. It takes time and patience."

"Stand up." She stood on shaky legs still trying to get her fingers between the rope and her windpipe. She began kicking him, using her hand to steady herself away from him for better leverage.

He eased the rope so she could breathe. Andrea, gasped air like a fish out of water, her fingers pulled at the rope. He used her acquiescence to zip-tie her hands behind her back.

Out onto the porch, his hand pressed her back, and his knees bumped the back of her legs. Evan locked the door. He took a fistful of the back of her jacket as he hurried her down the steps.

They didn't speak as he changed his grip from her jacket to her arm and pulled her beside him through the woods. She stumbled on a fallen branch. Evan held on to her and swore at her. "I hope you don't think that trick is going to work. I'll carry you over my shoulder if you do it again."

She watched the ground until the trees thinned, and they stopped by an ATV. The same one she'd seen through the gate earlier.

Evan helped her into the front seat and snapped her into a seatbelt. It was similar to a car one, but this one didn't give. It locked her into place. He didn't have to reach across to buckle it.

He looked around the woods before getting in and putting the vehicle into gear. It shot forward. It wasn't a road just grooves in the leaves.

At the end of the forest, a fence rose before them. How come she hadn't a fence at the edge of the property?

Evan stopped at a gate. While he unlocked it, Andrea rubbed her hands together behind her back. The red gloves stuck on her wrists. Keeping her movements as imperceptible as possible, she worked with precise movements until she felt the first glove slide off her hand. Gritting her teeth, she leaned a little to her left side to keep her hands out of his sight as he slid into the seat.

The ATV choked and didn't start when he returned. He fiddled with the knob and gas pedal. When the vehicle choked and jerked again, she took the opportunity to jerk the remaining glove off. Gripped in her right hand, the motor caught and moved forward, she moved to the edge of the seat.

As he drove through the gate she pushed the gloves onto the ground. She held her breath he wouldn't go to the lock. He pushed the gate and it closed with no notice the gloves. She sighed.

They drove through another wooded area. "Where are we?" She couldn't keep the question inside.

A smile spread across his lips. He threw back his head and gave a loud guffaw. "You never looked here." He turned to look at her for a moment. "You didn't look at all the properties around the lake even if they weren't connected to the family?"

Andrea mentally pulled up maps she'd studied. The lake with its plots around it became clear. There hadn't been any plots beyond the solid line denoting the Saunders property and the roads that outlined the other parameters. They hadn't looked at the properties that didn't access the lake. There was no reason to. She'd concentrated on the satellite maps that included the lake and roads. She remembered the trees behind the Saunders property. There had been a housing development to the north and east of the lake properties.

Her thoughts were interrupted when the ATV turned into an open area. The back of a two-story home lay in front of her. A triple car garage sat between them and the house.

Evan pulled to a stop next to an addition to the garage and house. Evan gripped her arm and pulled her from the ATV. With long strides, he marched her to a door to the addition.

Inside, she could smell bleach. A metal counter like a morgue table occupied a short wall. A morgue table on wheels stood next to it. White subway tile covered the walls. Knives and an assortment of power saws lined the shelves and wall.

Andrea took a step back, jerking her arm from Evan's, who tightened his grip so that pain shot up to her shoulder. "OWWW!"

She stepped toward him, hoping to ease the grip. He didn't.

"Don't do that again." He spoke through gritted teeth.

She nodded, and he eased his grip. He continued to a chair similar to the one she'd sat in at the well house. This one was metal, and the sight sent visions of possibilities and fear through her.

Chains hung from the ceiling; she could see it was some sort of restraint made for a head that could be adjusted. Right now, it was at its full height. She began to shake inside. She bit her lip to keep from screaming and crying.

He pushed her toward the chair. She began to fight him with all she had. She arched her back and kicked him. When he dodged, he elbowed her into the wall. Andrea threw back her shoulders, and while he tried to regain his balance, she kicked his knee, trying to unbalance him again. His knee buckled, and he swore, falling against her. With a flash of anger, he slapped her across the face.

Andrea fell back. He took advantage of her momentary stillness to push her onto the chair. She tried to fight but he had one hand clamped down. She continued to try to stand and fight with her right hand, but he fought her, overpowering her into the chair. He overpowered he and clamped her right hand in place.

"Sorry about that." His lips smiled, but it didn't reach his eyes. His rapid breath blew hot on her, "Don't do that again." With a quick motion, he had a band clamped to one wrist.

She bent one knee and leveled a powerful kick at his groin with the opposite foot. He swung to the side, narrowly avoiding the blow. Andrea recoiled her leg but she wasn't fast enough to reset. He moved out of range. She growled at him.

He strapped her ankles to the chair. She fought to get away, but it was no use.

"Oh, I like that." His face close to her's as he breathed on her cheek. "Keep it up, and I'll forget I like you."

Andrea twisted her face away. He moved across the room, opened a metal door, and disappeared.

While he was gone, she tried to find a way to unlock the clamps. No luck. Anger and despair took turns with her emotions.

Andrea made a note of her surroundings for a possible escape route. There were two atrium windows bringing light into the room. If she wasn't in this situation, she would have admired the vintage doctor's office cabinetry against the wall, an examination table with the stirrups locked in the air. If she wanted to describe the furnishings, she'd have said they came directly from some old sanitorium sale.

A door caught her eye behind an old-fashioned privacy screen with its cloth curtains. One section was folded toward her revealing the massive walk-in cooler style door. Immediately she felt cold.

The room wavered like heat waves on the summer asphalt. A fast forward movie flashed before her eyes. Evan carrying a frozen body from the cooler to the table and strapping it down. He picks up a power saws-all and begins to cut a woman's arms off. Andrea squeezed her eyes closed.

"What's wrong with you?" Evan demanded.

Andrea opened her eyes, the vision vanished. He stood inside the room, looking at her, waiting for an answer.

"Nothing."

Evan moved around the room, placing instruments on the tray. He hummed an unfamiliar tune.

"Are you too warm?" He moved toward her, and Andrea shrank back into the chair.

Her heart beat faster with each of his movements. She tried to think of some way to distract him.

"Stop it. I'm just going to take off your coat. You'll be more comfortable." He let go of her one hand at a time, standing behind her until he'd taken her coat off and hung it on a hook next to one of the doors.

He ignored her as he went back to arranging the room to his satisfaction.

"Where's Kaeli?" Her voice sounded strident in the silence.

He turned his head to look at her. "Kaeli? Kaeli, who?"

"You know who she is. You were driving her car. You left it at the airport." She leaned forward; her eyes met his.

Evan sat on the edge of the table and rested his arm on his leg, "So you found her car? How clever. What makes you think I had anything to do with this woman?"

"Evan! I know you took her. I saw you driving her car, and we met Brian Wilson, who you paid to play a little car swap game."

He shrugged and continued to watch her saying nothing.

"Well, where is she? Is she still alive?"

After a few minutes, he dropped his leg to the floor and stood. "Yes, she's here."

"Alive?"

"Yes."

"Can I see her?"

He stopped in front of her and shrugged, "Why not. She's here because of you."

"Evan! What do you mean she's here because of me?" *What did I do to cause him to kidnap her?*

"She was harassing you."

"So? It's part of the job. Reporters do it all the time."

Evan glared at her. "This was different."

Andrea didn't answer because she knew that to be true.

She could see the white around his eyes as he leaned closer. She pulled away from him. He held a scalpel and used the tip to raise her chin. "That woman wasn't letting you do your job. She had it in for you. She constantly accused you of being some freak." He stared at her for a long moment, then appeared to change his mind. He removed the sharp blade from her skin and straightened his body.

Turning away, he walked to the metal door, unlocked it, and left the room.

Chapter 36

ndrea could hear his steps fade, and another door opened and shut.

Andrea tried to get her wrists from the clamps, but all she did was rub her skin raw, breaking it, so it began to bleed.

Her phone pinged, then pinged again. It was in her coat, hanging on a hook with her purse. *DAD! Where are you? Do you hear me?*

They didn't have telepathy, nor did she believe in it. Andrea hoped he had some sense she was in trouble and contacted the station.

Evan returned with a sandwich on a plate and sat on a rolling stool. The rollers squeaked when he rolled closer to her.

"I like you," he said while chewing.

"Really?" She raised her eyebrows in disbelief.

"Really. When I saw you on TV, I knew I'd met someone who would challenge me. There was something in your eyes. Then I saw Kaeli began to harass you." He shook his head and set the plate on the floor.

"Do you have juju?' Evan leaned his elbows on his knees, watching Andrea.

"Juju?" Andrea feigned surprise.

"Yeah, what Kaeli said you had."

"You mean am I psychic? No."

"So, what was she after you about? Why did she keep accusing you of having powers?

"Evan, it's a long story." Andrea thought about what she would tell him. "Her brother went missing up north. She contacted my dad. He sometimes can find people when others can't."

"He has the juju."

"Some people think so."

"You don't?"

She shook her head. He continued. "You're his daughter, you'd know."

Andrea didn't answer right away. Then as if pulled from her a deep dark place, she answered. "My dad has a unique ability to find people."

"You already said that." He interjected.

"Yes, I can't tell you for sure that my dad is a psychic. I've seen things happen I can't explain. If you saw things like that, would you believe he's got—juju?"

"Probably."

"Okay, then you can believe it. Can I go now?"

He rolled back from her. "No. I like talking to you."

"Evan, what did you do with Kaeli?"

"You're psychic, you tell me."

"If I was, I'd know where she was, and we wouldn't be having this conversation. At least not here." She cocked her head as she made the point.

Evan stood and took his plate to a counter. "That is true. You must have had an idea, or you wouldn't have been in the woods."

"What were you doing there?"

This time he cocked his head and smiled. "For me to know and you to find out."

Andrea nodded. She needed to keep him talking. Surely someone would miss her by now. "Evan, why did you kill all those women?"

"You think I killed anyone?" He crossed his arms and waited for her answer.

The sound of a ping then the phone began to ring. Evan looked at the coat he'd taken from her. "Someone wants to talk to you."

She didn't answer and wished she'd silenced it.

Evan pulled the phone from her pocket made sure it was off. Taking it to a counter, he stuck a pin in the side and pulled out the sim card. Leaving them there, he returned to sit facing her again.

"I'm not usually that scatterbrained. I should have taken it from you at the well house and left it there. It's fine." He shrugged. After a moment, he asked the question he'd asked before. "You think I killed someone?"

"Yes."

"You think your so smart."

"All the evidence points to you. My guess is when the police start passing your picture around to the places that women went missing, someone is going to recognize you."

"Naw. I'm invisible. No one remembers me. I went back to some of the places where the women went missing. No one put two and two together. Some of the people remembered I'd been there. They remembered me as the father of a child or wife with cancer." He grinned.

Andrea remembered the people in the bars that had been interviewed. They described the man they'd bought a beer and dinner for. He'd told them that story, and they didn't consider him a suspect. No one did. He'd committed the perfect murder.

"How long have you been doing this?" Andera kept her voice friendly.

Evan opened the fridge and snagged a beer, and popped the cap on the opener attached to the side.

At the sight of a woman's head on the shelf next to the perfectly aligned beer bottles, Andrea recoiled. A picture of Evan using the head flashed through her mind. Andrea stared at Evan in disgust.

"Sorry. I didn't mean for you to see that." He slammed the door before sitting on the stool.

She moaned and turned her head trying to unsee that picture in her mind.

"What?!" Evan whirled and examined the room for intruders. Finding the room empty except for the two of them he calmed down.

"What was that all about?" He swiveled on the stool to face her and took a swig from the bottle.

"Nothing." What could she say? After a few minutes of silence, her mind whirled with thoughts. "I've been studying you."

"You have? Why?"

"How do you think I found you?"

"You didn't find me. I found you." He countered.

"When did you start doing this?" Andrea changed the subject and asked the first thing that came to her mind.

"You want to know how I started--this?"

She nodded, "Evan, can you take this off my hands?"

Evan gave her a sad expression and shook his head, "I'm sorry, but listen, you're going to love this story." He rested his arms on his knees and smiled at her. "I've been killing since I was a teenager. There was a runaway girl I met and killed. I cut her up and buried her. Unfortunately, she was found when animals drug her out into a field. They never found out who did it. I got better at killing and hiding it. Although that wasn't my first."

"Why?" The question came out as a whisper from her dry throat.

Evan stared at her for a long moment. "You want details, don't you?" he grinned at her. "You're my kind of woman."

She didn't, but if it kept him talking and not killing her, she'd keep him talking until he fell asleep.

"Okay." After a long pull on the bottle, he hung it from his fingers. "My mother." His voice hardened. "It's always the mother, isn't it? Well, not so much in this case. It started with her boyfriend." His voice became hard. "He lied to me. For six long years, he lied and abused me. Told me all fathers taught this to their boys, and if no father was around, the man in the house was responsible.

When I was eleven when I discovered the lie. It took another couple of years before I dared to make him stop." Evan grimaced as he continued. "He was the first human. The old man taught me to hunt and skin wild game. He had no idea how useful those accomplishments would come in handy when the time came to dispose of him."

Andrea shivered at the implication. "What about your mother?"

His expression became hard as his eyes narrowed and his jaw locked. He didn't look at Andrea, but looked at something far away. "She was either drunk or high. She didn't care what happened to Roxie and me. As long as HE gave her what she wanted, she was happy to put me in his care." He gave her a slight smile. "After Mother left us, my sister and I. You know I have a sister here." Andrea nodded. "Mom, disappeared one day." He paused. "I killed her too." He waited for Andrea to respond. She couldn't.

"After she was gone." He took a long drink from the bottle, letting the liquid slide down his throat. Andrea focused on his Adams apple as it bobbed.

He continued, "The state was going to put me into foster care. My sister got custody of me and made sure I went to school. I got a job as an apprentice butcher." This time he grinned as if he'd revealed the prize behind door number three.

"That particular expertise came into good use.

One day I came home from work and Mother laid into me wanting money. When I wouldn't give her any she went off in a rage. She grabbed a mop and began beating me with it."

Andrea felt his hurt and anger. The heat of his rage filled the room and she recoiled. Would he kill her now?

"I grabbed ahold of the handle before she could hit me another time. We fought and she fell. I pressed the handle over her neck and watched as her anger changed to fear. I loved watching her try to plead for her life, then fight for air until the life drained from her. I took her out to the garage and cut her up. Took the pieces to work and threw them in the scrap bucket that went to a local farm. The head I buried in the garden outside."

Andrea shuddered as he leaned back and crossed his leg, resting his hand and bottle waiting for her reaction.

"How did you find the women? Do you know how many there are?" Andrea hoped as long as she kept him talking, she'd learn more about him and keep him from hurting her.

"Andrea, you ask too many questions." Evan gave Andrea a long look. He stood and stared down at her.

Andrea began to shake. Fear coursed through her veins, and her fingers curled, her heart beat he thought he could hear it.

He swore and stomped out a side door slamming it behind him. His steps could be heard until another door slammed, and it was quiet.

Andrea sighed. Her body still shaking from the prospect of being killed. She wiggled her hands, trying to find some weak area to slide her wrists from the restraints. It was no use.

Oh, Dad, why am I here? Am I going to die like all those women? Don't let him cut me up and put me in the lake. The image of the head in the fridge flashed in her mind. *God in heaven, not that either!*

She heard a commotion outside the door Evan had exited. Banging and a woman shouting. Could it be Kaeli? Andrea leaned forward, straining to listen to what was going on.

The door burst open. Evan dragged a woman in and dropped her arms, letting the chains clank to the floor.

"Let me go!" the woman screamed. Her wet hair hung in ropes around her face. She wore an old hospital gown that fell off her shoulders as she rested on her knees and fists on the floor.

Evan didn't answer. He took the end of the chain in his hand and fastened it to a clip on the wall. Pulling the chain through a ring caused the woman to struggle to a half-standing position. The force of the chain being pulled forced her to stand with her hands raised in the air. She hung off the cuffs around her wrists, limp as if they were the only thing keeping her upright.

Andrea gasped at the blueish tinge to the skin on the other woman. As if sensing another person in the room, she raised her face and looked around the room. Her eyes focused on the figure chained to a chair.

"You!" Kaeli screamed and tried to take a step toward Andrea. The chain whined as it rubbed against the ring and came to an abrupt stop. "Oof!" She gasped and fell back against the wall.

Andrea tried to stand but fell back into the chair. "What are you doing to her?" She shouted at Evan. "Let her go!"

He turned his head to face Andrea, "How nice. You demand her release and not your own?" He shook his head and locked the chain in place. He moved toward the examination table.

Kaeli struggled to stand. She glared at Andrea. "Why are you here? I thought you could read minds. How did you not know he was after you?" She made a rude noise. "Now we're both in trouble.

Maybe you should telepath your dad and see if he can come and rescue us. Oh yeah," she sneered, "He isn't a psychic."

Andrea watched Evan as he moved to stand by Kaeli. He ran the back of his fingers to her chin and pinched it hard. While she fought to hold her head away from him screaming. He cocked his arm and slapped Kaeli across the face. "Shut-up!"

Kaeli whipped her head back to face Evan. She arched her back and hocked a spit at him. Evan evaded her projectile and pulled the chains, so her arms were spread even further apart, and her toes rested on the floor. Pain etched her face.

"Evan, no, please, don't do that," Andrea begged.

Evan turned to look at her. "Why are you concerned about her? She's done nothing but harass you. She hates you. You're wasting your feelings on her." He turned away and began to adjust the instruments on the tray.

Andrea took a breath and chose her words carefully. "Evan, she didn't DO anything to me. They're words, just words. People choose to believe her or not. I can't change that now. I'm sure after this, she isn't going to say anything or do anything like that again." She didn't look at Kaeli but spoke to her, "Right, Kaeli." It was a statement, not a question. She saw Kaeli give a brief nod.

A chill and shiver started at Andrea's ears and moved through her body to her now cold toes. She began to shake with the cold. Even though she had her clothes on, she couldn't stop the shaking. The possibility of what would happen in the next few minutes had her on edge,

Evan ignored the two as he walked around the room, pulling instruments from drawers and cupboards.

Thoughts of what Andrea could say to distract Evan whirled through her head.

"Evan, how did you get those women back here?" *Now, why did she ask that?*

Evan turned to Andrea. "Why do you want to know?"

"I'm curious. If you're going to kill us, then satisfy my curiosity."

He gave her a long look then nodded his head. "Okay. It was simple. I built a false bottom in my SUV. I insulated the space then packed dry ice into it. I put the body into a center section, so the body didn't get ice burn. It stayed cold and sometimes froze a little. I planned each kill, so I'd had time to leave the area and drive back here." He shrugged as if it was a simple process.

"That reminds me, you never told me how you came to have this house? Did you kill the owers? Will they be found at the bottom of the lake?" Andrea felt horror at the thought. *Who owned this house?*

"Now that was a stroke of luck." Evan rolled a cart holding several power tools to the metal table attached to the wall on her left. He picked up a tool from the cart. It looked like a reciprocating saw but had a blade like a crosscut saw.

She shuddered.

"One day, when I drove the ATV down the track next to the fence, I thought I heard someone yelling. After stopping, I heard a man yelling for help. I stood on the ATV and looked over the wall. I saw a man lying under an ATV.

After climbing over the fence and getting the ATV off him, I helped him onto the four-wheeler, and he directed me to the house. His wife had Alzheimer's and wasn't any help. I called an ambulance." Evan walked back to the table where he'd left his second bottle and took a long drink. He sat on the rolling chair, looking at Andrea and ignoring Kaeli.

"Elmer Hansen was released, and I took him and Patricia home. He was so glad I was there, he offered me money. I told him no, that wasn't necessary. Over the course of the next few years, our friendship grew. Patricia died. Elmer built this addition onto the garage so we'd have somewhere to dress our deer, turkey, pheasants, or whatever we killed. It worked out well for both of us."

"I take it your brother-in-aw and his family didn't know about your relationship with Elmer and his wife?" Andrea slipped in when he paused.

"Nope. I kept that our secret. Elmer knew Dan's parents when they bought their property. Elmer bought his land first."

"Where is Elmer?" Andrea asked. *Maybe he'll change his mind about killing us.*

"He died." The answer was short.

"On his own?" Andrea raised her eyebrow at him.

"You think I killed him?" Evan's expression showed his surprise.

"You have no a lack of compulsion to kill."

He shook his head. "Not Elmer. He died in his sleep. I came back from a trip and found him dead in his recliner. Luckily he'd only died the night before."

"How did anyone not know you and Elmer were friends? I mean, who came to the funeral? What about his family?"

Evan didn't answer. He stared at Andrea until she asked, "You said you didn't put him in the lake."

"I didn't." He stood.

Andrea tried to find something else to say, "Then where is he buried?"

'He was cremated, and his ashes scattered here on the property with Patricia." Evan leaned back, his fingers laced around on his knee. "He left everything he had to me."

"It was the perfect set up. You killed the women, brought them here to dismember them, and then drove through the fence to the lake. Then took a boat or drove onto the lake and dropped the weighted parts in. No one questioned you because everyone knew you fished the lake." Andrea nodded as she spoke.

"I knew you were a smart woman." Evan pulled the chain connected to Kaeli's arms, moving her toward the examination table.

Andrea wanted to scream. Her breath came so hard she couldn't breathe. She strained at her restraints. He was going to kill Kaeli right in front of her eyes. Squeezing, her eyes shut against the scene.

"Please, don't kill me. I promise to apologize and never interview Andrea." The pleading tone sounded heartbreaking to Andrea. She opened her eyes.

Evan had Kaeli sitting on the table. Her hands were free, but she was so intent on pleading with Evan she hadn't realize it.

While Kaeli shivered, Evan walked around the table behind her. Like a flash, Evan wrapped his arm around Kaeli and pressed a syringe into her neck. She fought against him, screaming. He tightened his arm, cutting off her air. Her eyes bulged as she fought for air. After a moment, her eyes closed, and she sagged against him.

Andrea fought the chains crying. Tears falling, and her chin dropped to her chest. "Kaeli!" Her voice rasped. "Evan, did you kill her?" She screamed.

The sound of the saw pierced Andrea's heart and she let out a long scream.

The door burst open and flew across the room and crashed to the floor. Men in black tactical uniforms rolled, flipped, and crouched as they entered the room. All came to a halt with their guns on Andrea, Evan, and the now reclining Kaeli.

"Put your hands in the air!" A muffled voice ordered Evan.

Evan's eyes narrowed at the man kneeling, then at the one standing directly behind the officer. His head moved slightly to take in more officers entering the room. They filled the room.

Andrea repressed the grin of nervous relief. They were on her side. She was saved, but Evan still held the vibrating saw.

"Put the saw down, Evan." A familiar voice ordered the man.

Fletcher! Her hands shook with relief. *He found me.*

Chapter 37

Andrea stood outside of the addition where she and Kaeli had been held. Shivering despite wearing a silver thermal sheet. She hugged it around her. She looked for Fletcher, wondering if he could bring her coat.

"Andrea!"

This time tears flowed as her father rush around a cruiser and took her into his arms. The smell of old pipe smoke, sweat, and bacon caused her to hug him like she wasn't going to let go.

"Ah, Honey Bear." His arms tightened around her. "Are you okay? I can see you aren't hurt. Tank goodness."

"How did you get here?" Her voice muffled in his jacket.

"I drove."

Andrea leaned away from him. "When did you leave? It's a four-hour drive down here."

"Ja. I left dis morning." He tilted his head a little watching her expression.

"You knew?" She asked, "You didn't call me."

"If I called you an' tol' you, I felt someting terrible was going to happen to you, what would you have told me?" He pulled away to look at her face.

She mulled over her response. "Okay, I would have said I was fine and I didn't need any interference."

"Yep, dat's for sure." He gave her another hug.

"How did you find me?" she whispered against his chest.

"Sorry to interrupt." Bob, her fellow officer, stood next to her. "We need to get you to the station to debrief."

"I can take her." Donald offered.

"Sorry, Sheriff, I have to keep her separated so she doesn't say anything or tell anyone something she shouldn't." He held out his arm to steer her to a car.

"I'll see you at the station Dad."

He nodded, then looked back to where Steve Totts and others were guiding Evan into a cruiser.

"It'll be okay, Dad." She saw Kaeli being pushed into an ambulance on a gurney.

At the station, she was taken to an interrogation room and left alone. After what seemed to be an hour, Chrissy stuck her head in the door and slipped in with an insulated tumbler. "Here's some hot chocolate. You probably need something to eat too. The guys are all discussing the press conference." She hugged Andrea. "I can't talk long, but are you okay?"

Andrea nodded and gave her a weak smile. "I have to process it. At least we were rescued before he had a chance to kill Kaeli. How is she?"

"I haven't heard, she's at the hospital. I'll bring you a sandwich or something in a minute." She headed out the door.

Andrea sat in the postage stamp size room. Time passed with no one coming in. Chrissy didn't come back. Walking to the door, she opened it, surprised it wasn't locked and looked down the hall. No one was there.

"I guess they forgot about me." Walking toward the squad room, she saw the office cubes were empty. She heard a smattering of officers talking into phones, so someone still worked around here.

In the lobby, her father sat slumped in a chair, snoring softly. No-one stopped her as she slipped by the empty desk. "PSST! Dad!" Her father's eyes opened, and he looked around. Seeing her, he hurried to her side. "They all done with you?"

"They never came in. I think they forgot about me. Have you seen Fletcher? Never mind, you never met him."

"Yes, I did when I got here." Her dad took her arm. "Is there a back door we can sneak out?"

"Yes, follow me." No one stopped them as they left the station.

"You should go to the hospital." Her father maneuvered the truck through traffic to the freeway, and they soon arrived at her townhouse.

Andrea took a hot shower while her father puttered around the kitchen. She came into the living room to find him nursing a mug of coffee.

"What do you want for dinner?" Andrea asked as she popped a pod into the coffee maker.

"Fletcher called. He's coming over with dinner."

"You talked to Fletcher?" Andrea leaned against the counter and folded her arms, waiting for an explanation.

"He texted me." He didn't look at her and took another sip of coffee.

"What aren't you telling me? Dad?"

"After we eat, Fletcher's here." He set the cup down and made his way to the front door as the bell sounded.

Andrea shook her head as the two men greeted each other as if they were longtime friends.

Fletcher entered and set the bags on the counter. He waved her to the living room. "Go sit. Donald and I will take care of everything and call you when it's ready."

"Okay, I'm going." She took her cup and wagged her finger at her father. "You know where everything is." She looked at the two talking with such ease. They got along; her lips curved to a smile.

"Yes, and so does Fletcher." He wiggled his bushy eyebrows at her and jerked his head for her to go.

Andrea pulled the lap blanket over her and relaxed as she listened to the banter between the two men. Taking a sip from the cup, she wondered at their camaraderie, it felt natural.

The three ate chicken dinner with small talk about Fletcher's past and observations of the Twin Cities.

"I'm getting used to this big city community with a small-town feel. People can dress up and attend the opera or a Broadway hit and the next day go down a ski hill on a mattress." He looked at Andrea, "Who does that?"

"It's all for a good cause and so much fun. You laugh so hard, your stomach aches." Andrea answered as she pushed the plate of barely eaten dinner away. She ignored the questioning look from her father and the look he gave Fletcher.

Her phone vibrated on the table next to her. Steve Tott's name flashed. She took a deep breath and exhaled. The phone vibrated again. No one spoke. Andrea took another breath and exhaled. The phone gave a more insistent vibrate. She breathed in, connected the call, and pressed the speaker icon. "This is Detective Watson."

"WHERE-ARE-YOU?" Steve punctuated each word loud enough for all of them to hear without the speaker.

"I'm home."

"Why aren't you in the interrogation room?" His voice didn't change tone or volume. "You know the rules."

"After two and a half hours without a single officer checking on me, I stepped out of an unlocked room to find everyone otherwise occupied." She didn't mention they were huddled around the monitors watching Evan talk. "I was cold and hungry after not eating all day."

"You were to submit evidence for collection." He shot back.

"My clothes are bagged and tagged. I'll bring them in tomorrow."

"Get down here now. There will be someone there to debrief and question you." The sound of children in the background gave her the impression he was at his own home.

She looked at her father who shook his head no. After another breath and exhale she answered in a calm even tone. "I will be at the station tomorrow morning to answer any questions you might have for me."

Steve paused before he answered. "Do you have me on speaker?"

"Yes."

"Who's there with you?"

"My father, a retired Sheriff and Agent Fletcher Peterson."

Another moment of silence then Steve spoke. "Fine. Be there early."

"Yes Sir, I'll be on time for my shift." She could almost hear Steve's teeth gnash at her response.

He disconnected without another word.

"Nice boss you have." Her father intoned.

"He's not her boss," Fletcher stood and took his and Andrea's plate to the kitchen. "Technically, he's above her in pay, but she could be a team leader if Conrad decided to give her a case to work."

"Like that's ever going to happen," Andrea snorted. She stood, giving her shaky legs a moment to adjust to her weight, then made her way to the living room and sat on the couch.

"Do you want a cup of coffee?" Fletcher asked.

"No."

"Why don't you just go ta bed?" Her dad suggested as he followed her and sat in the recliner across the room.

She heard Fletcher rinsing dishes and loading the dishwasher. She felt relieved and guilty he was doing an act she should be doing but was thankful for him.

After starting the dishwasher, Fletcher pulled a blanket from the tote on the floor and covered the two of them. Andrea leaned against him when he curled his arm around her shoulders. She didn't look at her father, knowing he had a satisfied smile on his face.

"Dad, how did you get here in time? It's a four-hour drive from Bemidji to St. Paul." Andrea asked.

"I woke up dis mornin' wit a bad feeling. I wasn't sure who it was connected to, but you didn't answer your phone when I called. It didn't go away, and I kept seein' you in a woods wit' danger. I got in da car and started driving down here." His voice sounded like it was an everyday occurrence. "It wasn't da first time. I'd been having flashes of evil toughts but not directed at you. Da toughts were about someone else."

"You didn't call me?" She raised an eyebrow at her father.

"You rarely believe anyting I tell you about my feelings," he countered.

"I believe you when I can verify with facts."

"Dat's the problem. Sometimes you have to go wit' your gut feeling den find if da facts follow da clues. Dey usually pan out in my experience." He looked at Fletcher as he spoke the last sentence. "It could have been because he was focusing on you, Andrea. Da closer I got to da Cities; da feeling of danger got stronger. I called your phone again, but no answer." He gave her a pointed look.

"Sorry, Dad, I was busy with the case." She didn't tell him she'd seen his first calls but didn't want to talk to him. She felt a twinge of guilt.

"When I got to da station, I asked for Agent Fletcher," He grimaced, "Dat jerk Steve Totts came out and blew me off when I said you were in danger. He said you were out interviewing property owners. When I pitched a fit in da lobby, sorry honey, your friend Chrissy heard me and slipped me Fletcher's phone number. I left da station and called him." He nodded to Fletcher to continue.

"I got a call from a number I didn't recognize. I almost ignored it, but something prompted me to answer it." He gave her dad a look. "I'm glad I did. He told me about his feelings, and I drove to the station to pick him up. We headed to the lake. When we got there, we found two boys wandering around the parking lot, trying to talk to someone, but no one was listening.

"Your dad met them and brought them to me. You made quite an impression on them. One of them is the grandson of Dan Saunders. He told us they'd seen you, and you'd headed into the woods. They doubled back along the shoreline. When they didn't see you walking along the edge of the water, they looked for your footprints and found them leading to the well house.

When you weren't there, they said they had a bad feeling and ran through the woods to the front gate leading to the parking lot. They remembered the police parked there. He stopped and took a drink from his cup.

"Hey, no stopping. I want to know what happened." Andrea urged.

Fletcher hugged her. "Give me a moment, my throat's dry thinking about your capture." He took another drink. "I guess no one would listen to them until they met your dad."

"Dad, thank goodness. What happened next? How did you find me?" She leaned a little forward as her phone buzzed. "It's Chrissy," she announced as she picked up the phone. "Hi, Chrissy."

"Hi, how are you? You caused quite a stir when you weren't in the room."

"I'm doing good. I've got my dad and Fletcher here to keep me company."

259

"You might want to turn on the TV. Steve and Conrad are having a press conference. I guess they finished with Evan Morrison, for now."

"Thank you." She indicated the remote, and Fletcher picked it up, turning on the TV. "Oh, Chrissy, what station?"

"Well, which one do you think?" Her voice suggested it must be Kaeli's station.

Andrea held up six fingers. "Thank you for giving Dad Fletcher's phone number."

"You're welcome. I'd be careful tomorrow. My guess someone might leak that despite what is said tonight, you were on the case and, in fact, a victim."

"Thanks. I'm taking tomorrow off. I think I deserve it. That is after I go in for the interview I skipped." She gave a little chuckle and disconnected after she said goodbye.

The three watched the empty podium and the reporters milling around.

"I wonder if Kaeli is watching," Andrea offered.

There was a flurry of movement when Steve Totts, Conrad Bellows, HD, and other detectives who worked on the case juxtaposition around the podium.

"I'm so glad I'm not there," Andrea whispered.

Conrad stepped to the podium and addressed the reporters. He gave a recap of the case and what transpired that day. Andrea snorted in derision as he glossed over how her father and Fletcher assisted in finding the killer.

Steve stepped forward and fiddled with the mic. "We have apprehended the man who killed women across state lines. We don't know how many he killed, but we will be diving to retrieve what's at the bottom of Blue Lake, then evaluate the victims' DNA. Now, are there questions?"

"Who is the man you have in custody?" Someone in the back of the shouted.

"The man in custody is Evan Wayne Morrison."

"How did you find this guy?" A reporter shouted.

"We had excellent cyber detectives who pinpointed times and areas. I can't go into detail, but he thought he was smarter than our profiling team." Steve leaned into the microphone.

"We were told Evan Morrison kidnapped two women. One we is our reporter Kaeli Meyers. Who was the other woman?

"I think we will keep that evidence to ourselves for the time being. I'm sure she wants to keep her privacy as long as she can.

"Detective, Chanel 11 news. We heard this killer has been stalking local women. Were there other women he was going to kill? Did he have a kill list?"

"We're still collecting evidence," Steve answered and looked around for other questions. "Yes?" He nodded to another reporter.

"I've been following this case. We've heard one of your detectives might have a paranormal ability she used on this case. Can you comment on that?" The man's coat pocket sported a national affiliate tag.

Steve's jaw clenched, and he picked up the papers on the podium.

"He's composing himself. The guy got under his skin. I wonder how he's going to get out of this?" Andrea watched the TV.

"He's going to smile and tell dem dey found de killer with excellent forensic detection," Donald added dryly.

Steve repeated what her father said almost word for word. The three watched for a little longer, then Fletcher turned the TV off.

"Steve is going to take credit for the case." Andrea stared at the black screen.

"Andrea, does dat matter? You have a gift for dis." He held up his hand to stop her as she opened her mouth. "Dis isn't about your "gift," he crooked his fingers to indicate quote marks. "You are smart when it comes ta using computers to find tings. You're letting da past keep you from using your natural ability to push you into being da best detective you can be. Even if you choose ta stay in dis precinct, you can go far. No one likes a braggart. It can be a detriment to moving up in de department." He leaned back and crossed his arms, giving her the look that meant they knew who he was talking about.

"Okay, Dad. Let's go back to telling me how you found me."

Chapter 38

Fletcher crossed his leg under the blanket and gave Andrea another hug, pulling her close to his side. She felt him kiss the side of her head.

"Your father talked to the boys. Here's the odd thing. Why did they double back? They'd started toward home as you said, but they told us they felt they should follow you to be sure you made it back to your car safely."

"That does seem odd." Andrea commented, "Why would teenagers be concerned about me? Did they have any concern about Evan?"

This time Donald answered. "No, I tink we'll find dat da man is a loner but moved in and out of da communities wit ease, friendly, and at ease wit dose around him."

"One boy called his grandfather and, after talking to me, allowed us to access the property." Fletcher continued. "We began walking back toward the end of the cul de sac in front of the house. Andrea, remember we parked in front of the house the day we went to interview Daniel Saunders? That road ends further into the woods. Once the boys showed us there was a path to the well house, we sent them back to the parking lot with an officer.

The whole time I had the picture of Evan, we had on file, in my mind. We got to the well house, but it was empty. We saw your footsteps leading to the house and those of another individual. That had me worried." He reached for his cup and took a sip. "Steve showed up and started ordering the guys to check the woods. Daniel showed up and unlocked the well house. What I saw inside that room had me more than worried.

Daniel said he hadn't been in the structure for years.

Donald and I saw tracks leading away from the building. I had to order the guys to stop walking around. Your dad and I followed the tracks. Good thing you dragged your feet and made some odd steps. It made it easier to follow the progress.

Once we got to the edge of woods, we found the fence."

"That was a surprise to me. How did we miss that?" Andrea wondered. "I can't believe I never saw the fence or that property."

"I was surprised too. We stood looking at the fence, and I thought, where did this come from? Your father walked along the fence line and called me over. We saw the gate, and on the ground stuck in the gate, your dad saw your mittens. I never felt so glad and scared at the same time when he said he'd told you to wear them." Fletcher hugged Andrea closer. "The officer with us radioed to Steve, and he called the drone operator at the parking lot to fly over the property. The rest is us getting the team together to rescue you."

"I'm so glad you did." Andrea looked up at Fletcher. He leaned in and kissed her.

Donald gave a knowing grin at the two.

Lightning Source UK Ltd.
Milton Keynes UK
UKHW041834050421
381487UK00001B/27

ENTROPY

"Maximum entropy is achieved when nothing else happens, nothing ever can happen again. Energy is so dissipated, the effort to reassemble some order, is simply too great to overcome the inertia.

Maximum entropy is the death of the universe. Maximum entropy on this planet would be death of all living things, no earthquakes, no weather, an eerie silence, the thermal death of maximum entropy where nothing happens, where there is no time, for nothing changes."

Anthony Harris

ENTROPY

by

Anthony Harris

Madeleine Shaw • Publishers
London

© Anthony Harris 2000

ISBN 1 9007 3730 2

First Edition
First Published in the UK, 2000

Published by
Madeleine Shaw Publishers
PO Box 10024
Hackney
London E8 1PT

Printed and bound in Great Britain by:
Madeleine Shaw, PO Box 10024, London E8 1PT

INTRODUCTION

I learned about entropy when I read chemistry at Kings College London. The three year course was called Special Chemistry, an honours course which took no hostages. About a third of us got degrees. I learned the heat concept of entropy, the statistical concept. I was able to calculate the increase of entropy in a chemical reaction. I regarded the three year course as a study in the humanities, because chemistry was always stimulating my imagination.

As the years passed, I saw that the notion of entropy could be developed to include more than mere chemical collections. Indeed, I saw that *we* are chemical collections, and that large numbers of *homo sapiens* are statistical collections. Having seen that, I hoped that someone else would see it, and so I would not have to write a book about it. Three decades on and nothing came forth, so I wrote this book to share with you the fascinations that the concept of entropy is capable of bringing to so many different aspects of life.

I have not burdened the text with calculations or technical detail, which I have reserved for the *Notes and References*.

Anthony Harris
London, 2000

CONTENTS

CHAPTER ONE

ENTROPY

Chaos, anarchy, rioting, war, are all very high in entropy. Entropy can be intuitively grasped as disorder. A crystal lattice, a stately building, a tree with its wonderful design and stateliness, a mammalian cell with its intricately interconnected chemical reactions, are all examples of low entropy. High entropy is found in a rubbish tip, the aftermath of a bomb explosion, a rotting corpse. All industrial processes produce huge amounts of entropy, and so do all living things.

Stephen Hawking, the renowned Cambridge mathematician, has done a neat calculation which emphasises just how hard-won order is. He contrasts the amount of decrease of entropy in the brain as a result of study, and the increase of entropy around the student as he radiates heat, and loses it through sweat. Within a given time, the increase of entropy is billions of times greater than the decrease within the brain.

To get deeper into the concept, some familiarity with attendant notions is useful. The notion of *there is no free lunch* is contained in the First Law of Thermodynamics, which states that energy cannot be created or destroyed. We now know that a better formulation is that the sum total of energy and mass in the universe cannot be increased or decreased. One might be chary about applying this to the whole universe, but here on earth, and in our solar system, this law has never been seen to be broken. The introduction of mass, matter, is there because we know about the break up and fusion of atomic nuclei, where small changes of mass produce vast quantities of energy.

But what is energy? Put simply it is merely the ability to do work, and that can be any kind of work, electrical, mechanical, physiological, and so on. Work is the product of force times distance. You push a brick along the floor with your foot, you are overcoming friction over a distance, you do work. Water cannot flow uphill by itself, it has to be pumped, or hauled: here the force you are overcoming is the attraction of the earth to the water, usually called gravity.

This whole business of work, energy, force, fills entire libraries, but the basic idea is easily grasped: if you want something to happen, you have to expend effort, and effort always means you pay for it in some way. And effort always means heat, always, and there is the nexus with entropy, for entropy can be measured as a heat flow divided by temperature. You attain by the sweat of your brow, and so does nature.

Energy is never lost or gained, it merely transforms, and ultimately it involves a heat exchange from one place to another, one system to another, and that means entropy is created. The fact of this planet, this solar system, and as far as we know the universe, is that there is never any event which does not involve an increase in entropy. This finding is summarised in the Second Law of thermodynamics which states that the amount of entropy in the universe is increasing, and never decreases.

But what is heat? *Heat is movement of molecules.* Hence the notion of entropy being disorder; there is little order in boiling water, even less in steam. Cool steam down, in other words take entropy from it (which does not disappear, but adds on to the global total which is always rising), and the molecules of water slow down until they are liquid; cool some more, and you have the low entropy order of perfectly formed crystals of ice, where water molecules do not rush about but vibrate at a point.

Often crystalline structure is very beautiful, as exhibited in snowflakes, but just a little heat passing into them destroys the order, and in the destruction of order there is the concomitant inevitable increase in entropy, shown here in the transition from exquisite patterning in three dimension of the snowflake to the formless blob of water in which the water molecules rush about randomly. Randomness is the very stuff of entropy.

The molecules in the air around you vary not only in their chemical nature, oxygen, nitrogen, carbon-dioxide for instance, but they also differ in their energy. Some oxygen molecules are moving around at a vast pace, tens of times faster than the majority, while some sluggards barely move at all. For any given temperature there is a specific share

out of energies amongst the molecules. The higher
the temperature the more of the sprightly ones, the
lower, the more of the staid ones. Cool them down
sufficiently, and they fall into each other's arms and
form a liquid. Despite this inner randomness, this
togetherness of the mixes, the air obeys certain laws
- the classical gas laws - to a fair degree of
consistency. Here then we have the paradox of order
out of randomness. Get a sufficient number of
molecules together, and they obey statistical laws.
We cannot say anything about an individual
molecule, indeed if we know where it is, we do not
know how fast it is travelling, and vice versa; indeed
if we know its energy, we don't know when we did.
In the same way, I suggest, when dealing with huge
numbers of objects, and living things, there comes a
time when laws become apparent if the numbers are
large enough, even though you cannot tell what any
particular individual is going to do. Insurance
companies make a living, and more, by studying
trends in huge numbers of people. They see the death
rate, calculate how many of millions will die, and set
the premium accordingly so the pay out is less than
the pay in. We do not call what insurance companies
do *laws*, we do not call their statistical results and
findings laws either, but if they were scientists, they
would. The so-called laws of nature are apparently
statistical, and certainly for many purposes these
laws (these actuarial findings in nature) are sufficient.
Why then should we not seek more laws, as it were,
of large numbers of human beings? After all, if we

already admit we cannot tell what a single molecule is going to do, we need not assume the absence of free will in a human person of a billion population.

The chemical processes of life are fuelled by energy from oxidising food. Large molecules such as proteins and nucleic acids are made from smaller molecules ultimately derived from food. Large molecules are constructed so that the constituent parts of cells, the organelles, can be made, and these carry out much of the cell's work.

If these chemical processes were entirely efficient and error free, then there is no reason why life should not continue indefinitely in an individual. However, the reactions are not free from error. For example the error in protein replication is of the order of .0001%. Thus, the individual living entity will accumulate mistakes, and therefore *age*, and this means an increase of entropy, and so the Second Law is ultimately obeyed. Cellular life forms get round this by replicating individuals through maturation of fertilised eggs, which develop into fresh new individuals. The old accumulate entropy through chemical error, radiation, disease, mechanical insult and so forth, while the newly formed, the birthlings, start with a relatively clean entropy balance, only to run up against the creditor who will brook no departure from its entropy books. It would seem that the dance of life is between the dying and the about to be given birth.

A lifespan is only possible because the rate of accumulation of entropy is kept low at the expense of the systems outside the life form.

If heat were not lost from living tissue temperature would rise due to metabolic activity, the chemistry of being alive, and the living tissue would be killed. Proteins coagulate at quite low temperatures; the heat in boiling water is sufficient to rapidly increase structural morbidity in living tissue, we call it scalding. Heat is lost from living tissue by radiation and by water loss, the latter being very efficient since water has such a high heat capacity: you burn your tongue on the jam of a hot jam tart, because the jam contains more water than the pastry. In mammalian species water loss is effected by sweating, whereby tissue water evaporates through ducts in the skin. Heat loss has then been reasonably catered for during evolution, thereby reducing entropy in living tissue.

Blood heat

Insects, reptiles, unlike mammals, cannot control their own temperature. If the ambient temperature is low, their metabolisms are low, and hence they are sluggish. Mammals however have evolved a system of homostasis, they maintain their own internal temperatures at a constant level, which means they can operate in a variety of temperatures with vigour.

Blood heat for *homo sapiens* is about 37 degrees Celsius; a few degrees above or below this temperature means death. When the temperature is too low, metabolisms slow down according to the law: a halving of rate for every ten degrees Celsius fall. If the temperature is too high, heat cannot be expelled quickly enough, which means that entropy is not being expelled quickly enough, so the internal structures begin to break down into chaos, and death intervenes. The most common ploy of germs is to cause fever, which is an increase in entropy. With lower temperature death, as in hypothermia, it might appear that there has been a decrease in entropy, but this is not so, for although the temperature is less than blood heat, the dissynchronisation of the billions of chemical reactions means huge amounts of entropy are locked into the cellular structures; this cannot be eliminated, death results.

A nice problem is this: why is the blood heat 37 degrees? If it were possible to have living tissue as we know it able to sustain 47 degrees we would be twice as metabolically active, and could supply muscles with energy at twice the rate we do. However, with the proteins we are made of, this option is simply not viable, since the higher heat would mean breakdown of the configuration of our proteins, and that would mean they cannot do their jobs, structural or chemical. A temperature of 27 degrees would make us half as quick, and perhaps we would have succumbed long ago to non mammalian predators in hot climates. Our blood

7

temperature appears to be a compromise of several factors, some of which are: the need not too lose too much heat when we are in the cold, the need to lose sufficient heat when in the warm, the need to be able to function in many different ambient temperatures.

A precise and dramatic proof that increase of entropy reduces lifespan

I have argued that life forms must export entropy to their surroundings if they are to escape the consequences of the Second Law, albeit for a finite time. Mammals maintain a constant temperature, but insects do not. What happens if we input entropy into insects? If they are put in environments of slightly increased temperature, their lifespans should be reduced by precisely graded amounts with the increase of entropy flowing into them. I found that entomologists had subjected Daphnia Magna to heat experiments. They set a thermostat on the bugs' cage and waited for the insects to die. They concluded that hotter bug accommodation reduces lifespan, but they had no idea why, and did not moot the notion of entropy. However, analysing the results, I found a direct incremental fall of lifespan with input of entropy.

Limits of longevity

Since a lower temperature means lower entropy in insects, it might be thought human beings could in some way exploit this and so live longer. However, if we wish to live like human beings, we cannot gain longevity in this manner, since our biomachines are finely tuned to our constant blood heat, indeed the structure of living matter within cells, although jelly-like, must be highly organised because of the observed speed, very rapid, of biochemical reactions.

Simple life forms can be frozen, they do not deteriorate, and can be reanimated by warming, very slowly. Indeed, very simple life forms can be frozen, and then dehydrated, stored, and then reanimated by water dosage and improvement of temperature. This cannot be done with complex multi-celled mammals. Lowering temperature would mean cessation of metabolism, the lack of vital energy to fuel the cell mechanisms would mean gaps appear in the machinery, which is the beginning of entropy. Here the entropy increase occurs because of chemical disorder, not heat increase. So complex are the spatial interactions of proteins, which have water molecules attached to them, that lowering temperature would clog them with more water, malforming their three-dimensional structures, and hence their energetics. The structure of multi-celled animals is too complex for a reversible cooling then rewarming to occur. Damage is inevitable. As for dehydrating, death would ensue no matter how cold the process was, simply because cellular architecture at the organelle level would collapse. People who have themselves frozen at death should ponder the fact that immobilising water in cells, which is freezing, means an irreversible damage to cell architecture at the molecular level. If revival did occur, a headache would be the least of your worries.

Cosmic death

The current notion is that the mass of galaxies and nebulae are exploding outwards. We are not sure what they are exploding outwards into. Is it space? But what can that be, for it is something into which matter is passing, whereas what we know of space is that populated by matter. However, no doubt this conundrum will be eventually and dutifully solved. So we have matter flying out from what is supposed to be some kind of central point. In time the force of the outward plunge will weaken for it is pulling against gravity, and once slowed to zero, will reverse direction. After a while all that matter will be concentrated in one tiny point, and the whole thing of explosion, expansion, fall back, and so on will occur wearingly again and again. However, this conclusion is most certainly flawed, because it

10

ignores the effect of entropy increase, until it can increase no more. We do not know how many dilations and collapses will be required to reach this stage of maximum entropy, but reach it matter must. When maximum entropy is reached, there will be no more big bangs. The universe will be dead. There will be no motion. Nothing happening, not even the ticking of a cuckoo clock. This will be the thermal death, death not by fire, but the death *of* fire. The universe will be at the absolute zero. The dead of night.

Maximum entropy is achieved when nothing else happens, nothing ever can happen again. Energy is so dissipated, the effort to reassemble some order is simply too great to overcome the inertia. Maximum entropy is the death of the universe. Maximum entropy on this planet would be death of all living things, no earthquakes, no weather, an eerie silence, the thermal death of maximum entropy where nothing happens, where there is no time, for nothing changes. If it were possible to have a clock face in a world of maximum entropy the hands would not move, and there would be no tick. Maximum entropy is the equilibrium of zero action. And maximum entropy is also the condition of absolute certainty; the higher the entropy the more likely the situation is. Maximum entropy is maximum probability. And the information content is zero. No books, no computers, can exist in such a world, no transmission of knowledge can occur. Maximum entropy means zero knowledge, timelessness, and an ever on-going sameness.

The universe will reach it sooner or later, and we won't be there. But what is of concern now and for the foreseeable future is that unless we mend our ways we will turn this planet into an entropy swamp in just a few generations.

CHAPTER TWO

EXPORT ENERGY OR DIE

Life forms are chemical systems which export entropy outside themselves by utilising energy from molecules released from carbohydrates by the oxidation process of respiration. Plants are a special case since they attain order and cohesion not only through respiration but use energy from the sun to make molecules from which energy can be obtained. *Homo sapiens* has increased average life expectancy in general measure as it reduces the insults which increase entropy by improved sanitation, nutrition, and the use of medicines to combat germs and parasites, as well as replacing body parts which have become dysfunctional through an increase in entropy, for example, diseased hearts can be transplanted with healthy ones. However, the end is always reached, and death intervenes when the capacity to export entropy falls below that of processes increasing entropy in the living system.

Since trees can live for hundreds of years as cohesive organisms, attempts to increase the intrinsic lifespan of *homo sapiens* are not foredoomed, but it would require selective genetics. If people whose families show centenarians only mated with people whose families showed the same trend, longevity in that group would increase. Random mating means diffusion of low life expectancy genes, as in congenital diseases. It is interesting that people have

13

never, on any appreciable scale, chosen mates for longevity; if they had, centenarians would be commonplace. However, if substantial increase in longevity were achieved, disaster would result unless we in the meantime as a species reduced our population by not breeding so quickly. A race of *homo sapiens* which lived to several centuries would produce even more massive amounts of entropy than we do now. If we want long life for our descendants there must be fewer of them.

That longevity can be dramatically increased cannot be doubted, if the resources, and they would have to be huge, were devoted to it, since molecules are long lived. Molecular systems design is the challenge here. The links between atoms in large molecules are extremely strong, many times the strength of the linkage between water molecules, for example, in liquid form, and several times again stronger than the vague pulsations between the molecules of a gas as they hurtle about their apparently regardless and random ways. Since the relative position of atoms in large molecules is fixed, this means information can be stored, and stored safely. Hence the blueprints for proteins which make up any particular species are stored as large molecules of DNA in the chromosomes.

Life strategies at the molecular level combating entropy

There are millions of different proteins which make up the biomass on this planet, but each type is drawn from only twenty-three constituent units, the amino acids. Each acid has a code in DNA, chosen from the four letter alphabet of the constituents of DNA. This means that there are 64 codes, 4 x 4 x 4, rather more than required. Oddly, this excessive capability, called rather quaintly *degeneracy*, is also a feature of most written human languages. Write a sentence, then write it again without the vowels. Try: *th ct st n th mt.* Give it to someone else - usually they can make a gist out of it. Entropy destroys information, and this is probably why bio-information systems are degenerate. Degeneracy seems an ill chosen word for such sturdiness of information keeping, so perhaps we might call it sturdiness instead.

The approximate diameter of a mammalian generalised cell is about a thousandth of a centimetre, with a volume of the order of one billionth of a cubic centimetre. Although minute, this volume is large enough for many of the molecules inside the cell to behave statistically, which means that although we do not know what a particular water molecule is going to do, we do know the properties of a large collection of such molecules and can give numbers to such properties as density, temperature, freezing and boiling points.

In order to understand the processes of life, we need to grasp the notion of increase of entropy. If two containers, one containing oxygen gas, and another nitrogen, are connected by a tube with a tap in it which closes the connection between the containers, nothing happens. If the tap is opened, then immediately oxygen passes spontaneously out of its container into the nitrogen container, and vice versa. Depending on the temperature and the amounts of gases, there will come a time when the gases are thoroughly mixed, the ratios of gases in both containers being exactly the same. This happens faster at higher temperatures, and faster the bigger the cross-section of the open connecting pipe. This mixing process is spontaneous, and involves an increase in entropy of the system, since prior to mixing there was a simple order, pure oxygen, pure nitrogen; after mixing there is the disorder of mixing, and if one tried to de-mix the mixture, it would involve a great deal of effort, expenditure of energy, producing ever more entropy. Similar remarks apply to two materials, A and B, dissolved in water, in different containers. If they are connected, they spontaneously mix.

It is this spontaneous increase of entropy by mixing that mammalian cells have to prevent, since otherwise the blood and the cells would have the same concentration of salt and other minerals, as well as other dissolved nutrients. To do this, special chemical pumps are present in cells to increase absorption of potassium from the blood, but pump out sodium from the cell into the blood. It is this maintenance of gradients of concentration of hundreds of different ions and molecules that most of the energy consumed in living is used. As you sit reading this, 80% of your living activity is simply maintaining these gradients. If the process failed for even a few moments, severe discomfort of temperature change, and flooding of the lungs would occur, leading to death.

There are approximately ten trillion water molecules in a mammalian cell, more than enough for it to behave as water as we know it. This means that the billions of molecules, like amino acids, and ions like sodium, calcium and chloride, behave as if they were in a beaker of water. The amounts of materials in a cell are, however, not random; there are more sodium ions than potassium, while ions of zinc, iron, copper and manganese tend to be at the heart of large protein molecules and not in "free" water, where you find sodium and chloride in the cell.

When there are a million *freely* dispersed molecules the departure from statistical behaviour is about one in a thousand, which means to all intents and purposes the molecules obey the laws of solutions, osmosis, diffusion, and so forth. But for ten thousand molecules the departure is about a per cent, and so we see that in cells quantum effects rather than classical effects will be expected, and so they are. Classical here means we can predict very accurately the course of a chemical or physical change; but when only a few (relatively) atoms and molecules are involved we cannot be certain of the outcome. However, nature minimises mischievous effects in living things by employing large molecules such as proteins and nucleic acids (DNA, for example) which have fixed individual properties rather than statistical behaviour. Most chemical reactions in living cells are made to go faster by enzymes, huge molecules which do not show statistical error because of the strong chemical links within them, that is, they are not freely dispersed so are not random in their behaviour.

Even rigidly preserved molecules like DNA have ultimately to be replicated, while the minerals cannot be obtained except from dietary sources. Iron requirements for example can only be satisfied by intake of iron, whereas fats can give rise to carbohydrates, and vice versa. The vitamins too are a class of molecules which cannot be synthesised in the body, and must be absorbed from the food. A million molecules of niacin, ascorbic acid, and a million ions of calcium, and a million atoms of iron, are required each day by each of your individual cells. Both the B vitamin riboflavin and retinoic acid (vitamin A active) need to be replenished to the extent of ten thousand molecules per day per cell. So does thiamine, vitamin B1. A mere thousand molecules of folic acid are required, while only a hundred of vitamin D1. Departure from these values, either much higher, or lower, results in severe disruption, increase in entropy, within the cell.

Evolution has thinned the various chemical possibilities to the ones we observe today. It is noteworthy that order out of such seeming chaos has emerged because of large biomolecules, molecules found only in living systems and replicated by living systems, and these molecules are primarily the nucleic acids and proteins.

Molecular biology over the last forty years has been very successful in determining the structures of the large molecules found in cells, in particular the genetic material DNA, many proteins, and RNA, the important information carrying go-between genetic blueprints and the sites of protein construction. Alongside this the anatomy of cells too has been probed, so that we understand better now what the aggregates of large molecules in cells are doing. Thus the mitochondria are small factories in the cell which derive energy from carbohydrates for the working of the cell, while the ribosomes are sites of protein manufacture using blueprints derived from the gene DNA carried to the ribosomes by RNA. We can now see the cell as machinery which can replicate itself, and it does so by replicating its structures via its genetic component DNA. But all this requires not only information, which is in DNA, but huge amounts of energy, and cells obtain energy by breaking down carbohydrate molecules to carbon dioxide and water, thereby releasing the energy that was in the molecules as chemical links. This breaking down process, called respiration, is a controlled fire. Just as you obtain energy in the form of heat and flame by burning sugar, releasing carbon dioxide as you do so, so cells burn sugars and fats, but in a multi-step controlled process. It is best to concentrate on one of these processes, to get the general idea.

Carbohydrates are the source of much cellular energy. They are produced by plants by taking carbon dioxide and water from the air and the soil respectively, and using light energy to make sugar molecules, the light coming from the sun. When the plants want energy to build new cells, or just to run the machinery of existing cells, they burn the sugars they have produced. So do all life forms, but only plants can make the sugars trapping sunlight. Turn the sun off, and life will cease on this planet.

The energy in sugar molecules is released in several stages. There are six carbon atoms in glucose and these eventually end up as the gas carbon dioxide, so there are at least six stages. The machinery which breaks, burns the molecule, is called the citric acid cycle. It is a production line dedicated to producing energy, and it is a cyclic production line. It spins on and on, sucking in glucose molecules at the beginning, and spitting out carbon dioxide. The energy that held the carbon atoms together is not all dissipated as heat but captured in molecular packets, referred to as high energy packets, molecules of ATP, adenosine triphosphate. These ATP molecules are then used to power life processes, such as the replication of genetic material, cell division, growth, protein formation, and the repair of the large molecule aggregates, mitochondria and ribosomes.

This process of building and regeneration is exquisitely accurate, but not one hundred per cent so. Mistakes do occur, and this is partially the reason we have, like all species, finite and characteristic life-spans. The chemical reactions of life inside cells proceed efficiently enough for you to have a life-span, but these same chemical reactions produce entropy, which must be dumped outside of your body if it is not to grind to a halt. This dumping is in the form of carbon dioxide emission, heat loss, and various excretory processes. A life form is an entropy generator simply because life itself is highly ordered and low entropy in content, and hence by the Second Law of Thermodynamics, produces a disproportionate amount of extra entropy in its environment. You do this, your cat or canary does this. Your family does it, and your neighbourhood too. And so will the town. The greatest producers of entropy are the living entities we call cities. Just think of the persistent and steady effort which has to be made to keep the streets free of garbage and from getting holes in, the constant repair of buildings, the constant tearing down, and building up. All these processes are not merely metaphors of what happens in the living city of your body, *but analogues.*

Entropy and the embryo

As soon as the ovum is penetrated by a spermatozoon, an entropy increase occurs. Thereafter, as the fertilised ovum divides, the entropy per cell increases relative to the entropy of the ovum, however entropy is exported via the umbilicus into the mother, and she in turn exports it to the home she lives in, the city she lives in. Babies develop because they export entropy via their mothers. There is an increase in entropy per cell as the child develops, but there is also much synthesis of ordered molecules, organelles, tissues, and organs. The developing foetus is in negative entropy with respect to its mother, who is in negative entropy with respect to the place she lives in.

When the first membrane was formed in the dividing ovum, that membrane between the two daughter cells, the fight for life was on, since even at the very early stages, each cell is differentiating from the other, and therefore there will be a spontaneous mixing process across the membrane, which would of course, if allowed to happen, reduce the differentiation of developing cells. There would be no distinction between the cells of liver, skin, nerve and so on cells. So, from the beginning entropy increase has to be steadfastly resisted by the developing foetus. It is resisted, at great cost to the mother, and to the environment. Entropy is exported out of the foetus.

This process is continuous after birth, and, for a while, until sexual maturation, the increase in entropy per cell relative to that at birth is small. Maturation is a kind of entropy increase, and thereafter the increase in entropy appears to accelerate. We all have had the experience of seeing how people we have not met for some time appear to have dramatically aged, and that sense of shock is increased the older they are.

The metabolic rate, which can be measured as heat production, decreases throughout the lifespan. People literally slow down. In old people the fall can be quite substantial relative to their teens. This means that entropy is less and less successfully exported, and so entropy builds up in the tissues. This is ageing. More and more proteins are cross linked - wrinkles in the skin! - more of them are produced with errors; even DNA is time-damaged by chemical and radiation insult. Also there is the inherent imperfection of chemical life processes.

That we should take exercise comes directly from the need to export entropy out of our bodies. Exercise increases the metabolic rate during exercising, but it also increases the resting metabolic rate. A fit person sheds entropy more readily than an unfit sedentary one. However, a *caveat* here, it is possible to exercise and train to such an intense degree that the improvement of entropy export is vitiated by a rise in entropy caused by stress, which disturbs the partition mechanisms which keep metabolites and salts at correct but differing levels in different tissues. Shock is often lethal because it is registered as a breakdown of these mechanisms.

The large, tennis court, area of membranes of the lung in the human adult cannot be allowed to weep fluids or you drown, but that means fluid must be retained by the lung lining, and that requires various chemical pumps. Bronchitics suffer a temporary breakdown, and so have to cough up the excess fluid; such is the enormous energy cost in attempting to maintain fluid balance, bronchitics find themselves very tired and must take to bed. All this, even before opportunistic bacteria invade the lungs and multiply in the warm bronchitic fluids that should not be there so copiously.

The natural world seems to be a series of crises leading to other crises without permanent resolution. Individual biochemistry in every living thing is very finely balanced, and most balanced in mammals and birds which maintain their body temperature at constant levels against fluctuations external to them. But, these differences notwithstanding, life intrinsically produces entropy, and life-forms must export their entropy or die. Life is inherently at war with order around it.

As we have seen, life by its very nature produces entropy and must export it. Indeed, the fact of life on this planet means there is a much greater increase of entropy here than there would be without it. The moon is very near maximum entropy, very little happens there, a dead satellite.

One day, Earth will be dead too, and here is the paradox, because life teems here, it hastens the death of the planet. The more life there is here, the quicker it will die.

CHAPTER THREE

ENTROPY AND FOOD DYSFUNCTION

Chemical need

The chemical input we require to live is staggering. We need at least fifteen amino acids, but get on better with a mix of twenty-three commonly occurring ones, found in other animals' muscles and in plant cytoplasm. We use fats, the most common being the esters of glycerol and long chain fatty acids, but although we can nip and tuck with these there are several essential fatty acids we need, essential because we can't make them. We need them both structurally and chemically. Similar remarks can be made of the amino acids, some we can make in our cells, some we cannot. Carbohydrates really come down to three or four main mono-sacchrides, fructose being a common one in fruits, though we usually ingest our carbohydrates as dissacharrides, lactose in milk, maltose in honey - until the industrialisation of beet and cane we hardly ever ate sucrose, now found in most foods.

There are twelve molecules which we must have or become ill to the point of death, these are the vitamins, and the number of a round dozen is conservative. We cannot make these materials, but they are absolutely essential for our lives.

We need calcium, sodium, potassium, phosphate, chloride, and magnesium, usually in ionic form. These materials cannot be made from other materials, we have to ingest them or decline, to death, but the quantities daily are of the order of two grams or less, while vitamins are usually needed in milligram quantities, or in the case of B12, micrograms. The slew of diet, made up of fats, proteins, and carbohydrates, weighs several hundred grams. A good diet will contain iron, zinc, copper, manganese which, just like vitamins, are essential. We need these daily in milligram to double digit milligram amounts, we need more iron than copper for example. More exotic, but nonetheless essential, are molybdenum, nickel, iodine, fluoride, cadmium, selenium and cobalt in microgram amounts.

All these materials are not static, but are involved in a dynamic interplay amongst themselves, within the body and with the environment.

Though millions of water molecules pass in and out of a single cell per second, the level of water remains metabolically constant. Energy source molecules like glucose are consumed inside cells, and must be constantly replenished, or starvation results. The vitamin niacin is used up, and a net ten molecules enters each cell every second to make up for this; the same is true of ascorbic acid. Iron cannot be used up, iron stays iron, though it can change its positive charge; however about ten iron atoms enter the cell per second because iron can become unavailable in the cell when it is trapped in large protein molecules. There is a net loss of calcium in the urine, so loss from cells would occur, but a net intake of about a thousand calcium ions enter the cell per second. Vitamins B1 and B2 are not consumed at so great a rate as their vitamin cousin niacin, since repletion rate for B1 and B2 is one molecule per ten seconds.

Since there are about ten thousand million calcium ions in the cell, and repletion is at the rate of a thousand a second, only one ten millionth of the stock needs to be replenished, showing the fine tuning of cellular processes; however if the replenishment does not occur, the cell will began to dysfunction within just a few minutes. Cellular concentration of constituent molecules is not a hit or miss affair, but very finely calibrated. If the optimum number of materials are not present, dysfunction sets in, that is entropy rises. Too little of iron means anaemia, too much results in damaged livers.

Chemical reactions which occur in living tissue are all reactions which can take place in test tubes, there is nothing chemically special about the transformations of molecules and the synthesis of them which occur in living tissue. What is unusual is the *speed* at which they occur, many many many times faster than would occur if you simply mixed them in a test tube. The secret here are the enzymes, large molecules, proteins, which provide a nesting site for molecules to come together, and react. Part of the energy within the protein is used to facilitate these changes; each enzyme has its own special chemical reaction to facilitate. There are other molecules involved too, in this careful jig-sawing in three-D of molecules. Molecules cannot interact unless they meet. In test tubes it is merely a matter of thermal randomness, but when enzymes are present there is a meeting place. Reaction is also helped by medium-sized molecules, called co-enzymes. These are often vitamins.

We do not need large amounts of vitamins, a few milligrams a day usually, but if they are not present, then the various chemical reactions, that huge myriad host of different transformations, cannot take place. Vitamins and enzymes are the machine tools of the engineering of the cell, they transform billions of molecules without themselves being much changed; eventually some error occurs, eventually a co-enzyme is lost by diffusion, and so eventually since we cannot make these vitamins, they must be supplied by the diet. We can synthesise enzymes, but not their co-workers, vitamins. The disruptions in cellular activity following on a too small supply from the diet of vitamins are called deficiency diseases, and if prolonged, result in death. Vitamins then are essential for maintaining low entropy in organisms. Without them, entropy rises until it reaches such a level that death intervenes.

Man a sea-going vessel, provision it with hard biscuits, salt pork and beef, water, and set off on a six month voyage without landfall, and many of the crew will have died before journey's end. Those that remain will scarcely be able to perform. Those still walking will have loose teeth, bleeding from old wounds that healed years ago, while those in the sick bay will have bones broken, because although the fractures were sustained years ago, the substance of the re-growth of bone has dissolved away. Such is the inevitable result, and such was the result in countless expeditions of European seafarers before it was realised that fresh fruit and vegetables were essential. The symptoms are those of scurvy, and except in the worse cases where entropy has developed in the system so as to be irrecoverable, even those spontaneously bleeding will be cured once they get access to fruits, especially oranges, grapefruits, lemons, black and red currants. Fresh blood if effective too!

The crucial factor lacking in scurvy is ascorbic acid, vitamin C. We humans do not make it in our tissues, but it is necessary as a co-factor in the making of proteins for skin, joints, and critical connecting tissue, and the very walls of cells. The minimal amount daily required is thirty milligrams, but a variety of factors make this value too small to maintain truly robust health. Pregnant women require at least three times; people who smoke, too have an increased need, presumably because smoking destroys tissues, there being in smoke very active and degenerating molecules. These can be mopped up by vitamin C. The contraceptive pill also increases need.

The precariousness of life is revealed in the human being, requiring something of the order of one millionth of its body weight in the form of a white powder dissolved in various vegetable and fruit juices to stay in good health. The membrane, the cell wall defences of the body, crumbles when it is not repaired with vitamin C-dependent maintenance systems. Bacteria enter easily, the immune system is devalued - we may say that the walls against external entropy entering our bodies are only sustainable with vitamin C. Furthermore, the spontaneous breakdown of tissues within the body begins when tissue levels of vitamin C fall.

Vitamin C is lost without let, the rate of loss depending on concentration in the tissues and blood. It is lost in the urine, as well as being consumed during metabolic activity. This means a daily supply is necessary.

Since we evolved from the sea and have moved away from the aquatic environment, we might expect to find traces of this in our make up, since the first life in the sea would have been discrete pieces of living material whose inner composition would to some extent reflect the outer environment. We find that the mineral make up of the blood is similar to the sea, while the internal fluids of our cells are not. We have, as it were, evolved to live in our own sea, and the reason we carry it about with us is that we can control its composition, and hence control our metabolism. However, since the fluid composition inside cells is different from that in the blood, and since minerals can diffuse across cell membranes, the fact that the differences are maintained means that we preferentially pump some minerals out into the blood, while others are preferentially pumped into the cells from the blood. Usually this process is against the concentration of the nutrients. For example, there is fifty times more phosphate, seven times more calcium, and twenty times more potassium concentrated in cells than in blood, while blood has four times more sodium, reflecting our ancestral origin. Such maintenance takes a huge expenditure of energy, *indeed nearly eighty per cent of our total energy expenditure is used to maintain tissue and blood compositions at different but constant levels.* By preventing spontaneous mixing, we prevent spontaneous entropy increases in our bodies. In shock, this process is disturbed, and can be fatal. In death, the process halts, the tissues loose their integrity *vis à vis* the blood, and the blood loses its integrity *vis à vis* the tissues.

The source of these minerals is our food, and must be replenished since we lose minerals in urine, spittle, sweat, and faeces, as well as the constant abrasure of skin, nails, and the cutting of hair and beards. There are vital sexual differences: men lose B vitamins and trace minerals in ejaculation; women lose large quantities of many nutrients in menstruation and pregnancy.

Though our marine ancestry is obvious, we later evolved from hunters and gatherers, though gathering was the first form of nutrition, where wandering bands of hominids searched for roots, berries, eggs of birds and insects, fruits, and what was edible was eaten. Such a diet, unless on the sea shore, or large lake littoral, is necessarily high in vegetable material. The energy content is low, and Linus Pauling calculated that many kilograms had to be ingested to produce the required energy levels. This means that we used to ingest several grams of vitamin C a day, whereas in modern cities the value is so low, especially in high-rise apartments in inner cities where money is spent on colas, crisps, ice-creams and fast food, the intake is often so small as to produce sub-clinical signs of vitamin deficiency. Sub-clinical here means you are not so ill you need hospitalisation but your acuity and venturesomeness are reduced; the high-rise syndrome of lethargy, anxiety and often inability to cope is arguably partly caused by bad diet.

Using Pauling's diet analysis, I calculated that even if we were ingesting the recommended daily intakes of vitamin E, folic acid, iron, copper and potassium we would still be receiving less, by an average factor of four times less, than our ancestors would have obtained on their hunter gathering diet. Since a great number of people, even in the West, do not receive the recommended amounts, it is clear that there is something wrong with eating habits as well as the food consumed.

Most vegetable material we use as food, in the natural state, reflects our tissues more than our blood, however convenience foods and fast foods are usually highly salted. Bran from wheat before processing has one part sodium to forty parts potassium, but by the time it appears packaged as a cereal, there are three parts sodium to every one part potassium. Clearly this puts a strain on the body, because this balance has to be altered to fit blood and cells. Too much sodium is lethal, because it causes localised droughts in cells, by literally holding onto the water molecules, thereby sequestering them from vital reactions. The excessive use of salt by the food industry and personal preference for the salt cellar can lead to hypertension, again because salt attracts water and so causes pressure. As early as 1980 the National Research Council of America warned of this insidious process, but fast food continues to get faster and its consumers slower.

The amount of vitamin C is low in junk foods. For example, you find only negligible residues of vitamin C in the tiny shreds of lettuce leaf you get with fast food burgers. Western fast food culture is one low in vitamin C. For children, who need more of the vitamin than adults, a diet of cokes, burgers, processed food, is inadequate. Most of the little amount of vitamin C obtained in these circumstances come from chips.

Sub-clinical avitaminosis is the worry here: poor developmental rates, reduced energy, and increased vulnerability to minor infections are the results. Not so spectacular as the scurvy of the men o'war, but nonetheless high entropy which we can do without.

We may conclude that the fast food chains and the supermarket check-outs militate not *for* good vitamin levels, but *against*, and are therefore entropy producers.

Life is entropy-vulnerable; the resources of living tissue are finite, and so entropy wins in the end. Our challenge is to reduce our rate of creation of entropy. We cannot do that if world population continues to increase, but even now, in the advanced democracies let alone the Third world, our ability to reduce entropy is hampered by poor food.

Obesity

Obesity is the most commonly observed form of malnutrition in the west, but is not the only sign of high entropy diets: hypertension, vascular disease, cancer rates, are all increased on fast food, diets with little fresh produce; perhaps even motor and brain function are impaired.

Obesity is life threatening when gross, and de-enhancing when merely excessive. Obesity is the stockpiling of fats under the skin and around organs. The condition is associated with increased fatty acid and cholesterol levels in the blood and lymph. The heart has to pump blood through a vastly increased networks of capillaries in the fatty tissue to keep it alive. *Fat is entropy stockpiled.* To lose gross fat deposits means a massive biochemical campaign which produces much heat and uses up mineral stores and demands increased vitamin intake.

A sedentary adult female in the west will produce about 2,200 kilocalories daily. Entropy can be measured as heat change divided by the temperature at which it occurs. In thermodynamics the convention is to use degrees Kelvin, and since this means very approximately that the temperature of our bodies on this scale is 310, our sedentary female is expelling 7100 entropy units per twenty-four hours. Sedentary males, being on average larger, but having the same blood heat, expel more entropy than this. Active people expel even more, good for them, but bad for the planet! The total bio-mass of human beings produce enough heat *every minute* from their bodies to boil one hundred million 2-pint tea kettles. I am assuming boiling from room temperature, and six billion people as world population. Or, to put it another way, the average adult produces enough heat every ten minutes to make a cup of tea.

I say entropy units merely for illustration, in science we would not use this term but heat units per degree Kelvin; I use entropy units here merely to emphasise that entropy is measurable, is a quantity, that it is real. Further, my use of tea making is not merely for amusement, we make tea by boiling water, that is, we put heat into it and make the water molecules move around faster and faster until they escape into the atmosphere: that is, we boil water by increasing the entropy in water from the tap.

However, if you take in 1,000 Calories of food a week more than you utilise, you stockpile, as fat, 3,230 entropy units. Many people are many pounds overweight, and statistical studies show that overweight people suffer from many diseases more than people at their ideal weight. Note that a person 14 kilograms overweight has stockpiled 35,000 entropy units. It is little wonder then that such people have health, that is, high entropy problems.

Inuits when living their traditional life eat large amounts of blubber from whales and seals, and much fat from polar bears. Because they, the Inuits living in this condition, rely on their own emulsifiers for fat digestion, little of the saturated fat is absorbed into their blood streams, while the liquid fats, the useful polyunsaturates are. *Homo sapiens* cannot digest fats of the solid type unless the fat is broken up into droplets, and this job is done by bile fluids, which are sluiced into the alimentary canal with finely regulated feed-back mechanisms, so that excess fat is not absorbed. The result is that although Inuit children and adults ingest thousands of fat calories, they do not enter their biochemical systems, but pass unprocessed out via the faeces. Inuits are well covered with subcutaneous fat in their traditional way of life, but are seldom obese in the grotesque Western sense: you can hardly paddle a kayak, hunt, and maintain agility if you are grossly overweight.

Contact with Western foods has however produced the same problems amongst Inuits as we find in affluent societies: heart disease and diabetes being front runners in this entropy race. If you look at the label of bread sold in supermarkets, you will find there are emulsifiers present. In the manufacture of many mass-produced meat products emulsifiers are used. These emulsifiers make the fat globules very small, and digestion is easy. The result is that fast foods and ersatz bread short circuit the regulation mechanisms of our digestive tracts. Industrial emulsifiers mean we absorb more fat than we would have done. This is probably why obesity is associated with the gobbling of fried hens and burgers, with so-called French fries. The reason for addition of these emulsifiers is to enhance easy eating. When you eat food that has not been much degraded by chemical and physical means, such as fresh fruit, lean cuts of meat, fish, and pulses, various vegetables, we are quickly satiated. Fast food, it seems, is designed *not* to satiate, and so it is easy to go to one of the chains and simply gobble the stuff up. Your body does not tell you when to stop, because it has been fooled. Is this a deliberate policy on behalf of fast food chains to increase profit? They may profit, but what of the cost to society? The connecting link between entropy increase and profit seen so clearly here, is something I will revert to.

The enormous transport systems, the cold stores, the chemical and mechanical preparations needed for fast food, produce huge entropy in the form of heat, because of the intense requirements for energy and fuels. The fact that these massive chains give people throw-away plates, bags, cups and containers, adds to the detritus of this planet, and usually the throw-away stuff is not biodegradable. We can only conclude that the big fast-food chains provide poorish food at the expense of massive pollution, and pollution *is* entropy increase.

Imagine a culture where people eat good fruit, vegetables, meats and fish, and do so eating well-prepared meals attended by wine. In this Utopia culture children drink wine, usually watered, so they do not need sleeping tablets, nor do they suffer from anaemia - wine contains many minerals. Imagine this culture invaded by many objects: millions of TV sets, billions of cans of cola, hundreds of millions of battery chickens and hundreds of millions of burger bits. Have this stuff consumed before TV in fifteen minutes, or in a car, or even sauntering down a fume-filled street. The result is a massive increase of entropy in the people of our imagined Utopia, and in the very structure of the Utopia. A huge increase of entropy results from the purely mixing process itself, that is, the pollution. This mixing is driven by millions of pounds of advertising, and the destruction of hundreds of thousands of small businesses: fishmongers, grocers, greengrocers, fruiterers, bakers. There is another entropy cost however, anaemia, and the poor diet leads to general ill health later. Again, we have to ask: Is it moral, or even sensible, to allow high profit, high entropy businesses, to pollute on the scale they do? A little thought will show the answer to be inescapably no.

If we grow bacteria in a flask with a fixed amount of nutrient, at first the cells divide 2, 4, 8, 16 and so on. However as the numbers increase they consume the nutrient, and so growth stops. Often the bacteria die poisoned by their own waste products *before* they have eaten all the nutrient. *Death intervenes for that system because the entropy could not be exported.*

Keep rats in a fixed area, but provide all the food and water they need. They reproduce until they are stressed by overcrowding. Tough harem king rats raise litters with several females. Bands of homosexual rats kill females, and bands of female rats kill anything they can. The system has collapsed because of unexported entropy shows not only in the death of so many rats from fighting, but also in bizarre behaviour patterns. If the rat mistreatment is done without all the food and water they need, they simply die of starvation, though cannibalism is an option.

The condition of human beings on this planet is similar to that of the bacteria and rats: we will reach sooner or later, a limit in our ability to grow food; we certainly have a fixed planet size, and *we cannot export our entropy off the planet, because the very effort of trying to do so would produce even more entropy.*

CHAPTER FOUR

THE ENTROPY TRAP

We have already seen that living things produce entropy, and we can now refine the idea. Consider, there are more cells in your body than there are people on this earth, about ten billion times more, and each cell contains trillions of atoms, *yet the human body functions as a coherent whole*. Clearly this implies exquisite organisation, order at the molecular level, and hence the tissue level, thence to organs, and systems, and finally the coordinated whole. *Such order can only exist by producing great disorder around it*. This is so because entropy *must* increase for any change on this planet, and since our bodies can only exist in low entropy, we are entropy machines which dump our disorder outside us.

To do this we need energy, and we get that energy from our food. We kill things to live, whether animal or plant, and so in the very act of obtaining energy produce entropy. These comments apply to all life forms on this planet, though plants do not produce so much entropy per gram of biomass as we do, since many have the capacity to obtain energy freely from the sun.

In order to eat, we grow food and kill animals. As our population rises, so must the animal and the plant population. Since there are only so many nutrients for plants in the soil and water of the earth, plus some from the atmosphere, and since solar

41

energy is a finite transmission, it must follow that there is a limit to human population.

It is fashionable today to decry Malthus, the Victorian who suggested that since population with sufficient food tends to increase as $1 \rightarrow 2 \rightarrow 4 \rightarrow 8$ and so on, while food production follows $1 \rightarrow 2 \rightarrow 3 \rightarrow 4 \rightarrow 5$ and so on, population will outstrip food production and famine will result. It is certainly true that his bald statement does not follow from the method he used to prove it, but it is incontestably true that if *homo sapiens* is going to live a recognisably human and decent life in terms of space, shelter, sanitation and food, the planet can only sustain a certain number of us. Faced with that fact, it is pointless to argue about Malthus, history has passed him by, he is even, in academic debate, irrelevant.

What I am trying to impress is that we need to understand the role of entropy in our lives, for we cannot brook the impact of entropy. It is to me astonishing that otherwise able and learned people think that we *homo sapiens* can always reverse what we have done as a species on this planet. What we have done in the past decade is *already* irreversible. The awful fact of this planet with its teeming life is that events occur daily which can never be reversed. We cannot get back the oil we so recklessly burn, we cannot reverse pollution without making more pollution - it takes energy to disperse oil slicks, and energy produces more heat, more entropy.

The higher the population, the greater the amount of entropy formed, the greater the amount of entropy the less utilisable are the planet's resources. For example, Europeans use phosphate mined and then concentrated as fertiliser; Asians use the phosphate contained in human waste, thereby producing less entropy. Europeans pour phosphate in faeces into the seas, where it forms calcium phosphate. This phosphate is only recoverable by expenditure of energy which produces more entropy.

The growth of population results in a great acceleration of the rate of increase of global entropy, however the rate of increase of entropy of a developing foetus, per capita, is many thousands of times greater: from one cell to trillions in a few months. After birth, there is a further increase in size of a factor of about twenty. Growth necessarily means global increase of entropy. The more entropy the more energy needed to utilise resources. The more energy utilised, the greater the production of entropy. This is similar to the myth of Sisyphus. He carried or rolled a bolder up a hill, but it always ran down again. His fate was that of perpetual futile striving. In our case, as we increase in numbers, as we use more and more energy (electricity, burn petrol or oil) the steeper our hill becomes the hill of entropy, so that soon we will not have the energy to climb it, and hastening the arrival of such a time is our interference with natural cycles.

Natural cycles

Unlike animal life, plant life maintains its integrity without creating so much entropy mayhem around it, and this is because plants get a free supply of energy from the sun. Light is trapped by plants using a variety of pigments, the most common being the green chlorophyll, and this energy is used to make sugars from water and carbon dioxide in the atmosphere. The extraordinary result is that trees pump oxygen out into the atmosphere, a net amount, during daylight hours. In the dark, this photosynthesis ceases, and although respiration occurs during the daylight hours, it takes on a greater importance in the economy of the plant during darkness. The sugars formed by photosynthesis are burned, using oxygen, to produce chemical energy which is used to translocate food materials and grow new tissue, and for reproduction. Here then we have a beautifully efficient cycle of carbon. We have nothing so efficient in any of our industrial processes.

Humans have subverted this cycle. Wood itself is made from the trapped carbon from the atmosphere. When wood is burned, and we humans have been doing that for tens of thousands of years, the entropy of the planet is increased; we do it for the energy released. Wood is the raw material from which coal, gas, and oil is produced. We have consumed billions of tons of wood, thereby breaking the cycle and releasing vast quantities of heat and carbon dioxide. Since we are also destroying plant life, reducing forestation, the rise of carbon dioxide, and the fall of oxygen, results. Carbon dioxide produces a warming effect since the molecules absorb solar energy rather better than oxygen or nitrogen which make up much of the atmosphere. In the atmosphere, carbon dioxide increase then has a disproportionate impact on global thermodynamics. It also contributes to the so-called greenhouse effect. Many units of energy, photons, from the sun would reflect on surfaces on the planet and bounce back into space carrying their energy with them. Carbon dioxide and many industrial effluent gases prevent this, usually by direct capture of the photons. Pollution is seriously interfering with loss of entropy through photons escaping from the planet into space. This so-called global warming effect has implications for water levels, and storm trends, all increasing global entropy.

The atmosphere, upon which all life depends, is relative to the earth in thickness not as an orange skin, but an onion skin. Go up from Earth's surface a little over seven miles, and oxygen runs out. When Saddam Hussein set fire to the Kuwait oil wells he irretrievably damaged this planet, *for all time.*

On that basis alone, it is clear there is a new international crime: The reckless criminal damage to the environment.

Energy sources

The potential entropy locked up in nuclear waste is vast, it merely needs for the nuclear cesspits in which it is stored to leak. But where is safe for this material? Clearly nowhere, the risk is too high. The stuff is entropy active for hundreds of years. What a bequest for generations yet unborn! Clearly, if we have any respect for ourselves, this planet, and the implacably unbreakable truths of thermo-dynamics, no more nuclear fission reactors should be constructed. If that is not achievable now, it must be a long term aim.

The most efficient energy supplier is the chloro-phyllic plant. It is cyclic, and is fuelled by radiant energy from the sun, which comes free of transportation and import tariffs. If *homo sapiens* were really wise the wealthiest parts of the globe would be where there is most sun, but the tropics and sub-tropics contain most slums.

Another clean and efficient energy supply is available from the moon. The moon makes tides, and tides represent more energy than we shall ever get from nuclear fission, since we would all be dead by radioactive poisoning trying to match such a colossal and energy production, which at present is ignored and wasted.

Other energy sources are minor in comparison to solar and lunar forms. The great energy companies, oil, gas, coal, nuclear are hardly likely to view lunar and solar power with a friendly eye. Why, wars are fought over oil, usually in countries where the sun beats down all day. If solar panels were produced in industrial rather than DIY quantities, they would be very cheap indeed, and so the demand for fossil fuels would fall drastically. However, oil, coal and nuclear cartels have a vested interest in not supporting tidal or sun energy sources; they want their return on their oil, coal and nuclear investments.

The nitrogen cycle

Another cycle we subvert is the nitrogen cycle. Nitrogen is an essential constituent of living things, making up part of the proteins and other important molecules, including DNA. As a living thing grows it stockpiles nitrogen in highly organised structures such as proteins and nucleic acids. When it dies, bacteria decompose the flesh and release ammonia, and this can be absorbed as ammonium salts and used by plants to build their own tissue, which can provide food for animals. Furthermore, there are bacteria in the soil, often associated with clovers, which can absorb nitrogen from the atmosphere, and form proteins. Nitrogen then is in cycle. This cycle is not as entropy low as carbon because it is not driven by free energy from the sun, but is nonetheless a true cycle.

The entropy trap

There are dove Darwinians who hold that nature is a balance. There are hawk Darwinians who hold that nature is red in tooth and claw. You can find things in nature to support either view, but the total picture is one of change and ever increasing entropy. What nature achieved before *homo sapiens* began their deadly work was keeping entropy increase to a minimum. The biomass rests on two cycles, that of nitrogen and carbon, the latter being more fundamental since it is the conduit through which energy from the sun flows. Life has evolved to be able to cope. Predators increase in numbers the better they become at preying, but then the prey population goes down, and so some predators will die. Observations of this kind lead to the balance notion, but there seems little balance in microbes which kill their hosts.

Wild fluctuations occur in nature, for example locust numbers, blotting out the sky in one season, absent the next. In all, little irreversible damage appears to occur to the biomass as a whole, that is until *homo sapiens* arrived. Slash and burn in Africa helped produce the Sahara desert.

Once the rain forests are destroyed, they cannot be regained. Chop up a rain forest, and the rains wash the soil away. The Amazonian areas won't become prairies, but deserts. Reclamation of fertile soil once covered by concrete may be irreversible because of costs. The concentration of radioactive isotopes is proving irreversible, witness the Selafield debacle: where to put the waste? The fossil fuels, billions of years in the making, are being consumed at a rate which must lead to depletion.

The reclamation of polluted rivers and lakes is sometimes possible, but always at enormous cost, *and that wealth can only have come from other wounds on the planet*: whatever we do we always increase global entropy, our challenge is to slow the rate of acceleration, and slow it drastically.

CHAPTER FIVE

THE BODY NATIONAL

So far what I have said is basically orthodox chemical and biological science, it is just that I have teased out the implications of entropy in these sciences and referred them more directly to life as we commonly experience it. Now I would like to show that the concept of entropy is universal, and so are its applications.

It is not original to observe that there are similarities between nation states and the mammalian body, but it is probably original to assert that the resemblance is not one of metaphor or analogy, but real. If indeed this were the case, that the relationship between the nation state and the mammalian organisation was real and not merely apparent, then we would have a new tool for understanding the health and wealth of nations.

The brain would be the government, though that might cause amusement in certain cynical Western quarters which regard governments as brainless; the nerves, media, including telecommunications and postal services; the vascular system would be the canals, roads, airways, and railways. Cities could be regarded as organs of the state, though it would pressing analysis too fine to assume say that Birmingham were the liver of England, and London its heart, but to some tastes this might be palatable. Basic packing tissue would be the countryside. The

50

armed forces would be teeth, nails, fists; the police would be the immune system. The bones presumably would be the actual solid earth and buildings. Individual persons would be the cells that inhabit and make up this body national.

Just as the individual person, the individual mammal, has internal economies, commonly referred to as metabolism, so does a nation state. England imports many materials, just as each human ingests food. England exports material, just as each human being excretes urea and breathes out carbon dioxide.

If indeed a nation is a living organism it must perforce face the same pattern as any other life form, the build up of entropy. Nations must export entropy, or die. We should also expect that just as mammals develop and age, then die, so would a nation. A nation is in a constant battle against the entropy it inevitably produces. Successful nations succeed by dumping their entropy onto other nations. This leads to a new view of economics and warfare, which is discussed later.

People as mammals have interests which are essentially unchangeable: the need for food and water, the need for shelter; these needs cannot be wished away, indeed much suffering occurs if these needs are not met. In like manner all nation states have interests which cannot be altered no matter what complexion of government is in power. For example, England must trade, must import raw materials and export finished goods. Much trouble has been caused globally by governments taking an ideological line which seeks to ignore the essential needs of their nation. What American national need was served by landing ground troops in Vietnam? No one has found a positive answer. Ideology called the tune the piper played, and much did America pay for that dirge.

In economics, nature's laws are often ignored for ideological reasons, even to the point of commandeering the economy so that it is no longer a market, and so cannot compete and cannot be measured. Nature is always pragmatic: if something does not work it dies. Ideology, rather than pragmatism, of whatever hue, left or right, is akin to mental illness in a government.

The notions of egalitarianism and socialism appeal to a sense of fairness. The idea of equality has become current in Europe now. However, appealing as such ideas may be, they do not represent a mirror of reality, but nonetheless are stubbornly held on to against evidence of their dangerous impracticality. Socialism as practised in command economies has in the last half century beggared the nations which practised it. Currently egalitarianism in education wastes the clever, as they are taught in the same classrooms as children who find learning to read difficult.

This is not to say *laissez faire* capitalism is a natural law, the fact is that unfettered capitalism leads to as much chaos and degeneration as unrestrained socialism, the systems of extreme left and right politics are entropy makers *par excellence*.

Although increase of entropy is inevitable, cooperation of the parts of a nation can reduce the rate of production of disorder. Human beings are social animals, the family, the community, the township or borough, the city, the nation, and the relationships of nations reveal this. Irrespective of what ideology is taken up, these facts remain.

The recognition that cooperation can yield dividends in the fight against entropy is being played out as never before in scale in Europe. Individual European states are not strong enough to individually dump their entropy onto other parts of the world. America is strong enough, she sequesters more energy and goods than any other nation, and there is little any other group at present can do about it. America's entropy export is pollution, war and usury.

The likelihood of a majority of the nation states in Europe, in the West, maintaining their standard of living *individually* against the world, for European wealth concentration is at least five times higher than its population would suggest, is small; hence the drive towards closer ties. If you wish sovereignty, it is as well to ask what use it is if you cannot do anything although you want to because you are too poor or too weak; sovereignty as discussed in the nineteen nineties by Portillo and Redwood, is a chimera. This is something French and German leaders, for different reasons, have understood for some time. The Franco-German axis is a recognition that they cannot go it alone against the world.

Clearly these are political questions, but their reality is based on the biology of nations, and biology is ultimately based on the laws of chemistry, and chemistry has at its heart the Second Law of Thermodynamics, entry increases with time, *inevitably*.

The notion of a nation being comparable with a life form, in a real rather than a metaphysical sense, can lead to insights into political and social issues, and below I touch on some of these views.

Criminality in the body national

Crime, such as theft, vandalism, murder, rape, fraud would appear to bear relationship to the body national that cancer does to the body biological. In cancer, cells no longer participate in the bodily economy but disrupt it, and if unchecked, kill the body. Crime increases entropy in the body national.

Cancer is a life form. Its organisation depends on disorganising the tissue it lives on. Organised crime is the exact counterpart to a nation as a malignant tumour, and cancers expand by splitting off parts of themselves to grow elsewhere in the body: this metastasis and its counterpart in organised crime is in setting up new cells and offices in other cities than the origin.

There are two defining features of organised crime: the threat and use of violence and the breaking of laws. The first feature is universal, usually threat is sufficient to bend people to criminal will, but violence becomes actual when threat is insufficient. The use of violence naturally increases the power of threat. The second feature of breaking laws seems to be a truism, but in a spate of books on organised crime, especially those on the Krays in London and the mobs in New York, this feature is glossed over. Laws at their best are entropy restrainers just as good parenting teaches children not to eat faeces and play with fire. Criminality is always the breaking of law and increases entropy in the body national, just as cancerous cells damage the body natural.

Revolutions

A revolution may be expected when citizens demand reform or change, but the government refuses to accommodate this, and does so by force. A revolution is certain if the citizenry insist on change, and are prepared to force change. It seems that the greater the desire for change times the resistance to it, is the measure of the drive to violent revolution, and violence is an increase in entropy.

Does this theorem fit history? I believe it does. For example, Cromwell was confronting a king who would not brook change, even though parliament wanted it, the result was a revolution, the second only major civil war in England; the French king Louis XIV would not countenance change, and so the French revolution occurred. Tsar Nicholas of Russia would not brook change either, thence came the Leninist revolution.

Entropy and civil unrest

The product of the number of strikes times the violence of the pickets increased under the UK Labour government before Thatcher's. The increase of entropy was such that garbage clogged the towns and cities, rats scuffled on main streets, and the dead were unburied. This was in 1979, and called the Winter of Discontent. It was also one of the most obvious examples of social decay, the entropy literally spewing out into the streets.

Global entropy

When the number of people in a nation is larger than their ability to feed, clothe, and shelter themselves, then clearly a pathology has arisen. Overpopulation is a catastrophe in a nation state, but other factors leading to increase of entropy play their part too.

If people in a nation consume more than they produce, poverty is inevitable. If they produce more than they consume, standard of living increases, but the cost is increase in *global* entropy.

Just as in nature there is no free lunch, so in the world no nation will get a free helping hand. You can get loans, but you have to repay the principle, and with interest.

Germany, France, America, Japan, England have large numbers of *technically* skilled people: engineers, industrial chemists, agricultural biologists, systems managers, the list is very very long. These skills are hard won: a research scientist will have to study from age about fifteen to twenty-six to be recognised by the scientific community as properly trained. To be an adequate engineer you need advanced mathematics, at least three years' undergraduate training, and several more learning the industrial ropes. Such training is expensive, and is backed up by an industrial technical infrastructure. Advanced nations consequently produce more entropy than unindustrialised nations.

Just as life forms compete, that is endeavour to keep their entropy down by shifting it to their competitors, so do nations. Charity and overseas aid appeals to the affluent West, but only as long as its standard of living is not threatened by such largesse. The Third World person lives in dire entropy, he dies early, proving that he has absorbed more entropy than the affluent Westerner, but he does not export entropy in terms of industrial pollution.

CHAPTER SIX

ENTROPY IS A FACT OF LIFE

The condition of the poor in late Victorian England was so bad that English boys in the East End of London were two inches shorter and several pounds lighter than their age counterparts at Eton. The Beveridge Report recommended medical services being supplied to the poor, since the nation's human stock was severely debilitated. Aneurin Bevan pushed through the National Health scheme. The thrust of the reforms was to increase working efficiency of the employed to improve child health; it was not envisaged that people would be turned into super Britons who would live for ever. Such schemes reduce entropy in society, for disease is certainly an increase in individual entropy, often to the point of death. Death is inevitable, ultimately, in the very old, but premature death is certainly not countenanceable in a civilised society amongst children.

As the years have progressed so has medical intervention. We have now moved away from mending a child's broken arm for free, or giving him dental treatment, free, so that he has teeth at age forty and beyond. Cocktails of drugs, costing upwards of twelve thousand pounds a years are now demanded by AIDS sufferers; sexual surgery is practised at state expense to put penises where vulva were, and vice versa; hips are replaced in old people;

lungs, livers, hearts are replaced. Intervention often begins very late in life and is sequential: a hip replacement, then a liver transplant; perhaps a heart transplant when the patient is bed-ridden? The permutations are endless, the cost escalating, and who is to make the decisions? If a person will die if they do not have a heart transplant, and a heart transplantation is done, and it is subsequently found that a liver transplant is also required, subsequent to the first transplant, who shall deny a subsequent lung transplant? Who shall insist? And so here is the paradox: the National Health was put in place to reduce entropy in the nation, but now, by keeping people alive at great cost to the nation and often great pain to the patient, the entropy in the population rises, not falls. This paradox is compounded fiendishly by medical intervention itself producing intractable diseases and new threats: hospital intensive care units offer a wide variety of drug resistant bacteria, while we now have strains of TB which are resistant to conventional antibiotics.

The gleaming modern hospital, with its rooms dedicated to keeping unviable foetuses alive next door to operating theatres where tens of thousands of healthy children are cut to pieces in the womb, and then the parts sucked out to be consumed in the hospital crematorium without rite, is the modern church of health - or is it institutionalised disease? In these huge complexes, agonising treatments are carried out leading to persistent nausea, hair loss and weight loss, with a gain at best of a few months of life. These cathedrals of advanced intervention feature old people being kept alive by technical wizardry which elevates the professional status of the wizard. These ideopathic emporia where the sick and the merely pregnantly healthy go to be confronted with the drugs and scalpels of modern medicine, seem to be a church of technique without moral content.

Ultimately the cost of these places as now run cannot be met, the demand is unquantifiable, yet who can stop this entropy-creating colossus that is the NHS? Would the highly paid surgeon? The cancer specialist? The politician who if he squeaks "thrift" will lose his credibility? Who? Religious leaders?

For the National Health to grow cancerously all that is required is that sane men and women stay silent; but who of us would pass up a free medical intervention if it meant we might have years more of productive life? As things stand, the hospices, which actually recognise the fact that we *die*, if not of disease, then old age (not recognised by the World Health Organisation) are beacons of sanity and dignity.

It is a truism that the NHS consumes vast quantities of money, and we have seen that the NHS produces entropy, can we conclude that cash movement is inescapably linked to entropy increase? Certainly that is the case with the NHS, but it is also true in general, since we live by exchanging cash for goods and services, and living increases entropy. The trick is to be sure *your* entropy is kept to a minimum.

Here then is an apparent paradox: if *you* have cash, you can reduce entropic effects on you by improving your way of life, but this produces entropy, and someone somewhere will absorb it, and so age quicker, die younger. Cash can help an individual, but ultimately the entropy it represents to others will be felt by others. The planet is finite, entropy increases, wealth can stave it off for the few, but the planet has to absorb what the wealthy do.

The cruel dilemma

If we assume that the movement of cash implies an entropy increase, then the payment of benefits involves a rise in entropy. But where is the rise? Cash flows from central government to the accounts and pockets of people who are not earning money. The government raises the money by taxation of individuals and companies who are earning money. The work ethic is known to have been undermined, and in such areas where welfare payment is high, there is also much crime and a general running down of public behaviour, with squalor and graffiti commonplace. There is a further retreat from stable families, with children being born to parents who cannot have any realistic likelihood of ever paying for their housing, food or clothing. All these factors, and this list is not exhaustive, represent a higher entropy in comparison to life lived with higher income and stabler families. Thus, we observe that the general assumption that movement of cash as welfare usually means an increase in entropy.

However, who would it be who would suggest that children of feckless adults should not receive free dental treatment? Only a cruel and heartless faction. Who would suggest that children of non-working parents be un-housed and un-fed? A despot only, surely. And so we have it: *the problem in a democracy is insoluble by its very nature.*

Nature solves such problems because nature has no conscience. Animals born of inadequate parents do not learn the skills necessary to survive, and so fail against more rugged individuals of the same species and other species. There is no welfare in nature, in human society there is welfare because of the observed needs of the weak. In nature when weakness it observed, it is immediately exploited. Western democratic capitalist states, insist on helping the weak within their borders, and in so doing create more entropy in their very vitals.

The problem is compounded by the competition between welfare giving and non welfare giving countries. Already the resources of the planet are inadequate for all. If China, if it were possible, began to consume energy and raw materials at the rate the Americans do, for example, the rest of the world would have to starve. It is impossible that the Third World can ever reach the consumption of the West, because there simply are not enough planetary resources. Import from space? When? The ineradicable fact is that every human being is fighting against entropy, and so increases it. The devil gets the hindmost. Nature has the most effective ploy: it simply lets the weak go to the wall to be crushed by entropy.

Meanwhile the inexorable entropic production of population increase continues. What will the West do, scale down its consumption? What will the Third World do, resist the temptation to ape the West? Intractability is a fact of life when the way of life produces the intractable problem. Human beings produce too much entropy for this planet to be healthy. The accelerating increase of entropy can be reduced only by reduction of population increase. However, it may occur to another Hitler that such is only palliative, and the search will be on for the final solution. Future Hitlers are inevitable unless the fact of entropy is recognised, unless its inexorable nature is accepted. We can as a species reduce the rate of increase of entropy without resort to extreme dictatorships, but only if democracies reduce their populations, and the Third World would follow suit. However, the runes do no appear propitious.

The Welfare State in Britain is heading for £100 billion a year, and that does not include education. The UK simply does not *earn* enough to support this figure without borrowing. A rich *enough* state can afford to spend on ever burgeoning welfare. There is however no such state in the world. Debate on welfarism usually, and rightly, focuses on the inability to meet demand. The debate is made difficult because civilised countries insist that the weak, the old, the young, should be helped. Can France, can Britain, can Germany live with the notion of having starving children riddled with disease simply because their parents have not the skills to support them? Politically the notion is absurd, but unless something is done in the major economies, a shift to the conditions of the Third World where the poor do die of starvation, exposure, and disease without help, is inevitable in the advanced countries of the West.

At the centre of this Gordian knot is a concept: it is not right that some people live well, and others do not: hence the level of benefits are arranged to approximate to the average. It is not enough that children are sheltered, they have to be housed as well as the average working family; it is not enough that children get free medical care, the care must also include what middle class children have, too; it is not enough that old people are rendered comfortable, they must have free access to expensive operations. The equality concept is an ideology, and ideologies by their very nature ignore realities. But there is a deeper fact: reality never ignores ideologies, and reality always wins in the end. The crunch with welfarism comes when the working population has to pay more than it is prepared to pay in taxes. Result, an explosive rise in entropy. The poor will riot for welfare, the working taxed will resist tax levels, which may involve a riot or two. Judging by the resourcefulness of well paid people in reducing their tax bills, they may not have to resort to street violence, but the money needed for welfare will not be forthcoming.

No easy solution

To recap, welfare, as originally conceived by Beveridge in the UK, was to reduce hardship in the poor, especially in the young, who had done nothing to deserve their miserable diet and medical services. After Prime Minister Wilson, the notion of Welfare as Equality began to take hold. The former view of welfare reduces entropy in the body national; the latter increases it. I suggest this idea has the status of an inviolable natural law. There is however an alternative: the *Attila the Hun option*, whereby the G7 agree to export their entropy out into the world by commerce and warfare. This would meet the fiscal needs of welfarism at home, but turn the planet of the Third World into hell. It may be unthinkable at the moment, but the Hun option has showed itself very attractive to many states throughout history.

But some Hun aficionados do not stop at exporting entropy, they think that health services should be entirely privatised, and so should education. This would make Britain, for example, rather like Victorian Britain, where millions were undernourished, ill-clad, ill-housed, devoid of medical care, illiterate, and oppressed.

Nonetheless, the choice seems to be - export entropy or see your institutions fall to pieces under the pounding of social entropy waves. Meanwhile we can expect to see an ever vigorous acceleration of free trade by G7 with the developing world which is nothing other than the commercial face of the Hun option.

Faced with the cruelties of rampant capitalism which turned men into adjuncts of machines, Marx proposed the abolition of private property and the introduction of state ownership of industry and utilities. The result was a near century of strife, with millions of people living repressed and drab lives. Meanwhile capitalist societies strove for a better distribution of wealth, for example F D Roosevelt's New Deal, and Attlee's nationalisation of the welfare system in Britain after World War II.

Excesses there were in these social experiments, but there is within capitalism, if unchecked, a pitiless urge to *do anything* for a profit. That an industrialist is paid millions to sack huge numbers of his workforce, thereby injecting massive entropy into the social welfare system, is clearly a form of rampant capitalism; call it downsizing, it is nonetheless a hearkening back to *laissez faire* capitalism of the last century.

In contrast, increasing the level of welfare to such a point that an economy fails, is similar to the command economy of the failed communist systems.

Neither extreme can ever work, and no compromise can either if the level of population increases.

Today there is emerging in America and Western Europe a super rich class, while the lowest paid workers can never expect to own their own home, and are fearful of loosing their employment. Since unfettered capitalism leads to massive injections of entropy into the social fabric, child labour for example, and since communism leads to high entropy creation in inefficient industrial practices, there is little merit in lurching from one system to the other, and back again. The sense of balance achieved fitfully in the Western democracies is the best hope.

CHAPTER SEVEN

SEX, RACE AND ENTROPY

Unless Draconian measures are taken to keep different ethnic groups apart, they will mix, and they will bear children. In time the population will be homogenous, it will have reached a genetic equilibrium, and so race tensions will disappear. Any attempt on creed or race grounds to separate people must involve a huge investment of energy, and is doomed ultimately to failure, since expenditure of energy here is policing, law enforcement and so on, which creates further partitions to be broken, further "membranes" to be passed through. Apartheid was therefore doomed, and so were Hitler's policies. It can be done for a limited time, but always the cost is high, not least in misery, but always in terms of increase of entropy.

If, as in tyrannies or slaveries, severe compartmentalisation methods are used, the resultant pressures, potential releasable entropy, must, perforce, lead to the destruction of such a regime. Ultimately such regimes fail, and always must. The American slavery system was based on colour, and in that regard was a most peculiar institution, slavery historically being colour-blind, as in Islam, or Rome. The result was that the South in its doomed effort to retain its race compartments, actually tried to destroy the federal American states by secession, and so a civil war followed in which the entropy rise was

enormous: 750,000 soldiers died. It follows from this entropy picture of regimes and societies that rigid systems are *inherently* unstable, since compartments in the form of dogma and bad law, as well as physical separation of peoples, are barriers to mixing, while mixing is spontaneous, and so unless the barriers are maintained a sudden mixing occurs in a rigid society - and sudden means a riot, a civil wary. Rigid societies always change dramatically, not gradually as in a democracy, which will attain racial equality if these principles are understood, since there is no way the human race can ever alter the laws of thermodynamics. And here is the paradox: all mixing processes involve an increase of entropy. *But the energy required to stop mixing between ethnic groups creates more entropy than the mixing.*

The preaching and practice of racial hatred is an attempt to prevent the spontaneous mixing of peoples. We know now that in the US at least half of different white ethnic groups marry outside their ethnic groups, English descendants marry German, Italian and so on, descendants. For Hispanics, the figure is nearer one in four. Blacks somewhat less. It is pointless for racists to attempt to stop this, it is a spontaneous process.

The Bosnia and Kosova experience shows that if mixing does not occur, savage increases of entropy result: massacre, rape, torture, destruction of infrastructure. Tolerance is the only way out of this problem, since to de-mix a partially mixed system, whether animate or not, requires a massive injection of resources - energy in other words - and that always means huge entropy increases. When Hitler tried to de-mix Slav from German, Jew from German, he did so with concentration camps, torture, and genocide. Increase of entropy of this order is rightly conceived as atrocity. At a time when Germany needed every soldier, every train, hundreds of trains and tens of thousands of soldiers were used to de-mix. A wise nation would not have tried to undertake such a scheme, let alone one with a humane government. South Africa's apartheid system is another example of the futility of trying to de-mix. The pluralistic tendency of the Western democracies, those stemming from English migration to Australia, New Zealand, Canada and the United State of America, and democratic European countries, is a hope for the world. If an attempt to forcefully prevent mixing is made, the tragedies of Bosnia and Kosova are inevitable.

Bigots and entropy

So strong is the drive to mix, that bigots have to use force has to be used to prevent sexual relationships between different races. Technically, inter-marriage - or at least inter-ethnic breeding - does increase entropy, but much less than the entropy created by trying to stop the interbreeding, as shown in Apartheid, the Southern States of

America and Nazi Germany. When force is not used, it is implied, as in the social shunning of white women in southern states who consorted with black men. Totem and taboo is used extensively whenever creeds and or ethnicities are restrained from mixing. The result is always worse than if natural sexual dynamics were allowed their free play. It is the attempt to segregate races that leads to violence. The partitions are not only costly, but lead to huge increases in entropy. The wounds of slavery in America are still apparent, while in the Dominican Republic and other parts of the South Americas colour was not a partition; the Spaniards were cruel, but they had no women, and the Catholic Church was converting the few natives that remained, and so a new true-breeding Spanish-Indian ethnic group was created. As race becomes less of an issue in the Dominican Republic, the partition of wealth becomes a greater one: the rich sit in houses guarded by armed guards. Something of the same is occurring in America. In the UK we have security patrolled leafy suburbs of the affluent, and unpoliced inner cities. Race, creed, wealth all can be partitions, and like all partitions they will be swept away by violence. The end result is never in doubt, change will occur: the choice is violent upheaval, or incremental changes along the way. The French and the English are now both democracies, but the English aristocracy adapted, and so survived, while the French were slaughtered because they insisted on the unchanging partitions of wealth, privilege and class.

71

It is instructive here to note that the people who understand all this perfectly, are also those who deliberately confound the natural process in order to gain power and wealth. If things are not perfect, and they never are, it is easy to whip up racial hatreds, blame one ethnicity for the troubles of another, or blame one religion for the troubles of another. Bigots thrive on these divisions. They represent all that is unnatural. It may be useful to view racists and intolerant clerics in this way, so as not to be seduced by their specious arguments, which are always *ultimately* unworkable.

The insistence I make here on the folly of trying to defeat natural laws is perhaps best proved not by referring yet again to the suicide of Nazi Germany, but to the success of insisting race was not an issue. When William, Duke of Normandy, conquered England he found a land where *constant* warfare had been going on for six centuries, after the Romans left: Angle against Dane, Dane against Saxon, Jute against Viking. William recognised that he would not have a kingdom without the King's Peace, which meant only he had the right to use violence. He married his retainers into the Viking and Saxon nobility, the Vikings were christened, and on top of the various laws practised amongst the different ethnic groups, placed the King's Law. On these foundations, the English emerged as a breeding population, a vigorous people, eventually homogeneous. England might have been a Balkans for centuries if William had been a racist bigot.

A thought experiment

Charles I insisted that since he was chosen by God, he need not bother to listen to parliament. In order to make parliament do what he insists, he brings in foreign mercenaries, in other words injects entropy into his kingdom, the very opposite of what a leader should do. Cromwell pleads, to no avail; as a result the military option is taken. Battles ensue. As a thought experiment, suppose after one battle the United Nations went into England, intervened, and made the Cavaliers and Roundheads stop fighting. This would have led to dislocations anyway, but let us suppose the fighting was prevented. The United Nations would have to stay in England for many years, and when they left the problems between monarch and parliament would still not have been resolved, and so another civil war would ensue. We know from history that the civil war was not all that costly in comparison to continental civil wars - compare the German 30 years war for example. In England the parliamentary side won, and the Protectorate installed. England prospered well, respected for its new Model Army and its vigour. When Cromwell died, the monarchy was restored, but this time constitutionally, no more divine rights, no more inviting foreign soldiers in to kill Englishmen. UN intervention would have been a disaster.

The ethnic and religious divisions in the former Yugoslavia go back to the beginning of the Ottoman Empire, at least. Ethnic cleansing and communal strife was not tolerated by the Yugoslav communist government, but when that government lost credibility at the beginning of the nineteen nineties Serb, Croat and Bosnian unleashed the hatreds of centuries. These peoples had existed in a metastable stand-off, rather as a saturated solution of various salts still does not form crystals, although it should. A situation of great instability, for all you need to do to cause precipitation is add to the saturated solution one tiny crystal. And so it was in Yugoslavia, the problems between Serb, Croat and Bosnian had been frozen, not solved. There then followed the predictable sorting out: Serbs in Bosnia were killed, Bosnians in Serbia were killed; terror was instilled by torture, rape, and incarceration, the aim - to get your enemy out of your territory. The maps shown at this time reveal enclaves of Serbs in Bosnia, Croats in Serbia, and so on. A distinctly unstable situation because the dogmas of religion and race were barriers to interbreeding of the various peoples, and the politicians riding the horses of hate, ignorance and fear insisted on "ethnic cleansing" which is none other than de-mixing, a process always associated with great effort, therefore great entropy, with its expression as destruction of people, livestock, crops and infrastructure.

This process had gone along with some alacrity, and no doubt if no one had interfered, Bosnia would have exchanged its Serbs, for Serbia exchanging its Bosnians. Possibly they would now be independent states with tourist industries, and trading with one another. However, TV images and photos so upset the affluent peoples of the West as they chewed chicken in front of TV sets, or drank coffee over the morning paper, that they felt something must be done. When this happens, politicians have to respond, because they think they will otherwise lose votes. So here we have an uninformed emotional response predicating national policy with no regard to national interests. The result was a flagrant invasion of Bosnia by vastly superior Western forces, demanding that the self-determination of the regional peoples cease forthwith. At the time of writing, enclaves of ejected people are being bussed back to where they were ejected from. This means at great expense, and at a total waste of all the suffering and effort of these peoples to self-determine their futures, *the prior condition which caused the conflict is being forcibly re-instated.* How long can Western forces stay in former Yugoslavia? As long as the money holds out and the need to get votes? Obviously if you were a Serb, Croat or Bosnian you wouldn't trust such interlopers, and you would be right. When these "keepers of the peace" leave, they will take the peace with them, for they keep it, and once they have gone the indigenous people will get on with their own affairs.

I say *keep it* ironically since none of the barriers the Serbs, Croats, Albanians set up on the form of religions and ethnic intolerance have been broken down. The UN is yet another barrier, an interdiction.

Since I wrote the above paragraphs, the Kosova tragedy was sprung. Nato forces bombed a European city, damaged the industrial and ecological systems of the Danube, and this damage - entropy - can never be totally eradicated. The effort to make good the damage will turn up more entropy elsewhere. Arguably the worst case has been enacted. The Balkans will have to be policed for decades because the underlying barriers of racial and religious intolerance are still there, and have been made more rigid. An appreciation of the workings of entropy in human affairs would have at least cautioned against forceful intervention.

Racism

Liberal scientists assure the media there is no scientific basis for thinking human beings are made up of different races. Hardly two generations ago scientists and politicians could be found a-plenty who passionately declared for racism. What is the fact of the matter? Are white supremacists any more cogent than black supremacists? Or yellow Asian supremacists? And what of the caste system in India? All so-called races of mankind can inter-mate, and the progeny is capable of mating with any other human being. The skeleton is essentially the same, so is the metabolism; there are deeply embedded cultural traits shared by all human beings, for example language making and tool making. It would appear tedious to go on. Biologically there is only one species, *homo sapiens*, culturally however, individual groupings differ vastly, and this must have implications, particularly so where people think themselves as a distinctive *race*.

We *homo sapiens* carry in our genes a wide variety of debilitating diseases and malfunctions. These inheritable conditions increase in density the more a breeding populations confines its matings within itself. The consequence is that any group or sect which only mates with itself will certainly have an increasing incidence of congenital disease and inheritable deformities, and will through ill health eventually become extinct. We are therefore led to an extraordinary paradox: *peoples who wish to remain healthy and vigorous must mix with other peoples*. And this applies to all human populations.

Even the most reactionary of Popes, if not some Baptist divines in the Southern States of America, concluded early on that Amerindians, blacks, Chinese, were all human beings possessing immortal souls. Islam is literally colour blind. Islam sees people as two groups, Moslem and Infidel, the latter also called Kaffir. It is amusing to note that the Afrikaaners on hearing Moslem merchants speak of blacks as Kaffirs, introduced the word in their own speech to refer to blacks, not realising that to Moslems they themselves were Kaffir, in Islam,

Kaffir is not a racist term. Nonetheless, if we do not speak of race, we speak of ethnicity. In the UK there are laws about incitement to racial hatred, but nowhere is race defined. Is an Englishman a white descendent of white forebears, inhabiting this island for at least three thousand years, and having an admixture of blood from Phoenicians, Celts, Romans, Angles, Saxons, Vikings, Normans? Or is he an Englishman whose father came from Jamaica and who was black and married a white woman from the intermixed Celts, Romans and so on, breeding population? Is English an ethnic or a national term? If it is the former, what is the ethnicity? If the latter, who are the English?

If the concepts of race and ethnicity are complex, and often obscure to other people who are sure of their own ethnicity, but inclined to doubt the claims of others, the concept of a breeding population is biologically clear.

A few generations only are all that is required for a group of people, who without large admixtures of new blood from other groups, to subsume physical and cultural characteristics, they are a breeding population. When such groups confront others, equally distinct in their own right, a peaceful future is acquired when interbreeding occurs so that a new breeding group is formed. It is in this way that nations are formed. Political conglomerates such as Yugoslavia tend not to survive a fall of central government, and "Balkanise" simply because there are several breeding populations arising from religious and cultural bigotry. The spontaneous nature of human sexuality, evident even when an attempt to control it by religious and so-called racial precept is ever present. Attempts to separate people have inevitable results, most of which are horrendous; slavery in the American south, the blood laws of the Third Reich, apartheid, and the Yugoslav tragedy.

When people enter a country peacefully, or are invited, as they were by America, and by Britain just after World War II when West Indians were enticed into Britain and then ignored, there are still problems of adjustment. If immigrants are not invited, but come, and are successful in entering despite protests and resistance, it is called an invasion. Invasions when successful from the point of view of the invader usually means an infliction of entropy on the host nation. Often this is fatal, and the host nation is destroyed. A new body national is created. The destruction is usually more complete when the invaders have a greater capacity to wage war, that is inflict entropy, than the host peoples have of inflicting, or sustaining. Cortez destroyed the Aztecs in less than a generation. Within a century a new breeding population, most of whom had Aztec blood, was established, but the richest and most powerful citizens had more Spanish blood than Aztec.

Often the clash is so dramatic the result is genocide. The Spanish destroyed all the Indians on

Hispaniola (now the Dominican Republic and Haiti) in a generation. White Americans took vast tracts of land from Amerindians in the latter half of the nineteenth century, destroying whole breeding populations. When the invaders and the hosts are more nearly the same in breeding populations *and* culture, as when the Viking Normans invaded England, which had large Viking settlements, the result although profound, leads to a new breeding population arising from intermarriage between the hosts and the invaders. It is an interesting fact that the English are called English from the tribal word "Angle", although the people on the island are often referred to as Anglo-Saxons.

William of Normandy when he invaded, successfully, England in 1066 brought concepts of a united kingdom, feudalism, central power, heavy cavalry. His adventurers sired a new aristocracy on English women (Jutes, Saxons, Vikings, Celts, and so on). The dogged agricultural leanings of the Anglo-Saxons, the Viking expertise at sea combined with the mercantile flair of Celts, and the expansionist policies of the Normans, to produce though intermarriage and sharing of culture, a distinctly English civilisation, a distinctly English nation, a distinct breeding population, peculiar to England, separate but linked to the continental breeding populations. These English, who stood at their height of power in the middle of the nineteenth century, were a breeding population founded on new forces that battled their way onto the island, and whose energies were released throughout the world. For the sake of neatness, we can date this process to the first century AD when the Romans came. The influx of new ideas and culture, and the taking up of them by a homogenising breeding population is one of the sagas of world history, producing a breeding population so skilled and vigorous that it exported thousands of its stock to form new populations in America, Canada, Australia and Africa.

The question no one has sought to ask, let alone answer is this: are there any signs that the several millions of immigrants in Britain, who came here peacefully during the last forty years will be incorporated into *one* breeding population? If so, there clearly will be no problem. Or will the people on this island be facing the same problem as the Irish in Northern Ireland, which appears to be one of irreconcilable cultural differences? After all, would DNA testing reveal a great difference between Protestant and Catholic? Are the people of this island going to face the problems of Serb and Bosnian, where most people cannot see the physical difference between the two groups, but religion provides the identifying factor? The potential entropic explosion did occur in Yugoslavia once the restraining force of the Communist government was removed. There is a potential entropic explosion in England. Pious references to multiculture, juggling with minority rights and bafflement of majority rights, will not solve the problem, the only solution, permanent and dynamic at the same time, is interbreeding.

The spontaneous move by sex to the mixing of peoples can only be frustrated not prevented by the constructing of partitions. The attempt to stop a natural process has a cost; the bill is presented in civil unrest, expensive security arrangements, as shown in Apartheid, and even genocide, as shown by Nazi Germany. Unless caste, creed, and colour barriers are removed, potential entropy accretes, and finally becomes real in social explosions.

That real progress can be made is revealed by several incidents I saw in the summer of 1997 in multi-ethnic inner city Hackney. Apart from Inuits, and I cannot be sure there are none in Hackney, nearly every breeding population in the world is represented here, and it is a small borough, and it showed that *race is irrelevant - culture is pre-eminent.*

Someone ran over with his scooter a 14 year old Yoruba schoolboy - he was born here. The scooter driver absconded. The police were called. Two cars turned up. Out of one came a tall, large Sikh PC and a short blonde WPC. From the other car came a five foot ten blond, blue-eyed straw-headed PC with his partner, a five foot six Caribbean WPC. The school kids, of many genotypes, that is many ethnic backgrounds, clustered round. They obviously saw no difference between any of the cops - they were cops only, and the kids expected them to sort the situation. They did. Where is race here? It would seem that the overriding societal factor present here was an expectation of help and resolution from the police irrespective of *their* ethnic origin, or the observers' ethnic origin.

However, I have also witnessed gross insensitivity.

Kids were coming from school. Two 15 year olds starting fighting. They were black. They fought just outside my flat in a main street. The paddy wagon came. Eight 13 to 15 stone blond blue-eyed cops piled out, faces contorted with hate. At one time they threatened a 15 stone schoolboy who had tried to stop the fighting. Meanwhile, the two boys were forcibly arrested, each with two large white policemen frog-marching them to the police van. This was not anything more than two youths having a fist fight, and it would have been stopped had the police not come. All that was needed was a good talking to about fighting in streets. The arrest was surely over-kill.

It looked like a race incident because the boys were black and the cops white. At least one young man in four in London is brown or black, or at least not Anglo-Saxon. That less than one policeman in twenty is not Anglo-Saxon suggests the people who are in authority are not discharging their duties. If the armed forces and the forces of civil peace are not fully representative of the biological mix of the nation, then this is evidence that a barrier exists which is preventing representation. It would appear there is a barrier in the predominantly white organisation of the armed forces and police, but so too are there forces within ethnic minorities which militate against joining the police.

Now, what happens when certain clans, creeds, classes do not want the barriers removed? Are they to be forced? And here is the nub of the problem: entropy will increase anyway, all we can do is minimise the increase. On balance, invasion of other people's territory, as with the European diaspora, has spelt disaster for the host peoples, often to the point of extinction. Will the English be the aboriginals in England in ten generations? The Welsh the Zuni of Snowdonia, the Scots the Massai of the Grampians? Or will there be a *new* English?

What is however less open to debate is the changing genotype of the breeding population in England. Although non-whites are only about 20 per cent of London's population, the majority of children born are non-white, or admixtures of Asians and blacks with original white breeding population. Since the whites have a greater proportion of old people throughout the country, and whites have fewer children, it seems that a new coloured phenotype will preponderate in three generations. This means that more than 50 per cent of young people available for all jobs, including the judiciary, the armed forces, the police, teachers and so on, will be of the new breed. Within less than a century the English breeding population will be transformed, unless bigotry, fear, intolerance and hate are allowed to grow, singly or severally, in any of the ethnic groups.

A major biologic change has occurred in England, a change far greater than ever happened before. The population of a *peaceful* England will not be Asian, nor Anglo-Saxon, nor black, but a new mixture; the culture will be a new culture. If we do not want our grandchildren to experience the Yugoslav debacle, fraternity is the order of the day.

A paradox of some importance

I say 'of some importance' because this single fact puts the lie firmly in racism. A breeding population which continues to interbreed for religious or ideological dictats will inevitably accumulate disabilities because persistent congenital defects will concentrate, not dissipate. White racism which views a person born of black and white as coloured, and not a variant of white, would lead to an increasing population of blacks, and in comparison a decreasing population of whites. In this century, Nazis had to learn the hard way that calling vigorous peoples like the Poles and Russians inferior because they were Slavs was nonsense. Through Nazi policies the German people are much less numerous now than they would have been: policies which many thought would make Germany strong, enfeebled her, and contributed much to her defeat. And yet some countries still attempt to deny racial mixing. The Japanese frown on inter-marriage, and though active and often successful, it is a nation which finds fundamental innovation difficult, so unlike the interbreeding peoples of Europe and America.

These factors have impact on the rise and fall of nations and empires, and will be reverted to in a later chapter, but their full analysis cannot be undertaken without an entropic examination of another factor in the fate of nations, economics.

CHAPTER EIGHT

ENTROPY AND MONEY -
A NEW THEORY OF ECONOMICS

A man with a suitcase full of dollars (or pounds, marks, francs...) is shipwrecked on a desert island. There is no water on the island and he dies of thirst, as he does so he laments: *What is money?* This anecdote, and it has a myriad of forms, but the same point, is a long lived one. The implication is that money is somehow valueless, an abstraction. It is - *on a desert island, and you are the only one there.* In other contexts, money is real. Money has a value because people agree to give it a value. The value will depend on time, place, and what kind of money (specie) it is. Capital is an accumulation of money. It is real, its value can be reckoned in terms of labour, land, food, mineral resources, finished goods. Neither money nor capital are abstractions, as Marx appeared to have thought.

However, capital can represent theft, as when a robber increases his capital by taking money from someone else, but capital itself need not necessarily be theft. However, when a society is characterised by excessive difference in wealth, trouble is usually on the way in terms of social unrest, because this excessive concentration of capital in a few hands means that those few hands have erected partitions against the free flow of money, for money is meant to diffuse through a society, not stagnate, or be used to enslave by credit and usury other members of the society.

Creditors and debtors

Debt in financial terms is someone owing someone else money, where the someone can also mean other than a person, since legal entities can extend credit, for example banks, and enter into debt. On the surface debt is then a simple concept, but the fact of it is often far from simple, and in many cases is catastrophic.

The debt of a seventeenth century aristocrat who bets his estate upon a show of cards, is his estate. It passes to the gambler who beat him. This sort of debt is often thought of as the debt of the fool. Compare it with the debt of an Indian untouchable in the Deccan borrowing money from a higher caste Indian in order to pay for rice so he and his family will not starve to death. He cannot ever repay the debt, since his earning capacity is so small and so he usually loses what land he may have had, and gives himself up to indentured slavery, and often makes arrangements, or they are made for him, for his children to go into various kinds of servitude, most of which are unpleasant, some, like prostitution, vile. The debt is never discharged. Indeed, the system is such that it cannot be discharged. The poor in this system are smaller physically than the creditors, less healthy, die earlier. The creditor reduces his entropy by passing it on to the poor. It will be noted that such a society does not increase its net wealth.

But there are other kinds of debt. An inventor, a salesman, an industrialist, people of ideas, can obtain money from venture capitalists without any surety of the monies other than a written agreement that the lender will have rights to the business so engendered. This is perhaps the plus side of debt: the debtor gets to do business he could not have done without the capital injection. If he succeeds, he and his creditor make a profit. Here is growth. It is not always achieved. Most people who go to banks for start-up loans do not seem to realise that the bank is more interested in what collateral they have, rather than the business plan. Hundreds of thousands of businesses of this sort fail every year in the Western world, many after paying huge interest on modest overdrafts, vis £9,000 on £10,000 over three years. When the crunch comes, they repay the capital out of collateral, their home, which usually means they then have nowhere to live. The bank never loses, since the bank has always got the debtor's house, land, the very clothes he stands up in, as collateral against the loan. Such banking practice is indeed nothing more than asset stripping; it is a lucrative trade. It is not growth, it is not wealth, it increases social entropy.

Although most Western banks would never lend to small businesses unless they had at least a house to serve as collateral, they have, during the last decade, sold off billions of debt owed to them by Third World countries, and others, to debt buyers. Often they do not receive more than a few per cent of the debt. No matter how the debt may be marketed from one group to another, the debtor still owes. Some commentators believe that the Third World will never pay off its debt, and the debt is serviced by the starvation of children, and the general running down of the debt nation into savagery. The effect, world wide, is that debt increases entropy in the indebted and is expressed in poor health and low longevity.

The paradox of usury

One man has spare capital, he lends it to another who buys a boat and fishes wild fish out of the sea and sells them in the market, thereby earning money with which he can pay off the interest on the loan. The lender has gained more capital by the destruction of fish, a natural resource; he does nothing to replenish the stocks. Indeed, huge fortunes have been made in depleting North Sea herring and cod. Our capitalist next lends money to a logger, who proceeds to destroy forests. He lends money to a developer who builds luxury homes on agricultural land, thereby putting pressure, ultimately on food production, and so food prices rise. He has diminished the amount of land, and he takes his interest, and so land prices go up. The very fact of taking interest is inflationary; the very fact of taking interest depreciates the earth's resources. In other words, the paradox is that in gaining more capital through taking interest his capital is worth progressively less because the planet is being destroyed. But one way of ameliorating this ghastly spectacle is to tax interest, and in the West this is done. If the tax is too high, economies falter, since the money won't be risked, but experience has shown that taxes of up to fifty per cent are easily sustained by capitalists. Clearly, it is up to governments to let citizen entrepreneurs get on with business, but it is implicit that governments have the right and duty to reallocate wealth, and to take steps to repair as much of the damage caused by speculation and expansion. It is true that the healing can never be total, since if it were, the Second Law of Thermodynamics would be broken, and no one has ever seen that happen.

Usury is denied Jews, Muslims, and Christians, if the strict letter of the Bible is adhered to. However some of these children of the book keep other books, ledgers with loan and interest accounts. Christian used Jews, Jews used Christians, Moslems used both, and were used by both. But not only religion views interest taking as bad. Marx was so appalled by capital and interest he tried to wish them away as abstractions. Adherents, if not strict disciples of his, did away with private property, and constructed command economies like Stalinism and Maoism. Such non-market led economies were bound to fail, and have done so. Why? Because markets were replaced by bureaucracies who assigned a monetary value to goods and services on whim, I say whim because there is no way of assigning value except by markets.

What is a market and how does it assign value?

We have seen that money is real, and that it has a value, and the value it has comes about by agreement between people who are in a trading relationship. A trading relationship is when money is exchanged for goods or services. In that respect, everyone in the West is a trader, but not everyone is a true trader. If I am starving I will work for less than a man who is not, and so I am under a kind of duress. Western economies through welfare try to ensure that no one is in that position of duress. Well and good. However, there are millions of people in Britain who do not work, yet receive monies from government, with which to buy food and services. There are no free lunches, so someone somewhere is paying for this, and that person is not necessarily a tax payer, it may be a tribe in the Amazon rain forest, or people living in the chemical sludge of a multinational company. There is always a cost for every activity. A market is merely a device by which people can trade and come to some agreement however fleeting as to the money value of goods and services. That value can change by the hour, or in the case of shares by the second. The principles are simple, the results appear chaotic, but at base over a longish period, say five years, a market trend will reflect an underlying reality, namely the value of particular goods or service against other particular goods and service. That underlying reality is why markets are essential, they are the only way we have, or will ever have in anything like a free and democratic society of determining value. Command economies do not use markets, they don't understand them, they disdain them, and so their economies fail.

Command economies cannot know the monetary value of anything. They can only assign value, but since the element of trading, that is of agreement between traders, is not operating they, the bureaucrats of command economies, cannot possibly have any real idea of what value to assign to a goods or service. What figures they come up with are inherently whimsical.

Viewed from an entropy viewpoint we can now see that capitalism assigns value by markets; this involves entropy increase, but it is less than the inevitable chaos command economies, usually socialist, but not always, produce: factories are badly run, pollution is high, productivity low, unrest kept in check by expensive police forces.

What is poverty?

If you are not getting enough food, you must be in poverty; if you have no shelter against the elements and have no clothes, indubitably you are in poverty. Having these two criteria of poverty is probably something everyone would agree with; the problem is that other criteria are added: in the UK and the US not having a TV set or a washing machine, even though you are housed, fed and clothed, constitutes poverty, while in most of the world being fed, housed and clothed would mean you were rich. The absence or presence of TV sets seems hardly relevant when the basic necessities of life are concerned. You cannot live without food, and will not remain healthy unless you are clothed, and so notions of poverty based on lack of a second car appear vexatious. Nonetheless they have a relevance, since it is the mass proliferation of such goods which threaten this planet. The notion that everyone on earth can have cars, TV sets, and consume vast amounts of energy on non-life supportive features such as luxury goods, is unsustainable. Given food, clothing, housing, fresh water, sewage treatment, law and order, one can suppose a defeat of poverty; that much is sustainable if population increases are halted.

However, if the gap between rich and poor continues to increase, then the poor, in great numbers, will want more. And the rich will become more fearful as the get richer. A crisis in the making. Gross inequality of wealth, or to put it another way, gross inequality of poverty, must mean wars, civil and international. We understand this, we protest at inequality, but the Second Law of Thermodynamics is operating: *mixing is spontaneous, so if you wish to keep your money from mixing with other people, you'll need security.* In the past, armed guards and police who favoured the rich against the poor were ultimately of no avail. Revolutions did occur, riots did occur. They will occur again. Entropy must increase, and inequalities speed the increase up.

What is wealth?

Tom Wasp drives his car to work, sits at a desk all day, drives back home. Because he does not walk anywhere, he has a treadmill, at no small cost, installed in his bedroom. You see such advertised in the truly obscene pages of the colour supplements of the so-called quality Sunday papers all across the Western industrialised world. Piped or beamed into Tom Wasp's home weekly are more TV bytes than he could ever digest in a lifetime. He spends several hours a day looking at the world as other people called editors make him see it the way cameras see it. Images change in milliseconds. The material looks structured, it is, but the effect on Tom's brain is to decrease his neuronal ordering, in other words increase his brain entropy, because he has no time to digest the information. Eyes that evolved to detect where a rabbit had walked on grass, are now sacrificed to adverts, and ears that can detect nuances in bird song now jangle with jingles. Since he eats from Marks and Spencer's, and goes on holiday to identical hotels in different locations he would be hard put to identify the country he is holidaying in. He is living, our Tom Wasp, an affluent lifestyle. His female counterpart, Mary Bee, lives similarly. It would be more apt to call it the life style of effluence, since pollution stems from such living. However, these people are said to belong to wealthy economies, so what is wealth?

CHAPTER NINE

WEALTH AND ENTROPY

The reality of money is brought home to a citizen when he discovers that there are systems which force him to pay off debt. Loan-sharks use direct violence, ordinary creditors have recourse to bailiffs, and the courts. Similarly, the reality of money is clear to those who have it: they can exchange money for goods and services. Since profit is measured in money, the contemporary obsession in companies for profit is easily understandable, but profit is not always wealth.

What is wealth? I distinguish three broad types of wealth. *Primary*: this would include forests, mines, livestock, fruit and vegetable produce; it even includes a good climate. An increase in wealth can be acquiring such things, it can also be exploiting them as, say, the Americans did with the prairies, running vast herds of cattle, planting millions of acres of wheat. Wealth too is the possession of mineral resources, which, even if they do not yield a profit because they have not been exploited, are nevertheless wealth.

Secondary Wealth: infrastructure such as railroads, motorways, sewage systems, electrical grids, factories, airports, are all wealth, and so are schools and so is an educated, skilled, population.

Primary and secondary wealth may or may not yield a profit, but without them a profit is impossible, is indeed meaningless, for what would you spend your profit on?

From primary and secondary wealth come goods and services, which may be thought of as *Tertiary Wealth*. The lubrication, the connector, of all three wealths is money, which can increase as wealth increases, but that is not the same as profit. Profit today is often generated by destroying wealth, for example profits can be generated by sacking large numbers of people - the company may profit, but the polity as a whole is impoverished. I conclude that the pursuance of profit as a goal by companies and nations is misguided, and in the absence of an increase of wealth must mean that someone somewhere has less money. Today that means the Third World. The Third World is characterised by disease, war, crime, all contributing to the entropic total of the globe, and mostly felt as misery by the Third World peoples. The pursuit of *profit* instead of *wealth* in the developed nations inevitably produces entropy in the Third World.

It will readily be seen that such terms as chaos, anarchy, decomposition, riot, disorder, *und so weiter*, connote increases of entropy. However, mere heat production means an increase of entropy, so every industrial plant consuming energy, of whatever kind, will increase the sum total of global entropy, but industrial activity can only occur though the use of money. It follows therefore that rich nations will inevitably increase global entropy. Indeed, we can say that a part of global entropy increase is in direct proportion to GDP, such that entropy increase equals GDP times some factor, or to put it more succinctly: *Increase of entropy is directly related to wealth.* Economic growth as practised by the industrial northern hemisphere means increasingly rapid irreversible despoilation of the planet, for the way to enjoy wealth is to ensure you dump the entropy you have made on someone else. You do not dump it in your own back-yard, you export it elsewhere.

Hundreds of millions of women every day forage for fuel, spend hours carrying water. Hundreds of millions of children go to sleep hungry every night. At least a third of the human population of this planet have no running water and no sewage access. It is in precisely these areas that catastrophic increase in population is occurring, while in the most affluent of countries there is standstill or decline; the Germans, for instance, are not replenishing their numbers, and the once fecund Spanish and Italians have drastically reduced families. The imbalance is unstable. The natural forces of migration from high to low concentration of human beings will put pressure on the West from the East, and the North from the South. I have personally observed young men in the Dominican Republic being ferreted out of stinking bilge holds, winkled out of rudder housings, crowbarred out of lifeboats, and then beaten senseless, before being thrown over the dock wall. These young men risked their lives - they are often reduced to a pulp in rudder housings - to get out from a land where hunger stalks, and employment is low. Their aim: *to get out, anywhere.* They even climb into the wheel-housings of airliners, and so freeze to death when the jet reaches high altitude.

If happiness, or at least contentment is low entropy for the individual, which it is; if being adequately fed is low entropy for the individual, which it is; and if reasonable health means the absence of high entropy, which it does, then we find these aspects of low entropy in the majority of people only in the North and West. In the Third World disease, malnutrition, parasitic infestation, exposure to the elements, is the fate of most, not the few. Had these people been left alone and lived their lives of pastoral economy, they would be far better off, but their way of life, as has recently happened to the Massai, has been destroyed, and entropy put in its place. The demands of the northern Western peoples not merely to have enough food, good health, and infrastructure, rich cites with electricity, water supply, sewage treatment, and transport, but to have richness in culture, entertainment, and consumer affluence, necessarily means that entropy is exported to the Third World. You can see it there: in the pavement hordes of Calcutta, in the shanty towns of Africa and South America; you can see it in the diseased bodies of the people who exist in these slums.

There is nothing infinite in nature

It is a truism that the earth's resources are finite, and for that reason no doubt the West appears to believe it can ignore the truth of it. All wealth comes from the earth, its biomass - agriculture and wildlife, both plant and animal - and mineral resources. Plants plug us into the energy of the sun, while the dynamo that is the moon lifting trillions of tons of water as it rotates around the earth has yet to be properly used, but used it must be one day, since fossil fuels are running out, while fissile nuclear energy represents a level of entropy that cannot be contained. It follows then, that wealth cannot keep on increasing. It is possible, but surely not probable, that exploitation of space may alleviate the crisis, one day, but that does not excuse the destruction of the planet, since that solution may not come quick enough.

The difference in living standards on this planet are very great, with, for example, Canada having a GDP *per capita* of $21,646, *fifty-three* times more than citizens of Sierra Leone. A Canadian consumer earns in a week in services and goods than a citizen of Sierra Leone does in a year. In general, two figure multiples apply in the West's economies in comparison to the Third World. There is constant agitation for something to be done, but the brute fact is that there is not the capital in the entire planet to industrialise even a small fraction of the Third World - and even if it were, the planet's water and fuel resources, as well as its capacity to absorb pollution, would not meet the need. What is agitated for is thermodynamically impossible.

India's population may well reach 1.2 billion early in the 21st century. Food production cannot, and has not kept up with population growth. Most of India's citizens are illiterate, have no running water or electricity supplies, nor is there sewerage provision. The countryside is a picture of poverty of the many, affluence of the few, while the cities are shanty-towns clustering to a collapsing Raj nucleus. India is close to chaos. Since there are not enough resources on this planet to solve India's economic problems, population growth must be halted. Unfortunately, no one knows how to do this. India, like China, has tried but failed. Crises have a way of creating leaders who balk at nothing. They would know how to solve the population problem, and like Hitler and Stalin experience few scruples.

It may be objected that since the West with a minority of world population but a great majority of its wealth, there is sufficient resource to remove poverty - all that has to happen is the West gives away most of its wealth to the third world, but dumping of wealth would exacerbate poverty, as it already does when charities literally dump tons of cereals and meat into countries thus destroying indigenous arable and livestock farming. Furthermore, transfer of wealth is often technically impossible - does one move New York skyscrapers to Somalia? Tower Bridge to Bangladesh?

People who are desperate, in their billions, for food, clothes and shelter, may yet go to war to sequester these from richer nations. China and India have nuclear capability, and desperate problems seek desperate remedies.

Export of entropy

When a British man-o'war, or even a frigate, turned up at some hitherto unclaimed island in the seventeenth and early eighteenth centuries, the indigenous peoples soon learned that it brought with it in the form of powder and shot, sword and musket, and marines, concentrated potential violence, entropy in other words, such that the people upon whom it would be unleashed would have no answer to it: they would simply have no way of sustaining such an accelerated rise in entropy in their lives.

However, the same effect can be obtained by trade. The injection of money into newly discovered territories has the same effect, though not so quickly, as military power. A mercantile nation is therefore a conquering nation, and this would be so even if that nation did not think to protect its assets in the new territories with garrisons; that it did so choose meant an empire was created. The French and the Dutch were also entrepreneurs of entropy. To export entropy and reap the benefits requires a superior technology and an audacity of spirit, the mercantile view of life. As a result, Europeans waxed rich. Nations which contained their entropy, as the Japanese did, eschewing external contact, burying their heads as it were in the snows of Mount Fuji trying to maintain a mediaeval style of life, were at the mercy of the first visiting European. Shades of *Madam Butterfly*. Alarmed, the Japanese underwent industrialisation, and embarked on a series of wars which culminated in their defeat, because with the exception of inflicting maximum entropy on POWs at their mercy, *the Japanese were never able to mount a sufficient export of entropy* to defeat the British, let alone the Americans.

Viewed from this perspective, the success of nations up to the twentieth century depended on who could export the most entropy. This trend will no doubt continue in the third millennium. It is noteworthy that whereas military war was lost by the Japanese, having learned a lesson, they concentrated on trade war and succeeded brilliantly. They recognised that trade was war, and concentrated not on profit but market share, which is nothing short of colonisation of their customers, indebting them. We have already seen that debt is entropy, and entropy weakens nations. Clauswitz famously said that war was policy carried out by force; trade is war too. What Japan could not get by war, viz iron ore, coal, oil, she obtained by trade, by destroying other nations' market share in finished goods. All mercantile nations export entropy. Japan is a nation which seems to have understood rather more cogently that trade is another form of war, and war is the infliction of entropy upon opponents.

The industrial West and the Third World

The greater the industrialisation, which includes use of information technology, the greater the monetary wealth. The greater the industrialisation the greater the destruction of the planet, since entropy is accelerated. The more money, therefore, the greater the increase of global entropy. When the industrial West enters Third World countries they bring with them entropy. Interdiction by the industrial west into Third World affairs must inevitably cause dislocation of Third World economy and culture. Their natural resources are consumed. This applies even when the interdiction is undertaken for a benign motive, as in aid programs.

The concept of progress is now recognised as mischievous. The few tribes in the Amazonian rain forests not yet contacted by Western mores and methods are doing very well, judging by the state of those tribes which have been contacted. Within months of being "discovered" such tribes move from self dependency, low entropy ways of living, to disease ridden, welfare recipients. They don't need the West, just as the plains Indians of America did not need the white man's ways either. To destroy such noble ways of living so that Europeans and those who copy them can devastate this planet is clearly a crime. Non industrial people will inevitably be destroyed by high entropy industrial people, even if the latter do not intend to hurt them.

Consumerism

A major supermarket chain is highly organised, and in the extent it is successful, it has low internal disorder, low entropy. However, in order to attain low entropy, entropy has to increase elsewhere, or else the Second Law is broken, which it has never been observed to be. Supermarkets in their search for profits *must increase entropy elsewhere*.

Having deduced from first principles that supermarket chains must produce disorder in the environment around them, what are the disorders - entropy - they produce? Here is a partial list:

Destruction of small businesses. Nearly two hundred thousand small business have been destroyed by the food supermarkets in Britain, to date. This has entailed not only unemployment, but bankruptcy, mental ill health, grief, anxiety.

Degradation of quality. If you have never known real bacon, then the cardboard chemically infested products on sale in supermarkets will ensure you never know real bacon, and perhaps a whole generation will ensue supposing that what is purchased at the check-out is real bacon. Bacon is of ancient provenance; it is a technique whereby pork may be kept in wholesome condition some time after slaughter. Supermarkets, however, because shelf life is so important to them but not to you, want an ever longer period. They put bacon into airtight packets. The most dangerous bacteria are those which cannot live in the air we breathe, and they are the ones likely to be in airtight packets. Because supermarkets deal in billions of pieces of bacon they have to have suppliers who do so too. This means factory farming, with an increase of entropy in the pigs in terms of their poor health and ghastly lives. Hormones, antibiotics are liberally dispensed and pour into our systems. Lower quality means lower nutrition; antibiotics and hormones residues are pollutants. *Our* entropy rises.

We now see further evidence for the principle discussed earlier that profit usually means an increase in entropy, viz: destruction of high street butchers in their thousands by the supermarket chains. Butchers were about a family earning a living, supermarkets are about profits, and profits alone. Earning a living is not the same as profit. Earning a living is an expression of a need; there is no ratio of profit and need. Profit is a product of business whose sole and only aim is to make profit, and that profit is not measurable as need.

Why, even the seasons have been banished. Supermarkets do best from their point of view when they have monocultural products. It is economically more viable, that is profitable, if you get in a harvest of say, peas, within weeks, and market them. This means the peas must be the same variety. Vast storage shed, kept at low temperature, and their atmosphere devoid of oxygen, are used to store "fresh" vegetables and fruits for months. The cost in pollution of the atmosphere in running these facilities is not born by the supermarkets but by the planet's population in respiratory anguish.

Supermarkets are not happy places. Has anyone enjoyed the checkpoint? In Dalston the huge Sainsbury's is not full of happily chatting people. The cost of vegetables and fruits is more than in the nearby bustling lively market of Ridley Road, and I for one see the produce in the market as fresher, and better quality, because most produce there comes from a quick turnover from producer to wholesaler at New Covent Garden, not from central storage sheds.

When a supermarket opens it spells the death of many livelihoods. Grocers, and now newsagents, feel the pinch. In Well Street, Hackney the Tesco, in 1997, seemed always to have little activity at the meat counter, while the local butcher always has a queue. He learned how to respond to the challenge. But thousands did not. They are gone, the families have lost their pride and their living. At another branch of Tesco there is a man who serves pre-cut pieces of pink meat at the "Deli". He is dressed up in straw hat and butcher's apron. He looks the part of a butcher with his huge hands and forearms. He is very miserable, not unpleasant to customers, but is clearly a saddened man. I asked him what he had been before he took this job. He said, 'I *was* a butcher.'

Destruction of a way of life. The entropic costs of supermarkets are not only unaesthetic and socially numbing, they are quantifiable. For example, there are hundreds of thousands of dispossessed people, people who used to run their own little business, their pride and livelihoods destroyed.

The modern standardised uniform food retailing system is motivated only by profit, and the profit thereby made is directly related to entropy increase. Supermarkets pollute with their vast logistical system of lorries and warehouses. Supermarkets degrade the quality of food. Supermarkets take away livelihoods of small traders. All this for profit. Such profit is therefore a direct measure of entropy, the modern equivalent of Blake's *Satanic Mills*.

Monoculturism in this Country and Abroad. So huge is the appetite for goods that intensive farming is required to meet it. This has led to prairie farming in Britain, uprooting of thousands of miles of hedgerows, erosion of soil. In Third World countries traditional farming has been destroyed, and vast acreages of one crop planted, leading to unemployment, migration to cities where shantytowns house millions. Disease, malnutrition, crime are results, all are high entropy conditions.

Production of waste which is not part of the natural cycles. Whereas degradation of fruit skins and the like is easily accomplished by nature, plastic and other polymers used in packing persist for decades. In-fill sites of these materials are a nice example of high entropy. Waste production seems to be an industry of itself.

Fast food chains, many of the biggest of which have tens of thousands of "restaurants", and junk food manufacturers, are like supermarkets, highly ordered, and also like supermarkets are conceived for the express purpose of maximising profit for their owners without any equal commitment to maintaining the fabric of the communities around them. Because they are so highly organised, they have a low internal entropy, which must mean they spew out entropy onto and into the communities around them. Because it costs money to wash up crockery, fast food junk empires use throw-away plastic utensils and throw-away plates and containers. These usually find their way to in-fill sites after they have been picked up from the streets by communal garbage collectors. You can engage in a plastic and paper chase in any city high street, and the trail always leads to a fast food source, high in fat, sugar, but low in nutritional quality. The figures for rubbish and waste production are numbing: the UK produces two tonnes of domestic, industrial and commercial waste per capita each year. America produces even more. Burning waste will produce heat for central heating or electricity production, but even more pollution. The core of the problem is profit seeking at the expense of the planet. Furthermore, the rate of waste increase is at least 3 per cent per annum.

The problem of divisive wealth

If Jefferson had given every American citizen fifty acres as he once proposed, what would the position be five generations on? Some citizens would be large landowners, many others would have no land, and would live by labour on land they once owned. Such is the dynamic of human frailty. It is because human beings differ in ability that democratic governments have to keep an eye on forceful individuals who apportion wealth to themselves.

The disparity in wealth between individuals can graphically be seen when the richest are given a height according to wealth, and the poorest also; the result is a few individuals of several miles high, while hordes are hundredths of an inch. The inherent instability of such inequality is patent, after all Gulliver was tied down easily enough by Lilliputians.

Judging by the present circumstances in Western Europe and America, huge fortunes are tolerated if earned. Gates, founder of Microsoft, may have grotesque riches, but the law of copyright made it so; who would repeal private ownership attained within the law? However, the much smaller monies that directors of utilities receive have caused fury in the UK. The British Gas executive Cedric Brown had a pig named after him. Disparity itself then is not the essence of instability; disparity can be sustained, if the populace as a whole feels it is receiving a fair share of the economic cake. Entropy in fiscal matters involves a sociological dimension, a moral aspect: people ask the question, Is this situation fair? Once the guns come out to guard private mansions, the situation suggests remedial action. The high to low ratio of thirty times in salaries within an organisation appears to be easily accepted, while vast private wealth is tolerated, if it is not flaunted. Entropy in these circumstances appears to have a sense of justice as well as sharp eyes.

In America because the average man can live reasonably well, inequality is less likely to cause unrest; however, in most of the world's poorest areas gross inequality exists, and has to be maintained by force. When inequality becomes grotesque armed guards are necessary at house gates. Such arrangements usually end in blood-baths.

That forceful individuals set up empires of wealth is an observable fact, but it is also true they have to be watched carefully otherwise they will dump their entropy on the people they employ and the community around them. The mill owners and factory czars of industrial Britain did not stop using child labour because they were suddenly inspired by love of their fellow man. The English polity was such as to demand humanity, and the capitalists seeing trouble ahead, acceded to reform. The aristocrats of France did not, and lost not only their wealth, but their heads, the latter being proven to have lacked flexibility in thought and were probably an evolutionary *cul de sac*. *Laissez faire* capitalism brings home the bacon for the many if only the few are watched by governments who understand there is a nice balance to be had between profit and exploitation. Tax has always been bearable by businessmen, while regulation upsets them. Certainly no Western country could possibly tolerate a Rockerfeller again, with his cartels, his hiring of Pinkertons to shoot and burn men women and children; nonetheless the energy of the businessman is useful, and can be entrained to the better good. Certainly governments with command economies have proved incapable of making wealth.

However, the profit motive, which is what drives all businesses despite their protestation to the contrary that they are really philanthropies in disguise, is a potent entropy creator. It was bloody minded profiteering that led to the deregulation of foodstuff for cattle that led to the BSE crisis. The feed manufacturers cut costs by lowering the temperature of the autoclaving of sheep flesh, and so the prion which causes BSE was not extinguished. A few hundred pounds profit led to a multibillion pound disaster, and the human costs have yet to be computed.

It is consumerism, which is a kind of secular rite, whose intended outcome is profit, which leads to the destruction of small family shops, the corner newsagent, the barrow stalls of town markets. To facilitate consumerism, costs are cut. This usually means a decline in quality of food, in particular. The food industry is more like a chemical industry than much to do with fresh produce.

The irony is that supermarkets have become mausoleums, acres of trash. Who needs forty feet of crisps in a supermarket? And why do we need cars to get to these crisp shelves? Food distribution has been more efficiently solved in the past: every village had at least two market days, and you walked just a few yards to get to the stalls. London still has street markets; if you live there, try the quality and price, both far more acceptable than the sprayed and fungicided produce of the vegetable and meat counters in supermarkets. But you may have to hurry, in London and other cities, because supermarkets hate street markets, if only because they sell you better fruit and vegetables at a lower cost than they do, and offer so many varieties. Cheaper, better, more choice! Why then do we have supermarkets? Because they are profitable to their owners. No one ever needed them.

CHAPTER TEN

ASCENT, DECLINE, FALL OF EMPIRE AND CIVILISATION AS ENTROPIC PHENOMENA

Many commentators have attempted to explain the undoubted cyclic nature of civilisations and empires. There is the moral school: Rome fell because it was immoral. The Religious school: their god became angry with them for their iniquities. There are other schools, as good or bad as the ones I mentioned, but there has been some persuasive work done. For example, we can trace the rise of the Han people in China against other ethnic groups because of their efficient growing of rice, or the initial success of the Hittites against the Egyptians because of their ability to smelt iron and so produce harder, sharper weapons and armour than the bronze and copper equipment of the Egyptians. Nonetheless, no general theory of ascent and decay of empires and civilisations has found favour generally. An entropic analysis might yield such a thing, and I give the main notions here, beginning with an analysis of colonisation.

Two broadly separated forms of colonisation can be identified: *settlement* - an imperial policy which leads to settling of foreign lands by citizens of the imperial power; *administration* - a policy which leads to an administration of a foreign territory, the number of imperial citizens being confined to officials and troops. Clearly these two can overlap.

115

Examples of the former type of colonisation are afforded by British policy during the colonial era in North America, Australia, New Zealand; of the second, British policy in India.

Settlement policy

The effects of this colonial mode is the destruction of indigenous culture, if not its people, a rapid rise of population by immigrants, followed by industrialisation and efficient agriculture. These features mean a great increase in global entropy. Settlement and colonisation of North America led to a republic which produces more entropy *per capita* than any other major country.

Administration policy

The effect in India was to build roads, railways, ports, and other infrastructure, paid for by British capital, and not recovered wholly. However infrastructure building always means expenditure of energy, as it does of money, and hence an increase of entropy.

The conclusion is that colonisation damages the planet. It may be that, say, if the Amerindians had been unvisited by any other power, over the course of many centuries, perhaps millennia, they would have created significant amounts of entropy as they moved from hunting to agriculture, and then to some form of industrialisation, but hunter gatherers do not have much impact on an environment until population is high. What colonisation does is accelerate the rate of entropy creation vastly - often in the imperial state itself.

The paradox of empires

When the permanent way for railroads were already old and not well maintained, Britain spent billions in today's money on rail in India; when the British road system was poor, with barely double lanes serving the gigantic London docks, Britain poured capital into road-building in Africa and the sub-continent. While millions of Britons in the East End of London lived in squalor, without health or education provision, hundreds of millions of people in the Empire were being given free education by Britons who were therefore not available to cater for the masses in Britain. Here is an example of entropy developing at home, because *order* was being exported out of the country. We can say, from the British experience, that an empire must decay unless it exports entropy from the centre to the colonies.

Empires never pay for themselves, unless as with the Spanish plunder is the sole motive, not empire building: the Spanish empire was never anything like the British, and when it was, it went bankrupt. Attila the Hun is probably one of the few incursives to always make a profit, but then he did not intend an empire. The inexorable working of entropy dooms all empires. As Santayana the Spanish observer noted of the British Empire, "Never since the heroic days of Greece has the world had such a sweet, just, boyish master." That Britain exported order, not entropy, but imported entropy from her empire, is perhaps confirmed by what has happened in her former African and Asian colonies: almost without exception there has been corruption, war, civil war, famine and plague. I say 'perhaps' because it may be objected that by colonising, always disruptive of the colonised, Britain set a new order in motion, and was forced by local agitation to leave the job unfinished.

The rise and fall of empires

It has often been observed that empires decline, and so regular a phenomenon as this suggests that a common principle is being enacted, though hitherto such has not been identified. The rise of an empire is often from small beginnings, for example that of the Roman empire from the inhabitants of the seven hills of Rome. The emergence phase leads to greater and greater consolidation until a plateau is reached, which is maintained for a shorter or longer period, and then decline sets in. The emerging process is one of transferring entropy or disorder to other civilisations, that is conquering them, absorbing them, so they follow the *mores* of the conqueror, the imperial power. A limit is always reached, since the internal creation of entropy, the burden of empire, cannot be exported quickly enough, and so the empire crumbles from within. During this period great efforts are made to maintain the *status quo*, but in that very effort more entropy is created, and so decline occurs. It will be entertaining to apply this set of concepts to some examples.

The rise and fall of Rome

The cycle of Rome was: from the Latin states to Africa, to Germany, France, even Britain, and then collapse circa 400 AD, a process of approximately eight hundred years. Arguably the pinnacle was reached with the Claudian Caesars, but the decline also began with Augustus with the destruction of two legions in Germany, which were never raised again. Reproductive vigour was being sapped not least by the nobility seeing children as encumbrances, and the policy of not recognising a legionnaire's right to marriage until he was retired. Augustus tried to maintain the boundaries, and maintaining a *status quo* meant a profitless expenditure of energy since boundaries are an invitation to those outside to cross them. To prevent this needs a vast apparatus of border protection against incursion. This requires money, and money-making creates entropy, which if not diverted externally, as in conquest, must perforce turn inwards. This is what happened to the Romans. On this basis, an empire must inevitably decay.

The destruction of the Aztec empire

Cortez destroyed the Mexican empire of the Aztecs by injecting huge amounts of entropy so that the ruling class and much of the elite were destroyed. He did this through sword, lance, cannon and mastiff, but the greatest amount of entropy came from disease, in particular smallpox, which by some estimates killed a third of the empire's soldiers.

At this juncture we might examine why there are empires. The Spanish set out the exploit, to loot, but became entangled with settlement because the supply of Spanish women was inadequate in the New World, and through Christianisation of the native women. Spanish soldiers were forced by the Church to recognise their children, and former concubines as wives, since these women were now baptised Christians.

The English took their women to the New World, and founded colonies which later became independent, marginalising the indigenous peoples. But the experience in India was different: there, a huge population thrived in an ancient civilisation. The Indian experience was a commercial one which, fatally, became an imperial saga. Setting out to change other people's cultures seems an act of decadence, since quite clearly someone has got to pay for it. The slums of London, Birmingham, Manchester and Glasgow are perhaps tangible evidence that someone did. It may also be observed that attempting something so quixotic pointed to a weakening in facing reality in the British. Had they become too interbred by the 1850s? After all, from a few million to some 25 million over a period of a thousand years from William's conquest, must, in the absence of immigration, mean precisely that. Certainly debacles of the Crimea War, the Boer War, and then the suicide of World War I, suggest a less than acute grip of the realities of national interest.

Lebensraum

If Britain gained an empire by mistake, mistaking commerce for an imperium, then what of German attempts at empire? Why did they try so hard? As Germany's technical and industrial base increased, during the time of Bismark, so did its population, but its territory did not. Germany went to war against its western neighbour, France. In the early years of the twentieth century Germany's industrial might surpassed that of most of Europe. Her population was larger than France, the once most populous western nation. To increase territory, Germany invaded France and struck east as well. The Versailles treaty severely reduced German territory, but its *per capita* area of living also went down because of population replenishment. Hitler came to power on a platform which promised to decrease entropy in Germany, which was suffering from riot, inflation and debt. His solution was to export entropy. Germany invaded Poland, then France. Is there some kind of dynamic process here with simple themes? It appears that if you multiply the GDP by the population and divide by the territory occupied by that population, the higher the figure, the greater the chance that nation wages aggressive war - or is a great trading nation - or both. In the latter case, the British expansion provides an excellent example, with its small territory at home, its rising population, and its increasing trade and industrial power. Japan, boxed in by American naval forces and trade embargoes, had a very high GDP but small territory. It attacked America.

As Hitler expanded, the value of the quotient: GDP of the conquered territories including Germany times the total population, divided by the area occupied, went down. In other words, the ability of Germany to expand, that is conquer, was decreasing as she expanded, and so would eventually lose the initiative. As this was happening, America was making rapid increases in GPD and so could wage war effectively.

The British empire ceased to grow by the end of the nineteenth century, so huge were the territories, so small the GDP occupying those territories, that shrinkage became inevitable.

The rise and fall of empires then is not so much a mystery but an inevitability, the working out of simple themes of entropy increase in the imperial power, and its export, followed by a failure to export entropy, leading to an internal increase of entropy leading to collapse.

I would like to suggest that these themes have been intuitively recognised by the Germans and the French. They have wanted for some time to grow closer. Euro-federalists recognise a simple fact: none of the sovereign states of Europe, not even Germany, has the capacity to inflict entropy on other nations of the world with sufficient devastation to be victor in trade wars. The fear indeed, is that the dreary round of continental wars will begin again.

Without border controls people will cross borders. This is a spontaneous process, and is driven by the general force of the Second Law, namely entropy will spontaneously increase. However, if border controls are installed, the cost of preventing a spontaneous process in terms of entropy increase is usually higher. The free movement of goods and people across national boundaries in the EU is consequently something to be valued. The pressure

for increasing mixing in Europe, perhaps to a federal
level is not so much a question of political will,
(though such when negative can stymie it), as a
natural process. A federalisation in Europe would
present the rest of the globe with a gigantic force for
creation of entropy outside Europe. Small sovereign
states will not only inevitably fight one another in
trade and perhaps in war, they will not be able to
compete with the emerging titanic forces of the
Pacific rim. There is then, no choice for Europe, the
drive to a federal state, or at least greater mixing, has
its own inherent energy; attempts to prevent the
merging will of themselves produce even greater
entropy within Europe itself, as is show by the
Conservative Party, which is riven because it is
attempting to halt history.

The solution of the European problem of
smallish states is to create a new entity, one with
sufficient internal energy and scope to produce an
economy which cannot be ignored. You can ignore
the UK, but the world cannot ignore a united
Europe. Here then is survival by joining, here is the
push for mixing, so central a feature of
thermodynamics. It appears to operate on nation
states when in world terms they are no longer
thrusting and entropy exporters. The notion that
sovereignty is being lost, as we hear brayed in the
shires of England is quaint, alarming in its
obscurantism, and grotesque. Weak countries have
no sovereignty worth speaking off, they can be
pushed around economically, and if need be,

124

militarily, by stronger countries. Despite the United Nations, it is still a dog eat dog world. The west did not defend Kuwait because it loves a loser, but because of oil interests. The UK is simply not viable alone, and if not part of a unified Europe, will simply be an off shore island whose influence bleeds away by the hour, indeed a banana republic *without* bananas but *with* a monarch.

There are no doubt difficulties with this analysis in detail, but the over-riding notions commend themselves. The notion that the Americans simply had to expand west because of their much greater value of GPD times population divided by living space than the Amerindians refines the model a little. As individuals, we are perhaps as unpredictable as individual molecules, but in the mass our behaviour is statistical, just as all large aggregates, living or inanimate are. This is probably why democracy works, it is a statistical notion.

Democracies imply a mixing of people, the notion of equality; true this does not work out perfectly in practice, but citizens are custom and honour bound to be aware of one another's dignity, rights and responsibilities. Such cannot occur if barriers are made between different classes, races, creeds. Tyrannies and dictatorships are by their very nature partitionists, they pit citizen against citizen. Rigidity, the attempt to stop intellectual, physical, and genetic diffusion amongst the citizenry must necessarily result in tension, and this is probably why dictators and tyrants either invade some other country, or set up witch hunts in their own. There is, then, in dictatorships, in tyrannies, an inherent, intrinsic, push to increase entropy, and it will be experienced as human misery either outside that state, or inside, or both.

Democracies change their rulers, which is a very good thing to do if they need changing, which they usually do, since politicians seeking elective office are often not the most able of men, and this soon becomes apparent, and the dead wood can be got rid of. In tyrannies, and kingdoms, the ruler usually cannot be got rid of except by force. The inherent instability of rigid system states has been shown by the collapse of the command economies of communist Russia and the eastern European communist states. A huge empire constructed and fallen in less than a century! Democracies may have many faults, but they are correctable; those of rigid states are often fatal, not only to the state, but its citizens. The fall of the Aztec empire, and the Inca empire, was not inevitable given the resources of the invading Spanish armies, although in time it would have been, but that time might well have been as long as a century; but those absolute rulers, Montezuma and the Inca, went against the advice of their own military aristocracy, against the interests of their people, and such was the savageness of the Spanish grabbing of opportunity, there was no time to recover from the mistakes these rulers made. Reliance on one man, even one party, is bound to lead to disaster, since this militates against spontaneous mixing of elements within the nation. Alexander knew this when he threw his main effort at Darius the Persian ruler: Darius fled, and the Persians followed him. Darius was the army, was the state. It is instructive to compare such a system with that of the Royal Navy. Many British seamen knew Nelson by sight, but the value he was held in was in direct ratio to his ability within a system. When the British Jack Tars learned at Trafalgar that Nelson was mortally wounded, they redoubled their efforts to beat the French. They were seaman of the Royal Navy, Nelson was an Admiral of the Navy; the Navy was the reality. This is worth exploring: the British man o'war was a near perfection in order and discipline as human beings can make such a system: in other words, the British warships contained less internal entropy than French or Spanish ships. As a result, the British man o'war could inflict more entropy per battle-hour than its enemies and so destroyed tens of ships at Copenhagen and Trafalgar. By discipline and training, the entropy of the British gun crews was lowered, and that resulted in increased efficiency (which is inevitable) which meant they could fire cannon much more often in the same time as their foes.

CHAPTER ELEVEN

AN ENTROPIC THEORY OF WAR

The most concentrated form of potential entropy, or entropy locked up but releasable, we *homo sapiens* possess, is the hydrogen bomb. We have seen what the atomic bomb can do: set off, it consumed tens of thousands of people, and converted large areas of Japan into entropy rich areas which were only reclaimed, just, by enormous expenditure of energy, which again produced more entropy in the form of pollution, as all industrial activity does.

During the Cold War, had the arsenals of nuclear west and east been triggered, the resultant release of entropy in these potential entropy systems might well have killed the planet.

The development of such awful weapons of war provides an insight into the very nature of war: *it is the visiting of entropy upon an enemy.*

Principles of warfare

Clauswitz's well known observation that *war is the pursuance of policy by force* is I believe basically correct, and is, as I hope to show, a statement of political thermodynamics.

It fails however in not being deep enough as a principle on the nature of war. War of its nature is entropic. I have previously argued that a nation is an organism not by analogy, but actually *is* an organism. Further, because it consists of millions of citizens, the mass behaviour of the citizenry can be treated on a statistical basis. The probability of a system departing from the laws of thermodynamics is proportional to the reciprocal of the square root of the number of entities in that system. This means that a system of one entity cannot be treated statistically, since the probability of departure is 100 per cent. A system of a million has a departure rate of point one per cent. For large nations the divergence from the laws is so small as to be irrelevant, and this is the reason why empires can be treated as thermodynamic entities with intrinsic instabilities of their very nature.

The organism which we call a nation has certain needs: water, food, raw materials, the ability to trade, and police itself. It needs to be able to control emigration and immigration. These factors constitute the basis of the national interest, which are unvarying over centuries, although they can develop nuances when new alliances, changes in population, alterations in environment and so forth come into play.

A nation which attempts to obtain the maximisation of its national interests can often do so by trade, as shown particularly clearly by England, Germany and Japan. When these interests are threatened the response is either to increase trade, and thereby dominate events by money, or to use force, that is, make war. War and trade are inseparable, those nations you fight, are also those you trade with. Hence Clauswitz's dictum.

The death of an organism by violence occurs when the entropy injected into the organism is so great as to overwhelm the organism's ability to contain the increased entropy. German military theory says it clearly enough in the concept of the spear point, whereby force is concentrated on a small front or area to such a degree as to overwhelm the capacity of the victim to diffuse, re-export, assimilate the havoc caused. It follows from this that if a nation contemplating war has not the ability to provide a sufficient number of spear points, then either stalemate will result, or the aggressor itself will be defeated. A nice example is that of Japan attacking the United States in World War II. To conquer America a majority of the main cities, centres of industry, would have to be destroyed or captured. The Japanese had no such capacity, and consequently were doomed to failure, and so the Pearl Harbour attack was futile. Great leaders appear to grasp these laws intuitively. However, I am suggesting that thermodynamics, the concepts of entropy, can help in making decisions, particularly by leaders who may not be very intuitive, and since great men are not numerous, most leaders are in need of guidelines of an objective kind: the entropic concept of war may prove helpful.

Trade as a means of satisfying national interests is also about increasing the internal entropy of your trading partners. It is misleading to speak of competition, one does not enter a boxing ring to compete, but to beat. Japan seems to understand this. She has flooded the world with her constructs, called consumer goods, when most of these could easily be built in Europe or North America. The introduction of objects by one country into another is aggressive in nature, since mixing always means an increase of entropy. The essential difference about trade and war is that in the latter the hope is to bring about dependence in the enemy quickly; in trade it is advantageous to have your partners, or your dumping grounds, as complaisant as long as possible. Recall I have argued that debt can result in increased entropy in the debtor.

GDP ratios as entropic indicators in warfare

The GDP of the Sioux nation in the last quarter of the nineteenth century was a pitiful fraction of that of the US. These Amerindians were destroyed in a few months. It would therefore appear possible to suggest that the ability to inflict entropic damage on an enemy depends on the ratio of your GDP to theirs. Equally, if you attack someone of greater GDP, you are likely to be annihilated. How well does the measure stand up? We must first make the proviso that the GDP is being used to manufacture entropy producing materials, bullets, bombs, warships, warplanes and, of course, used to train and organise men and women as combatants.

When Britain was the richest nation in the world it won most of its wars, most of them easily. By the turn of the century, Britain was not overwhelmingly rich, and Germany had huge resources. German efforts to overwhelm France allied with Britain failed because her GDP was not large enough to visit sufficient entropy upon her enemies. Germany could not manufacture sufficient entropy in 1914 to 1918; France and Britain absorbed its impact. Stalemate between Britain allied with France resulted, and was not broken until the huge entropic input from America, while the German entropic production at the front faltered because of strikes and war-weariness at home: entropy was not being exported but internalised. Defeat was then inevitable. Japan, with but fractions of the GDP of America, and despite a vicious aggression, failed to conquer America in World War II. Germany defeated Poland easily, the ratio of GDP was by far in favour of Germany, in World War II. As soon as the powers of Britain, Russia, and America, were arrayed against that of Japan, Italy, and Germany the result was foregone since the capacity by the allies to inflict entropy was far greater than that of the axis powers.

Terrorism

It may be observed that the IRA has a tiny GDP, if we may apply such a term, and we may, for all we mean is its economic base, in comparison to Britain. But the IRA year in year out has inflicted immense damage on Britain, much greater than Britain has inflicted on the IRA. By the GDP ratio alone, the IRA should have ceased to exist within weeks of the first offensive. However, there is an added factor, *the IRA is protected by British Law*. In other words only a small part of the GDP can be deployed against the IRA. Indeed, the Department of Social Security supports IRA men, and their wives and children are treated free by the NHS, and their education is free too. This is a new principle, and its implications will not be unobserved by the terrorist of whatever hue of the future. A democracy with its insistence of what it calls human rights of the terrorists (which effectively denies human rights to its law-abiding citizens at the hands of the terrorists) and its desire that no one shall be treated cruelly or inhumanely (except the victims of terrorist attacks) can never defeat terrorists of the calibre of the IRA, who in any case regards itself as made up of soldiers. The entropic view clarifies why: since the principle of war is to inflict maximum entropy on the enemy, then it implies the enemy has no human rights. You cannot wage war in half measures; the opposing soldier must be captured or destroyed.

Consequently, a democratic government *cannot* wage effective war against terrorists in its midst. The IRA have proved that, and so has HMG, for thirty years.

The Republican movement in Northern Ireland has a political wing, Sinn Fein, and military wing, the IRA. Republicans have recognised the need for both, since a democracy confers power to politicians by vote, hence Sinn Fein; but Republicans have also discerned, and they were the first to combine both ballot and bullet, that terror *terrorises*. Governments must do something, and since a *democratic* government insisting that the rights of terrorists and law-abiding citizens are *equal, cannot* defeat a well-organised terrorist group, the political wing will inevitably gain concessions.

This brilliant, if unappetising, set of entropic principles was developed by leading Republicans in the past few decades, and in doing so they have produced a technique that can be used by *any* minority in a democracy to gain concessions for itself at the expense of other minorities and the majority. All that is required is the will to organise themselves on the model so resoundingly exhibited in Northern Ireland. With separate organisations for political and military wings, they can simultaneously terrorise, and play "democratic" party politics. Eventually their demands, or something approaching them, will be conceded. All you need is the will, and *separate* organisation for your political and military wings.

Information and war

It is a truism of military science that an infantry line cannot be broken by a cavalry charge if the line is thick enough, and the soldiers stand firm. Royalist cavalry charged in vain against the long-piked parliamentary infantry in the civil War in England. Most of the squares of British infantry at Waterloo withstood the heavy cavalry of Napoleon. The logic is simple: the thundering horses cannot continue to thunder at the point of the pike or bayonet. The shock dissipates. Horses rear, shy. As infantry, hold firm, and you survive - break, you will be cut down. Parliamentary and Wellington's officers knew this, and had instilled it into their men. The correct evaluation of the information available then, dictates resolution; an incorrect, or refusal to sieve out information, leads to panic. There is a direct link between correct evaluation of information and low entropy states - the infantry standing steady - and the incorrect evaluation of information and high entropy states - panic leading to route, leading to massacre.

When large numbers of people are congregated, there is always the danger that panic can result; there is often no command or management structure in place to check the development to panic. At Hillsborough, stampeding worsened the situation; at Mecca distraught crowds trample. Here there appears to be no informational content, except that of reading the situation as one in which you must panic. The genesis of panic is fear. Fear then, as well as ignorance, are directly correlated with the potential of high entropy, and high entropy is the essence of war. This is also the theory and practice of effective terrorism.

Disinformation is entropy

In World War II dummy planes, tanks, and assembly camps were erected in the south of England to lure the Germans into believing that the invasion would take place at the shortest point across the channel. In the event, Normandy was attacked, and the Germans were wrong-footed. This disinformation had the same effect as material destruction of weapons and the killing and maiming of men: it reduced the effectiveness of the German army. This observation has important implications for other fields of application of the entropic principle: advertising and education, for example, which will be discussed in a later chapter.

Goebbels, the Minister of Propaganda for the Nazis, fully understood what could be done with distorted information. Jews were depicted as sub-human, Russians as barbarians; this disinformation was part of the unleashed entropy against Jews and Russians, along with starvation, disease, torture, gassing and shootings. Again we see that war is about visiting entropy on the enemy, and disinformation is entropy-making, just as a high explosive shell is. It is interesting to observe that since disinformation is high entropy, and hence true information is low entropy, it follows that lying to your own soldiers and people will be counter-productive.

Boundaries and the spear point

When you do not have the ability to deliver a charge of entropy to your enemy such that the impact is overwhelming, and when the enemy finds himself in the same position as you, the result is attrition, with little hope of a decision in the short term. Such was the situation in World War I. Neither side could concentrate sufficient force to break the lines and achieve deep penetration. Tragically the tool was there, and had been advocated by Liddell Hart - the tank, but the British High Command did not perceive that to use tanks effectively they had to be concentrated at a small section of the front line. Although new American blood was decisive (and in the end the Allies would have won), if there had not been a revolution in the fatherland of Germany, how many more millions of men would have died in those appalling trenches? One of the worst kind of enemy you can have is one who attacks you with insufficient strength, because it will lead to the same terrible scenario of World War I.

Some Germans if no one else, had learned the lessons of World War I. Hitler's generals wanted to storm the Maginot line, that system of deep dug forts and guns defending France. It would have lead to terrible casualties, probably without result. Instead, Hitler adopted the Manstein plan - ignore the Maginot line and sweep through the Ardennes. In this way enormous entropy discharge could be concentrated against the French armies. Without fortification the French were effectively in the open. A swift decision could be reached if the piling up of entropy was remorseless. It was, in the form of co-ordinated, and therefore concentrated, air attacks, artillery, and fast-moving armour. France fell. The casualties were much less for the entire campaign than a few weeks of the slugging matches of World War I.

There is another method of inflicting unacceptable entropy upon your enemy, and it is something only highly disciplined and valorous armies can do: mount a fighting retreat. Such was the skill of the British retreating to Dunkirk, along with units of the French Army, that Hitler was concerned these beaten men would chew up his panzers. He called them off. He was right to. The power of the fighting retreat, used in the Peninsular war by Wellington, and the British forces in Crete in World War II depends on the low entropy of the retreating force: it is highly ordered, hence it must *ipso facto* produce much entropy in what it opposes. It is costly for the rearguard, but it saves armies.

For a campaign to be decisive it has to deliver, or threaten to deliver, such huge destruction, in other words entropy, in the enemy, that the enemy sues for peace, or is rendered impotent by attack. The attacker must deliver an incapacitating stroke. Hitler did against France in World War II, but when it came to conquering England, he had to master English air space. If he had, he then he could have destroyed not only British cities, but the Royal Navy, and so starved the island to submission. He failed to gain mastery of British air space because he lacked machines to inflict sufficient entropy on RAF fighter command to destroy it. And with that, he lost the war. Had England lost control of its air space, it would have been invaded.

It is an interesting insight into the Japanese mentality in that though their air force was destroyed, though any part of their country, mainly two islands, could be bombed, they still fought on. It took the seismic shock of nuclear fission to force surrender. Application of maximum entropy for decisive results would appear to concentrate the minds of even the purblind.

The entropic calculus of attack

If the ability to inflict entropy upon the attacked by the attacker is greater than the ability of the attacked to inflict on the attacker, then the attack will probably be successful. The entropy can be measured in a variety of ways, but would always include in land warfare the fire power of the attacker, and the retaliatory fire power of the attacked. For example, in the Battle of the Somme, the attacking British, after initial bombardment, walked with rifles over open land towards German trenches protected by barbed wire several metres deep. This wire had not been pierced, and so the British soldier could not close with the enemy. His entropic factor as ability to kill Germans per second per British soldier was effectively zero. The Germans however had many machine guns, and so their entropic factor was high. In the event the entropy total for the British was very high, some 50,000 killed and wounded in the first hour, or 14 per second. The entropy wreaked on the Germans was a fraction of this. Clearly, the British Generals were guilty of gross negligence, a charge of incompetence is insufficient. A simple analysis as I have put here, merely comparing sighted and set machine guns with rifles carried by walking soldiers would have been sufficient to call the attack off. The British soldier tore his hands to shreds in frustration at the barbed wire in not being able to close with bayonet. Had he got through, then his entropic effect would have been great. That the barbed wire was still there vitiated this, and so again on entropic principles, the attack should have been called off. German soldiers, hands seared on their red hot machine guns, after the euphoria of victory looked upon the swathes of brave men slaughtered and were filled with awe, and a kind of rage: for as soldiers, they too might face such a terrible death, moreover a futile death, a death directly resulting from orders given by a high command which was not only criminally negligent, but criminally culpable to the point of mass slaughter of its own men.

Montgomery was put in charge of the British Eighth Army in Africa by Churchill to attack Rommel. Two of Montgomery's predecessors had been moved out because they did not attack. Neither did Montgomery. He, like the generals before him, insisted that no attack would occur until he had machines and men with such entropic capability, Rommel would be defeated. Churchill had to give in, though he wanted an attack, because here was the third English general stating military realism. When he had the force he wanted, Montgomery attacked, and the victory at El Alamein, given bravery and devotion to duty, was assured. Rommel was broken. It is by such victories wars are won, for such is the scale of entropic disintegration of the attacked, they cannot recover.

A fascinating example of the entropy of attack is given by a defence, that of the English at Agincourt.

Eight thousand Welsh and English archers were there, skilled in firing heavy arrows from longbows which had a pull of at least a hundred pounds. These archers, trained from boyhood, could fire at least ten aimed arrows every minute, and the armour piercing range began at two hundred yards. This meant that the French nobility as they came in on horseback met eighty thousand aimed arrows, aimed at individual horses and men, in the first minute once they were within two hundred yards. Thereafter, their rate of progress was slow because of ancillary troops retreating. Three minutes would mean a quarter million arrows, dozens each for even mere knights. The result was the near elimination of the nobility of France.

Body counts and entropic costs in war

Verdun was the longest running battle of World War I and consumed over a million French and German young men, an irrecoverable cost to both nations. War fought in this manner, for it was in the large scheme of things a battle leading to no gain, only loss, on both sides, is something no sane government could ever lead its people into again. But this phenomenon of equal entropy infliction by one army against another is not new, it happens when sides are evenly matched. It always has and always will inflict grave entropic damage to the nations involved and should never even be countenanced by governments. When Spartans fought Athenians in the Peloponnesian wars, the method was for one phalanx to fight another, the order of battle being each tight-packed mass would *run at the double* with their fourteen foot spears levelled. Physically, the men on both sides were similar and had the same equipment. They collided, with many deaths, and then set about one another with swords. Result: the destruction of two phalanxes. Further result: when the Romans invaded Greece, their task was the easier because of the loss of manpower, also they did not send their phalanxes at Greek phalanxes until they had thrown their javelins, three to each legionnaire, javelins with iron points but a very thin soft iron haft attaching the head to the shaft so that on striking the target the javelin bent, which meant the advancing - running - Greek who had fielded the javelin on his shield, tripped. The body-count of Greek dead was higher than the Roman, since when the phalanxes did meet, the Greek was weaker. Result: a true victory to the Roman army because the entropy on the Greek side was much greater. However, later when Pompey and Caesar clashed, pitting Roman Legion against Legion, the result was the virtual destruction of both. How can leaders be called great men when they weaken their country in this way? Caesar and Pompey permanently weakened Rome, for when Augustus was Emperor, such was the dearth of

Roman manpower, he could not raise his Eagles lost in Germany, *two* legions.

War, from a thermodynamic viewpoint, is inflicting entropy on the enemy, while keeping your own damage to a minimum. The NATO air war against Belgrade, although not leading to victory, as at Agincourt, nevertheless keep NATO entropy low. However, the cost of munitions, missiles at a million a shot, also implies an entropic cost on the home front, namely pollution and the destruction of wealth, and so the NATO war cost more than was achieved, and as discussed earlier, the effect on other people's minds is an entropic factor in war: the cost of Chinese suspicion, to mention merely one disaffected nation in the NATO air war will be a long time in the paying.

CHAPTER TWELVE

THE MIND, BEHAVIOUR AND ENTROPY

There has been much debate in the UK and the USA on teaching methods. Out went rote, in came "creative expression." The result, it appears, has been wide-spread illiteracy and innumeracy, poor spelling, bad grammar. At the tertiary level the liberal mode of thought in education has led to relativism, embodying such notions as that there is no essential difference between different opinions, that a poem in street argot is equivalent, perhaps even more "relevant", than a sonnet of Keats, that there is no such thing as an objective body of knowledge, and so on. The debate on the merits of such are likely to continue, after all the proponents are in important citadels of academia, but what is interesting about this position of relativism is that it embodies notions guaranteed to produce maximum entropy in a student's mind, this inevitably means poor logic, jumbled and distorted facts, and decreased ability to identify rhetoric, and to confuse suggestion with proof, exactly what a consumer society needs.

The assault begins early, with a refusal to teach by rote, so that primary pupils fail to learn grammar, pronunciation, spelling, and arithmetic. This has been a feature of British education of the last forty years. Instead of children learning, as they sat in rows, obedient and attentive, little play group tables are set up and children encouraged to be "creative". The result, not surprisingly, has been a vast increase in entropy within the children's heads, often the result of frustration and anger too, since the insistence on creativity is no less formalist that the old rote reaching, since what is "creative" is defined and insisted on by the teacher, who does not agree that little Johnny's notion of creativity being to fight, shoot elastic band catapults, and to engage teacher in verbal duels, is acceptable as creativity. Classroom tyranny indeed. The old rote techniques at least made you literate and numerate.

Relativism in educational theory suggests that nothing is better than anything else, that one opinion is as good as another, that there is no objective knowledge. The result of such assertions must be high entropy within the mind, since there is no structure. I cited Hawking's neat little calculation of real knowledge meaning low entropy in the brain in Chapter One.

It is to have been expected that classroom disorder would increase the more trenchantly the new doctrines were imposed. This has been found to be the case.

Teachers have been taught that they are teachers, as if teaching were some arcane profession which does not have to be rooted in knowledge. Thousands of teachers left teacher training college without any real grasp of grammar, or numeracy. The notion that you had to actually know some chemistry, for example, to teach the subject, appears to have been regarded as a kind of heresy.

The result of such nostra has been increasingly apparent: increase in illiteracy, lower standards in the three R's, and you can't do much unless you have the three R's, and a rising proportion of young people who are unemployable.

The educational debacle is one of professional fostering of entropy. The problem is that no nation is the world is going to pay for England's rich level of living - except England. And this statement applies to any and all of the rich Western states. If entropy is cultured and grown and not exported, ruin is the result. It may be fairly said that countries of the world are ganging up together to fight off entropy importations from other blocs, and the game is in deadly earnest. Those countries which receive more entropy than they export will descend into chaos. Entropy feeds on itself. It always increases. With education, America and England have shown themselves devoid of even the most basic notion of health in the nation state.

Political correctness is part of this morbidity: the notion here is that you do not say or write anything which might offend someone. Since in a population of hundreds of millions any statement containing a noun, a verb, and an adjective may very well offend some one person, adherence to PC means stifling the ability to think, let alone express that thinking in words written or said. Any large group of people who did follow PC would end up in a cocoon of non-communication, though it might be observed that most PC supporters go around offending the rest of us with their notions.

Variants of politically correct educational theory has been around since the early 1900s when the American John Dewey, who wished for socialisation of the child, and was not concerned that any child should reach a higher level than another; indeed, he regarded that as socially divisive. His thinking is described in a massive output in tomes such as *Discovery and Education*. Accretions to the Dewey model have occurred, since his influence is vast, given that many professors were once his pupils, and these professors laid on hands, as it were, and the Dewey accord became endemic in America, and since the War increasingly influential in the UK. This increasing weight of misinformation and ideology is in itself a frightening example that entropy increases spontaneously.

Why would educationalists set out to cripple minds? *Cui bono*? Those whose intellectual accomplishments did not really equate with their important academic positions? I do not know the answer, but it might be observed that PC must necessarily collide with science, since you might discover something which is objective and it may offend someone. It is as if certain sections of *homo sapiens* don't want to be able to make judgements, or analyse, but sink back into a soup of deep entropy. We might recall that maximum entropy is death. In love with Thanatos? However these questions are addressed, there is one that is pre-eminent, any nation which puts up with an education system which is setting out to increase the amount of entropy in the brains of the young will not last long against nations which train their young people to think, to weigh, to analyse, to speak and write clearly, and who know there are bodies of real knowledge.

That the drift to maximum entropy rather than order in education is occurring needs no conspiracy theory to account for it. We do not need to invoke the spectre of fiendish nerds and geeks writhing in their anoraks as they contemplate their own shortcomings, and resolving no kid is ever going to call them nerd or geek because no kid is ever going to form a judgement after they've been through their programs.

No, since the natural, spontaneous trend of nature is to increase entropy, we should expect it to happen if a *laissez faire* attitude prevails. Just as our bodies by constant effort, bestowed to us through evolution, throw off entropy and try to maintain coherence and order, so we can insist that education is structure-making, coherence-making, judgement-making, choice-making as a species. Leave these agendas out, and the drift is towards intellectual and moral vacuousness even without the apparatchiks of PC and relativism.

Nature is not interested in your opinion

The doves of Darwinism try to reassure us that nature is really very cuddly. There is competition, yes, but it all to a good end. Everything is all right, really. You see, when a lion pulls down an antelope, it means the faster ones get away, so that can only improve the antelopes, really, can't it? And if a lion is so old he can't make it, well, that means a younger lion does the mating (whoops!). Everything is good, the best of all possible worlds. Switch on the telly, and see yet another eco-guru talking about our cousins, as he sits with a bewildered primate. What horrors of iniquity did that chimp / gorilla / monkey commit to deserve such a fate? Well, he is helpless against us *homo sapiens*, we can do what we like to him, we even vivisect him. Nature *is* red in tooth and claw, and when it isn't, it is poisonously fanged, and noxiously barbed. The least chance, and a parasite will come and live with you, trying to break the universal law: there is no free dinner. Even the parasite, though, must pay for it, exchanging its freedom to get its food.

Nature is not politically correct. The old are left to die, bull elephants having reached a certain age and having spent their sperm are bullied out of the herd by matrons who never reach that certain age, that is, they still have a function. Clearly, a case of sexism. Male lions when they no longer can beat up younger males are driven off by lionesses and the young new king, to live a lonely life, often resorting to eating carrion, or a human child or young woman - an adult man is often too much for them. In nature there are no drones, those that we call so in beehives are sperm-bearers, they get fed so they can function.

The competition, the struggle between species, is an entropic war where the aim is to deliver as much entropy into your competitors as possible. Carnivores are luridly exhibitionists in this, they sink claw and tooth into soft flesh, rend it, importing so much entropy into the prey that it dies, and then the carnivore eats it, using the low entropy tissues of the prey to lower *its* entropy. Herbivores do the same things to plants, which are the beginning of nearly all food chains because they photosynthesise, but even they compete with one another for light, water and air.

Entropy and gene manipulation

During the last ten thousand years human beings have moved from hunting-gathering to highly technical industrial civilisation. As animals we have not changed much; as cultural creatures the change has been vast. The rise of the great monotheist religions was pre-eminent in cultural change, while the ever accelerating increase of scientific knowledge has provided an alternative, some think, to religion. But now we face, as a species, more dangerous challenges, for we can radically alter our genes, and in doing so, the challenge is directly to our human nature.

One of the defining characteristics of a species is that is breeds true to itself. Darwin recognised this, and also observed that variations can creep in, and these variations if useful in reproduction and competition would eventually become preponderant in the species. This, rawly, is the basis of Darwinian evolution. However, there is an underlying assumption here, namely that species do not interbreed, and indeed this is an observable fact. Even when cross species fertilisation occurs, a rare event, the result is often sterile, as in the mule, progeny of horse and donkey. Evolution then has not favoured the entropy increase of interspecies gene mixing, for the simple reason that when it has occurred it has entirely been disastrous, yielding progeny so bizarre and incapable, that extinction of the line was certain, or it was sterile in any case. When we observe the millions of species and the billions of years of evolution we note that there must indeed be very deep reasons why interspecies gene mixing is unworkable, and in evolution, *verboten*. However, sinisterly, some people have been mixing human genes with pigs, and with sheep.

The reason given for these potentially dangerous excursions is familiar, they may help this or that person to live a life better than they would otherwise. This kind of reason is never balanced against the potential harm for the society as a whole.

Never, since individuals' whims and desires are now considered *rights*, and besides, since the scientists responsible for these developments are busily patenting what they do, there is a vast fortune to made by the more successful Frankensteins. It is noteworthy that the profit motive is evident here in actions of deliberate entropy increase, the mixing of genes. In Chapters Eight and Nine, I argued that profit-making itself was inherently entropic.

The lure of money, the bedazzlement of the ordinary person by the possibility they may get something out of technical change, has led to an outlawing of common sense, that low entropy making facility of the mind. Relativism in league with profit and aspirations will, it may be predicted with some confidence, lead to the birth of monsters that Goya's *Sleep of Reason* could never conjure. After all, sleep of reason only produces nightmares.

The notion that given enough money and time most technical problems can be solved is now being questioned on the grounds of environmental cost, which is wise scepticism, for as we have seen, industrialisation is always paid for in increased entropy. The notion that technology can be applied to such features as fertility is not questioned. Why not have *in vitro* fertilisation? Why not clone? Why not grow children in bottles? Or in sheep? As if these possibilities did not provide sufficient material to affright our waking hours, not to mention their impact on our sleeping hours, some people blithely talk about inserting human genes into pigs. This is entropy increase with a vengeance! This is mixing of a kind we have never seen before. What horrors lurk in this new exotic entropy jungle? We shall soon find out, since these possibilities will be embraced, and religion will be powerless to prevent them happening somewhere, sometime. Curiously, there has been a much greater outcry against tampering with potatoes, tomatoes and soya beans, but the reason is not sinister. No transgenic company has yet run big advertising campaigns telling an unknowing public that pig~human organs will be available at your local NHS surgery; however Monsanto *did* run ads about its GM foods. The result has been uproar with Sainsburys and M & S hand in hand saying GM shall not pass. Monsanto appears genuinely surprised. What is sinister is this: perhaps transgenic companies dealing with medical products obtained by genetically mixing human and other animals (snakes? millipedes? etc) will not tell us until we've signed the dotted line. By the way, they are patenting these developments.

Criminal justice

This phrase appears to contain a flagrant contradiction of terms, or even a meaning opposite to what is intended. Surely no one would wish to have a *criminal* justice bill? Of course not, we conclude, which merely makes the paradox worse. It seems at the heart of much of what society does to try to be right and good ends up with the reverse effect, and that words are so mutilated in meaning would then cause no surprise. What is the mechanism here?

It may be something of this sort: since disorder spontaneously increases, and since any effort to reduce entropy in one area, inevitably means a greater increase elsewhere, any attempt to increase disorder is likely to create an explosion. Have we seen this in the treatment of criminal justice?

Certainly there are unpleasant aspects of the criminal justice system. That a woman may spend time in Holloway prison for not paying the BBC compulsory TV licence may seem bizarre, especially is she bought the TV for the independent stations! You have to pay the salaries of BBC mandarins even if you don't want their shows. There she is, often a single parent, in with murderers and poisoners. Yet I have heard few criticisms of this grotesque criminalisation of citizens who have done no one any harm. Could it be that BBC executive spare no thought, as they open their second bottle of claret, for our TV *criminals*?

But the difficulty goes beyond a repellent *class* based judicial system, and lies at the heart of the thinking which has led to the present system. *Lex talones* took the view that if you tear out someone's eye, you should have yours torn out. The thinking here is that the entropy you create should be visited on you. It is curious that egalitarians do not enthuse on this barbaric law, since it demands equality of entropy in the criminal and victim. Over centuries, the view in England was that the law made you pay a tariff, increased your entropy, for what you did. You damage property, people, the state, *you* must pay. Payment could be painfully entropic - flogging, racking, hanging. Less serious crimes have tariffs of loss of liberty, which in as much as this led to frustration, anger, helplessness and often poor diet and instant victimisation by warders and fellow prisoners, was also painfully entropic. Lesser crimes still attract fines - which if they are not paid transform into incarcerations. Taking money from criminals decreases their ability to inflict entropy on others, and may actually be a hardship in some cases. The problem with the idea of a tariff, a restitution, today is that truly vile crimes such as child rape and torture are viewed restitutional by process of incarceration, since capital punishment and physically painful tariffs have been outlawed. This leads to child murderers and torturers to insist that they can pay for their crime after a number of years spent in prison. Murder can mean freedom in less than two decades. The issue here is that the entropy such people inflict is vastly greater than is inflicted on them, and in the case of notorious child torturers, rapists and murderers, we are constantly reminded of what they have done by themselves and by people agitating to have them released. This means grave suffering in the victims' families and a sense of disgust in most of the population. People are being made to absorb the entropy the criminal has unleashed.

Furthermore, many psychopaths are released several times and each time commit terrible crimes, until they are incarcerated for life, or at least, said to be. I am suggesting that such a system damages the psychic health of the polity, when surely the function of criminal justice should be to reduce the entropic ravages of criminals.

Just as a democratic society is incapable of defending itself against well-organised terrorists, because *their* human rights are, in effect, regarded as more important than the public's, so the public is helpless against the worst kind of criminal. The child torturer, rapist and murderer Dutroux in Belgium was in police custody and he knew two little girls were starving to death. They did die. He said nothing. His human rights were meticulously observed, while two children were abandoned by the criminal justice system.

Such criminals, small in number, have affected the lives of millions of children: they are not even allowed to walk to school. This is terrorism too. Paedophiles are terrorists, and they often work in organised gangs.

The conclusion must be that Western democracies have rendered themselves impotent against terrorism and terrorist crime; and have done so by failing to recognise that terrorism is an entropy manufacturing activity, and as in war, the only means of defeating the enemy is to visit greater entropy on the enemy than the enemy can inflict on you.

A stable method of response to violence

If your first act with another person is a benign one, and their response is malign, and if you respond with a malignancy equal to their malign act, they will tend to recognise you mean business. Such strategies do not work with the mentally deranged, but may very well work with many criminals, and most ordinary people. This tit for tat, this variant of *lex talones*, has been studied extensively and is found to be stable, namely it does not lead to escalating violence, and so is superior to other forms of response. It is a technique which tends to decrease the rate of increase of entropy.

When young offenders commit acts of brutality and are rewarded with safari holidays, when murderers are out after a few years, when child molesters' rights are respected over victims and parents, not only are the perpetrators pleased, but the victims and the victim's families traumatised. Physical and mental trauma means increase of entropy. The fact is that criminals are being allowed to create more entropy than will ever be visited on them. The result has been an explosion of vile crime throughout the Western world. One would have thought that the evidence was plain, but the capacity of people in authority to abuse those they rule appears limitless. They are supposed to protect the polity, but in effect they see little difference between victim and perpetrator. You had better understand that when you are next attacked, for if you hurt your attacker, you may very well be imprisoned.

Contempt for law as entropic

Drunkenness is not a function of the availability of alcohol. Outlawing alcohol does not outlaw alcoholism. The grape civilisation of the Mediterranean goes back to the bronze age. Mediterranean civilisation to this day regulates the use of alcohol by simply having a time-proven social attitude to wine consumption. If you are a wino, you are not to blame the wine, since the same wine has supported labourer and prince during their lifetimes, providing energy, solace, and relaxation. Moralists who will be outraged to see Mediterranean mothers give their five year old children watered wine with the evening meal, may in fact not worry they might be given high-sugar nutrition-low carbonated drinks instead. Wine is rich in minerals, is a food; carbonated drinks are not only expensive, but harmful to teeth and the acidity balance of the blood. The abuse of alcohol has penalties both in health and law. The balance of its use is positive, and one of the reasons for this is that society has developed *mores* of use over the centuries.

There are some drugs which can never be legalised, LSD for example, since that leads to schizophrenia - but cannabis? Clearly there should be regulations concerning use of cannabis when driving or working. The trouble arises because this mild drug is in the control not of the authorities but vicious drug gangs whose profits from trafficking give them immense influence, most of it malign. It may be thought, therefore, that it is mere folly to allow such predators to gain mastery when they can be virtually destroyed simply by having cannabis use legalised, and its sale and distribution legitimised in the same way alcohol and tobacco are. The present situation is creating drug traffickers who are so wealthy, so influential, they will probably never be indicted, while tens of thousands of ordinary citizens are criminalised for a roach.

The specific case of outlawing the manufacture and the retailing of alcoholic drinks in America serves as a concrete example of the principle that barriers erected against spontaneous processes must lead to an increase in disorder. Millions of people wished to drink beer, had been drinking beer for centuries, this was particularly so of the Americans descended from English and German stock. The Italian immigrants had a wine culture thousands of years old. Wine in southern Europe is regarded benignly. It is served with most meals, and some labourers begin the day with bread and wine. Italian immigrants who had made their own wine in their tenements stood incredulous as federal agents smashed their wine barrels and poured the bubble-beaded liquid down the sewers. How could such madness be tolerated? The prohibition statute was a barrier between people and what they wanted, and so since a majority of them saw no sin in drinking they set about trying to find supplies. These were supplied by hitherto small-time gangsters of several ethnic strains, who became, through selling beer and wine as well as spirits, very rich, and hence very powerful. So rich were the pickings, or perhaps we should say slops, that gangs fought for territory and market share. People still got as drunk as they ever did, if not more so, but now extra entropy was being created in American society by the clash between law enforcement agencies and the drink gangs, not to mention the confrontation between police and ordinary citizens who did not regard themselves as criminal just because they had a few beers. Finally, the madness was perceived for what it was, and the laws repealed, but they left behind them huge highly organised criminal gangs. It seems the bigots will never learn that there are natural spontaneous forces at work in human affairs.

In *A Man for All Seasons*, Thomas More points out that if the thicket of laws in England were abolished, a wind would arise that might be devastating. Well enough, obviously we must have laws against burglary, violence, theft and so on, but Dickens' Mr Micawber pointed out that the Law could be an ass. When the courts pronounce what seems to the "right thinking person" inanity, there is a risk of increasing entropy in the polity. A truck driver in the USA was awarded over five million dollars for being discriminated against by his company who suspended him because he had epilepsy. On suspension he drove for some other company and went into a tree. In another case, a Judge ruled that the body-carrying test for firefighters was unfair because women couldn't do it as well as men. Gloucestershire police in the UK felt they could not tell the leaders of youth clubs that they were employing a convicted paedophile because they risked suit which would be successful if the paedophile decided to bring it. Such a state of affairs leads ordinary people to disrespect the law for they see some of it as contemptible, and dangerous to children. There are now shrubs and scrub amongst More's trees, and a match applied to them, as contempt may be, could well burn even higher trees down.

Poverty of view

Human eyes can pierce distance in a three dimensional world, but the television image is two dimensional. Not only is this degrading of our vision, but we degrade the physique as well, sitting, often chewing nuts or popcorn, often drinking beer, adding pounds which are either stockpiled, or nudged a little by working the treadmill in the bedroom. Passive, the viewer even allows the editor to select views for him; when outside, or working at some motor task, the individual selects his material, tests his environment. That children watch hours of TV every day must mean that motor ability, self-dependency, and richness of experience, all suffer.

Television news is a nightmare for the brain: how can you reconcile a story about an old lady's cat with pictures of the latest terrorist outrage? Or form a coherent view on seeing, in no order chosen by you, scenes of war, society weddings, sports and famine? If you don't cohere the material so that it makes some sort of sense to you, there is an even higher entropy increase in your brain - all those unconnected thoughts mean unconnected neurons. Similar remarks apply to radio, papers, and magazines news material.

Viewed from the entropy viewpoint, unassimilated information affects the brain, it is disorder. Damage is done by the sheer entropy increase by exposure. It is curious for example that the visual information conduits feature much pornography, and much of that the basest kind, that involving children. Just as subjecting prisoners to persistent noise can break resistance and lead to confessions, or betrayal, may it not be the case that the white noise of persistent unchallenged information may numb sensitivity, and so allow imprinting of the mind with the foulest images? And if not foul, may not the images chosen by advertisers also go unchallenged? And is this why advertising time on TV is so expensive? Because it works, and TV people know *why* it works?

When the internet was born, a vast new source of global entropy was created. Than many of the websites are sources of bestiality and paedophilia is a sorry commentary on our species. The damage, entropy inflicted, on children by all kinds of abuse persists, and leads to abuse later in life by the abused. It is a doleful wrong that *homo sapiens* has used its technological expertise to damage its young. If a species wished to commit suicide, it does not need to jump into the sea as do lemmings, who are actually following a migration route that has since flooded, it can invent an all-pervasive foulness in its technologies.

These are deductions from entropic principles, and since I have set them out, the American Association of Paediatricians have said on behalf of its 55,000 members that children under two should not be exposed to *any* TV. Older children too should be encouraged to limit watching. The reason is that brain development is impaired, and inter-personal skills unlearned.

IQ and entropy

The average IQ is 100, the mean deviation about ten, which means that about two people in three have IQs between 90 and 110. The result of this is that road signs, laws, consumer goods, films, radio and TV are on average geared to this massive majority. However, top scientists have IQs of at least 135, particularly in the hard sciences where the calculus must be well grasped. The very infrastructure of Western civilisation, based on engineering, physics, and chemistry, has been created by people with IQs of at least 135 but geared to the average IQ. To make this point concrete, just consider a main street in any Western city. There are traffic lights, parking restrictions, shop and street signs, laws governing speed and direction of motor traffic, advertising, public transport, displayed time-tables. The level of intricacy must not extend beyond that level which most people can grasp. Few people understand how a telephone or a car actually work, but they are designed in such a way so that most people can *use* them. The fifteen per cent of the population, with IQ scores below 90 may have difficulty, without help, using these infrastructures and systems.

However, illiteracy and innumeracy is at a higher level than inherent learning disabilities, which means that in most Western countries their educational systems are not successful. There are more illiterate and innumerate people than there need be. The so-called underclass contains many of these people and they are there for reasons other than low IQ. The main road described above is to many citizens meaningless, a chaos, being unnamed and unnumbered to the illiterate and innumerate. This, I suggest, is alienation, and alienation is associated with crime. There is within the Western democracies a group of people who do not work, who commit crimes, the alienated who alienate everybody around them. This entropy-making group of people present one of the greatest social problems to the West.

As technology increases more and more of us understand less and less of what we see around us in our great cities. It follows then that the mechanisms which result in an underclass are increasing in strength. The so-called underclass is therefore endemic, and burgeoning. This underclass is probably what Marx would call "lumpen" and Stalin's plans for them were not benign. Not wanted by increasingly technically sophisticated industries and services, the underclass is unemployable. Democratic principles will nonetheless mean that governments will subsidise this class, and continue to do so until the wealth creating class refuse to support them. We cannot be sure when this will happen, but that it will seems inevitable. The prudent conclusion is that the nature of Western civilisation is entropic, and as I have argued, consumerism and welfarism are part of the problem.

There are few signs that governments and sociologists are aware of the inherent nature of many social problems, but there are warning signs that a culture of blame is arising, where the alienated and alienating are thought to be guilty of original sin, rather than as they are, the inevitable result of the entropic nature of Western civilisation.

Debate, often inane, often inflammatory, about the IQ status of different ethnic groups proceeds apace. It would seem that Asians score higher than whites, who score higher than blacks, even when cultural asymmetries or bias are eliminated from tests. However, all ethnic groups have gifts to offer society. It is mischievous of the authors of *the Bell Curve* to say that blacks are at a disadvantage without emphasising that is not a natural law but a social construct, rooted in economic structures.

Attention is drawn by several observers that US blacks earn less than whites, and conclude this is because blacks, allegedly, have lower IQs. In setting earning power as a function of IQ (and it seems that siblings of all races who differ in IQ go on to differ in earning power, thereby eliminating the culture factor in assessing impact of IQ) the message is that socio-economic status is all that matters in human life. If wealth is the measure of human beings, then Mother Teresa is demeaned. Rather the emphasis should be on the brute and inescapable fact: *if any basis is used to segregate people, then entropy will rise in an explosive manner.*

The distribution of IQ in Third World countries is as far as we know the same as in the west, indeed certain Asian peoples score a higher average. Unfortunately, education is so expensive, and therefore often lacking in the Third World, that this potential brain power, a loss to mankind, is not realised. The Third World, then, through no fault of its own, is lumpen, as defined in industrial terms. Lumpen, *through no fault of their own*. Democracies continue to insist that material standards in the Third World must be raised to that of the West, but the West cannot bear the cost, and if it could, would it? Indeed, the cost may not be bearable by the planet, let alone some section of it.

It is clear that a situation of potentially explosive entropy is being reached. Already, Western governments are cutting back on welfare. What chance then, has an increase in aid? If you responded to charity demands on the media, your purse would never be full enough to meet the demands. When your purse is empty, there will still be demands. The problem is only soluble by a fall in birth-rate, a realisation that we are mortal, and that in no manner can this planet have a global Western economy and infrastructure.

As a species, we expect to bring nature to our heel, forgetting we cannot do that. In the end we must somehow live within nature. We have at best a generation to stop the entropic upward spiral. Thereafter it is irreversible.

The choice is between our descendants for many many generations living sustainably on this planet, or laying on our grandchildren an entropic curse, more savage than any retribution the world has ever known.

NOTES
AND
REFERENCES

CHAPTER ONE
ENTROPY

Reference to Hawking: S Hawking *A Brief History of Time* Bantam Books 1995 p169-170.

Limits of physics: Whereas I can see no reason for expecting the laws of thermodynamics to hold other than in the kind of space and matter we know about, what do we know of the space outside the most far flung, and flinging, lumps of matter? Nothing. There are serious problems here for physics. Are we to assume that infinity exists in nature? Everything so far shows that nature is finite.

The chemical processes of life: The synthesis of nucleic acids and proteins, and from them the make up of organelles within cells requires a source of Gibbs Free Energy. This is an odd term, since the energy is not free, and it is not Gibbs; the term comes from the name of the thermodynamicist, Gibbs, and is the energy available to make a reaction occur. The activation of these complex processes is facilitated by enzymes, which lower the energy threshold for the reaction to take place. However the difference between the starting materials and the resultant materials in terms of the Gibbs Free Energy remains the same. The drive for vital reactions comes from the breakdown of ATP, these molecules in turn being synthesised by the oxidation of carbohydrates.

The relationship between the Gibbs Free Energy, G, the heat content, and the temperature and entropy of a system is G = H-TS. For homothermic mammals we have H maintained constant by body weight constant, and loss of heat. For the body itself, we have dG = -TdS, and since for a chemical reaction to proceed dG must be negative, it follows that the life process involves the creation of entropy, for dS must be positive for dG to be negative.

Error in biochemical processes: See review *Nature* 30th Nov, 1978, vol 276, pp 442-444.

Blood heat: Depending on size and work rate, human beings expel 1000 to 3000 kilocalories per 24 hours. This rate cannot be obtained by radiation, rather it is done by evaporation of sweat, utilising the large heat capacity of water, and the latent heat of vaporisation of water. Since even in temperate climes the sweat loss is of the order of litres, such heat loss can easily be attained. In the tropics, because the temperature differential between ambience and body heat is much less, the rate of sweat production markedly increases. If the human blood heat were ten degrees higher than its usual value, about 37 degrees Celsius, we would be much quicker, (See R D Martin, *Nature*, vol 283, p335,1980) but the metabolic requirement to produce such large quantities of heat to maintain a temperature of 47 degrees Celsius, other things being equal, and they are not, would be quite beyond any known mammalian metabolism. Birds do manage a few degrees higher than most mammals, but suffer for it in having to perpetually forage, and are extremely vulnerable to low temperatures.

I am indebted to Professor Antonio Braibanti,. Faculty of Pharmacy, University of Parma, Italy for bringing to my attention: R L Biltonen and G Rialdi, *MTP Intern. Rev. of Science, Series 2, Physical Chem.* Ch 5, pp 148-189, 1975.

Life-span and entropy: For details of the experiments on Daphnia see *Biology of Ageing*, Inst. Biol. Symp. No 6, p 28)

Using this data, I found that I got a straight line, where $T = .65 \times (1000/t)$ where T is the temperature of the insects' ambient temperature in degrees Celsius, and t the lifespan of the insect in days. If we assume that the heat capacity of the insect is not temperature variant, the incremental input of entropy dS caused by an increase of dT of temperature is proportional to dT/T, whence it quickly follows that $dT = -\text{constant} \times dS$, which means that there is a decrease in lifespan directly proportional to the input of entropy, the specific heat of the ambience remaining constant.

Limits of longevity: Since the drive to form H-bonds with residue side chains is of the order of $10-20$ ergs, while the thermal energy of translation, that is random movement, of water molecules is of the order of 10^{-14} ergs per water molecule per degree of freedom, at physiologic temperatures, very few water molecules of the cell would loose their thermal movement. However, in the regions of net electrostatic charge on proteins, there would be water-protein interaction, for example, between protonated water and the negatively charged carboxyl radical, the drive to form the link, that is the drop of potential energy, is of the order of 10^{-12} ergs per radical. This would mean such water is translationally static. These observations, along with the 10^{-19} ergs of the solvation of the peptide link probably accounts for proteins precipitating with between ten and thirty per cent of their precipitated weight as bound water.

The polar side chains of amino acid residues form hydrogen bonds with water molecules, with a heat of formation of about 1 kilocalorie per mole of water. On average about half the available residues will form such links. Since in the generalised cell there are 10^{14} water molecules, while the number of amino acid residues in proteins is 10^{13}, and the number of ATP molecules is 10^6, the ratio of energy in water-protein H-bonds is about a thousand times greater in total than energy in ATP.

Taking average figures for the volume of the mitochondria, there is sufficient space for 10^{12} water molecules. This figure is large enough for the water to behave as free water, since probable departure would be proportional to inverse square root, namely 10^{-6}, or one molecule in a million. However in the convolutions of the mitochondria, the cristae, the volume of their lacunae may be less than can accommodate 10^8 molecules, or perhaps several orders less. Hence in these lacunae the concept of pH is not valid, since the water molecules would be bound.

Since there is a fall of potential energy of the water within the double membrane of the lacunae, there will be a net drive for free water to enter. This means that water has to be pumped out of the lacunae; this is another way of saying that the topology of the membrane, and the enzymes within them and the lacunae, have a source of energy. Since the potential chemical energy available is of the order of a thousand times that of the total from available ATP, this *water engine* may be of considerable importance in the economy of the cell.

For data on H-bonds and amino acid residues see Frank, Water, *Plenum* vol. 2 pp 1-113; vol. 5 pp 293-330. Wolfenden et al, *Science* vol. 206, p 575, 1979. For dimensions of mitochondria see Novikoff and Holtzman, *Cells and Organelles*, p 110, Holt-Rinehart, 1976.

It should be observed that the model I have propounded suggests that charge transfer can occur in lacunae and in bound water on proteins, by resonance, as shown over, rather than direct proton transfer.

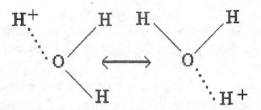

A simple test of this would be to use tritium in peptide acid groups, and see if in charge transfers the tritium migrated across lacunae and along peptide chains, or simply the *charge* migrated, which would be a resonance effect.

Speed of reactions within cells: Even for a relatively large molecule as an amino acid, in average terms the cell is 100,000 times its diameter. Spatially, an amino acid occupies volume the order of 10^{-15} that of the cell. It thus, as it were, experiences being in a vast space, but biochemical reactions are extremely fast. The rate limiting step in any reaction involving enzymes will be the rate of arrival of the substrate to the enzyme, since enzymes are far too large to wander thermally, and are in any case usually attached to an organelle, or at least the reticulum. Yet the reactions are fast. How can we understand this paradox?

Suppose, for example, and taking a liberal view, there are 10^8 substrate amino acids and the same number of enzymes which catalyse a reaction with this amino acid. Since the cell volume is of the order of a millionth of a cubic centimetre, or a billionth of a litre, the molarity of the enzyme and the amino acid is of the order 10^{-6} (one divides by the Avogadro number to find molarity when dealing with numbers of molecules in a volume). In the synthesis of haemoglobin (see Novikoff, loc cit p75) amino acid residues are added at a rate of about two a second. For the enzyme and amino acid with a molarity of about 10^{-6}, this would mean the rate constant would have to be of the order of 10^{12}; however the empirical findings are rate constants of 10^{6}. Since the reactions do take place about one a second, it can only mean the concentration of the amino acid is many orders enhanced in the vicinity of the enzyme. However the amino acid must come to the enzyme, not the other way about. Random thermal diffusion cannot produce such concentrations as are required, and so mechanisms must exist which transport amino acids to the enzyme. These comments also apply to other molecules, essential for enzymic activity, such as FAD, NADP which have molarities less than the values used in this analysis.

Proteins are helixes, even though the helix may convolute on itself. The helix is not isotropic electrically, because the residues differ along its length. Certain sequences, involving acids with polar groups, would be anisotropic providing an electrical potential, and so a charged free molecule would experience an electromotive force, and the particle would move along such pathways.

That ribosomes are found on the reticulum, which is formed by proteins, may fit in with the notion that pathways in the reticulum recruit amino acids for protein synthesis. Furthermore, proteins have partially bound water, and through such loci amino acids would not freely diffuse, and so a further element of pathways may be so constructed, since where the water was not bound, diffusion, even accelerated diffusion, would occur.

These ideas, reflecting the delicacy of cellular architecture, are now finding routine application in molecular cell biology, see review by R A Cross, *Nature* vol 389, 4 Sept 1997, p 15 *et seq*.

CHAPTER TWO
EXPORT ENERGY OR DIE

Sense of shock: The genetic code is written in words of three letters drawn from an alphabet of four, A, G, U, T, corresponding to the four distinctive moieties, adenine, guanine, uracil, and thymine within genetic material. Proteins have nearly two dozen different kinds of amino acids to choose from. The information in a protein then is written from an alphabet approximately the same size as the English alphabet, however, up to now we cannot discern words in a protein. I would guess that we will eventually. At present there is the dogma, *proteins read DNA, DNA does not read proteins*. However since much of the cell's activity depends on reversible reactions, powered in one direction by enzymes, it is not unlikely that we shall find that DNA reads information from proteins. After all, it is not as if the protein were short of potential messages.

Sense of shock when seeing people after a while: This would suggest that entropy is not a linear function of time, but time indexed. A relationship such as $S \propto t^2$, where t is age, is probably too strong.

Hence $S \propto t^a$, where $a > 1$, $a < 2$, probably obtains over much of the lifespan, but a probably increases with age. Indeed during the last few hours before death, a probably increases dramatically beyond two.

Notes on the calculations: I have assumed amino acids to have average molecular weight of 100, that of nucleotides, 300. Both phosphate and protein values include cell membranes. Idealised cell derived from data in Biochemists Handbook, Spon, London, 1968, pages 78,678-686. For the calculation of daily molecular and ionic requirements of cells, I used DHSS Report on Health and Social Subjects, No 15. All figures rounded to nearest order of ten. I have assumed the number of cells in the human body to be 10^{14}.

Information: Mammalian neurons either send a message or they do not; they either send an impulse along the nerve highways, or they do not; they cannot send half an impulse. The neuronal system is binary, either on, or off. Computers work on the same principle, the electron is on site on the disc, or it is not. In computers and brains we can write 0 for no signal, no electron, or 1, for signal or electron. Binary is what nature seems to like. Their are two sexes. The DNA molecule is a double helix. Enzyme A will either transform molecule B, or it will not. A cell is alive, or it is dead. Divisions of a fertilised ovum go in twos: its sequence of cell numbers goes, 1, 2, 4, 8, 16, 32... and so on. Bacteria replicating in adequate nutrient surrounds go the same way, each cell splitting into two, in the sequence 2, 4, 8, 16, 32, and so on. Binary in nature, binary in fact.

It is intriguing to note that there can be no simpler numbering system than binary. There are an infinite number of numbering systems above binary, but none below it. That 0, 1, 2 is the simplest numbering system, and binary events are what nature likes, it might be thought that nature is trying to tell us something. What is this information? Curiously, information itself is always reducible to a binary system.

CHAPTER THREE
ENTROPY AND FOOD DYSFUNCTION

Chemical need: If we have too little iron in the diet, anaemia results; too much, and poisoning of the liver occurs. This is a general principle with essential nutrients, too much, or too little leads to increased entropy. The optimal level is when use of the nutrient is equalled by its intake; departure from this balance on either side leads to increased entropy. Fortunately the limits are somewhat elastic, which is just as well, since we only have rough rules of thumb for dietary needs, expressed as Recommended Daily Allowances. These differ from country to country, though the WHO attempts some standardisation. Needs, rather than allowances are what we should really be concerned with. The needs of children differ markedly from adults, while pregnancy affects needs too.

The shape of the entropy versus intake curves will differ from nutrient to nutrient, but they will all basically have the bell shaped curve, though usually it will be slewed.

Lifespan is a function, among other things, of dietary intake. As time goes on, the amount of irreducible entropy in the living organism increases until it reaches saturation level, and death intervenes. The vitamins when in too small a supply cannot dampen down entropy increases, and specific diseases emerge, characteristic of the deficit. Luckily there is some leeway, and uptake of the vitamin, if the deficiency has not been going on too long and too drastically, can reverse the symptoms. However, there always remains some residual entropy as a memorial to the deficit.

The hunter-gatherer diet: For Pauling's analysis see L Pauling, Ballantine Books, 1972. *Impoverished intake of other essential nutrients;* see A Harris, *Human Measurement*, Heinemann Educational Books. 1978, p77-86. For a survey of deficiencies in modern diet see *Nutritional Deficiencies in Modern Society*, Ed Howard and McLean Board, Newman Books, 1973.

Imagine a culture...: *Survey Familles de France. The Times*, June 18, 1997.

Obesity: When an amount of heat dQ moves out of a reservoir at T degrees absolute, the entropy change is $dS = - dQ/T$. Since the human body is at 37 degrees Celsius, entropy changes can be calculated from the metabolic rate. Since we know the heat content as energy producing materials of foodstuffs, we can calculate their entropic value. Fats have higher values than proteins, which have higher values than carbohydrates. Thus an overweight person is more at risk of increasing obesity eating fats than carbohydrates per unit weight of each food. A starving person, however, would reduce his entropy by eating high heat content food. Clearly, the notion of high entropic foods is merely metaphorical, and must be used with context in mind.

CHAPTER FOUR
THE ENTROPY TRAP

The values referred to in this Chapter were calculated from reference data referred to in the notes for Chapter Three.

CHAPTER FIVE
THE BODY NATIONAL

Criminality in the body national: For the Krays: see Tony Lambucanon *Inside the Firm* Pan London, 1992. New York mobs: see Peter Maas *Underboss* Harper Collins, 1998.

Revolutions: If we put D as desire for change, G for wealth gap, and willingness for change as W, then the drive for entropy, entropy itself is $S = DG/W$. These may be quantified. D can be obtained by polling, for example the percentage of population wanting change; G is directly computable and expressible as a percentage, eg per cent of wealth owned by the top five per cent, where the bigger the wealth gap the bigger this per cent will be; and W obtained again by polling, what popular measures have not been enacted expressed as a per cent of measures passed by the government. The resultant number can be compared, providing the same methods are used for different periods of modern history, and for different countries.

Concerning the internal entropy of a country using number of strikes times violence of pickets, it would be interesting if some economist would calculate these numbers for France, UK, Germany for the past ten years, for they would be directly comparable if the same techniques of measuring were adopted, and then relate that to national earnings. The prediction is that for the seventies Germany would show little internal entropy, and large earnings. Internal entropy can also factor in crime by addition, but except in near anarchic states, the crime factor would be small in comparison to number of strikes times violence of pickets.

CHAPTER SIX
ENTROPY IS A FACT OF LIFE

The cruel dilemma: For welfare costs, see D Smith, A Grice, and C Hastings, *Nanny Britain*, *Sunday Times*, 6 July 1997. *Privatisation*, Norman Macrae, *ibid*.

CHAPTER SEVEN
SEX, RACE AND ENTROPY

Andrew Sullivan remarks that blacks are not marrying outside their ethnic group as quickly as other groups. However, the rate is still over ten per cent. Given the inter-rate figures, mixing is merely a few generations away. Such a society would be stable, and numerous, and surely the odd genius will be found if necessary, and no one would be able to predict their sex, or their colour. See *Sunday Times*, 25 May 1997.

CHAPTER EIGHT
ENTROPY AND MONEY -
A NEW THEORY OF ECONOMICS

Third World Debt: For the crippling effect of debt on the Third World see E J Lerner *The Big Bang Never Happened*, Simon and Schuster, 1992 pp 408- 418.

Entropy and political change: That quantitative treatment of the entropy build up for political change is feasible, consider the following data from J Mackay, *The State of Health Atlas*, Simon & Schuster, 1993, p 99. At the beginning of the 1990's the ratio between average income of the richest countries to the poor was 50. On average rich countries donated about a per cent of GDP to poor countries. We may assume a figure of 100 per cent for people in poor countries desiring change, while the driving force for change is 50. If we see the percentage of GDP of rich countries given as aid as a measure of desire to make beneficial changes in poor countries, then the drive is 100 x 50/1 = 5000. The UK actually reduced the percentage of its aid as measured by percentage of GDP as the decade progressed. Suppose the reduction was 25 per cent. Meanwhile the ratio of incomes has increased, and assuming that ratio is now 70, the drive towards change in the poor countries would now be given as 100 x 70/.75 = 9333. Clearly, even on this simple index, the push towards change is increasing.

Against a background of 14 per cent of all children in the world living in dire poverty in the sixties decade, as compared to 22 per cent in the nineties, and rising, it is clear that unrest, entropy, will increase, eventually to an explosive form.

Presumably the effect of TV shows of Third World children in parlous state on middle class citizens of rich countries will either result in agitation for something to be done, or apathy. If the former, the living standards of rich countries must fall, and drastically, if any real amelioration is to be achieved.

CHAPTER NINE
WEALTH AND ENTROPY

For a penetrating insight into the actual fiscal nature of wealth distribution see: A B Atkinson, *The Economics of Inequality,* Clarendon Press, 1983.

For a fiscal analysis of consumerism, and the deleterious effects thereof see: B Fine & E Leopold, *The World of Consumption,* Routledge 993.

Public concern over waste is growing, see *the Times,* July 1, 1999, p 21.

CHAPTER TEN
ASCENT, DECLINE, FALL OF EMPIRE AND CIVILISATION AS ENTROPIC PHENOMENA

A nice example is that currently occurring with the British Empire. See Andrew Roberts on the End of Empire, *Sunday Times,* 6 July, 1997.

Good background reading for this chapter would include Gibbon's *Decline and Fall*; the works of Suetonius and Tacitus.

CHAPTER ELEVEN
AN ENTROPIC THEORY OF WAR

A visit to the Imperial War Museum really brings home the influence of technology on war. For wars of attrition, see A Horne's *The Price of Glory*, Macmillan 1962. For differing notions of concentrated force, as developed by the Zulu, Shaka, see D R Morris's *The Washing of the Spears*, Cape, 1966.

CHAPTER TWELVE
THE MIND, BEHAVIOUR AND ENTROPY

The Evolution of Cooperation, R Axelrod Basic Books, NY, 1984.

For strange litigation see *The Excuse Factory*, W Olson. Free Press NY 1997.

Paedophiles: see N Lawson *Times* June 18, 1997.

The Bell Curve was co-authored by Charles Marray, who insists that partition is inevitable. See *Sunday Times*, 25 May 1997.

***High entropy statements*:** I have seen this argument many times: *Your religion doesn't matter because where you were born was a sheer accident of birth.*

It has been trotted out so often by agnostics and atheists it is almost a mantra, but it is certainly wrong. Where I was born depended entirely on where my parents were, where my mother was at giving birth. I could not have had any other genes than I did have because I was born of that woman and that man. Since they, and their parents, and so on back, were all English, that was not subject to chance. The religion of these people was Protestant Christianity, and I was brought up in it. My religion of birth was not a matter of chance. Such apparently reasonable statements as *your religion, your race, your intelligence...* and so on are all a matter of accident of birth, are high entropy statements in that they lead to confusion.

INDEX

Also by Dr Harris

A Sceptical Chemist

In this important book, Dr Harris Points a way to break out of the paradigms which now straight-jacket scientific thought.

Dr Peter Melrose, King's College, London, writes-

"This book will encourage the growing number of chemists who feel that physics has given them some unwieldy or even intractable methods of calculation without a comprehensible model.

"This fascinating book does contain a very important concrete achievement. Dr Harris' theory of Mister Cubes, a combination of the *mister particles* and the symmetry properties of a cube, leads to the prediction of the relative abundance of the elements. This startling result can also be reached from quantum mechanics, although, as Dr Harris wryly remarks, it takes a lot longer."

£9.99   ISBN 1 9007 3722 1